THE DAY THE RAINBOW DIED

Book Two
The 90's and Beyond

James Bellis

Take a Peek Publishing—Conway, SC
Paperback ISBN: 979-8-9859469-7-0
eBook ISBN: 979-8-9859469-8-7
Title: *The Day the Rainbow Died: The 90's and Beyond*
Author: James Bellis
Digital distribution | 2026
Paperback | 2026

This is a work of fiction. The characters, names, incidents, places, and dialogue are products of the author's imagination, and are not to be construed as real.

DEDICATION

I would like to thank my fabulous daughter Isobeil for her belief and her skill at editing this novel.

Special thanks to Susan Benade, Anne Streaton and Margaret Sweetnam for their encouragement.

Although this is a work of fiction the period of time that it covers in the narrative highlights what was the situation around the world that we as white South Africans grew up in. The characters in the book are made up of composite people that passed through my life.

PROLOGUE

The dawning of the new millennium had brought the feeling of a new beginning, of an excitement never before felt in this young nation. A new start. A time to forget past bitterness. A time to embrace racial harmony; walk together into the future as brothers, equals in the eyes of all.

The start of a New Year, new century, and celebrations had begun in the east less than eight hours ago. On Islands of Tonga the local Tongan people will be among the first to usher in the new century. Celebrations will move west in an unstoppable march encompassing all in its wake; no one will escape the euphoric dawning of a new century.

As the gray light of a summer dawn begins to creep across the African continent to herald the start of the first day of this new century, one man sits surprisingly calm in his small 9 by 9 cell on the once infamous death row at Pollsmoor Prison. The one certainty he has is that the coming millennium will play no part in his life.

The sounds of a prison stirring brought unease to him and a knowledge that the last hope of a stay of execution has passed. His mind drifts back to the previous evening and the final visit of his lawyer and friend Desmond Rabinowitz and the inevitable news of a failed appeal to the president for clemency. Despite a growing public opinion on the way the original trial and appeal had seemed to ignore all evidence, and the passing of the shocking sentence, the appeal for clemency had been rejected out of hand.

He had read of the final moments of condemned men and how some accept their fate, or, of others making their peace with God in hope of forgiveness and absolution. The speed of events leading to this point and the unrealness of everything make it seem that this is happening to someone else and he is just a spectator watching from the sidelines.

He cannot remember what his final meal was but that he had slept soundly the previous night, they must have put something in the food. The priest had tried to speak of the forgiveness and love of God and of his journey to an eternal life. He would be here this morning to pray for his soul and accompany him the final twelve steps.

The other cells on death row were not empty, but once moved to the execution cell no contact could be made with other inmates; he was totally isolated. The prison guards offered little or no conversation or solace. Those guards who avoided his eyes, both black and white were ashamed by the trial and the verdict, and those who weren't were openly aggressive and felt he deserved his fate. There were no fence sitters in this situation.

This would be the first execution performed since the re-instating of the death penalty and would make history. The bleeding hearts of those who opposed the death penalty were silently demonstrating outside the prison. Those who agreed and welcomed the re-instating of the death penalty were also present although more vociferous and walked in an endless circles with their placards saying "No Reprieve" or "All killers must Hang."

Wasn't it Andy Warhol who said everyone has fifteen minutes of fame? Well, his will last a little longer than that.

It was impossible to know the exact moment when the door would open and the short journey would begin. They had taken away his watch and he had no way of knowing the time.

The execution was scheduled for seven am. How much time did he have? He had made peace with God, or at least that was the impression he had given the priest, now it was time to make peace within himself.

He could sense a presence, probably the hangman preparing himself, and wondered if it would be soon. The cell seemed to crowd in on him, was this the first signs of panic? They said it would be swift and painless. Hell, how did they know, nobody had come back to confirm this. What would he feel the moment the trap door opened and he fell that short three feet before the thick rope took up its slack with the weight of his body? Was the effect of whatever they put in his food subsiding? The time must be near. He looked around his cell and tried to find some indication of the time. The gray walls and lowly dimmed light in the ceiling gave no indication.

He wondered about the other men and women who had passed through this cell on to the unknown. The cell had been repainted, not been in use for a good number years, no indication of any previous occupation. No names etched on the walls, no dates, no messages. Hell, what would one use for etching, everything sharp, blunt or otherwise had been taken from him. All he had were the prison shirt and pants, no belt and slip on shoes with no laces, as he might try to preempt the hangman. He had read that at the moment of death that your bowels released. Well, they tied your legs together when they hung you didn't they, was this to stop the shit running out the bottom of your pants or to prevent you kicking out and struggling?

Pull yourself together, he thought, these panicked thoughts are causing you to lose it. A feature of your life had always been calmness under pressure, but don't let everybody down by breaking up now. You have no control over the situation and no matter what you do; nothing will prevent your life ending. Accept it, if you cannot show courage now at least try to show calmness, don't let them see you break down. I wonder if those present will tell the outside world of my behavior in my final minutes. I have brought enough shame to friends and family already, no more! Christ, what is the time? How much longer? Should I be thinking of the four men who died because of my actions? The priest asked if I had any remorse, God would forgive me. My answer seemed to please him. I just wish I could convince myself of any remorse. No, they deserved to die.

The sound of a key being inserted to the lock of the cell door snapped him back to reality, this was it. The door silently swung open and the somber figure of Father Seamus Rogan appeared before him. Behind him stood what looked about half a dozen prison officials. The priest approached, bible clutched in his hands and placed a comforting hand on his shoulder.

'It is time my son', said Father Rogan.

Jesus, he calls me my son, I must be fifteen to twenty years older than him.

Four of the prison warders circled around behind him, three black and one white. He felt his hands pulled behind his back and immediately secured. The two remaining officials turned as did Father Rogan, and the small procession moved quickly forward. They moved out of the door, turned sharp right and immediately right again. With a swiftness that came from a well-rehearsed routine, he was turned; his legs were pulled together and quickly bound. A white cotton bag was placed over his head and he felt the noose being pulled down to his neck. He sensed the people present moving away from him as he braced himself for that short sudden drop into oblivion.

'They say your life passes before your eyes just prior to the moment of death', he thought.

The final sound he heard was one of a metallic click as the floor beneath his feet opened and sent him on that final journey. Death was instantaneous. The clock on the prison wall registered 07:00:14. A satisfactory job by all concerned.

The lifeless body was lowered and placed in a cheap coffin to be prepared for collection by family members. In the event of no one claiming the body it would be cremated and disposed of by the State.

CHAPTER 15
The Times They Are Changing - 1969

Jan 1, 1969
Thousands of Asians leave Kenya for the United Kingdom as the government takes away their trading licenses.

Having grown up in South Africa under a National Party Government with an apartheid policy in place, most of the white youth of the country had a blinkered view of race relations. With no television and biased, often censored, reporting they had little idea of how the rest of the world viewed South Africa and its white population.

Black Africans were seen as second-class citizens, uneducated, fit only for menial work and not capable of governing themselves. Coloureds, being mixed race, were more tolerated by the whites and less tolerated by the blacks. Indians, most of whom were initially brought to South Africa from India to work in the sugar cane fields, were difficult to pigeonhole. Many still worked at low paying unskilled jobs, but there was a growing community of educated Indians who became doctors, lawyers and other professionals. Much of the clothing and textile industries in the Durban area were dominated by Indians. They, along with a growing Chinese and Malayan population, cornered the fruit and vegetable market. The entire 'non-white' population were regarded as second class citizens with no voting rights.

1969 would see the continued escalation of the rest of the world speaking out about the hateful apartheid policies of the South African government. As the year progressed, change would be attempted by applying sanctions and political demonstration but more effective would be the sport boycotts.

Gus and Jimmy returned to work on January 3. Gus had to be in Cape Town to start university by February 17 so would need to hand in his notice at the bank in two weeks' time. Ian got ready to write his National Technical Certificate II (NTCII) and if he passed he would be able to complete his apprenticeship by the end of the year. Chubby was due to register for his Bachelor of Commerce (B. Com.) degree at Natal University by January 27. Only Jimmy had no long term plans.

Coral returned to work on Monday, January 6, the same day that Cathy Bright returned. Cathy had been away on vacation since the New Year's party. Jimmy was the first to notice she was no longer wearing a wedding ring; he made a note to check with Gus during the lunch break.

Lunch break arrived and Jimmy headed out to find Gus. Before he got to the lunch room, Coral intercepted him. 'Jimmy, I need to speak to you, it's important. Can we go for a walk?' Jimmy was more concerned about Gus and Cathy but reluctantly agreed and they headed for the lift.

Once outside the building, she turned to him with a serious look on her face. 'I don't know how to tell you this without hurting you so I'll just jump in. While I was on holiday at home I met someone. He saw me on the beach and walked up and just asked me for a date. I was a bit startled but I said yes. We went for a long drive in his Alpha Spider and I am sorry but he just bowled me off my feet. I spent every day of the holiday with him and he drove me back to Durban yesterday. I want to spend my time with him so I am sorry, I cannot see you socially any more. Can you forgive me? I want us to stay friends.'

Jesus, thank God for that! I was wondering how I was going to break up with her. It's a blessing in disguise, he thought. 'Oh no, this is a bit of a shock. I spent most of the time thinking of you, New Years was lonely with just Gus and me, I am sad this happened but there is no point in moping. I am sure I will find someone. I wish you the best,' Jimmy said, pretending to hold back his tears. 'I have to go now and talk to Gus. Goodbye.'

Tracking down Gus to the lunch room he said, 'Coral just dumped me, as you can see, I'm heartbroken. What's going on with Cathy? I didn't see a wedding ring.'

'She had a big fight with her husband and kicked him out of the house. She said the fight was about him seeing another woman. It has been coming for a long time now and nothing to do with me. She doesn't seem too cut up about it. The house is in her name and she has been paying the mortgage so he has no claim on it. We are going out for a drink after work so I'll see you at home.'

When Jimmy got home that evening there was a note from Dog telling him Koz had phoned and to call him back ASAP.

Jimmy dialled the number and after a couple of rings Koz answered. 'Howzit Koz, what's going on? I got a message to call you.'

'Bad news I'm afraid; my cousin says he has a buyer for the flat. In the unlikely event you and Gus can meet the same price and buy it, you will have to vacate the place.'

'Shit! When do we need to be out by?'

'He would like you out by the end of Feb; if that's a big problem for you then end of March would be okay. Hey, sorry about this, I had no idea he would want to sell.'

'No problem, Koz. We've been so lucky to have had the opportunity; it was a great help. Gus is off to Cape Town mid Feb, I have a bit of cash stored and I'm sure I can get fixed up by end the end of Feb. Tell your cousin thanks for letting us stay, it's a cool place. I'll let Gus know. Cheers Mate!' he said, putting down the phone.

Dog and Mickey arrived home accompanied by Sandy, who appeared to have moved in despite all agreeing that no girlfriends were allowed to be living in. Jimmy decided to wait for Gus to get home before dropping the news.

Gus arrived home just after eight with Cathy in tow. Before any discussions could take place regarding Cathy and her situation, Jimmy called everyone together, 'I have had a call from our landlord and there is bad news, he is going to sell the place and has a buyer already. If we can't afford to buy, and I know we can't, we have to be out by the end of February. I am sorry but that's it, it was good while it lasted and who's ever going to forget that party? Gus is off to Cape Town so he was moving out anyway. What about you, Dog, Mickey, will you be able to make a plan?'

'Man, this place is perfect. It's a pity we have to move out. I reckon we'll look for another place nearby otherwise it's back to the "Y.",' said Mickey. Dog just nodded while Sandy had a mournful look on her face.

There won't be much shagging at the 'Y', thought Gus.

With everyone in the picture, Dog, Mickey and Sandy headed for the roof to chill out, Gus, Cathy and Jimmy sat down at the kitchen table to hear what had happened at the Bright household.

'When I got home from Lynne's place on Wednesday lunch time, he wasn't home. I was quite glad as I was still on a high from the party. He eventually arrived home at 3am the next morning. He smelt of booze and sex and wanted to get into a discussion with me. I kicked him out of the bedroom and locked the door. When I got up that morning, he was gone again. I left him a message and went back to Lynne's place. He called me there and told me he was leaving me. I told him to pack his stuff and be sure to be gone by the time I get home. I hung around with Lynne until about eleven and then the two of us went back to my place.

He was gone and so was most of his clothing. Lynne spent the night just in case he came back and started up his nonsense. He never came back thankfully. On Friday I contacted a lawyer and started divorce proceedings, I just want that man out of my life. I am tired of being humiliated and beaten down by someone who cannot hold down a job and blames me for that. I have been the breadwinner ever since we got married, I can survive quite nicely on my own.'

'I have to thank the two of you, and especially you, Gus, for letting me be myself and showing me that I can have fun again. Jimmy, my friend Lynne thinks you are the greatest, I think you should call her. Gus told me about Coral and how sad you are about the breakup. Just joking but do call Lynne. If you boys are stuck for accommodation, you can move in with me until you get fixed up.'

'Thanks Cathy but we will still be here until Gus leaves for Cape Town. I daren't take up your offer on my own. Gus is my best mate but even he knows it would be dangerous to leave me alone in a house with you. Friend or no friend, you are way too gorgeous to be left alone with me, you'll need to get a restraining order,' said Jimmy laughing. 'I will make a plan but thank you for the offer.'

'You could stay with her but only if I can cut off your junk. Make a move on her and you are dead.'

'You two make me feel so wanted. You have seen me bare arse naked and made no judgement, I love you both; you have opened my eyes and made me feel special, I'm going to miss you so much. Gus, pour me another glass of wine, let's celebrate life.'

'Oh, you are wrong about us not making judgements, we both did and came to the same decision. You are absolutely fucking beautiful and completely natural, Gus is a damn lucky bastard to have met you. Me, I'm just jealous, I'll just have to settle for Lynne. Gus, raise your glass and let's toast to two of the most unreal women we could ever have hoped to meet. Cheers.'

Jan 12, 1969
**London police battle with over four thousand demonstrators
trying to enter both Rhodesian House and South African House.**

First thing Monday morning, Gus walked down to Les Sharpe's office and handed in his notice. Sharpe, strangely enough, wasn't that surprised, 'Take a seat Mr. Stewart and tell me about your decision, which unfortunately I have been expecting.'

'Well Sir, I have a full bursary to UCT to study medicine. My late father was a doctor and ever since I can remember I have wanted to be one as well. I am sorry to leave the bank but I need to follow my dream. I hope you understand.'

'When I first saw your Matric results, I had a feeling that you were likely to leave for university. If it had been for a commercial degree, I am sure the Bank would have helped fund you.' Standing up, Sharpe offered his hand. 'I wish you all the best for the future, and I suppose your friend Wilson will be down here shortly offering his resignation.'

'Thank you Sir, I can't talk on Wilson's behalf but I am not sure he will be.'

With Gus' resignation in the system, the news spread rapidly. The billing department, apart from Cathy, were surprised and disappointed. All said it would be hard to replace him. Coral heard the news and came over from her desk to check if it was true, 'Is Jimmy going to resign to?' she asked.

Gus, getting a sarcastic dig in, replied, 'Why do you want to know, I heard you dumped him? He is heartbroken. I have never seem him so unhappy.'

Coral just blushed and returned back to her desk.

Cathy decided to lay low until she knew what her husband's movements would be. She told Gus that she had to stay away from seeing him outside of the office, as she didn't want to give her husband any cause to challenge her reasons for divorcing him. She wouldn't put it past him to have her followed.

At the Friday social event both Coral and Cathy were absent, leaving a clear path for Heather, Gillian and Meg to join Gus and Jimmy, who, devoid of any female commitments, decided to get trashed.

The following morning, much the worse for wear, they headed off to NMR headquarters. Dressed in civvies, they pulled the same stunt as before at the previous parade. The results were the same, clean the Officer's Mess. Gus noticed the Administration Office was open so decided to go in and change his address. Moving to Cape Town and attending university precluded him from attending parades and any three week camps. He also found out that if you lived more than twenty miles from NMR headquarters you did not have to attend parades. He passed this information on to Jimmy.

When they returned to the flat there was a message from Ian that read, 'If you are both home tomorrow, Chubbs and I want to come around. Be there by ten, make sure you have beers. Phone if you will be out.'

Nine thirty the next morning they were awoken by loud knocking on the front door. Without waiting for an answer, the door was flung open and Ian and Chubby walked in. 'Come on, wake up you lazy bastards, the A team has arrived,' shouted Chubby at the top of his voice. 'Let's crack an Ale.'

'Fuck off, it's too early for beer, make us some coffee,' replied Gus, 'and then you can tell us what's happening in your lonely miserable lives.'

Ian went to the kitchen to boil the kettle, 'Mr. Williams over there has got himself a car, and we are now mobile,' said Chubby.

'Yes, the boy is correct. I have a Renault Gordini 1963 model. I got it from Steyn; it needed work so it was cheap, but it's all fixed up and goes like a bomb. We can go for a trip later. In the meantime, Chubby has been bullshitting me about what went on at the party.'

'Tell the man, guys, he thinks I am making up stories.'

'Not much to tell. After you left with Dee and Kerry, Chubby tried his luck with one of the chicks and she brushed him off. He spent the whole night bitching about it,' said Jimmy, shrugging his shoulders.

'Hey, fuck off Wilson, tell him the truth.'

Between the two of them they went through the night's events in graphic detail as to Chubby's conquests, right up to the naked breakfast, but did not include any of their own. Ian listened with a look of disbelief.

'It's a pity we brought Dee and Kerry with us! Kerry hasn't spoken to him since, but I hear from Dee that she has declared her love for Benny again. I also heard James, that she is not too thrilled with you either. Who were those gorgeous creatures you were with, are you still seeing them?'

'Nah. They were just two ladies from work, out for a bit of fun. It was just a one off,' said Gus, not wanting to give out too much information. 'We have been given notice on the flat and have to be out by the end of Feb. I'm heading for Cape Town before that. Jimmy hasn't made up his mind what to do yet.'

'Hey, why don't you come and board at my place? George is still in Jo'burg and Mary is in London. I'm sure my Mom won't mind a boarder. I would love to move in here but it wouldn't work with me at varsity.'

'Thanks Chubbs, but I will probably move into the "Y" while I look around. Come on, let's go and check out Ian's new jammy.'

They followed Ian downstairs where he proudly showed them his 'new' car. He gave them the grand tour, showing off the engine, wide wheels, new blue paint job and his in-dash radio. Shunting them into the car, he started up the engine and tapped the accelerator. The exhaust had a throaty sound which Ian explained was due to the twin carbs with an overhead cam and straight through double barrel exhaust. None of it made any sense to anyone but Ian.

Ian put the car in reverse and pulled out of the parking; he made a left turn and headed for the North Coast road. They took a trip up to Stanger where they stopped for a lunch time beer before heading back to Durban. Ian dropped Gus and Jimmy off with the promise that now he had wheels, they should get together more often.

With Gus due to leave for Cape Town on the February 10, they decided to have a farewell party at the flat on Saturday the 8th. An early birthday party for Jimmy and a farewell for Gus. Bring your own booze and dates if you want. Plan to sleep over as you will be in no condition to drive.

Jimmy had tried calling Lynne a couple of times but never managed to find her at home. He had an office number but was reluctant to call her at work. He decided to try again. The phone rang a couple of times before being picked up and answered by a voice Jimmy didn't recognise, 'Hello, who's calling please?' Jimmy, thinking he had dialled the wrong number, put the phone down in a panic.

A few seconds later the phone rang; Jimmy nervously picked up the receiver and stuttered out, 'Hello.'

'Hello Jimmy, I hoped that was you calling. My neighbour answered, sorry about that. I've been dying to call but didn't want you to think I was hounding you. I am so pleased you called; how are you keeping?'

'Sorry, I panicked when I heard a strange voice. I have tried calling a few times but never got you at home. I was worried you were ignoring me so I have been a bit unsure.'

'Oh no, I want you more than ever. When can we get together? You know about Cathy, I hoped the two of us could get down to your place but she is being careful with her divorce coming up. Her husband is a real arsehole.'

'The reason I called is because we are having a farewell for Gus on the 8th of next month and I would love you to come. I am sure Cathy will find a way as well.'

'It's a date. I will talk to Cathy and I'm sure she will make it. I would love to see you before then if possible. Give me a call and let me know, maybe we can go out for a meal, I can pick you up. Behave yourself until I see you next time. Bye.'

Dog and Mickey found a two bedroom flat just off Point Road and said they could move in there on February 15. Mickey asked if they could only pay half a month's rent for February as they needed to pay a deposit on the new place. To avoid any drama, Jimmy agreed, they had been paying the total rental after all. Jimmy decided that he would stay in the flat until the end of February and look around for a place of his own, if nothing appropriate was found he would check in at the 'Y'.

The next couple of weeks went by quickly and with Gus' departure looming, all attention was on having one last bash. Jimmy was feeling Gus' departure more than anyone, it was over six years since they first met and this would be the first time living apart in that period. It would be a major change in both of their lives and a big adjustment was going to be needed.

Mickey confirmed that Dog, Sandy and he would attend the party and if okay, he would bring Denise. He said he could get hold of Tina and Mandy if needed. Jimmy agreed with Denise but said a couple of girls from the Bank would be coming and he didn't want too many females. They had posted an open invitation at the Bank but didn't expect a big turnout.

The first arrivals were Chubby and Ian, Dee having been told it was a stag night and they would all probably get roaring drunk. It was after all a farewell for Gus. The next to arrive was the Bank contingent; Heather, Meg, Gillian and strangely with Coral in tow.

Coral walked over to where Gus and Jimmy were standing, turning to look Gus in the eye, 'I hope you don't mind me coming. I wanted to see you off. There was an open invite so I hope it's okay.'

'Absolutely fine. There are snacks in the kitchen and plenty of drinks so help yourself and enjoy.'

Coral turned to Jimmy and handed him a small wrapped gift, 'I know I am a day early, but here you are, Happy Birthday for tomorrow.' She gave him a hug and peck on the cheek.

'Oh. thanks Coral. you shouldn't have. Thanks for coming; you should have brought your boyfriend along.'

'Well, that's all over, we broke up.'

'I'm sorry to hear that, what happened? You seemed so sure it was the real thing,' Jimmy said with a slight dig.

'I think he was pretty much after one thing and didn't understand the word "No". He tried to force himself on me and when I wouldn't give in, he called me some bad names that I can't repeat. It made me realise what a gentleman you were; I think I made a big mistake. I regret us breaking up.'

'If you remember it was you who broke up with me. I was very hurt and I am having trust issues and need time to get over the hurt,' let her suffer a bit, he thought. 'Who knows, maybe one day I can feel trust again. Thanks again for the present. I will open it tomorrow, it's bad luck opening a present before your actual birthday. Have fun tonight, as the host I need to circulate. Maybe we can have a dance later?'

The next to arrive were Dog, Mickey, Sandy and Denise, followed minutes later by Lynne and Cathy. Lynne was wearing a very short mini-skirt and a bright low cut blouse. Cathy, aware that there might have been Bank staff present, was more conservatively dressed but still looked amazing. Lynne was first to greet Jimmy and Gus, just a warm hug and peck on the cheek, very low key.

The Bank contingent stared in amazement as Cathy walked over to Jimmy and wished him happy birthday and she then turned to Gus. 'Gus, I hope you don't mind me coming and bringing my friend, Lynne. I just wanted to thank you for the good work you have done, I am sure we will all miss you. I have a gift for you, the folks in Bills had a collection and we bought this for you as a going away present.' She handed him a small gift with a card attached.

'Thanks Boss. It was great working with all of you. I am sure I will miss you all.' He read the card out loud to applause and opened his gift. It was a gold Parker Pen, engraved with his full name. He leaned over and kissed her on the cheek. 'Right, time to party. Mrs. Bright, may I have this dance with you?'

Lynne, without the restraint shown by Cathy, grabbed Jimmy by the hand and whispered in his ear, 'Let's dance. I have missed you so much and have been looking forward to this for weeks. Cathy might have to behave but I don't. Is that your ex-girlfriend, Coral, over there? She doesn't know what she is missing.'

With Chubby and Ian zeroing in on Heather, Meg and Gillian, Coral looked left out and alone. 'I'm going to ask her for a dance just so she feels part of this,' said Jimmy.

'As long as you come back to me. Don't linger too long with her as I may be forced to find another man,' she joked. 'You are a real softy and that's probably why I love having you around.'

The song ended and Jimmy walked over to Coral, 'How about that dance then?' She smiled as he took her hand. It was a slow number which gave him the opportunity to talk while they danced. She beat him to it.

'Who is that older woman you have danced with? And what is Mrs. Bright doing here? I heard there were rumours of her getting divorced.'

'That was Lynne, a friend of Cathy's, I mean Mrs. Bright. I know her from another party we were at, I wouldn't call her an older woman though, and she's good fun. Mrs. Bright was Gus' boss, sort of: as far as her getting divorced I wouldn't know about that.'

'So, if you are not seeing anyone maybe we can get back together? I would really like that.'

'I don't know, that breakup was hard on me. Give me some time and let's see what happens.'

Coral held him close for the duration of the dance. As the song ended, Jimmy pulled back with the excuse that he needed to talk to Ian and Chubby. Playing the hosts, Gus and Jimmy first changed partners and then proceeded to ask Heather, Meg and Gillian in turn.

Cathy and Lynne were aware of the attempt to deflect attention away from them and it was further helped by Dog. Dog had taken a keen interest in Heather; he abandoned Sandy, who seemed oblivious, to the clutches of Chubby and kept Heather on the dance floor for several songs. Ian, like a kid in the candy store, did the rounds with Coral, Lynne, Cathy, Gillian and Meg, only missing out on Denise who was locked into Mickey.

As far as Gus and Jimmy were concerned, the party was going perfectly. Everyone dancing with each other and no one sneaking off to the roof or bedrooms; they were determined that this would not turn into the orgy like the previous party.

Just after ten o'clock, Coral approached Jimmy, 'I had better be going now if I want to make curfew at the 'Y'. I did enjoy myself and hope we can do something together soon. Happy birthday again for tomorrow, I hope you like your present.'

'I am glad you had fun. I'm sure I will like the present. Are you okay getting back to the "Y"?'

'Yes, thanks for asking. See you on Monday. I'm just going to say good bye to Gus then I will be on my way.' She leaned forward to kiss him and with a deft last minute move by Jimmy, she was presented with his cheek.

With Coral leaving, Gillian took the opportunity to leave as well, offering to walk out with her and waiting for the bus together. At this stage Cathy, Lynne and Gus were sitting at the kitchen table just drinking and talking. Mickey and Denise, accompanied by Dog and Heather, had gone up to the roof. Chubby was getting very friendly with Sandy and Ian slow dancing with Meg. Jimmy decided to join the three at the kitchen table.

'I hope Heather is okay up there with Dog. He really is a Dog, aptly named. I feel we should go up and check on them but I am afraid of what I'll find. She is a big girl. I hope she knows what she is doing,' said

Cathy. 'How does he leave his girlfriend down here? I see Chubby's not complaining.'

It was almost midnight when Dog and Heather reappeared. Dog looked over to where Sandy and Chubby were crawling all over each other and inquired, 'Hey Sandy, do you want to join me and this chick? We are going to hit the sack.'

'What do you mean "we"?' asked Heather angrily, 'I'm not into that shit.'

Sandy detached herself and headed over to Dog, leaving Chubby to his own devices. Heather gave Dog a dirty look and looking over at the group sitting at the kitchen table said, 'I think it's time I left. Thanks for the party, and Gus good luck in Cape Town. I hope you'll come and visit us at the Bank sometime.'

Chubby, always quick on the uptake, looked over at Ian, 'Hey Ian, what say we give these ladies a lift home? I'm sure Heather's not going to find a bus at this time of the night.'

Meg agreed immediately and the four of them bade their farewells. Ian and Chubby made plans to see Gus and Jimmy at Durban station on Monday afternoon, in time for Gus catching the 7pm train.

With all the guests either left or in their bedrooms, the four of them could relax. 'Thank God we are alone at last. It was difficult keeping my distance with all those young Bank ladies watching. Hopefully they keep it to themselves but I doubt it. I don't know about the rest of you but I am ready for bed,' said Cathy.

'Cathy, you beat me to it. I want to get this feller alone and really wish him "happy birthday". Come on James, let you and me catch up, it's been over a month,' urged Lynne.

While Cathy and Gus were working slowly to a deadline and savouring each other, Lynne and Jimmy were making love with gay abandon.

Just as Jimmy, having had his second orgasm, was rolling off Lynne, they heard a noise coming from Dog's bedroom. 'Damn, it sounds like Dog and his girl are starting up. What is wrong with those two? I'm going to bang on their door for them to stop.'

'Hold on, I will take care of it,' said Jimmy getting out of bed and walking naked out of the door. He returned moments later just as the cries started getting louder.

'What did you do? They are really starting to go at it,' said Lynne.

'Come over here and let's get ourselves distracted. We can move to the sound of their cries, see if we can get synchronised with them just for fun,' suggested Jimmy.

Lynne stared at him and just shook her head. She pushed him onto his back and climbed on, 'They say too much sex makes you deaf so be prepared to lose your ability to hear.'

By the time both had come again, the noises from next door had subsided and they both fell asleep. The next morning Lynne got up and pulling on her panties and Jimmy's shirt, she went to wake Cathy. Twenty minutes later to the smell of bacon cooking, Jimmy dragged himself out of bed and put on a pair of shorts.

By the time he reached the kitchen table he was joined by the rest of the crowd. Coffee was poured and everyone sat down to bacon, eggs and toast. Nothing was said about the noises from Dog's room last night.

'Hey Gus, do you fancy some music?' asked Jimmy with a grin.

'Good idea. I'll put on your tape recorder; we have some good stuff on there.' Gus left the table and reappeared a few minutes later with Jimmy's portable reel to reel tape recorder. He set it up on the table, rewound the tape and pressed start. Simon and Garfunkel's 'Sound of Silence' started up. Barely a minute into the song the tune stopped. There was what sounded like someone talking softly, which didn't last long before the sound of a women's voice gasping. This was joined almost immediately by a man's voice doing the same, only a bit louder. Within the space of about twenty seconds, the voices jointly rose louder and louder until a crescendo of calling for God and multiple yeses.

Cathy and Lynne burst out laughing. Sandy jumped up and attempted to switch of the recorder, Dog just grinned. Sandy eventually managed to get it switched off by pulling out the power plug. 'Why would you do that?' she cried.

'You both said that you never made any noise while shagging, so I did it to show you. I set the tape up under your bed with the record button pressed. I only plugged it in when you started up last night. Luckily Lynne wasn't too disturbed but you are way too loud and could have spoilt it for the rest of us.'

'Fuck, we really do get into it. I didn't believe you when you told me. Can I keep the spool as it kind of turned me on there?' asked Dog.

'Dog, you really are aptly named. Gus and I are going to miss you.'

After all the confusion Cathy remembered it was Jimmy's birthday, 'Happy Birthday Jimmy. Lynne and I have presents for you.' She left and returned moments later with two parcels. Cathy's gift was a bottle of Johnny Walker Red Label whiskey and Lynne's was a T-shirt with the logo 'The world's Greatest Lover'.

Jimmy thanked them both and then he remembered Coral had given him a present as well. He retrieved it and opened it. Inside he found a gold St. Christopher medal and matching chain. On the back of the medal were the engraved words, 'to Jimmy from Coral and a little heart'. He put it back in its box and put the box in his pocket without showing anyone.

Breakfast over, the couples returned to their rooms and took it in turns to shower.

Lynne was keen to find out about his gift from Coral and said, 'So, what did your girlfriend give you that you pocketed so quickly?' she asked with a grin.

Jimmy took the box out of his pocket and passed in to her without a word. She looked at it carefully and said, 'Wow, she is serious. Why did you not show everyone? Please tell me if you plan to get back with her.'

'I didn't show it as I felt embarrassed for her and myself. I don't know why she would do something like this. I don't want to hurt her feelings but there is no way I will get together with her again. She had her chance and pissed on it as far as I am concerned.'

'I am glad, although I wouldn't have held it against you if you did. I would have seriously missed being with you. Have you sorted out your accommodation plans yet?'

'I've looked around a bit but not found anything reasonable. Chubby has offered me accommodation at his house but I don't think that's a good idea. So I suppose it's the YMCA until I find something.'

'I have an idea and it's okay if you say no. As you know I live in Hillcrest and have plenty of room. You can share my bed or if that is too much, there are two spare rooms. I drive to Pinetown every day except Saturday so I can drop you off and you can take the short bus ride into Durban. I'll pick you up after work or meet you in Durban. What do you think?'

'How many miles outside of Durban is Hillcrest?'

'About twenty five but why do you ask?'

'I think I have died and gone to heaven. Not only will I be living with the sexiest and most beautiful woman in the world, but I will be far out enough not to have to do Army parades. Now I know why I love you. Yes, when can I move in?'

'Right now. Oh my God, you have made my day! I have to tell Cathy.'

'Hold on, as much as I would like to move right now, I had better wait for next Saturday. Gus is gone tomorrow, and I can't leave team Andersen here alone, they may just fuck the place up. They will be gone by Friday, so I can let our friend Koz know he can pick up the keys on Saturday. Come here wench, let's give ourselves a really good reason to need a shower.'

All showered and changed Lynne broke the good news to Cathy and Gus. Though happy for her friend, it brought home to Cathy that after today she would be alone. Jimmy suggested that as the Andersen's were out, that he and Lynne take a walk to the beach giving Gus and Cathy some alone time. They left saying they would be back much later, around supper time.

All alone, Cathy and Gus spent their final few hours between making love and talking about what they would do to keep in touch. Cathy knew Gus loved her but was maybe not in love with her and she was afraid that once he was living in Cape Town he would drift away. She vowed to herself never to pressure or to try and trap him emotionally. He had awakened parts of her that she thought were lost forever, she was grateful and would savour the memories.

Lynne and Jimmy returned later armed with hamburgers and fries for all of them. The rest of the evening was a sombre affair with both Gus and Cathy edgy and miserable. Finally, Cathy stood up and said, 'I think it's time we left, Gus, will you walk me down to the car? Lynne, give us a few minutes.'

Lynne waited until Gus returned before she got up to leave. 'Gus, I wish you all the best and I know you will be successful. My friend cares for you very much, just be kind to her.'

'Lynne, I love Cathy very much; she is a wonderful person. We both agreed to honour and respect each other and accept whatever life throws at us. Either way, I will never ever forget her. I hope I can be here for the July holidays. It has been great to meet you, don't let this idiot mate of mine give you any crap.' Gus, very close to tears, turned and headed for his bedroom.

Jimmy walked Lynne down to her car where they found a distraught Cathy. They tried to console her, but she brushed them off, 'Come on Lynne, time to go home. Jimmy, thanks for the party. I will see you at work on Monday.'

Jimmy went back upstairs to find Gus sitting on the side of his bed looking miserable, 'Hey man, I know it's tough; she is an amazing lady but from tomorrow you are gone. I will keep in touch with her and so should you. Let's have a couple of *dops* before we hit the sack.'

Gus was still asleep when Jimmy left for work. First thing he did when he got there was check on Cathy. It was obvious she was still suffering but put on a cheery face when she saw him. Twice during the day, Coral paid him a visit at his desk; fortunately each time he was busy and had no time to chat. As soon as four thirty arrived, Jimmy left work and headed for the station.

On arrival he found Gus waiting, his luggage already checked through to Cape Town. Ian and Chubby pitched up shortly thereafter and they all headed for the station bar. Jimmy, the only one with any cash, ordered four Lion Ales with rum chasers.

Jimmy raised his beer glass and proposed a toast, 'To our mate, Angus Ross Stewart, the cleverest bastard I know; soon to be a famous doctor. Cheers Gus.'

'Thanks guys, you are the best mates an oke could have, I sure am going to miss you bastards. You know, just over a year ago we were sitting in the same place waiting for the train to Bloem. I wonder where we will be this time next year.'

Chubby

With Gus moving to Cape Town, Jimmy living in Hillcrest with Lynne and Ian working and studying for his NTCIII, Chubby found himself at a loose end. He had started at Natal University and made the daily pilgrimage to and from the Berea initially by bus. Having signed up for cricket and practice twice per week, his days were long. The daily commute was causing an adverse effect on his social life.

Monday through Friday he left early and arrived home late, in no mood for going out. Every Saturday was taken up with a cricket match, leaving Sunday as his only free day. With Ian working part time at Steyn's Garage on Saturdays, he would spend his free time with Dee. Jimmy, not having surfed since moving in with Lynne, had no reason to visit the Bluff. Chubby decided that what he needed was a car.

Unable to finance a vehicle himself and with no immediate way of raising cash, his only hope was to convince his mother he needed transport. His early grades had not been that great and he decided to play on that.

Approaching his mother after arriving home late from cricket practice, "Mom, sorry I am late, cricket went on a bit. I am getting worried that I don't seem to find enough time to study, what with my long daily commute and my commitment to the Varsity to play cricket for them. I think I'm going to have to give up sports, my grades are suffering. With almost two hours each way on the buses each day, it's getting too much for me.'

'Oh Peter, giving up your sports would be a tragedy, there has to be a solution to this. Let me speak to your father.'

Val found her husband reading the daily newspaper, 'David, I think we have a problem with Peter. He is finding it difficult to keep up with his studies and he is thinking of giving up cricket. The daily commute is taking up too much of his time, I'm thinking of buying him a car or failing that, lending him mine. What do you think?'

'Giving up cricket? That would be a travesty, cricket teaches you many values that are useful in life, and he should keep on playing. You haven't had a new car in years, I think we should get you an upgrade and let him have the use of your current car. We make sure he knows it's still a family car and not solely his.'

'Do you think we have enough money to buy a new one for me rather than a good second hand car for him?'

'I am sure we will be okay. Go on, tell him the good news.'

Chubby was ecstatic; he had figured or at least hoped that his 'threat' to give up cricket would work on both parents. He gave his mother a hug and kiss then went looking for his father. 'Dad, thanks a lot for the car; it will make travelling a lot better and surely give me more time for study. I don't want to let you and Mom down.'

'I can't believe you wanted to give up cricket, I fully expect you to play for South Africa one day. You look after the car.'

Chubby phoned Ian with the news, 'Hey Ian, my Mom has given me her car, can you check it out for me? A Mini Clubman is better than nothing but maybe you can give it a bit of a tune up so I don't look like a complete *idiot* driving it.'

'The Clubman is not a bad car. Bring it round to my place on Sunday and I will see what I can do.'

Chubby arrived at Ian's place early Sunday morning and found Ian ready and waiting, 'Good to see you Chubbs, I've got the keys to Steyn's so let's get down there and see what we can do to spice up this cab of yours.'

They arrived at the deserted workshop, Ian unlocked the door and Chubby drove his car inside. 'I have a couple of things I can do. I will change the spark plugs and coil. Steyn has a carburettor that came off a Mini Cooper S and it will fit your car. Let's get started; you can pass me the spanners as I need them.'

Ian got to work. He changed the plugs and coil, removed the old carburettor and replaced it with one from the Cooper. He loosened and removed the exhaust pipe, replacing it with one more suited to the new carburettor. He changed the oil and air filters, drained and replaced the oil. He jacked up the car, removed the wheels and replaced all the brakes. Before replacing the wheels, he put spacers on each hub. He replaced the wheels and lowered the car.

'I can't do much with the overall look of the car, but the widened wheels at least make it look cooler. The carb and exhaust with give it more power and sound better. So, let's take it for a spin and see if I need to tune it further.'

With Chubby driving, they headed up Marine Drive past the Vermeulen's house, on towards the Bluff View site. Chubby could feel the added power and superior handling immediately, as a bonus it sounded great.

Chubby was ecstatic, 'Shit Ian, it's amazing; the car feels great. You are some kind of genius with cars, thank you, what do I owe you?'

'Nothing. All the parts were lying about, Steyn said I could take what I wanted. He knows he owes me big time. At least now you won't look like you are driving a little old lady's car.'

Chubby, excited with his new car, dropped Ian off and headed home. Val heard her son before she saw him, pulling into the driveway Chubby put the car in neutral and with a pump of the accelerator and one last blast from the exhaust, he switched off the engine. Val, looking out the front window to see where the noise was coming from, saw what looked like her car.

'Peter, what have you done to my car? Why are those wheels sticking out the side of the car? And what is that horrendous noise?'

'Mom, I thought it was now my car? Ian just tuned the car properly and he said it should be much better on fuel consumption' lied Chubby, he hoped his Mom would believe him.

'Well, I'm not driving that thing., it looks terrible and that noise. I am getting my new car on Wednesday so I'll just have to use your Father's car; he can catch the bus for a couple of days.'

Now with 'wheels' Chubby was keen to be out and about, so he decided to phone Jimmy whom he hadn't seen since Gus left. After a couple of rings, Lynne answered. 'Hey Lynne, how are you? It's Chubby, is Jimmy in?'

'Hello, it's good to hear from you. I am having a wonderful time. I'll call Jimmy. Jimmy, phone! It's Chubby for you.'

'Hey Chubbs, how the hell are you? Long time no see. What's new?'

'I've got wheels. My Mom's old car, Ian souped it up for me, it's looking good. I want to take it out for a long run to see how it goes so I thought maybe I could pay you and your lady a visit. How about this coming Sunday?'

'Yes, Sunday sounds good, maybe I can make a *braai*. Ask Ian if he wants to join you, we can catch up on the news.'

Mar 10, 1969
James Earl Ray pleads guilty to the murder of Martin Luther King Jr. and is jailed for ninety-nine years.

Just after ten on Sunday morning, Chubby arrived accompanied by Ian, Dee and much to Jimmy's surprise, Kerry. Handshakes and hugs all done, Jimmy took Dee and Kerry through to the kitchen where Lynne was busy putting together a salad and spicing the meat. Dee greeted Lynne warmly, Kerry, not so much. Lynne, bare-legged dressed in shorts and a halter top and wearing no makeup, looked the same age as her visitors.

'It's good to see you ladies again. Can I get you a glass of white wine or a soft drink if you prefer?' Both girls settled on the wine.

Meanwhile outside Chubby was giving Jimmy the tour of his car. 'What do you think of the job Ian has done?'

'The car looks great; I could hardly recognise it as your Mom's car. Why don't you two get the fire started and I'll get us a couple of Ales?'

Jimmy returned with ice cold Lion Ales and handed them around, 'Okay Chubbs, what's going on with you and Kerry? I thought she had declared her love for Benny.'

'Well, as you know, Benny is in the Army based in Kimberley. She gave me a call a few weeks back and asked if I wanted to come around to her place for coffee. I agreed and went around where we had a good chat. She questioned me at great length about you and Coral. She also wanted to know what you were doing with an old lady like Lynne. I told her Coral dumped you and as far as I knew, Lynne was just at the party as a friend of Cathy's.'

'Okay, first thing, Lynne is not an old lady; she turns twenty-two on December 3. Secondly, what the fuck is Kerry doing here?'

'Well, when I called Ian and suggested we come and see you, Dee insisted on coming along as well. Of course Dee told Kerry, Kerry called me and asked if she could come along as she hadn't seen you this year. How could I refuse?'

'Are you shagging her by any chance?'

'I never kiss and tell.'

The conversation was interrupted as the girls, having done all the necessary food preparation, went outside and joined the boys. The six of them were standing around the fire chatting about what was going on in their life. Kerry and Dee were in their Matric year and working hard at school. They couldn't wait for it to be over. Jimmy was doing okay at the Bank, having been promoted, but he really needed to find out what he wanted to do going forward. Lynne said she liked her job and it was going well. No mention was made about their living arrangements.

'Looks like we need another round of drinks. Same again everyone?' said Jimmy and headed for the kitchen.

'I'll give you a hand,' said Kerry and followed him to the kitchen. 'Jimmy, I've really missed you. I used to live for you coming around every day. My Mom and Dad asked after you. I assume you are living with Lynne; don't you think she is a bit old for you?'

'Lynne is two years, two months and six days older than me, so no, she's not too old for me. I have been living with her since we had to move out of the flat. She is an amazing lady and I'm going to stay with her for as long as she will have me.'

'I always thought that you and I would end up together, all our friends thought the same way. What happened?'

'Kerry, you know I was in love with you but when you dumped me the way you did, just before I left for the army, it was painful for me. I will always love you but will never be in love with you again. Anyway, why are you here with Chubby, I thought Benny was your guy?'

'He is in the Army and never seems to get a weekend pass. Chubby is just a friend and we hang out together.'

'What are you two up to? We thought you had got lost. Let me help you carry out the drinks. Jimmy, can you bring the meat? The fire is almost ready,' said Lynne, giving Jimmy a sly look.

With Jimmy cooking the meat, the rest of the party sat around the garden table, drinking and chatting. Jimmy noticed Lynne and Kerry both seemed to be summing each other up. He thought *what was Chubby thinking, bringing Kerry along?* Comparing the two was easy and he knew he was with the right one. Both blond, one 18 and the other 22, although it was hard to say which was which. Both supposedly in love with him, one who constantly changed her mind and one who remained constant. He knew he had made the right choice.

With the braai over, it was time for the Bluff contingent to head home. Ian, who hadn't drunk much, offered to drive, Chubby handed over his keys. All of them thanked Lynne for her hospitality, Kerry giving her an exaggerated hug and kiss on the cheek then repeated the same with Jimmy.

Waving their friends goodbye, Lynne turned to Jimmy, 'I hate to moan but what was going on with Kerry? She seemed unhappy about the two of us, I don't trust her at all, and I think she would love to undermine what we have. How do you feel about her?'

'Kerry is an old friend of mine; I spent a lot of time with her and her family. We were very tight as friends but then we got involved romantically. It ended for me when she broke it off a couple of weeks before I left for the Army. There is nothing going on between us as far as I am concerned, and I don't want anything going on.'

'Last question; did you ever have sex with her?'

'No, we came close a few times but never got there. You were my first and hopefully my last. Lynne, so help me, I am crazy for you.'

'I am glad to hear that, let's go and get naked.'

By the time Ian got back to the Bluff, Chubby felt fit enough to drive, Ian and Dee got out at his house and the other two headed for the Vermeulens. Kerry invited Chubby in for coffee and they took their regular place on the couch on the porch. Still feeling miffed by Lynne and Jimmy's relationship, she snuggled up to Chubby who put his arm around her shoulders.

'What do think of Jimmy's girlfriend? I don't think she is right for him, much too old. I cannot see it lasting. I think maybe I made a mistake breaking up with him.'

'What do I think? I think she is gorgeous and Jimmy is one lucky bastard. As far as being too old, did you see her in those shorts and halter top? She looked like the youngest one there. I have spoken with him and he is totally stoked. Dumping him a week before we went to the Army and then pitching up at the station with Dave when he got back wasn't a smart idea.'

'My folks will be home soon so how about you show me some TLC and make me forget about Jimmy and that woman?'

Chubby, not one to stand on ceremony, obliged and the two them locked lips. Before they got too intimate, they were disturbed by the Vermeulens arriving home from church. Chubby got up and greeted Kerry's folks, before he took his leave, he arranged to pick Kerry up next Saturday morning. It was the final cricket game of the season which would be followed by a presentation party. Free booze and food.

Chubby was now mobile but still lacking funds, kept his weekday activities to lectures and cricket practice. The only socialising he had was with Kerry at the house but even this was limited due to her needing to study.

On Saturday morning he picked Kerry up early and they headed for the University B field where he was due to play for NU under twenty side against Wanderers under twenties. Having only joined the side near the end of the season, he wasn't in a position to receive any awards. He had also made the decision to curtail his cricket activities in future and only play socially. He made the decision to concentrate on Rugby as there was more chance of success in that area and also the prospect of a bursary which would free up some funds for him.

The match turned out to be a wash out. Shortly after the game began the heavens opened, and the rains came. At four thirty the game was called off and both teams headed for their respective change rooms. At five o'clock the bar was declared open. Chubby was drinking his regular Lion Ale and Kerry, although not yet of legal drinking age, got started on the white wine.

With an early end to the game it was decided to bring the presentation ceremony forward. Once the awards and speeches were over, the crowd started to dwindle. By eight o'clock only a handful of people were left over. Both of them had drunk more than normal and Chubby suggested they wait for a while to allow them to sober up a bit. Helping Kerry along, he headed for outside veranda hoping the fresh air would help them sober up.

Less than twenty minutes later, they were the only two left at the ground. Standing up unsteadily, she declared, 'I need to pee, please help me to the toilets. I'm not sure I can find them myself.'

'The toilets are in the change room; come on, they should still be open.' With his arm around her waist, he helped Kerry to the home team dressing room and guided her to the nearest stall. He listened while she relieved herself long and loudly. Then there was nothing but silence. He waited for her to emerge but there was no movement.

Knocking on the stall door he called out, 'Kerry, are you okay in there?' Receiving no response, he pushed at the door, it swung open and there was Kerry, passed out with her slacks and underwear around her ankles. Taking her by the arms, he tried to pull her to her feet. With one arm around her thighs and face almost in her crotch he attempted to pull up her clothing with his free hand. Finding it impossible, he decided to lift her up on his shoulder and carried her out of the confined space and put her on one of the change room benches.

As he set her down, she suddenly became conscious of where she was. 'I'm okay, I can take care of myself. Can you get me some water to drink, please?'

Leaving her to get dressed, he went in search of something to use for a drink of water. He returned shortly afterwards to find Kerry completely naked. 'Hey, you need to get dressed, not undressed. Can you manage or do you need my help?'

'I'm not getting dressed. I want sex, then I'll put my clothes on. Take your pants off and come here.'

'You are drunk. I'm not going to have sex with you, you don't know what you are doing.'

'I am a little drunk but I know what I am doing and I want to be fucked by you. Don't you want to fuck me?'

Not bothering to answer, Chubby walked over to where she was sitting and stood directly in front of her. She reached over and undid his belt and top button, she unzipped his trousers and pulled them down and then did the same to his underpants. Giving his rapidly hardening cock one quick squeeze, she sat him down next to her. She stood up and straddled him and lowering herself, she guided his cock into her vagina. It was over in seconds, with no protection he came inside her before he realised what was happening.

Feeling the wetness of semen running out of her, she stood up and headed for the toilet to clean herself up. Chubby just sat there contemplating what had just happened. There was no blood so she was probably not a virgin: it happened so quick, no time to pull out. He stood up and pulled up his pants just in time to see Kerry, still naked, reappear. She walked over picked up her clothes and without a word got dressed.

They drove back to the Bluff in embarrassed silence. Thankfully, Kerry didn't invite him in for coffee. He walked her to the front door and then made a hasty retreat. They had previously come close to having sex with each other but until tonight had not made that leap. He consoled himself that it was her that made all the advances, and although he thought it wrong to take advantage, he had anyway. They were going to have to talk about this, they couldn't leave it hanging.

CHAPTER 16
Lynne

Lynnette Ann Zales, born December 3, 1947, was brought up as an only child to parents Cyril and Valerie. Val, as she was known, gave birth to Lynne a couple of weeks short of her nineteenth birthday, Cyril had yet to turn twenty-one. They had wanted another child but for whatever reason it had never happened.

Val was qualified as a Nursing Sister but had given that up to work on the local newspaper, reporting on local interest stories. Cyril had done his trade as a fitter and turner and then used those skills to open and run his own business. The family had spent their years together living in Benoni.

On leaving school, Lynne had followed her mother into the nursing profession. It was while working at the Benoni Hospital that she met her husband, Jaap. He, too, was a nurse and they found themselves on the same shift. He was sweet and caring and she fell for his charms. She had just turned twenty when he asked her to marry him. She agreed much to her parents' concern.

Cyril had doubts from day one. Jaap was from a well to do Afrikaans family and he had that arrogant attitude common to his background. He looked down on the Zales family but seemed to treat Lynne very well. Val just disliked him in general but for the sake of her daughter's happiness, went along with the wedding.

After a flashy honeymoon, they returned and moved into his apartment. The problems started almost immediately. Jaap, in typical Afrikaner tradition, wanted his wife to stop working. Lynne loved her job and saw no reason to stop work, they needed the money and there were no plans for children at the time. Jaap relented and for the next few months life seemed good.

It started falling apart when Lynne was given a promotion at the hospital which Jaap had believed should have been his. He came home ranting that if she had listened to him and stopped working when he ordered her to, the promotion would have been his. Lynne couldn't believe it; she knew she was far more efficient and hard-working than he was. She may have been three years younger than him but was more mature in her work and her life.

The final straw was when the two of them were placed on the same shift with Jaap having to report to her. At the end of the shift, they returned home and a raging argument ensued.

'You will listen to me! I am your husband and you will respect me. Tomorrow you will resign your job at the hospital and take up your duties as a wife full time. You are embarrassing me and making a mockery of our marriage. This will stop immediately.'

'You are being unfair. I love my job; I can't help it if I got a promotion that you think you should have got. I will not give my job.'

Jaap stepped forward and slapped her across the mouth, drawing blood, 'You will obey me or there will be more trouble for you.'

Lynne, licking the blood off her lips, stared at him and said, 'My Dad was right. You are an arrogant bully; I will not stop working.'

Jaap looked at her and in a fit of rage punched her on the side of her head, knocking her to the floor. Dazed, she got her feet, took one look at the raging Jaap and without a word turned and left the room. She got her handbag and car keys and left the apartment. Still shaking, she made the short trip to her parent's house.

Val answered the door and took one look at her daughter, 'Cyril, Lynne is here; she has been beaten. Come quickly, she needs help!'

Cyril ran into the room to find Val comforting his bleeding daughter, 'Did that fucking Dutchman do this to you? I will kill the bastard.'

'Yes Dad but leave it alone. I am leaving him, you were both right, what was I thinking?'

'Val, check Lynne out and take her to the outpatients at the hospital, I will be back shortly.' Before anyone could object, Cyril grabbed his car keys and left.

Cyril drove over to the apartment and knocked on the door, Jaap opened the door. Cyril, half a head shorter than his son-in-law, stepped through the door and grabbed him by the scruff of his neck and jammed him up against the wall.

'You fucking coward. You beat up my daughter and now stand there eyeballing me? I am of a mind to beat the shit out of you but I promised Lynne not to kill you. This is what is going to happen. She will serve you divorce papers as soon as she can get them drawn up. You will not contest a divorce; if you choose to, I will have her lay assault charges against you. You will have no contact with her, if you so much as look at her, I will come around here and fuck you up. Is that clear?'

Jaap, visibly shaking, muttered that he understood. Cyril loosened his grip on Jaap's throat, stood back and kicked him squarely in the balls. 'You remember what I said!'

Cyril headed for the hospital to check up on Val and Lynne. He found them just leaving for home, there were no broken bones and no stitches required. Being that it was Lynne's home hospital, word soon spread, and it didn't take a genius to work out what happened.

Lynne took the next day off to recuperate. She phoned in to her supervisor to request time off and was told to take as long as she needed. She was also told Jaap had resigned and was leaving immediately. Val and Cyril paid a visit to the apartment and collected all Lynne's personal items.

'Lynne, why don't you get away for a few days? Granddad's old house in Hillcrest is still vacant. Go down there and relax; we'll take care of things up here, the divorce will take some time.'

'Thanks Dad. I think I will. God, why did I ever marry that man? I should have listened to you both.'

Lynne made the five hour drive down to Hillcrest with the intention of spending ten or so days before returning to Benoni. The house was fully furnished and hadn't been occupied full time since her Grandfather had died nearly two years ago. Hillcrest is a small but growing town just outside of Durban. The pace of life was serene unlike that of the larger cities; Lynne fell in love with the place.

Desperate not to return to Benoni and any confrontations with Jaap, she decided to look around for job opportunities in the area. The largest hospital around was Addington Hospital, located on the Durban beach front. She decided to make a call and see what opportunities were possible.

Armed with her certificates, she made the twenty-five-mile drive to Addington Hospital. She asked to speak to the recruiting chief and was ushered in to see the Head of Personnel. Lynne explained that she was currently on extended leave from Benoni Hospital and wished to relocate to the Durban area. He took one look at her credentials and offered her a job on the spot. When asked when she would like to start, she replied as soon as possible. He said he would contact his counterpart at Benoni and make arrangements. Lynne thanked him and left her phone number.

Two days later she received a call from Addington with a job offer which she accepted. She started work the following Monday and was assigned to the emergency room.

Lynne settled into her new job, she loved the challenge of the emergency room, never a dull moment. The only negative was the daily commute. Many a day after a long shift, she would sleep over in the nurse's quarters rather than make the long drive home. She continued to wear her wedding ring as a deterrent to any male advances; she was not ready to date.

Four months later, Lynne's divorce became final. She continued to throw herself into her work leaving no time to socialise. Shortly before her twenty first birthday, an incident happened that would ultimately change her life.

She was working the late shift on a Friday night when a female patient was brought in suffering from a broken arm, cracked ribs and lacerations to her face and neck. Lynne took charge of the stretcher and wheeled the woman into the nearest examination room.

'Can you tell me what happened?' asked Lynne.

'I fell over in our driveway and I think I broke my arm and my ribs hurt.'

'What about your face and neck?'

'I think it's from the fall as I fell into the rockery on the side of the drive.'

'Okay, I'm going to get a doctor to examine you; I will be back in a few minutes to attend to the cuts on your face and neck.'

Lynne found the attending Doctor and gave him a brief description of the injuries; she also noted that she didn't think they were caused by a simple fall. In her opinion it looked more like a beating. While the doctor confirmed the broken arm and cracked ribs Lynne attended to the lacerations on the patient's face, none needed stitching. The neck injuries looked to be consistent with strangulation.

Later that night when Lynne made her rounds, she found the patient with her arm in a plaster cast sitting up in bed. Lynne lifted the patient chart and started to read the details; name Catherine Bright, married, twenty five years old, next of kin Joshua Bright, residence Durban North.

'Excuse me Sister, I am sure I know you from somewhere. You look so familiar. I noticed your name tag says, "Sister L. Zales". I was at school with a Lynnette Zales.'

'Where were you at school? I went to Benoni Convent.'

'Me too, it is you. I thought I recognised you. I am Cathy Jackson.'

'Oh my goodness; Cathy Jackson, you were a few standards ahead of me. I remember you; you were very nice to me when we had to catch the bus to and from school. Look, I have to finish my rounds, but I will call back later and maybe we can catch up.'

Being a Friday night the ER got hectic and by the time Lynne had a spare moment it was after three in the morning. She decided against looking in on Cathy. Exhausted, she decided to sleep in the nurse's quarters. Waking up just after nine she went to check up on Cathy only to find she had been signed out by her husband and had left. She walked over to the checkout desk and made a note of Cathy's contact telephone number.

Despite several calls in an attempt to contact Cathy, it was nearly a month before Lynne was able to make contact. They arranged to meet on a Sunday lunch time at a restaurant in Durban North.

Lynne found Cathy already seated at the restaurant, she still had her arm in plaster but her facial and neck injuries had all cleared up. She was a very attractive woman. Between ordering food and drinks they caught up with where their lives had taken them.

Cathy told of her leaving school and moving with her parents to Durban where she joined the Standard Bank, where she still worked. She had married Joshua Bright two and a half years ago, no children yet. They had a house in Durban North with a mortgage from the Bank in her name. Joshua worked as an Insurance Consultant and was between jobs at the moment.

Lynne detected some sadness in Cathy and felt she was holding back something about her situation but didn't push her on it. She went through the saga of her life right up to the present. The two of them made a pact of sorts; they would endeavour to get together at last once a month. A true friendship was forged that day.

Although Lynne loved her job, she found that the irregular hours and the long commute were wearing her down. She started looking around for something new in the medical field that would possibly interest her. She came across an advert looking for 'experienced medical practitioners to work in the challenging and well paid profession of Medical Representative'.

Thinking *why not?* She called the telephone number and arranged for an interview. She aced the interview and with all the necessary attributes; articulate, intelligent, confident and very presentable she was offered a position as a Medical Rep. Three weeks training on company products was scheduled at which time a decision would be made on her suitability to begin calling on customers. If successful, she would be given the use of a company car. Lynne was required to give one month's notice at the hospital. She accepted the offer and so started what would turn out to be a very successful career.

CHAPTER 17
Summer of Love

With the cricket season over, Chubby's attention turned to rugby. Having come from a school not known for its sporting prowess, he would have to go through the 'trials' route to try and establish himself. It would take only one training session.

Not one to stand back, Chubby informed the U20 coach that he was a fly-half and intended to play for the Varsity first team this season. The coach, thinking that he was an arrogant bastard, decided to put Chubby in as fly-half and wait for him to screw up. It didn't take long for the coach to realise he had a special talent on his hands. He immediately drafted Chubby into the U20 team.

It only took two matches for the Varsity first team coach to take notice. Pulling rank, he informed the U20 coach that he would be drafting Chubby into the senior sides. Chubby took the opportunity to inform his new coach that he may have to give up university as his parents were struggling to afford his university and sporting fees. The coach, knowing the importance of the college's sporting programs and the rewards a successful rugby team would bring, approached the Dean. After a discussion with the board, the Dean decided to award a full bursary to Peter Murphy.

The Varsity first team fly-half was the current Natal Provincial fly-half. He was in the last semester of his university career and was unlikely to be dropped for Chubby. The coach, recognising Chubby's ability with the ball, both running and kicking, decided to play him at full-back.

Jun 9, 1969
Enoch Powell proposes repatriation of immigrants from Britain.

Chubby is selected for Natal U20 at full-back. He scores two tries and converts his two and three others. He converts four penalties and kicks a drop goal. His performance generates rave reviews in the local newspapers, with suggestions he should be selected for the Natal first team.

Jun 30, 1969
Nigeria bans night flights by the Red Cross delivering food and medicines to the starving Biafrians.

Gus passes half year exams with six firsts and cancels his trip back to Durban to meet up with newly divorced Cathy in Jefferies Bay. For Gus, who had spent the last months since leaving Durban fully committed to studying, it was a chance to unwind. Cathy, on the other hand, had spent much of the same period in a bitterly contested divorce.

Joshua, who had originally stated he would not contest the divorce, decided to try and gain fifty percent of the couple's assets. Fortunately for her, they had signed an ante nuptial contract protecting her assets, but the added legal costs were a drain on her finances. Cathy was in the process of changing back to her maiden name of Jackson.

The two weeks they had together were spent rediscovering each other mentally and physically. On the last day of their holiday, Cathy broached the question of their relationship.

'Gus, you know I love you very much and I am sure your feelings towards me are genuine, but we really need to make a decision on our futures. There is the question of our age difference and the fact that you have six and a half years of study ahead. I am not looking for any long term commitment but I will be in my mid-thirties when you qualify. I have gone through a messy and emotional divorce and it's times like this that we have together that make it possible for me to cope.'

'What are you trying to tell me? Knowing you and making love with you have been the most important things I have.'

'What I am trying to say is that as much as I love and need you, I need us to be sensible. You are a young man with a great future ahead of you, I am a woman who would like a child, maybe a couple and this won't happen with us. Right now I cannot look at another man without seeing you. You are the single greatest thing that has happened to me, you have given me back my confidence which has allowed me to like myself again and for that I thank you with all my heart.'

'Are you saying that it's over between us? I need you in my life as this is the first time that I have been able to be emotionally attached to someone; we can't just give this up.'

'It will never be over between us. What I am saying is that we should both move on with our lives. I will always be there if you need me and as long as I am single and you are interested, my bed is always there for you. So, until we meet again, let's make love one last time.'

The following day Cathy left for Durban and Gus for Cape Town; it would be some time before they would meet again.

Jul 21, 1969
Neil Armstrong becomes the first man to set foot on the moon as Apollo Eleven lands at Tranquillity Base.

Ian passed his electricians NTCIII finals exam and began work on his mechanics equivalent with a view to being fully qualified by the end of the year. The credits he had already received meant that the new course could be completed in anything from six to eight months. He planned on doing it in six.

Aug 17, 1969
The Woodstock Music Festival ends after over four hundred thousand attend the "music and love happening."

Chubby is selected for the Natal first team at full-back to play the mighty Blue Bulls of Northern Transvaal in a Currie Cup match at King's Park in Durban. The Natal rugby team had never won the Currie Cup Final in their entire history, whereas the Bulls were perennial winners. Chubby was in for the injured regular full-back in what was the last game of the regular Currie Cup season.

The game started and within a minute Natal were awarded a penalty ten yards inside their own half. Much to the amusement of the Bulls players, Chubby indicated he would go for poles. Going through his normal routine he backed away, took three steps to the left, ran up and slotted the ball through the posts 3-0 to Natal. This was a wakeup call for the Bulls who proceeded to slaughter Natal to the tune of 42-6 with Chubby scoring a second penalty. Although on the side of a hammering, Chubby had had a decent game, steady if not spectacular and received praise for efforts in the press. He was called out as one for the future.

Nov 5, 1969
An anti-apartheid protest disrupts the South African Springbok rugby match at Twickenham. John Taylor as Wales and British Lions player refuses to play against the tourists.

Kerry, having missed her second period in a row and suspecting she may be pregnant, confronted Benny with the news.

'Benny, I think I might be pregnant. I am about six weeks overdue. I have always been irregular but never this much. It could have been when we had sex just after you got out of the army; I was worried at the time because I was sure you came inside of me. I need to see the doctor but my folks can't know.'

'How can this be? We only had sex that one time. I will get you an appointment with our doctor. Maybe it's the stress of the Matric exams; I have heard that can happen.'

Benny arranged the doctor's appointment and much to Kerry's horror, the Doctor confirmed her pregnancy. Based on his examination and the date of her last period, he put her at about eight to ten weeks. Counting back, Kerry realised that she may have been pregnant just before Benny got back from the army. In that case, it was possible Chubby was the father.

Nov 15, 1969
Police and anti-tour demonstrators clash at Swansea in Wales.

Monday morning November 24, Jimmy was called into Sharpe's office, ostensibly to do his annual review. Sharpe indicated that Jimmy should close the office door and take a seat.

'Mr. Wilson, it's that time of the year when I do staff reviews, we report on progress, areas of concern and general plans for your future. I am going to cut straight to the point. Although you are doing an excellent job in Foreign Exchange, I feel your talents are wasted there. Before I offer you a new challenge, I need to ask if you have any problems with travelling.'

'No Sir, I don't generally but I would need to know what that means.'

'Do you have your own transport?'

'I do have the use of a car.'

'Right. What I would like to offer you is the opportunity to join the Standard Bank Relief Staff department. What this entails is that whenever there is a need at any branch for temporary staff, usually to relieve someone who is either ill or on vacation. Initially you could be placed at any branch in Natal normally for a period of no more than three weeks at a time. As a single bloke it is a great opportunity to gain exposure to more facets of banking procedures. It is also the best way to advance your banking career. If you are interested we can discuss the details.'

Jimmy, not really liking the sound of this, answered, 'I would like the opportunity depending on what conditions are attached to the offer.'

'If you accept the offer there is an immediate two grade promotion which should be around R40 more per month. While on relief duties you will be paid a daily stipend of R10 per day. If the relief branch is more than thirty miles away from Standard Bank Main Street, your accommodation and travel costs will be paid by the Bank. It is a great opportunity to fast track you into a management position. Do you have questions or concerns?'

'If I turn this offer down will it impact my future at the Bank in a negative way?'

'No, it will not but it would definitely slow down your career path. You were selected as only one of two people in the whole of the Natal region for this chance. Think it over and let me know by the end of the week.'

'Yes, I will, and again thank you for the opportunity.'

As per normal, Jimmy caught the bus out to Pinetown after work and met up with Lynne. 'Lynne, I have something very important to discuss with you.'

'That's funny, so do I. You go first.'

'Let's wait until we get home then.'

It was a nervous drive back to Hillcrest as neither was sure what the other's reaction would be to the news. They pulled into the drive and Lynne immediately got out of the car and went straight to the kitchen emerging a few minutes later with a Lion Ale for Jimmy and a glass of red wine for herself.

'Ok Mr. Wilson, what is it you need to tell me? I can take anything but rejection, so please be gentle.'

'I will never reject you. You know how bored and unsettled I am at work. Well, I have been offered a new challenge and I want to discuss it with you before I accept.'

'I am glad that's all it is. So tell me all about it.'

Jimmy went on to explain in great detail what the job would be about. As he went through the details he tried to get a read on Lynne's reactions but was met by a solemn face. When he finished, he asked her what she thought he should do.

'I think the fact that they recognise your talents is great. More money and better prospects is a good thing. To make things clear for me; you could be away for up to three weeks at a time stuck in some backwater town somewhere in Natal? I don't know how happy I am that I will see so little of you, but I think you should do it if you want to.'

'I will only do this for a short time as I really want to get out of the banking world. I will come home every weekend or you could come and spend the weekend with me. I cannot go three weeks without seeing you. Maybe I could use the Beetle which would make a trip home quicker? I could just as easily be sent on relief to Durban North or Pinetown branches. If it does not work for us, I will quit. So that's my news, what's yours?'

'My folks are coming down here next Tuesday afternoon and plan to stay at least one week. They don't know too much about you other than I have a boyfriend who stays with me. I know it's short notice, but I am sure they will like you. My Dad's a good guy and my Mom is well, my Mom.'

'Oh shit! I will try and be on my best behaviour. I'll tell Sharpe tomorrow that I will take the job.'

The next day Jimmy informed Sharpe of his decision and was told in return that he would transfer to Relief Staff officially on January 5, 1970.

Dec 2, 1969
Ninety-eight people are arrested in Aberdeen during and after the rugby match against Scotland for numerous pitch invasions.

Jimmy and Lynne arrived home on Tuesday afternoon to find Cyril and Val sitting on the porch drinking an early evening cocktail. Lynne, anxious to see her folks after a long absence, leapt out of the car and ran over to her parents. Jimmy nervously followed her.

'Jimmy, this is my Mom, Val and my Dad, Cyril,' said Lynne, 'folks, this is my boyfriend, Jimmy.'

Jimmy stepped forward and extended his hand to Val, who ignored it and enveloped him in a bear hug. 'I am really pleased to meet you young man; my daughter has mentioned you and by the look of her, she seems very happy.'

'Thank you, Mrs. Zales, she makes me very happy as well. I know it's a cliché but you look exactly like your daughter and could be sisters. Wow!'

'Call me Val, please. I wish we looked like sisters; you are very kind. Cyril, what do you have to say for yourself?'

Cyril stepped forward with his hand extended, 'Nice to meet you Jimmy and what are your intentions with my sweet daughter?'

Taken aback for a few seconds, Jimmy answered, 'Sir, I am making it my mission in life to ensure Lynne is loved and respected forever.'

'Okay, I am just messing with you but that was some reply. Here, have a decent beer,' said Cyril, handing Jimmy a Castle Lager.

'Seeing I have just met you, I will be polite and join you with a Castle this one time, but if we are going to be friends, I will be drinking Lion Ale.'

'Lynnette, I like this one; he has a pair of balls, he may just be a keeper. Do you play darts? There is a board in the garage. I will be gentle with you.'

'I sure do, Cyril, but I must warn you, I am pretty crap unless I have had half a dozen beers.'

Cyril and Jimmy headed for the garage and for the next three hours they played darts only emerging to recharge their drinks. Val and Lynne in the meantime discussed the current living arrangements.

'Lynne, I like Jimmy, he seems a very nice young man, good looking and articulate. He was very relaxed in our company and I reckon your Dad likes him as well. How do you feel about him and the fact that he must be a bit younger than you? You seem happier than I have seen you for a number of years, is he good to you?'

'Mom, I'll make this easy for you. Jimmy is two and a bit years younger than me. He is the first and only man I have been involved with since the divorce. He is kind and considerate and has made me feel like a woman again, he has built up my confidence and made me happy again. I love him very much.'

'I am happy for you. You are positively glowing when you speak about him, long may it last.'

Back in the garage and six beers down, Jimmy was finally making some headway against Cyril. It was almost nine o'clock when Jimmy suggested they go into the house and find something to eat. 'Sir, I think it's time to call it quits, I am tired of being beaten up, I am hungry and a little drunk. While I can still talk sense, I have to say that Lynne looks just like her mother who is absolutely gorgeous. I am lucky Lynne takes after her mother and not you.'

'Cheeky bugger but you are right; my Val is beautiful, and you are lucky that you can see into the future and know what Lynne will look like in eighteen years' time.'

For the next ten days it was a bonding exercise for Jimmy and the Zales family. If they weren't playing darts, Jimmy and Cyril joined Val playing cards much to Lynne's annoyance. Darts were beers and cards were with Val's preferred drink which was brandy, lime and water. Cyril had found the son he had longed for and Val the person who would provide her with a grandchild. As much as she loved her parents, Lynne was not too sad when they left as she had Jimmy back to herself.

Dec 4, 1969
The police shoot dead two Black Panther members in Chicago.

Kerry and Dee write their final Matric examinations. Kerry decides to confide in Dee as to her current condition. 'Dee, I need to talk to someone, and I hope you can keep this to yourself. I'm pregnant, just on three months. I haven't told anybody. I am petrified to tell my folks. I don't know what they are going to do.'

'I suspected you might be but didn't want to ask. Have you told the father? Is it Chubby?'

'I sure it's not Chubby. I've told Benny that he is the father. We had unprotected sex the day after he got out of the Amy on September 26, the baby should be due around June 26. He has been really good about it and suggested we tell my folks together. He wants to get married.'

'In a way you are lucky, Benny is a stand-up guy; a lot of blokes would have done a runner. Tell your mom on her own. I am sure she will understand and will know how to broach the subject with your dad.'

That night Kerry and Benny told Mrs. Vermeulen, after the initial shock she hugged her daughter and whispered in her ear, 'I will tell your father; he will understand. After all, Ingrid was born just seven months after we were married.'

So, after all the drama was over, a wedding was arranged for January 17, 1970. At Mrs. Vermeulens insistence, it would be a white wedding with all the trimmings.

As the word got out, there were some surprise reactions. Ingrid and Dan were disappointed that younger sister Kerry had beaten them to it. Chubby was shocked but relieved that it was Benny's child and not his. Jimmy and Ian weren't sure that the right man was getting married but kept it to themselves. Lynne was glad that Kerry was now definitely out of the picture as far as Jimmy was concerned.

Dec 30, 1969
The United Kingdom Race Relations Board finds the
Wolverhampton Council guilty of racial discrimination.

And so ended a tumultuous year 1969 and the end of the swinging Sixties.

CHAPTER 18
The Seventies

1970

Thursday January 1 was the start of a new decade and Peter Murphy's twentieth birthday. A beautiful hot Durban summers day, perfect for a party at the Murphy household. The invitations were sent out to all close friends to join 'Peter' at a *braaivleis* and help him celebrate leaving his teenage years behind.

Ian and Dee, Jimmy and Lynne, and for some reason only known to Mrs. Murphy, Kerry and Benny were among the invited guests. Chubby was currently unattached and decided to invite Fiona much to the concern of his sister Mary who had recently arrived back from England.

Jimmy and Lynne were last to arrive and brought with them an unexpected guest in the form of Gus. Gus had hitch-hiked up from Cape Town, arriving only that morning. He had called Jimmy from the bus depot in Durban and Jimmy and Lynne picked him on the way to the Murphy's house. Gus had said he had hoped to make contact with Cathy but she was on three weeks holiday in England.

Of course, Gus had to give an update on what had happened to him over the previous year. He had passed his first year with firsts in all subjects. Due to his performance, he had been awarded a further bursary, giving him a bit more living money. He had taken a part time job at Groote Schuur Hospital which paid only a little but gave him some hands on experience. No lady or ladies in his life as he didn't have the time or the money.

Lynne, being the only real outsider, was introduced around. She was warmly greeted by Mr. & Mrs. Murphy but not so much by Mary and Fiona. At the first opportunity, she cornered Jimmy, 'Ok, what's going on here? Kerry, I understand, but what did I do to Mary and Fiona?'

'I am very sorry to have put you through this. I have been involved with both in the past. Mary chose to go overseas, and I barely managed to escape Fiona's clutches. I think the main reason is that you looking so fucking gorgeous has put their noses out of joint. Mary will quiz you at some point but Fiona might try and embarrass you, I have no idea why Chubby invited her.'

'I will be keeping an eye on you. I am glad you think I am gorgeous; you might just get lucky later on. Seems like the only one you've missed out here is Dee, you sneaky bugger.'

With lunch over, everyone settled into an afternoon of drinking and swimming. Lynne almost stopped the show when she emerged in tiny red bikini. Fiona, used to being the centre of attraction, was particularly miffed. Seeing everybody settled, Chubby called the guys together for a private pow wow. The four of them, armed with beers, retreated to Chubby's bedroom.

'Jesus, Gus, it's great to see you! Thanks a million for making the trip.'

'Hey, I wouldn't miss this for anything. I think we should make a pact. If at all possible, we should meet at the start of every decade and celebrate our friendship and also Chubby's birthday. Before we go on, what's with Kerry and Benny? If I had to make a guess, I'd say she's up the spout,' replied Gus.

'Right on there. They are getting married in about two weeks. From what Dee tells me, the baby is due sometime in June. Kerry says Benny is the father; he must have nailed her the day he got out of the army by all calculations,' said Ian.

'Is there some doubt?' inquired Gus.

'I think time will tell. If the kid is born with tight curly hair, one of this group is going to be in the shit,' said Ian.

'Chubbs, have you been a bad boy? Been diddling where you don't belong? You do know Benny is a Natal amateur boxing champ?' joked Gus.

'Hey guys, don't joke about things like this; I was sweating bullets when I heard about it. Let's stop talking about bad things, I propose a toast; 'To the best friends a guy can have, we must never lose touch with each other. Always be there, if needed'. Now, let's get vrot.'

'By the way, Wilson, what do you feed that woman of yours? She gets better looking every time I see her. I am sad I won't see Cathy this trip as I have to get back to Cape Town in the next few days,' said Gus.

Pow wow over, the boys headed back to the pool. There they found Mary and Lynne in deep conversation, the topic of which was Jimmy and her relationship with him. Fiona, on the other hand, was glaring at both of them. Kerry and Benny were sitting in the shade away from the rest of the party. Kerry, aware of her expanding physique, didn't risk wearing a swimming cozzie. Ian headed over to Dee and Chubby headed over to Fiona, Jimmy, not wanting to get involved with Lynne and Mary, grabbed a couple of beers and joined Gus.

Lynne eventually broke away from Mary with the excuse she needed the bathroom. She stood up and with a wink to Jimmy, made the walk around the pool heading for the toilet. Everything stopped and everybody present followed her every step; she really was a stunning creature and could work it when she wanted to. 'And I get to sleep next to that every night, what have I done to deserve that?' Jimmy thought, with a huge smile on his face.

The party eventually started breaking up. Kerry and Benny left first with 'see you at the wedding' ringing in their ears and an apology from Gus about not being able to attend as he was due back in Cape Town.

Lynne offered Gus a bed for the night and the three of them took off for Hillcrest. With Ian and Dee also departing, Chubby was left with his sister and Fiona. Mary and Fiona had never really made up since the last time they were all together, so a clearing of the air discussion was in order.

'Fiona, what are your intentions with my brother? You have a reputation of using and dumping men when you are done with them. I know he is not the most sensitive guy but I don't want to see him hurt.'

'I know you may not believe me, but I have changed a lot in the last year. I realised I was losing all my friends by acting the way I did. I don't know how your brother feels about me but I like him a lot, we have fun together. I want us to be friends again.'

'Well, as long as you are honest, I suggest we let bygones be bygones.'

Lynne, Jimmy and Gus arrived back at Hillcrest and settled down with gin and tonics. Gus was due back to work in Cape Town on Monday January 5.

'Gus, just how do you plan to get back to Cape Town? Please don't tell me you are going to hitch again?'

'Lynne, I don't really have an option. The reason I came up was to see my mates and also hoping to see Cathy. I haven't seen or spoken to her in six months and am not sure if she still wants to see me. I didn't have money for an airfare and the bus would take two days each way, so it's out with the thumb.'

'Jimmy, can you help me with another round and some snacks? Gus, we'll be back in a sec.'

Jimmy followed Lynne to the kitchen. 'You cannot let your friend hitch-hike back to Cape Town. I suggest we buy him a plane ticket. He will probably refuse but I am going to insist.'

'Okay, good luck with that.'

Lynne stepped back outside and honed in on Gus. 'I will not allow you to take your life in your hands by hitch-hiking back to Cape Town, we will buy you an air ticket tomorrow and you can fly out on Sunday.'

'I appreciate your offer but I cannot accept as I will not be able to repay you.'

'I am not taking no for an answer. When you are a rich doctor, we will remind you of this day, you can pay us then. End of discussion.'

Gus looked over at Jimmy who just shrugged his shoulders, 'Take it Mate, I have never won an argument with her yet.'

Jan 2, 1970
England cancels their cricket tour to Uganda and Kenya because of government pressures.

Bright and early Monday morning Jimmy reported for duty at Standard Bank Main Street. He was introduced around by his new boss, John Murray. Those in attendance were mainly the administration staff responsible for making staff travel bookings and generating payments for travel and accommodations. His first week was taken up getting an overview of the Bank's expectations and code of conduct. His first assignment was three weeks at Standard Bank Scottburgh as a teller.

Meeting Lynne in Pinetown after work, Jimmy broke the news of his first assignment.

'It's three weeks as a teller which is new to me, so good experience. The trip distance is about fifty miles from Hillcrest and about thirty five miles from the Main Street so the bank won't pay the daily mileage. They will pay for a hotel in Scottburgh and one round trip of seventy miles.'

'So, let me see if I get this right. You will be gone for three weeks, you won't be coming home each day and depending if you work Saturdays, you will be home Saturday afternoon and the whole day Sunday. Sounds wonderful,' replied Lynne, with just a trace of sarcasm.

'Oh come on! If you let me take the Beetle I can come home on Wednesday afternoons, sort you out and go back early Thursday morning. Saturday afternoon I'll be home by one o'clock, in bed by two minutes past and go back early Monday morning.'

'Sort me out, you cheeky bastard, you know me so well. What about Kerry and Benny's wedding? It's a two o'clock service at Saint James' on the Bluff.'

'No problem. I will meet you there. We can have a quickie in the parking lot just to calm you down. We will have two cars there, no problem.'

'A quickie in the parking lot, calm me down! In your dreams, buster, you know I don't do quickies. When we get home I'm going to give you a good seeing to so as you know what you'll be missing on a daily basis.'

Leaving early Monday morning, Jimmy headed for Scottburgh, arriving just after eight o'clock. He was met by the accountant who was obviously expecting him. He was briefed on the duties expected and would be introduced to the fourteen staff members before the bank opened. He was first introduced to Ronnie Smit, the chief teller, who went through the process of handing over the cash from the person he was relieving. All set up and ready to go, Ronnie took on the task of the introductions. Like all introductions, Jimmy immediately forgot most of the names until they got to the ledger department.

Ronnie walked up to the ledger check clerk and interrupted her, 'Coral, let me introduce you to our relief teller, Jimmy Wilson.'

It was difficult to know which of the two were more shocked.

'Hello Coral, it's been a while. I had no idea you had transferred to Scottburgh. How are you doing?'

Coral, blushing deeply, stood up and hugged Jimmy, 'Oh my God, fancy you being sent down to Scottburgh. I thought I had seen the last of you. We must have lunch and catch up.'

Jimmy, ever gracious, 'Yes, we must. I don't know what my lunch hour is yet but I am sure we can make a plan.' *Shit, just what I need* thought Jimmy.

It turned out they would be on different lunch hours much to Jimmy's relief but Coral would not be deterred. Jimmy was busy cashing up at the end of the day when Coral approached.

'I see you are staying at the Royal, it's really nice there. I am sure you will like it. Why don't we have a drink straight after work and then we can catch up?' Jimmy just nodded, realising that it would happen sooner or later so why not get it over with.

Jimmy had barely checked into his hotel room when the phone rang, he answered immediately hoping it was Lynne, it wasn't. Coral was downstairs, she said she would meet him in the bar. Jimmy finished unpacking before going downstairs. Jimmy went up to the bar and ordered a Lion Ale for himself and a vodka and tonic for Coral.

'So, how come you are working in Scottburgh?'

'Well, after we broke up, I had a couple of bad experiences in my social life and just hated living at the "Y" so I decided to get a transfer down here and live with my folks for a while. What's been happening in your life? Are you still going out with that older woman, what was her name, Liz or something?'

'Yes, her name is Lynne. We live in Hillcrest and I am madly in love with her. Just a point "we" never broke up, you did. So, how is your love life?'

'Pretty boring at the moment. You are here for three weeks, right? Maybe you can come out to the house over the weekend? I am sure my parents would like to see you.'

'Thank you for the offer but I am off home at every opportunity, Wednesday afternoons, Friday after work or Saturday straight after closing. Fancy another drink?'

'Yes please. What about a meal later?'

'The Bank pays for all my meals at the hotel, so sorry but I will be eating in.'

After the second drink, Jimmy stood up. 'Sorry, but I have to go. I need to phone Lynne for a chat before supper. It was nice to see you again.'

'Thanks for inviting me; maybe we can do this again?'

You invited yourself, thought Jimmy, 'I don't think that would be a good idea. When I'm not home with Lynne, I am studying for the Bank Exams so no time really,' lied Jimmy. 'See you at work tomorrow, good bye.'

Saturday morning directly after cashing up, Jimmy jumped in the Beetle and headed for the Bluff. By prearrangement, he met Ian and Chubby at the Harcourt hotel, they had two hours before the wedding but only one before he was to meet Lynne at the church.

Ian and Chubby were on their second round of drinks when Jimmy walked in.

'Ok Wilson, you have a bit of catching up to do. Chubbs here is drinking more in relief that it's not him walking down the aisle today. Barman, another round of Ales for us and two for this guy.'

'Hey boys, good to see you. I am going to have to neck these pints double quick as I am meeting Lynne in just under an hour.'

'Man, are you pussy whipped or what? How's it going in Scottburgh?'

'Shit, you'll never believe who is working there. Coral.'

'Coral, as in the one who dumped you? Must be a bit embarrassing for you.'

'No chance, she wants my body. I can fix you up with her, Chubbs.'

The banter went back and forth until it was time for Jimmy to head for the church and Lynne. Three beers down the throat in double quick time. When Jimmy pulled into parking lot he noticed Lynne's car already there. Pulling up next to her he climbed out of the Beetle and got into the passenger seat next to her. He leaned over to kiss her and was met with a dirty look.

'Have you been in the pub already? Couldn't wait to see me then? Is this what a week away is going to do to you?' she said with an angry look on her face.

Jimmy, taken aback, went instantly apologetic, 'I am so sorry. I met up with Ian and Chubby, they always lead me astray.'

'God, you are so easy. I' m just messing with you. Come here, you idiot.' Oblivious to anyone around them, they locked lips in a passionate kiss.

With guests arriving, they got out of the car to find Dee and Fiona waiting somewhat impatiently for Ian and Chubby. Jimmy and Lynne walked over to join them. By five to three there was no sign of Ian and Chubby, so the four of them entered the church and sat on the bride's side of the aisle. Up front stood a nervous-looking Benny with his brother Mickey as best man.

The organ struck up the bridal march and the congregation stood up and turned around. To everyone's surprise, they were greeted by the entrance of a giggling Ian and Chubby, followed directly by Kerry and her father. Ian and Chubby slid into the first available pew which happened to be on the groom's side. Dee and Fiona fumed while Lynne and Jimmy just shook their heads.

The wedding of 18 year old Kerry and 19 year old Benny went off without further incident. The happy couple left to have more photos taken and the congregation headed for the reception in the church hall.

With the speeches over, the party began. Jimmy was conscious of having to drive back to Hillcrest, so he nursed a single beer the entire time. Ian and Chubby, who were well on the way before they arrived, didn't hold back. By the time the reception was over, they were well and truly wasted; fortunately, Dee and Fiona managed to drive them home.

After wishing the bride and groom all the best for a happy future together, the three couples left for home.

Mar 2, 1970
Rhodesia becomes a Republic; the USA closes its consulate in Salisbury.

After his Scottburgh assignment, Jimmy's next relief was perfect; three weeks at Standard Bank Pinetown. Sharing his commute and lunch every day with Lynne, it was perfect; all was well at Casa Hillcrest.

Jimmy's third relief was at Standard Bank Durban North. He arrived at 8am Monday April 6. As per usual, he was met by the accountant and introduced around. The final person he was introduced to was one Cathy Bright, his new boss for the next three weeks.

Instead of the perfunctory handshake, he was greeted by a huge hug, 'Jimmy, when they said I was getting a relief I never imagined for a minute it would be you. Gosh, I haven't seen you for almost a year. How are you?'

'I am fine, Mrs. Bright. I thought you were still at ABC Branch?'

'No, I transferred here about six months ago. It's easier on the commute. Well, let's get down to business. You can call me Cathy, you know. We should get together after work, are you still seeing Lynne?'

'Yes, I am. I will call her and she can meet us here.'

Jimmy called Lynne and she agreed to meet them both after work at a nearby bar, Maggio's. Lynne and Cathy, although not having seen each other for nearly a year, still communicated regularly. After initial greetings, the conversation turned to Gus and how he was doing.

'I haven't spoken to Gus for a couple of months and haven't seen him since last July. He is doing well at UCT with straight A's. We didn't talk about his love life so I don't know. I was the one to suggest we move on but I miss him terribly, I don't know if I'll ever get over him. You two look perfect together. Any announcements on the way?'

'You sound just like my mother. We are happy as it is, aren't we James?'

'Sure.'

'So, what's she like as a Boss?' asked Lynne.

'Fantastic. I called her Mrs. Bright, which annoys her a bit, but she can't be too strict as I've seen her naked and I am sure she doesn't want me tell anyone at the bank. Isn't that right, Mrs. Bright?'

'Don't be cheeky, sonny, no one would believe you. Don't forget I have seen you in a similar condition and I can easily lie about how unimpressed I was. So behave. It's really good to see the two of you again, we should do this again soon.'

All agreed but as so often happens, it would be quite some time before all three would be together again.

Apr 16, 1970
Clifford Du Pont sworn in as the first President of the Republic of Rhodesia.

May 1, 1970
In Kampala, Milton Obote announces the nationalisation of all major industries.

May 4, 1970
During anti-Vietnam war protests at Kent State University in Ohio, four students (two of them girls) are shot dead by the National Guard.

May 22, 1970
The tour to England by South African cricketers is cancelled. Peter Hain and his anti-apartheid 'Stop the 70 Tour' members celebrate.

On June 1, 1970 after an eleven hour stretch of labour., Kerry gave birth to an eight-pound boy. The birth came nearly three weeks early but Mother and baby are healthy. Proud Dad Benny names the boy Lawrence.

Three weeks later the New Zealand All Blacks begin their Rugby Tour of South Africa. Protests over South Africa's Apartheid policies are seen around the world. Cries to cancel the tour are ignored despite threats of sanctions against New Zealand. Prior to the tour, the All Blacks played two exhibition matches in Australia amid huge and sometimes violent demonstrations.

With Chubby flip flopping between the Natal U20 and senior team, there is great hope that he may get a game against the All Blacks and impress enough to get himself in the frame for the November Springbok tour to the Wales and Ireland.

Jul 2, 1970
Mississippi has its first interracial wedding.

Ian, having written his final NTC III exam, got his results and found he had also qualified as a Motor Mechanic. He is now fully qualified as an Electrician as well as a Mechanic. The future looks bright.

Jul 9, 1970
Police and blacks clash during riots in Notting Hill, London. The Committee of Race Relations accuses Britain's beat policemen of being racially prejudiced.

On August 22, Chubby is selected at full back for the Natal first team to face the New Zealand All Blacks. New Zealand have never lost to a South African provincial team and Natal are seen as being no threat to that record.

To a full house at King's Park stadium, Natal take the field with no one giving them a hope; only they forgot to tell Chubby. The All Blacks kicked off and Chubby caught the ball on the Natal twenty-five-yard line. Taking two steps forward, he booted the ball back into their half going into touch ten yards from their line. There was huge cheer from the crowd and quizzical looks from the All Blacks.

From the resulting line out, the All Blacks conceded a penalty. The ball was thrown to Chubby who placed the ball five yards in from the left touchline and with his regular routine stepped up and slotted the ball through the posts 3-0 to Natal. The All Blacks looked shocked at the ease that the ball was struck and how accurate.

For the next twenty minutes, the All Blacks dominated the game and scored a converted try to go 5-3 ahead. The defining moment of the game came two minutes from half time. Chubby collected an All Black punt and took off towards their try line. Exchanging passes with his left wing he dotted down for a Natal try; 6-5 with the conversion to come. Chubby teed up the ball and calmly slotted the conversion; 8-5 for Natal.

From the kick-off, Chubby fielded the ball and made to kick it down field. No sooner had the ball left his boot than he was hit with a late tackle from the New Zealand flanker. Not braced for the tackle, he fell heavily to the turf with the weight of the flanker landing on his right knee. You could hear what sounded like bone breaking. Chubby screamed; initially there was a stunned silence and then loud booing at the blatant attempt to injure an opposing player.

The physio ran onto the field to check on Chubby. It was immediately obvious that he was badly injured so the stretcher bearers were called for. Chubby was gently loaded on to the stretcher and taken from the field. Back in the change room he was examined by the team doctor. His leg just below the knee was broken and the diagnosis was that there was probable knee damage as well. An ambulance was ordered and Chubby was shipped off to Addington Hospital.

The match was blown up for half time and the New Zealand team was roundly booed. The Natal team manager had to be physically restrained from confronting the guilty New Zealander. A half time replacement was put in for Chubby. The final score ended up 28-8 to New Zealand.

The local press had a field day highlighting the unsportsmanlike behaviour of the tourists. Putting a possible career-ending foul tackle on one of the most promising young rugby players in the country. The New Zealand team manager refused to condemn their player, saying it was an unfortunate part of the game. He sent his best wishes for a speedy recovery to Chubby.

Chubby was diagnosed with a fractured tibia just below the knee with possible cruciate knee ligament damage, which could only be assessed once the broken leg healed.

With public sentiment going against the New Zealanders, they lost the test series to South Africa by two games to one.

<h3 style="text-align:center">Oct 4, 1970
In Los Angeles, rock singer Janis Joplin is found dead from a drugs overdose.</h3>

A full two months after his leg was broken, the plaster was removed from Chubby's right leg. The muscle wastage made the leg look thin and weak. It was only now that the extent of the cruciate ligaments around the knee could be evaluated. X-rays revealed that both the interior and exterior have been damaged. The specialist explained that surgery will not be able to completely restore the ligaments and although extreme physical therapy will help strengthen the knee, it may never be strong enough to play first class rugby again.

Chubby, although devastated that his season and maybe his rugby future was over, vowed to get back to full fitness in time for the 1971 season. He would make the 1971 Springbok tour Australia or die trying.

With Jimmy still doing relief staff duty, things were getting a little strained at home. The past three assignments had been in Northern Natal with little hope of getting home on weekends. Lynne was getting frustrated with his continued absences and reminded him of his promise to quit if it wasn't working out for both of them.

Jimmy, not seeing a great future in the Bank in general and relief staff in particular, started looking around for alternative employment.

Looking through the classifieds in the Natal Mercury, he noticed an ad offering a career in computers. He called the number and was told that the company, Leo Computer Bureau, would be holding aptitude tests on the following Saturday. He gave his name and phone number and was told to report to a Pinetown address at 9.30am on Saturday. He figured nothing ventured, nothing gained.

8.45am Jimmy reported to Leo Computer Bureau to find around thirty other potential recruits. They were all seated in a large conference room and given an application to fill in. All the normal items: personal, vocational, military commitments and job history. When all attendees were done, the man in charge handed out what he called an aptitude test to see if you had the logic and aptitude to be a computer programmer. There were one hundred questions and you had three hours to complete the test.

Jimmy opened the test sheet and read the first item. It was very simple: you have three boxes A, B & C. In box A you had a 3 and in box B a 2. Using mathematical functions place 7 in box C. Easy enough. A+B into A; A+B into C. Two easy steps. The questions got progressively more difficult; Jimmy was in his element.

Forty-six minutes later, Jimmy completed the 100th question. He sat up and looked around him, everyone was busy, many looking confused. Figuring as he was done, he would just go and hand in his paper. He walked up to the man in charge and handed over his paper.

'A bit too difficult for you, young man?'

'No Sir, actually it was a bit of a challenge but fun.'

'You are the first person to call it fun. I will evaluate your test and let you know if we think you are a candidate for employment at Leo Computer Bureau. Good luck.'

Jimmy left the office and headed back to Hillcrest which was a twenty-minute drive. He was met by a very excited Lynne when he got home, 'Some guy from Leo Computers called and he wants you to call him back immediately. He seemed a bit excitable. His name is Al Spieth.'

'Jeez, I've only just left the place. I wonder what the problem is.'

Jimmy went inside and dialled the number. 'This is Al Spieth, who is this?'

'Jimmy Wilson. I got a message to call you, is there a problem with my test?'

'Thank you for returning my call. I'll say there is a problem with your test. We have never had anyone complete the test in the three hours allotted, let alone get all the correct answers and in less than an hour. What do you have to say about that, young man?'

'Lucky I guess, but I am a fast worker.'

'Lucky? Bloody amazing is more like it. How would you like to work for us as a trainee computer programmer?'

'When can I start?'

'Aren't you interested in the salary and working conditions?'

'Sure, what's the offer?'

'We will pay you R400 per month. The first month you will work in operations as a computer operator so as to become familiar with what we do here. It will be one week on day shift and one week on night shift. Three weeks paid vacation and an annual bonus depending on results, both yours and the Company. If this meets your requirements, we would like you to start on Monday January 4.'

'Sounds good to me. I will hand in my notice at the Bank on Monday; see you on the 4th then.'

Lynne, listening eagerly to the one side of the conversation, could hardly contain herself. 'Tell me! Tell me what's happening?'

Jimmy went through the details with her and ended with. 'Well, it's your birthday in three days so this is my birthday present to you; you can now have the pleasure of my company seven days a week again. Plus now I might be able to afford you financially.'

'You are going to have to get me another present as well, but in the meantime come with me and get your reward for making the decision to leave that fucking Bank.'

She turned and ran off towards the bedroom, by the time Jimmy caught up with her she was naked and on the bed.

Monday morning Jimmy handed in his notice at the Bank to no surprise; John Murray said he had been expecting it.

CHAPTER 19
1971

On New Year's Day 1971, as was the norm, everyone gathered at the Murphy home on the Bluff for Chubby's twenty first. The only absentee was Gus.

Chubby, still recovering from his horrific injury, was somewhat subdued. His sporting future in jeopardy, he decided to dedicate 1971 to his studies at Natal University. If he couldn't conquer the sporting world, he would conquer the business one instead.

On January 4 Jimmy reported for duty at Leo Computer Bureau in Pinetown. He was shown into Al Spieth's office who greeted him warmly. For the next hour he was introduced to the rest of the staff, all eager to see this guy who aced the aptitude test. He was then taken across to the computer room where he met the operations manager, John Coring, in whose care he was left.

John showed him around the computer room, pointing out all the main peripherals. He introduced him to the other operators and the shift boss, Mike Lowe, with whom he would spend the next four weeks. He left Jimmy with the parting words, 'We have you in here so that you can see how hard the operators work running around attending to various devices. So, when you write programs in future, take into account the actions the operators have to take and don't write fucking programs that chase the operators from device to device. Mike, he is all yours.'

'Don't take too much notice of John; he has a pathological hatred for programmers as he thinks they are all too full of themselves. You getting 100% on the aptitude hasn't helped his temper. How the fuck did you manage that?'

'Just good at Math, I suppose. Gee, this stuff looks great! I can't wait to get started.'

For the next four weeks Jimmy learnt the ins and outs of operating the Burroughs B3500 and B500 computers. He was a quick learner and was quite sad to have to leave operations and move over to the programming department. As he had no exposure to programming languages, he was put on a course at Burroughs in Durban. The course was scheduled to be completed by the end of July.

Jan 25, 1971
Idi Amin of Uganda ousts President Milton Obote in a military coup and assumes power. He immediately bans all political activity.

With Jimmy's twenty first birthday falling on a Tuesday, Lynne decided to throw him a party on the following Saturday. She invited all of his friends plus her Mother and Father, who travelled down from Benoni on the Friday. With all of the greetings done and presents handed out, Jimmy stood up and said he had an announcement to make.

'First of all, I would like to thank you all for coming and thanks for the gifts, even those inappropriate ones; I'm talking to you, Ian. I would also like to thank Lynne's parents, Val and Cyril, for making the trip down from Benoni. So, while I have you here Mr. Zales, I would like to ask your permission to marry your daughter.'

Val immediately burst into tears and ran over and hugged Jimmy first and then her daughter. Cyril, in an emotional state unable to talk, just grinned and nodded. Coming as a complete surprise to the gathered crowd, there was a huge cheer. The girls wanted to see the ring and the men wanted to congratulate their friend.

When questioned on a date for the wedding, they answered, 'When we have saved up enough money probably by this time next year.' Val, eager for some grandchildren, advised Lynne not to wait too long. Cyril, excited to gain a son, went around telling everyone what a fantastic bloke his future son-in-law was. Dee and Fiona wondered when their men were going to pop the question.

Feb 15, 1971
Enoch Powell predicts an "explosion" unless there is a massive repatriation scheme for immigrants.

Back at university, Chubby decided to test out his right leg and knee by turning out for the second cricket team. Batting first, he made a respectable thirty-two before being run out by his less than responsive batting partner. When it was their turn to field, Chubby took up his regular position as wicket keeper behind the stumps.

The position requires a lot of crouching and it soon became very obvious that his knee would not be able to take the pressure. He reluctantly gave up

50

the gloves and took a position in the covers. The first time a ball was hit in his direction, he had to make a sharp turn and chase it down. As he turned he felt a sharp pain in his right knee which brought him to an immediate stop. He knew at that moment if surgery was unable to fix his knee, he would not be able to play cricket at high level, let alone rugby.

Feb 20 1971
Idi Amin promotes himself to General and President for life.

Feb 22, 1971
South African Members of Parliament cheer when they are told that Britain will sell seven helicopters to South Africa.

Mar 3, 1971
Winnie Mandela, aged 36, wife of banned African National Congress leader Nelson Mandela, was jailed for one year. She was found guilty of violating a banning order which allowed her to see only a doctor and her two children.

Ian lands himself a job with ESCOM located at Maydon Wharf working on large transformers. With Dee working as a credit control clerk at Greaterman's and Ian earning good money, they decided to move out of their respective parents' homes and move in together. Thy secure a one bedroomed flat overlooking Brighton Beach. The flat warming party is attended by the usual suspects.

Apr 2, 1971
South African Prime Minister Vorster says South Africans will be allowed mixed race sport only at international level.

Jimmy completes his programming course six weeks early and returns full time to Leo. Still considered a trainee programmer, he is initially given mainly mundane maintenance jobs. Before being let onto any new projects, he would have to prove himself.

Jun 28, 1971
The US Supreme Court clears Muhammad Ali of draft dodging.

Chubby, having put his sporting activities to one side, completes his B Com. degree on December 3, 1971. With his mind set on conquering the business world, he commits to doing his Masters in 1972.

CHAPTER 20
1972

1972 began with more pressure being exerted on both South Africa and Rhodesia. More acts of terrorism being experienced in both countries.

On January 6 Ian is called up for what was termed a three-week army camp in Bloemfontein. As a former Parrabat, Ian had not yet been reassigned to his original unit, Durban Light Infantry, which would have been the normal course of events. He, his former paratroopers and those currently doing their National Service in Bloemfontein, were put through their paces in how to combat township rioting.

Emphasis was directed towards house to house combat. The feeling Ian got was that there was going to be a big increase in terrorist activities in and around the major cities of South Africa.

Jan 18, 1972
Ian Smith orders the arrest of former Rhodesian Prime, Minister Garfield Todd and his daughter, as they are seen as a threat to public law and order.

On May 6, 1972, thirty-year old Cathy marries Richard Wainwright. Both previously married but neither had any children. The wedding was attended by among others, Ian, Chubby, Jimmy, Dee, Fiona and Lynne. Gus sent a telegram with his best wishes and sorry he couldn't be there.

Jun 16, 1972
George Wallace, the segregationist Governor of Alabama, is critically wounded after an assassination attempt.

Aug 6, 1972
Idi Amin declares he will deport 50,000 Asians from Uganda to Britain within the next three months.

December 1972: Chubby completes Masters; he is now ready to find a real job and make his fortune. On December 3 Jimmy and Lynne announce that they will get married on February 10 the day after Jimmy's twenty third birthday. Gus agrees to be Jimmy's best man and Cathy to be Lynne's maid of honour with Dee and Fiona being bridesmaids.

Chubby, with his high profile from his Natal rugby days, joins the marketing and advertising firm of Miller, Keane and Bedford.

CHAPTER 21
1973

Jan 9, 1973
Rhodesia closes its border with Zambia in an effort to halt guerrilla attacks.

Jan 22, 1973
Former US President, Lyndon Bird Johnson, dies of a heart attack in Texas; he was sixty-four.

Feb 5, 1973
Twenty thousand black mine workers go on strike in South Africa.

Gus, now in his fifth year of medical studies, flew into Durban on the Thursday before the wedding. This was the first time he had been back in the area since July of 1970 which was also the last time he had seen Cathy.

The wedding rehearsal was set for that evening at the Catholic Church in Hillcrest. Expecting it to be awkward with Cathy and Gus, Lynne insisted that only those who were part of the wedding need attend. Val and Cyril had driven down from Benoni. Fiona and Dee drove over from the Bluff. Cathy arrived on her own from Durban North.

When Jimmy and Gus arrived at the church, they spotted Cathy talking to Val and Cyril. Jimmy walked over and introduced him to Cyril and Val, 'This is my best man and soon to be a world famous Doctor, Angus Stewart, you can call him Gus. Gus, these are Lynne's folks, Val and Cyril.'

Gus stepped forward and shook Cyril's hand and accepted a hug from Val. Gus stood back and stared at Val, not saying anything.

'Yes, I know, she looks like Lynne's sister, it's uncanny,' said Jimmy.

Gus turned to greet Cathy, 'Hi Cath, it's been a while, you look fabulous. Married life certainly agrees with you. Congratulations. I hope to meet your husband and tell him what a lucky man he is.'

It was obvious to all in attendance that there was still a spark between the two and probably always would be.

The following morning Jimmy picked up his sister, Maureen, from Durban airport and drove her back to Hillcrest. Maureen, working in Cape Town as a Medical researcher, would be Jimmy's only family member at the wedding. Jimmy introduced her to Gus and the two of them agreed to look each other up when back in Cape Town.

Although the wedding date had been known for months in advance, the bachelor party could only be held with the arrival of the best man. So, against all levels of common sense, the four guys and Cyril, the night before the wedding, set off for Durban. A room had been booked at the Cumberland Hotel where the plan was to spend the night if there was no one sober enough to drive.

Lynne had instructed her father to keep the boys under control and not let things get out of hand. It turned out that she had made a poor choice. Cyril, with the shackles off, was the worst of the bunch. The drinking started at the Cumberland and then they worked their way down the esplanade towards West Street, stopping for a drink at each pub on the way.

By the time they got to the Edward Hotel, they were all roaring drunk and were refused admission to the bar. Undeterred, Ian suggested they head for Smuggler's Inn, which is in the docks and red-light district. Hardly able to walk, they flagged down a taxi; five of them piled in and off they went.

Smuggler's Inn is probably one of the roughest pubs in Durban, if not the whole of South Africa. As it was a Friday night, it was packed, and one had to jostle your way to the bar to get a drink.

Cyril, feeling no pain, suggested it was his round and he made his way to the bar. Before he reached his destination, he was accosted by a scantily dressed woman who was employed to sell cigarettes, cigars and condoms, which she carried around in a tray which was suspended by a strap around her neck.

Cyril, much worse for wear, misinterpreted her intentions when she asked if he needed any of her wares; all he heard was, 'Do you need a condom?' Thanking her profusely, he said he was happily married and though she was a very attractive lady, he wouldn't be needing any sex tonight. Taking umbrage, she leaned forward to slap a surprised Cyril, who drunk as he was, ducked out of the way. This caused her to fall forwards spilling her wares onto the floor. Angrily, she shouted for help. This attracted the attention of the two huge bouncers who headed Cyril's way.

Ian, the least drunk of the group, saw a confrontation about to happen and moved to rescue Cyril. He got there a few steps before the first bouncer and grabbing Cyril by the arm, pulled him towards the exit. The bouncer lurched forward, missed Ian and bumped into another patron and knocked him and his beer to the floor. Wiping the beer from his shirt, the now very angry guy stood up and threw a punch at the bouncer, catching him squarely on the nose. Blood spurted everywhere; those in the immediate vicinity caught the brunt of it. Within seconds a free for all broke out.

In the ensuing melee, Ian managed to get Cyril and himself through the door followed by Gus and Jimmy. They started running down the road until they noticed Chubby was missing. They stopped and started to turn around and go back for their missing friend. They hadn't taken a step when Chubby appeared sprinting towards them, being followed one of the biggest brutes ever seen. Chubby, nodding his head, sped past at a speed none of them had seen since his rugby playing days. His pursuer, seeing Chubby disappear into the distance and now confronted by four guys who were obviously together, decided it was enough and he headed back to Smuggler's.

They finally managed to catch up with Chubby about a mile down the road. 'What the fuck happened there, Chubbs? I have never seen you move so fast?' asked Gus.

'Shit, Gus, I saw you Okes heading for the door but before I could make it, some bloke stopped me and asked why I was looking at his girlfriend. When I said I wasn't, he wanted to know why not was she too ugly for me? I said no, she was very nice. He didn't like that response either and grabbed me by the throat. It was at that moment I knew I was fucked so I kicked him in the balls and legged it out of there. I think it was his buddy chasing me.'

Deciding that maybe they were too drunk to drive home, the five of them headed back towards the Cumberland, stopping at three more pubs on the way. By this time, Jimmy and Cyril were well beyond help. With Gus, Ian and Chubby supporting the groom and the soon to be father-in-law, they managed to make it back without further incident.

It was left to Cyril to say the final words, 'Ian, thank you for saving my life and all you other blokes for letting me come along. Tomorrow my beautiful daughter will get married. I am so happy I could cry.' With those emotional words, Cyril fell onto the bed and totally passed out.

That night Cyril and Jimmy shared the double bed, Chubby got the single because he said his knee was sore; Ian and Gus got the floor.

It was just after ten the next morning when Ian was the first to wake up. Looking at his watch he realised the wedding was less than four hours away. He woke the other four, too much moaning and groaning. Having no change of clothing, it wasn't worth showering so they dragged themselves up and headed for the cars. Ian and Chubby headed back to the Bluff and Gus drove Jimmy and the still slightly drunk Cyril back to Hillcrest.

Arriving back in Hillcrest just before twelve, they were met by an irate Lynne. Seeing her father's condition, she angrily turned on Jimmy. 'I don't believe it! Look at my dad! How could you let him get like this and today of all days? As for you, Gus, I thought you would be more responsible.'

Before any of them could reply, she turned around and headed back indoors. So much for it being bad luck to see the bride before the wedding. Val, sensing her daughter was too angry to help, she decided to ply the three men with copious amounts of black coffee. While drinking the coffee, the story of the previous night's activities slowly came out.

On hearing what happened with Cyril, and suppressing a smile, she scolded him, 'Cyril, how could you lead these young men astray like this? When you are sober enough, you better own up and tell Lynne.'

Fashionably late, Lynne accompanied by her father, marched down the aisle followed first by Cathy and then by Dee and Fiona. The small congregation was evenly split between bride and groom. On the bride's side was Val, Cathy's husband, Richard, and a number of work colleagues. On the groom's side were Ian, Chubby and Maureen with workmates from Leo and a few from the Standard Bank.

Despite both Lynne and Jimmy being Catholics, the wedding ceremony was not the full Mass version, due to Lynne being previously married; a situation most of the congress was grateful for.

Cyril delivered Lynne to the alter, lifted her veil, kissed her on the cheek and handed her on to Jimmy. Lynne on any given day was a beautiful woman, on this day she took it up a couple of notches. One could feel the gasp when she was unveiled. Jimmy thought to himself, 'How did I get so lucky to meet this gorgeous creature?'

The church service was short and sweet with the priest extolling the virtues of love, respect, honesty and the love of God Almighty. Newly married, the bride and groom left the church and headed for the final wedding photographs. The congregation, after throwing the obligatory confetti and rice, headed off to the reception at the Hillcrest home of the new Mr. and Mrs. Wilson.

A large tent had been setup in the garden next to the swimming pool. A lamb was roasting on the spit which would later be served with a salad and vegetables in season. The tables had been setup and name cards placed. Drinks were served while the guests waited the arrival of the bridal party.

Photos over, the bridal party arrived. Lynne and Jimmy entered to a rousing cheer and prolonged clapping. They took their seats as did Val and Cyril, Gus and Cathy and the two bridesmaids. Maureen, as the sole Wilson family member, sat at the end of the table next to Dee.

Allowing the guests a few minutes to settle, Gus stood up and called for attention, 'At the request of both Lynne and Jimmy, we are going to break with tradition here today. We are going to get all the necessary speeches out of the way quick smart so we can get the party started. As soon as we are done here, food will be served. There is wine on the tables and an open bar; just flag down a waiter and order; hopefully we have your preferred poison. So, without further ado, I call on the bride to say a few words.'

'I know this isn't the way weddings go but I have to acknowledge a few people who have made this possible. Firstly, thank you all for coming.' Turning to her parents. 'Mom, you taught me to be kind, gracious, honest and caring, thank you; three out of four ain't bad. Seriously Mom, I love you so much. Dad, where would I start? You are always there for me, you picked me up when I was down and loved and supported me always, you are my rock, thank you for everything; I love you. Finally, to Cathy, my maid of honour and a true friend, I hope I can be as happy as you are. Richard, you are a very lucky man. I will leave the rest to the best man, Gus. Oh, by the way Gus, I am a little disappointed in the state you and the rest of them got my dad in last night.'

'Lynne, thank you for your heartfelt words. Just a point of clarity about Cyril and last night; Val, when your husband was approached by a lady selling wares at one of our stops, he unfortunately mistook her for a working girl and declared, *He was happily married and not looking for sex tonight but thanked her for asking*' and that's when the trouble started. Apart from declaring his love for you, the only other positive was seeing Chubby streaking past all of us, chased by a bouncer. We haven't seen him move that quick since his rugby playing days. Hopefully he can make a comeback. Natal sure needs him."

Turning towards Jimmy, 'It's at this point where the best man will tell an embarrassing story about the groom. I have been told I am only allowed one tale to tell, so unfortunately, I cannot tell the one about us finding him in a compromising position with a sheep; but I will tell how we all met. Back in January 1963 Jimmy, Ian, Chubby and myself ended up in the same standard 6 class. A week or so into the new school year, our friendship was cemented for all time. It was the day James here became a living legend at Grosvenor Boy's high school.'

To rapturous laughter, Gus related the story of the day Jimmy cleared the school hall with a single fart. Lynne, having not heard the story before, almost wet herself with laughter. Jimmy just shook his head.

When the laughter subsided, Gus continued, 'That was a true story. I have Ian and Chubby who can verify that tale. Lynne, Jimmy, Ian, Chubby you have been and still are my family. I love you all. Now I ask you to stand and join me in a toast to Lynne and Jimmy; may they have a long and happy life together. Cheers. I would like to call on Jimmy to say a few words; I hope he can because I think he is sitting there wondering just how the heck he pulled a girl like Lynne.'

Gus sat down and Jimmy stood up, 'Thanks Gus, but how can you tell that story? What can I say. Thanks Val and Cyril for producing such a beautiful person like Lynne. I am so lucky because in you, Val, I can see how beautiful my Lynne is going to look as she gets older. Cyril, I am not sure how we are going to get on, you are more like a buddy that a father in law, I hope you don't lead me astray too often. I would like to thank you for allowing me to be part of your family. Finally, I am so happy my sister Maureen could make it here today, thanks Mo.' Jimmy sat down.

Lynne stood up, 'Hey James, you forgot to mention the bridesmaids, so I'll do it for you. Dee and Fiona, thank you for making today so special for me. Also, thank you both for accepting me as a friend into your group. I hope to be attending your weddings one day soon. Ian and Chubby get a move on. As I forgot to do when I last spoke, I will do it now. Jimmy, I want to thank you for being there for me. When I met you, I was at an all-time low, you picked me up and gave me the confidence to be myself. You set me free and made me believe again. Thank you. I love you more than you will ever know.'

'Just don't put your contacts in and get a good look at him, you'll probably do a runner, He still can't believe he has hooked you, the lucky bastard' shouted out a voice that sounded very much like Ian's.

Formalities over, food was served, and the party began. Lynne and Jimmy did the rounds, stopping briefly at each table. Fiona caught the bouquet and Ian the garter. Gus and Maureen pulled up two chairs and joined Cathy and Richard; Ian, Dee, Chubby and Fiona got a table together. As the evening wore on and the guests started leaving, Lynne went to change out of her dress and Jimmy followed her.

'Cathy's bloke seems a nice guy and she seems happy,' said Jimmy.

'She does, though I am sure she is still in love with Gus,' replied Lynne.

'I think you are right. I know he does love her. What a pity that never happened,' confirmed Jimmy.

With Gus charged with getting himself and Maureen to the airport the next day, Lynne and Jimmy left to start their honeymoon. First stop was an overnight stay at the Edward Hotel then a flight to Salisbury and a week's trip to the Victoria Falls and Wankie game reserve.'

Jun 11, 1973
One thousand five hundred students expelled from university after demanding the appointment of a coloured Rector.

Ian was working the afternoon shift at ESCOM when he was called over by his supervisor to tell him there was a phone call from some lawyer guy who needs to talk to him. Ian walked into the small office and picked up the phone, 'This is Williams, who am I talking to?'

'I am Joseph Tillman and am calling on behalf of Mr. Jacobus Steyn. I have a document in my possession that has been drawn up on the instructions of Mr. Steyn, wherein he names you as one of his beneficiaries. I request you come in to our offices at your earliest convenience.'

'A beneficiary in what?' asked Ian.

'His last will and testament. Mr. Steyn passed away last week of a heart attack.'

'I did not know that. I am working afternoon shifts here so I can come in tomorrow morning, if that is okay.'

'It is; please be here at 9am tomorrow. Our offices Tillman, Tillman and Jackson are located at 155 Gardner Street.'

Ian grabbed a copy of the Natal Mercury and turned to the obituaries column and there it was; the death notice of Jacobus Steyn 58, died of a heart attack. At the end of his shift he hurried home to tell Dee the news.

'I got a call from Steyn's lawyer telling me that I have been named in Steyn's will. Maybe he left me some of those tools at the garage. I always mentioned that one day when I had enough money I was going to invest in a set like those.'

The next morning, bright and early, Ian arrived at Tillman, Tillman and Jackson and asked for Joseph Tillman. He was ushered into a conference room and a few minutes later Tillman entered. He shook hands with Ian and got right down to business.

'I have been instructed by the estate of the late Mr. Jacobus Steyn, that as he has no family, he wishes to bequest the deeds and title of Steyn's Garage, located at Crossways on the Bluff, clear and free to Ian Douglas Williams. He has also left you the property at 2625 Marine Drive. If you can show me some identification that this is indeed you, we can conclude this transaction.'

Ian, taken aback at the announcement, fumbled around in his coat pocket and managed to extract his wallet that included his driver's license. He handed it to Tillman, who after inspecting it, passed him the documents that needed to be signed. Ian signed the last page and handed them back to Tillman.

Tillman stood up and shook Ian's hand, 'Congratulations young man, you are now the owner of Steyn's Garage and the aforementioned property. Good luck. I hope you make a great success in your business venture.' He handed Ian a copy of both the title deeds and a bunch of keys.

Ian left the offices and instead of heading home, he made his way to ESCOM. Going directly to the personnel offices, he handed in his notice and asked if he could leave immediately. Not being a key member of the organisation, they agreed and arranged that his last pay would be processed at the end of the current cycle.

Ian picked up his car and headed back to the Bluff and Steyn's Garage. He unlocked the premises and phoned Dee at her place of work.

'Hey there, I am no longer working at ESCOM. I handed in my notice an hour or so back. I will be paid up until yesterday.'

'You quit ESCOM? Why?' she asked.

'Well, I am calling you from my new office at Steyn's.'

'Steyn gave you a job? Wow, things must be really busy there if he can afford to employ you full time.'

'He didn't give me a job. He gave me the whole business. I am now the owner of Steyn's Garage, how about that?'

'Why would he give you the business?'

'Oh sorry, I forgot to mention that he died last week and left it to me in his will. I have a meeting with the Bank this afternoon to transfer all the accounts into my name. I will let you know how that goes. See you this evening, just come straight here after work. Sorry, before you go, he also left me his house at 2625 Marine Drive.'

'We own a house as well? What are the monthly payments there? Can we afford it?'

'No monthly payments; the house is fully paid for. We can go and check it out tonight. If it's okay, we can hand in the notice on our flat. See you soon.'

Ian's meeting with the manager of Trust Bank Bluff Branch was an eye opener. Steyn's Garage had a substantial bank balance and a very positive monthly cash flow. Part of the instructions the bank had were to transfer Steyn's personal bank account to Ian as well. Ian was now a reasonably wealthy young man; more money than he had ever possessed.

All the paperwork done, Ian returned to the garage and went about contacting the staff, who had been locked out of the premises since Steyn's death. He contacted the three mechanics who in turn agreed to contact all of the black employees who wished to return. The lady who had answered the phone and did the banking had found another job and turned down Ian's offer.

When Dee arrived at the garage, she was greeted by Ian who announced Steyn's would be open for business from tomorrow. Ian wanted to show Dee around the premises, but she was too interested in 2625 Marine Drive to care about a garage.

Making sure everything was locked up, they headed out to see their new house. The house was a large three bedroom with a swimming pool. On entering, they found the place still fully furnished. They made the decision there and then that they would be sleeping in their new home immediately.

The following morning, Dee left for work and Ian headed to the Garage. He was met there by his workforce; the three motor mechanics and two of the four previous black workers. The other two were not able to be contacted. Ian thanked them all for coming in and promised that they would be paid in full for the days that the garage had been locked up.

Ian's next duty was to call the letting company and hand in his notice for the Brighton Beach flat, effective immediately and terminating on the last day of July. Almost straight away, the phone began ringing with people looking to book their cars in for a variety of mechanical needs or just plain services. Word had got out that Steyn's was now re-opening for business.

The first day was chaotic; the phone never stopped ringing and customers were ringing the bell in reception looking for service. By early afternoon it was clear to Ian that he needed someone to take care of the office and customers dropping off or collecting their vehicles.

That evening Ian told Dee all about his day and the need for help with the reception and the office in general, 'I just don't how I am going to find someone.'

'It's easy; just put an ad in the papers stating what the job is about and a contact number.'

'Then what? Do I just have them come in for an interview? I wouldn't know where to start.'

'Right, pretend I am coming in for an interview. I walk in and say: hello, I am Dee, here for the interview. Okay, now you interview me.'

'Okay. Hello, I am Ian Williams, the owner of this establishment. I am looking for someone to work a full day to manage the office part of the business. You will answer the phones, book in the cars, make out the invoices, collect the money or the cheques and do the banking. Also, you will help me do the weekly wages.'

'What is the pay?' asked Dee.

'Oh shit, I don't know. Let's say R200 per month,' suggested Ian.

'Make it R250 and I will take it. Just one more question, will I be able to sleep with boss?'

'Oh no, I have a girlfriend,' said Ian.

'You are such an idiot. I said I will take the job and was just checking if we will still be sleeping together. After all, R250 a month is way more than I am getting now.'

The penny dropped, 'You mean you actually want the job? I thought we were just role playing. You are hired! Hand in your notice tomorrow.'

Jul 6, 1973
Rhodesian guerrillas kidnap two hundred and seventy children and staff from a Catholic Mission.

Dee handed in her notice the next day and after explaining her situation, they allowed her to give only one week's notice.

At this time none of their friends had been told the good news so Ian decided it was time for a party. He called Chubby and Jimmy and invited them and partners to a party on Saturday July 14. He told them not to bring anything as he had a big announcement to make. Not fielding any more questions, he just gave them the address and told them to be there by 6pm, and bring a toothbrush as the party may go on a bit so they may want to sleep over.'

Both Chubby and Jimmy arrived at the same time and followed each other up the long driveway at 2625 Marine Drive. They parked one behind the other and got out of their cars. Jimmy surveyed the house and its large grounds, 'Ian must be house-sitting for someone, no wonder he wants to throw a party. Looks like a great place.'

The four of them walked up to the front door, before they could ring the bell the door was flung open by Ian who greeted them with 'Howzit. Welcome to my humble abode, come on in and have a *dop*. Dee is in the kitchen putting together a salad, we can head for the Den.'

They followed Ian through the lounge to the den. There was a well-stocked bar in the corner and Ian turned and said, 'Lynne and Fiona, what would you like to drink? Jimmy and Chubbs, a couple of pints?' suggested Ian.

With Fiona set with a dry white and Lynne a red, Ian passed the two men each a Castle Lager.

'Okay Williams, what the heck is going on here? Some dude lets you house sit and provides the booze; you lucky bastard?' asked Jimmy.

'No Jimmy, my mate, not quite. I am going to get Dee as I have an announcement to make. Hang on a minute.' Ian left his guests alone and went to get Dee. He returned moments later.

'Sorry to keep you all in suspense. You guys remember Steyn's Garage down the road at Crossways, right? Well it is to be renamed Williams Motors.'

'How come the new name?' asked Lynne.

'Well folks, old Mr. Steyn pulled the pegs and left the place to me,' said Ian.

'You lucky bastard, so you went and bought this place?' remarked Chubby.

'No, I didn't. He left me this place as well, lock, stock and barrel. So I figured it was time to celebrate with my friends. Cheers.'

'Well, that is a good enough reason to celebrate. Cheers!' said Chubby, raising his glass.

'Actually, the main reason for the party wasn't for the garage and house, it is for this.' Ian turned towards Dee and producing a small box from his pocket, got down on one knee. 'Dee, I love you more than you could ever know, please will you marry me?'

Dee, totally surprised by the request, burst into tears. Hardly able to speak, she just nodded. Ian opened the small box to reveal a sparkling diamond ring. He took Dee's left hand and slipped on the ring. Dee wiped away the tears and kissed Ian.

After congratulations all around, Ian went on to give all the details of Steyn's demise and the content of his will. He admitted he really was one lucky bastard; a Garage, a beautiful house and engaged to the love of his life.

The party raged on until the early hours and with none of the guests in any condition to drive, they decided to take up Ian's offer to sleep over.

Three weeks later, Ian filed the necessary papers to have the garage name changed to Williams Motors.

Oct 15, 1973
The South African Government extends racial segregation to all private gatherings.

On October 20 Chubby and Jimmy were called up by NMR and left on what was their first 'Three Week Camp'. Leaving from Durban Station, they were bade farewell by Lynne and Fiona as the train left for Bloemfontein. Chubby, who had a degree and was a regular at the Comrades club at NMR, had been promoted to a two-pip lieutenant; Jimmy, on the other hand, being safely out of range for parades had lost his corporal's stripes.

The camp was situated some twenty miles outside Bloemfontein in a military area known as De Brug. It was about a four hundred square mile tract of land where military exercises were carried out for the army and air force. NMR would be part of an exercise with two infantry units in a manoeuvrer to practice a mechanised battalion advance against a defensively dug in enemy force.

Chubby was the officer in charge of a troop of four tanks with two armoured cars as reconnaissance. His troop B squadron was short of a troop sergeant. Chubby used his influence to arrange a field promotion for Jimmy to troop sergeant. The manoeuvrer was a cock up as usual. Two of B squadron's tanks were not in any condition to take part. The one that Jimmy was tank commander of, developed gear box trouble the second day and he spent the next two and a half weeks waiting for spare parts. The second inoperable tank had radio problems; as a result it was unable to make radio contact with the rest of the troop.

So, for the duration of the camp, Chubby, Jimmy and their tank crews were confined to camp. They made the most of it by drinking duty free beers at fifteen cents to the pint. The only action they saw was qualifying with the R1 rifle at the shooting range.

They returned to Durban by train to bet met by Lynne and Fiona on Friday, November 16.

On arriving back home in Hillcrest, Lynne informed Jimmy that she had had a miscarriage. Unknown to Jimmy at the time, she was six weeks pregnant. Although disappointed, she was sure that it wouldn't be too long before she would be pregnant again.

CHAPTER 22
1974

1974 would turn out to be a year in which South Africa would be further ostracised by most of the rest of the world over their Apartheid policies. Sporting boycotts would remain across all sports, with the only exception being rugby. Demonstrations were continually being held outside the South African Embassy in London.

As an overflow from the bush war in Rhodesia, more incidents of terrorist activity were seen in South Africa. Labour problems, fuelled by black militants, were becoming more common. Pressure was being put on international companies to disinvest in South Africa but no official sanctions were in place.

The British and Irish Lions rugby team undertook a two and a half month tour to play South Africa in four test matches plus a number of games against the top provinces. Much to the dismay of the locals, the tourists were unbeatable. The only blot in their copy book was a drawn match against the Springboks in the last game of the tour. The general consensus by the media, both local and overseas, was that international isolation was the cause of the approaching demise of South African rugby.

Aug 8, 1974
Richard Nixon resigns as US President in the wake of the Watergate scandal. Gerald Ford sworn in as the next President on August 9, 1974.

Sep 16, 1974
President Ford pardons his predecessor Richard Nixon.

November saw the Springboks undertake a two match tour to play both matches against the French national team. The games saw the Boks win both games in spite of both games being marred by demonstrators. The Springboks returned home questioning what was the point in playing sport under those conditions; the rest of the world questioned why anyone would partake in a sporting contest with a country that selected their teams based on colour.

Dec 11, 1974
Ian Smith, the Rhodesian Premier, agrees to an immediate cease-fire with Black Nationalist leaders.

On December 15 Gus received his final examination results from UCT. He had achieved As in all subjects for the sixth straight year. He is voted top of his class and is awarded the Moss Trophy for highest marks scored by a medical student. The award named in honour of Doctor Theodore Moss, a famous doctor of the 1920's, came with a cash award of R10, 000. The following day, Gus signed on at Groote Schuur to start a one year internship which was a requirement to complete his qualification as a medical doctor.

CHAPTER 23
1975

1975 dawned and it would turn out to be a year of change in the lives of the four lifelong friends.

Chubby, realising that if he ever wanted to resurrect his sporting future, he would have to find a surgeon who could repair the ligaments on his right knee to allow the knee to stand up to the rigours of rugby. He was introduced to Doctor Steadman who had had success in repairing the knees of several well-known sportsmen. As a last resort, he made an appointment with the doctor to see him in his Atlanta, Georgia office.

With Williams Motors booming, Ian decided it was time to expand his business and take advantage of his electrical qualifications. The vacant property adjacent to his was up for sale. He decided to put in a bid which was accepted. He gutted the inside of the building and had it rebuilt to house an office and a workshop offering electrical services. The new business was opened under the name of Williams Electrical Services.

Keeping it in the family, he employed his older sister, Miriam, to manage the office and her eldest son, Clive, as an electrician. Together with Clive, Ian started tendering on small electrical contracts initially only on the Bluff. Armed with two fully equipped trucks, Williams Electrical became the go to company on the Bluff for household requirements.

Jimmy, now the top programmer at Leo, was offered the position of Manager of Programming Development. It would be more of a management position and less of a hands-on programming job. Jimmy's first reaction was to turn down the position as he loved writing programs but was not so keen on being just a manager. After much discussion with Lynne, she convinced him it was good experience and as a manager he could select the programming jobs he fancied for himself; she also realised that Leo was too small an organisation and the future would be limited. She didn't realise at the time just how prophetic that statement would be.

Apr 31, 1975
The Vietnam War is over. Saigon surrenders almost without a struggle. America's fifteen-year involvement in the war ends.

Despite Lynne no longer taking any form of contraceptive, she was unable to fall pregnant. Concerned that she was already twenty-seven and desperate to have a child, she convinced Jimmy that they needed to see a specialist.

They duly made an appointment with one of the top fertility doctors in the country. Lynne was examined and the doctor could find no physical reason why she could not conceive. Jimmy provided a semen sample which, after analysis, proved his sperm count was high and strong enough to not be the problem. The advice was for Lynne to take her temperature daily and when it indicated she was ovulating, have sexual intercourse on every day that she ovulated. After sex, she was to lay on her back with her pelvis raised, this was seen as the best way for the sperm to reach and fertilise her eggs.

Jun 1, 1975
Rhodesian police shoot dead eleven blacks during riots in Salisbury.

Chubby returned from Atlanta after having corrective surgery on his right knee. Doctor Steadman was quietly confident that the operation would strengthen the knee but only time would tell if it would be strong enough to play first-class rugby again.

The 1975 French rugby tour to South Africa would come too soon for Chubby but he was hopeful that he would be in shape for the 1976 All Black tour as he had some revenge in mind. With increasing pressure on sporting teams to boycott competition with South Africa, Chubby felt his chances of becoming a Springbok were reducing every year. With African countries threatening to boycott the 1976 Montreal Olympics if the New Zealand tour went ahead, there was a feeling that the pressure would lead to the cancellation of the tour.

Jun 11, 1975
British lecturer and author Denis Hills is found guilty of treason and is sentenced to death for criticising Ugandan President Idi Amin.

Jun 16, 1975
Britain and South Africa terminate the 1955 Simonstown Naval Agreement.

Britain's cancellation of the Simonstown Navel Agreement coincided with the cancellation of the order of five submarines and two coastal patrol boats that had been on order with France. An order with the French for ten Mirage Jet fighter bombers was cancelled by order of the French Government. South Africa's ability to defend itself was coming under threat as more arms manufacturers joined the UN resolution on arms sanctions against the country.

Jul 1, 1975
Uganda's military dictator, General Idi Amin, gives way to international pressure and grants sixty-one-year-old Denis Hills an unconditional reprieve from the firing squad.

The French rugby team completes a tour of South Africa. They lose both games in Pretoria and Bloemfontein.

Aug 12, 1975
Thousands of whites flee Angola as the threat of civil war looms. Although independence is still three months away, the exodus to Luanda begins with tales of rape, looting and murder by rival armies of black guerrillas.

August 14, 1975: Dee gives birth to their first child, a boy named Douglas John. Young Douglas was born into a far more affluent family than any of his male predecessors. Spoilt rotten by Grandmother Betty and his three aunts, he was the first grandchild in the Williams family.

Aug 25, 1975
In Rhodesia, talks between the government and black leaders take place in railway carriages on neutral ground near the Victoria Falls.

Aug 26, 1975
Rhodesian talks collapse.

With Jimmy being called up for a 26-day camp in October and November, Leo Computer Bureau management attempted to get him an exemption as a key member of a small business. They fail but make it clear that they had expected him to be more in favour of an exemption than he showed.

Sept 22, 1975
American President, Gerald Ford, escapes an assassination attempt for the second time in seventeen days; his assailant is Sara Jane Moore.

With the upcoming independence looming in Angola, the South African government hints that there is a strong possibility of National Servicemen being deployed on the northern border of South West Africa and Angola. The South West African People Organisation (SWAPO) strongly objects to the plan and vows to disrupt any SADF involvement in the affairs of a neighbouring country. South Africa has a legal mandate to protect the port of Walvis Bay, as per an agreement signed during the Second World War, to prevent Germany annexing it. This mandate does not extend to any other part of the country.

Sept 28, 1975
Joshua Nkomo is elected as President of the exiled United African National Council in Rhodesia.

Oct 26, 1975
London: Peter Hain, the Young Liberal leader and staunch anti-apartheid protester, is arrested for stealing four hundred and ninety pounds from a bank in Putney.

Chubby and Jimmy leave Durban Station with NMR for their second twenty-six-day army camp to be held in Bloemfontein. Rumours abound that with the tensions and possibilities of a civil war in Angola, they will be sent to the South West African border with Angola.

The rumours turn out to be partially true. Under South African Law, no Citizen Force soldiers may legally cross into a neighbouring country without declaring war on that country. What was allowed was the deployment of National Servicemen to protect the country's interest.

With Tempe's close proximity to De Brug, the powers that be decided that the young Armour troops doing their eighteen months National Service at 1SSB Tempe and those at the School of Armour would be temporarily seconded to NMR for additional training before being sent to Grootfontein

72

in South West Africa, where they would be held in readiness in case fighting spread across the Angola border.

What was supposed to be an extensive three weeks of training turned into two days of instruction by NMR on how to fire the 90mm guns on the Eiland armoured cars. This was the first and only time these young 18 and 19-year-old soldiers had fired these weapons before being shipped off to potentially fight a war.

Nov 14, 1975
Soviet advisors arrive in Luanda, Angola.

With NMR the only tank regiment currently involved in a camp of any sort, General Magnus Malan, chief of the Army, requested a demonstration of the Centurion tank in action. Major Hearn, the gung-ho officer in charge of C Squadron, was only too keen to show the Army Chief and his senior officers NMR's capabilities. Hearn's stated ambitions were to lead the first armoured advance against an enemy since the Second World War.

Hearn, eager to be seen by Magnus Malan, decided he would control the whole 'attack' by radio, while explaining to the General what was going on. One tank from each squadron A, B & C would do a drive-by, firing at targets on the range at distances of 1,000 to 2,000 yards. The Centurion tank was one of the few tanks able to fire accurately on the move. Hearn hoped this fact would impress the General in order to be considered for any future action. Hearn's wishes were not known to his troops.

Straws were drawn and C, A and finally B Squadron would show their firing abilities. Chubby, as senior officer for B Squadron, appointed his tank to be B Squadron's offering. The first thing he did was make Jimmy his gunner. Next, he and Jimmy, surreptitiously under the cover of darkness, paced out the distance between each firing point and marked the spot with an empty beer can. Making notes, they also paced out the firing range for each target.

On the day of the demonstration with all the dignitaries in place, Hearn got the show on the road. On his command, the C Squadron tank drove into view. Pulling up at each of the five firing points they stopped and fired two rounds and moved on to the next. Of the ten rounds fired, three were direct hits.

The A Squadron tank was next up. On Hearn's preset orders, they were to fire two rounds on the move at the third target and all the others

73

at stop, fire and go. The two on the move both fell short of the target but four of the stop and go rounds hit home.

For B Squadron's run, Hearn decided to put the tank's radio transmission on broadcast for the benefit of the attending brass. On Hearn's command, Chubby's tank moved forward.

With the first exact range already set into the sights and Chubby watching for the empty beer can, his voice came over the radio. 'Driver halt, Gunner target to the right ninety degrees infantry carrier, range 1,200 yards.'

Jimmy's voice, 'Range set, target acquired.'

'Fire two at will.'

'Firing now.' A direct hit; the target disabled. 'Firing now.' Another direct hit; target destroyed.

Chubby's orders were to have a firing on the move at the third target. Ignoring the order he had decided to try his luck at the second target. Knowing the range, Jimmy had set the sights in. Chubby, keeping an eye on the beer cans, ordered turret to right at forty-five degrees and on his order, Jimmy fired at the first target, a Bedford truck; a direct hit. A ten-degree adjustment of the turret, a new range and a second firing with no change in speed brought a second direct hit. All the while Chubby's voice echoed over the radio.

The final three sets of targets were all taken on the move and all were direct hits. One thing about the Centurion tank, if your sights were dialled in and you had the correct range you would hit every time on targets up to 2,000 yards.

Unaware they were on a broadcast speaker and the adrenaline pumping, Chubby's voice came booming over the loudspeakers, 'Fuck me, James, that was some shooting, I hope those fuckers were impressed. I wonder if they'll let us do it again. Jesus, that was fun.' Hearn, ten seconds too late, managed to switch off the broadcast.

Hearn looked over at Malan, who in turn walked over to the Major, 'Major Hearn, thank you for the demonstration. I would like to meet the crew of the last tank. Very unusual radio protocol.'

Hearn picked up the radio microphone and instructed Chubby to turn his tank around and report to the firing command post. A few minutes later, the tank pulled up with Chubby and Jimmy both standing up in the turret waving to the cheering watching NMR troops. The two of them accompanied, by the driver and loader, alighted the tank, came to attention and saluted the watching officers.

'Well, Major Hearn, introduce me to the crew.' Hearn obliged and introduce Malan to the crew.

'Chubby Murphy, now where do I know that name? You must be the same man that was at 1SSB around six or seven years ago. Played Rugby for the Army and then got taken out unfairly by those cheating All Blacks. Have you given up playing?'

'Yes Sir, that would be me. The knee is still giving me problems but I hope to be ready to take revenge on those bastards next year when they tour.'

'Well, I wish you luck. My officers and I thank you for your excellent demonstration. NMR should be proud of you and your crew.'

Malan returned Chubby's salute and as he turned to rejoin the dignitaries, he looked over his shoulder and said, 'Yes, you can be sure us fuckers were suitably impressed.'

Back at the base camp, Chubby was questioned at length by the other tank crews as to how he managed to shoot like that and on the move. The only answers they got were, 'Superior crew commander skills and the greatest gunner in the regiment.'

The festivities were interrupted by a private who informed Chubby that he was ordered to report to Major Hearn's quarters immediately. Chubby, well-fortified and feeling no pain, took his time before reporting as ordered.

Chubby walked into Hearn's tent and was met by a seriously angry man, 'Lieutenant, who the hell do you think you are disobeying my orders? Were you trying to make me look like a fool in front of General Malan?'

'If I have learnt anything in the Army, is that under battle conditions you take the initiative and engage the enemy as you see fit. After watching those clowns in A & C Squadrons barely hitting a target, I thought I would save the regiment and you from being embarrassed by hitting a few. If that was against your orders then I would apologise, but I thought the plan was to impress the watching Generals.'

'You know, Murphy, you have a real attitude problem, I am tempted to place you on orders.'

'Be my guest, Sir, it might just be the first time an officer is punished for saving the day. If there is nothing else Sir, I would like to get back to my men who happen to think what my crew did is worth celebrating. Good day, Sir.' Chubby saluted and left leaving Hearn lost for words.

For the rest of the camp, Chubby and Jimmy never had to buy a drink. Word had also got out about Chubby's confrontation with Hearn. The general consensus was that Hearn was an absolute cunt and a bit of a bully. The fact that Chubby stood up to him just added to the legend.

The camp broke up with the spectre of Angola hanging over them. Surely they wouldn't be called up as they had only just done a camp.

Jimmy returned home to find Lynne was six weeks pregnant, the baby due in the middle of June.

Nov 24, 1975

Two weeks after independence was declared, Angola reports an estimated forty thousand people dead and over one million left homeless. Marxist MPLA (Peoples Movement for the Liberation of Angola), the FNLA (National Angolan Liberation Front) and UNITA (National Union for the Total Independence of Angola) are locked in a civil war. UNITA is backed by South Africa and both UNITA and FNLA are backed by the USA. MPLA is supported by the Cubans, East Germans and Red China.

CHAPTER 24
1976

Jan 1, 1976: After three months of test programs, South Africa officially launch live TV. During the first live news broadcast, the lead story is that the Government announces the implementation of three-month call ups for Citizen Force units.

January 2, Jimmy and Chubby get call up papers for a three month camp starting on January 6. Based on the Post Office's crap service in delivering mail, it was obvious that the letters were posted well before the Government announcement on January 1. Gus gets the same call up and as a qualified doctor, gets rank of Captain.

After leaving Durban station on the morning of the 6th, the regiment arrived directly at De Brug the following morning, where they are met by those soldiers not resident in Natal. NMR is broken down into three tank squadrons A, B and C. Additionally, a mechanised support troop and a logistics section, each supporting each of the three fighting squadrons. 'A' Squadron was comprised mainly of those soldiers not resident in Durban.

Immediately on arrival, the whole regiment was lined up in front of Commandant Richard (Dickie) Bird. 'The Regimental orders are as follows. We will be completely kitted out in the new Defence Force "Nutria". Side arms in the form of Star 9mm pistols will be issued to all Officers and tanks crews, R1 rifles will be issued to the rest of the troops. Everyone will carry their weapons at all times and in order to simulate war conditions, live ammunition will be issued. The Regiment will undergo battle manoeuvrers for a period of no more than five weeks, after which we will be relocated to Grootfontein in South West Africa. Gentlemen, there we will draw our vehicles, after which we will be deployed on the border with Angola to combat both SWAPO incursions and any overflow from the Angola Civil war. That will be all; Officers, take over your squadrons.'

The advance party had drawn and pitched tents. The first night would be spent in those tents. In war conditions, tank crews were expected to 'sleep' with their vehicles. Tents were set up for 'non-fighting' officers and NCOs. A medic's tent was set up to house the regimental doctor, his orderlies and all medical equipment. Tents were set up for kitchen equipment and the cooks, plus tents for logistics and 'non-fighting' clerical troops.

One thing NMR are famous for is that placed anywhere on earth, they would find showers, a telephone and booze. On the first day, before the mess was set up, the scrounge was on to find liquor. Chubby and Jimmy had the foresight to realise that the old kit would be scrapped so they had loaded up their kit bags with bottles of vodka, rum and cane spirits. They had also removed the box part of Box Wine and between them, they had the insides of four boxes of wine. Word had circulated that there was a supply of alcohol in the B squad's tent.

A steady stream of non-B Squadron personnel made the trip to the tent and were not very politely told to take a hike or something along those lines. The booze was strictly for B Squadron. Chubby, being Chubby and not in the least rank conscious and with no other Officers present, was just one of the boys.

With the party well underway, Chubby was interrupted by one of the troopies, 'Sir, there is a Captain outside asking for permission to come in. What should I tell him?'

'If he is not from "B" Squadron, tell him to fuck off.'

'Sir, he said you would say that and if you did, to tell you to come outside to say it to his face, and in his words not mine, "You fat bastard."'

'Cheeky fucker. I will take care of this,' replied Chubby and getting to his feet headed for the tent flap.

Throwing the tent flap aside, Chubby stepped out ready for action. 'Gus, what the fuck are you doing here?'

'I thought calling you a fat bastard would get you out here. So, do I get a *dop* or not?'

'Sure, come on in. Hey Jimmy, look what the cat dragged in. Somebody get this man a drink.'

With Gus supplied with a mug of red wine, he and his two buddies caught up with their news. Gus, on his first camp, had been called up to 'A' Squadron. He was initially annoyed at the disruption to his internship but when told that the army camp would count towards it, he looked forward to meeting up with his two buddies.

Jan 26, 1976
Soviet built MIG jet fighters join the clash in Angola.

With over one month of the camp complete, Jimmy celebrates his twenty-sixth birthday by getting completely wasted and wondering just what the point of the whole exercise was. The news from Angola was troubling and here they were achieving absolutely nothing. Manoeuvrers were proving nothing, other than if this was the what would happen under battle conditions, they would be well and truly fucked.

Feb 14, 1976
Soviet T-34 tanks driven by Cuban troops and backed by MIG fighters sweep all before them as the MPLA forces drive towards UNITA-held strongholds. Thousands flee across the border into northern South West Africa.

With rumours circulating that the camp was being cancelled, finally some news was released. 'A' Squadron would escort twelve brand new Centurion tanks to Grootfontein. The train would be leaving from Bloemfontein via Pretoria. The camp at De Brug would be broken up and all other equipment handed back to stores, including small arms and rifles. 'B' and 'C' Squadrons would return to Durban and be called up at a later date to relieve 'A' squadron.

Feb 18, 1976
London, The Race Relations Bill is published, making it an offence to incite racial hatred.

Jimmy and Chubby bid Gus farewell as he heads for Grootfontein. Unsure of what the future holds, the two of them catch the train home.

Jimmy is met by Lynne who is barely showing her four and a half months pregnancy. The next day he heads back to Leo. The reception at work was cool to say the least. Al Spieth, who is an American citizen and very against Apartheid, does not approve of the SADF's call on Jimmy.

Mar 3, 1976
Mozambique President Machel puts his country on a war footing and sizes Rhodesian-held assets.

Jimmy and Chubby are called up with 'B' Squadron to report for duty again on April 6, no end date is given. With little or no news emanating on what was happening on the border, they were unsure if this was to complete the three-month camp or a completely new one. Leo management are disappointed to lose their Programming Development Manager for a further unknown amount of time.

Leaving Durban station, the train heads for Pretoria where a troop train is made up of 176 NMR soldiers and 550 Infantry men of the predominately Afrikaans Regiment Algoa Bay (RAB) from Port Elizabeth. While NMR were able to freely supply their troops with alcohol, RAB were under strict instructions that anyone found drunk or with alcohol on their person would be placed under arrest.

The train trip from Pretoria to Grootfontein would take six days and seven nights. Food was dry rations; loaves of bread that started out fresh on day one were rock hard by day three. For some reason, the labels on the canned goods had been removed; the only defining thing was the square tins were either bully beef or spam sausages, the round tins were supposed to be peas, corn, beans, potatoes, shredded beetroot or pears. Whoever had packed the tins had only included pears and beetroot. The majority of the square tins were bully beef.

With the incessant heat, stale bread and a poor selection of tinned food, tempers became frayed. Added to this condition was the normal antagonism between Infantry and Armour and the English and Afrikaans dislike of each other; when alcohol was added it was inevitable that friction would occur.

On the third day, a bunch of NMR men managed to disengage the back ten coaches from the train. By the time anyone in the front of the train was aware, the RAB coaches were some fifteen miles adrift. It took over three hours to reattach the coaches; armed guards were posted on the first RAB coach.

The train eventually arrived at Grootfontein where the troops joined a sprawling army base. There were over one hundred thousand soldiers made up of Permanent Force, Citizen Force and National Service men. The Armour, Infantry and Air Force branches were all represented. An airstrip had been made to service helicopters, transport planes and a squadron of Mirage fighter bombers.

NMR's B Squadron hooked up with their A Squadron colleagues who were thrilled to see them, as they had been instructed to hand over all equipment to the incoming troops, after which they would be leaving for home.

Chubby and Jimmy took the opportunity to seek out Gus.

'Gus, how the hell are you? You guys see any action?'

'I am good; happy to be soon the hell out of this shithole. Action? The only action we have seen is hurry up and wait. The entire squadron has been stuck here for six weeks doing absolutely fuck all. Fortunately, beer is 10c a pint and hard tack R1.00 a bottle. Rumour has it you guys will take over the tanks and head straight out to Ruacana 160 k's north of here on the Angola border.'

'I hear you lot will be leaving for home the day after tomorrow, so I reckon we spend the next day and a half necking some of those 10 cents beers,' said Jimmy.

'Funny you should mention that, James. I just happen to have a fridge full of Windhoek Lagers. I have the only fridge in the regiment; it was to keep medical supplies cool. As we have not been issued any supplies I thought why waste a perfectly good fridge; can I interest you fellows in a cold beer or six?'

They spent their first night in Grootfontein getting well loose, catching up on what was happening in their lives. The next morning the big handover got underway. The task went on well into the night and by the time it was over, A Squadron was ready to leave.

The departing troops were seen off by their B Squadron replacements. The comments of those departing were all derogatory. 'Don't worry boys, we'll take care of your women while you guard the border.' Some more personal. 'Hey Johnno, I'll look up Karen and help her out.'

Gus had told his two friends that he was getting off the train at Windhoek and flying back to Cape Town, as he couldn't face the train trip to Pretoria and then to Cape Town via Bloemfontein. He bade them farewell, not knowing it would be the best part of fifteen years before they would meet up again.

On returning to Cape Town, he applied for a grant to study at the famous Guy's Hospital in London. It was granted immediately and he left for London.

Apr 9, 1976
Young Liberal leader, Peter Hain, is acquitted of charges of stealing four hundred and ninety pounds from a Putney bank.

Chubby and Jimmy left Grootfontein for Ruacana in a convoy that included 12 tanks being transported on carriers, 6 armoured cars, 15 Bedford trucks, 12 Land Rover jeeps, 2 kitchen trucks and 1 Mercedes van carrying all personnel records, topographical maps and signal codes.

The 160km trip took twelve hours, as the tank transporters driven by National Service troops had to stop every hour to 'pump up the shock absorbers'. Each stop meant putting out a perimeter guard as the area was considered hostile.

B Squadron eventually arrived at what would be their base camp for the next six weeks. The site was located at the T-junction of the road that ran parallel to the Angola border which was just one mile to the north.

With typical NMR 'can do', somehow a front-end loader was located and driven by Staff Sergeant Basil (Baz) McMann, and a defensive position was dug. The tanks were dug in hull down; Troop 3 facing north, Troop 2 facing south and Troop 1 protecting the east and west perimeters. Three Armoured cars were spread between the tanks on the north and south sides.

Once the camp had been established, Baz dug a 30×50 six-foot deep hole in the middle of the camp. It was then covered by tarpaulins and filled with water. To keep the water clean and fresh, the camp's issue of water purification tablets was requisitioned. Who needed drinking water when you had beers at 10 cents each?

With average daily temperature in the upper 90's F, the days became one of lying in the pool cooling off or just hanging about in a pair of shorts getting a tan. The once a week trip into Grootfontein to get supplies proved a bit of distraction to two of the Bedford drivers and their 'copilots' plus the crews of two Armoured Cars.

As units in the field were only issued dry rations, there were only a limited number of ways the cooks could prepare bully beef into something resembling an appetising meal. It was after the latest offering that Chubby decided to intervene. He decided that he and his trusted sergeant, Jimmy Wilson, would requisition the two Armoured Cars and volunteer to accompany the convoy to and from Grootfontein.

The stores in Grootfontein were a drive through. The trucks would drive in one end, locate the food provisions pile marked 'NMR', load the two Bedford's and proceed to the beer issue and load that. On exiting the store, the two trucks would be checked that all was in order before allowing them to proceed. Nobody supervised the actual loading; they only checked the contents on the way out.

On this trip, the two Armoured Cars followed the trucks into the stores. With Chubby being an Officer, nobody questioned his presence walking around the store. With Chubby and Jimmy supervising, they raided the Officer's store and loaded up the Armoured Cars with cases of frozen chickens, eggs, bacon, *boerewors*, steaks and any non-dry rations they could lay their hands on. Following the Bedford's to the liquor stores, they loaded up ten cases of mixed whiskey, vodka, rum and cane spirits. Ten bags of ice were dumped into the vehicle carrying all the food.

The hatches were closed on the two Armoured cars, with only the driver inside the vehicle. The crew commanders and the gunners were perched on the turret. On exiting the stores, the Bedford's were checked, and the two escort vehicles were waved through. Once outside the Grootfontein camp, the convoy made it back to Ruacana in record time.

The convoy screamed into the camp, and with the armoured cars leading the way, headed for the kitchen. Never having seen an arrival quite like this, a crowd gathered. Chubby called the NCO in charge of the kitchen over and supervised the unloading of the pirated goods into the freezer. Chubby then approached the Squadron Commanding Officer and suggested a *braai* should be held that night. Knowing Chubby, the CO asked no questions; he called the Medic in charge and ordered that a pit be dug.

The plan was to cook the steaks, chickens and *boerewors* before any investigative search was done of their camp site. The eggs and bacon could be stored for later use. The hard tack would need to be consumed or buried somewhere. Never a unit to shirk a challenge, NMR decided the best way to make 120 bottles of booze disappear was to drink it.

Every one of the 176 men had at least one piece of chicken or steak and a piece of *boerewors*. The booze proved to be a too big a challenge with less than half the bottles being drunk. The empties were buried in one hole and the remaining bottles hidden in a hole outside the camp perimeter, right in the line of fire.

The inevitable inspection happened two days later. Although no direct accusations were levelled, the inspection covered more than just the troops and vehicles. No 'loot' was found but a new standing order was issued; in future, all supply pickups would be supervised by stores personnel.

Apr 20, 1976
Ian Smith calls up several thousand white reservists after black guerrillas blow up a key rail link with South Africa at Beit Bridge. The guerrillas are believed to have penetrated at least one hundred miles into Rhodesia from the Mozambique border.

The camp was put on high alert on May 1 as intelligence said the Communist-backed SWAPO and MPLA forces were likely to launch an attack. Throughout the day, signals were going back and forth but no attack happened. It was then assumed it would be a night attack.

Just before midnight, one of the guards atop the Armoured Car facing north heard what sounded like a large number of people advancing towards the camp. He called out that night's password and getting no response, launched a flare which sounded the alarm. In no time at all, the seven vehicles protecting the north side of the camp opened fire with 5.0 Browning machine guns and 60mm mortars.

Not receiving any return fire, the call to 'cease fire' eventually got through and all action stopped but not before over a thousand rounds of 5.0 bullets and forty mortars had been fired. For the rest of the night, vigilance was the key word. At first light, patrols were sent out to assess the damage and look for casualties.

Less than ten minutes later, the patrols returned with the news that there were at least twenty dead. The only problem: none were human; all were of the bovine variety. A team was sent out to recover the casualties, which were then skinned and cut up for consumption. All skins and bones were buried. Later that day, a delegation from the town of Ruacana arrived at the camp searching for any news on a missing herd of cattle that had escaped from a nearby *kraal*.

That was the last action B Squadron faced during the camp; at least they had fresh meat for most of the rest of the camp.

Jun 11, 1976
Angola: thirteen mercenaries go on trial for murder, looting and other crimes.

On June 13, C Squadron arrived to take over from their B counterparts. They arrived to find a well-fortified camp with a swimming pool. The first thing their commanding officer, Major Hearn, did was close the swimming pool and issue standing orders that full uniform was to be worn at all times. The highly tanned B Squadron handed over all equipment and headed back to Grootfontein. They were greeted there with the news that instead of a six-day train trip, they would be flown by military air plane back to Louis Botha Airport in Durban.

June 15 B Squadron arrived back in Durban to be greeted by their loved ones. Arriving back in what was the middle of winter, the troops looked tanned and rested, not what one would have expected after returning from a war zone.

Fiona and a heavily pregnant Lynne, met their men prepared to be shocked at their condition after being exposed to a war. Both were, if anything, a bit disappointed to see two tanned and relaxed soldiers; had they been on holiday? Fiona looked great, Lynne, on the other hand, looked huge and uncomfortable, there would be no homecoming sex on offer.

The next day Jimmy returned to a rather cool reception from his boss at Leo.

Ian had been returned to his unit at DLI as a Corporal and was given the news that he had to report for duty. It was a three-month camp based in the Pretoria area and would consist of patrolling local black townships as backup to the police.

Jun 18, 1976

Johannesburg. After three days of rioting by blacks in SOWETO, a black township south west of Johannesburg, over one hundred are left dead and thousands injured. Prime Minister, B.J. Vorster, announces that security forces have been ordered to restore law and order 'at all costs.' Police have been opening fire on crowds of mostly school children without warning. Two white men have been killed when they were dragged out of their cars and stoned and beaten to death.

June 21 after a short labour, Lynne gives birth to a daughter, who they name Sharon. With Jimmy feeling the heat at Leo, he decided against asking for time off to assist his wife. Fortunately, proud grandparents, Lynne and Cyril, made the journey down from Benoni.

Jun 28, 1976

Three British paratroopers and an American are sentenced to death by firing squad at the conclusion of the trial of thirteen white mercenaries in Angola. The nine others are given prison sentences ranging from sixteen to thirty years.

On July 1 Jimmy is called into Al Spieth's office and is told that due to cost reduction, he is being laid off effective immediately. He will be paid for the month of July, he can choose to attend work for that period or leave today. He chooses to leave immediately and leaves without shaking Spieth's extended hand.

Returning home to Hillcrest to tell Lynne about the devastating news; a new baby and no job. Lynne consoles him with the comment that Leo are a Mickey Mouse company and everything she has read says that small Computer Bureaus were unlikely to still exist in the near future. She would be proved prophetic as the Durban branch of Leo would shut its doors in less than two years.

Reading the Computing News, Jimmy finds a Senior Analyst Programmer job being offered at Southland Cables in Pietermaritzburg. He applies for the position and is granted an immediate interview. After an interview on July 5, he is offered the position with a salary of R100 more than he was getting at Leo.

On June 30, the New Zealand All Blacks begin their three-month rugby tour to South Africa. The five Maori players in the tour party are given honorary white status for the tour so as to not compromise the South African policy of only playing against white players. Although Chubby is playing club rugby, he is in no condition to play for Natal, let alone for the Springboks.

Jul 10, 1976
The three British and one American mercenary are executed by firing squad in Luanda.

On Monday July 19, Jimmy starts his new job at Southland. It would be a daily commute of just over sixteen miles each way, not much further than his daily commute was to Pinetown. Although the mainframe at Southland is different than the one at Leo, it gives him exposure to IBM equipment, which is by far the dominant computer company in South Africa and most of the western world.

Jul 31, 1976
The Montreal Olympic Games open despite the boycott of almost all of the African athletes who stay away in protest of New Zealand's continued rugby ties with South Africa.

Gus is arrested in London during anti-Apartheid demonstration outside South Africa House. Arrested with him are a number of Australians, one of whom is Stacey Packer, a native of Perth. Gus and Stacey are bundled into the same Paddy wagon and strike up a conversation. After their release Gus arranges to take Stacey out on a date.

Aug 13, 1976
Winnie Mandela, wife of banned ANC leader, Nelson Mandela, is held with twenty others as riots spread in SOWETO, Port Elizabeth and Grahamstown.

Sept 15, 1976
Two hundred and fifty thousand non-whites stage a strike in Cape Town.

The New Zealand All Blacks complete their tour of South Africa, losing the four-match series 3-1.

Ian returns to Durban after finishing his three month camp. He refuses to discuss the details with Jimmy and Chubby,

Gus is arrested a second time at an anti-Apartheid demonstration; this time he comes to blows with a police constable and is denied bail. His court appearance is set for three days hence.

Sept 23, 1976
The South African Government eases multi-racial sports contact at international level but strict segregation stays at club level (which forms the basis of international selections) remains.

Gus appears in Marylebone District Court where he is fined 1,000 pounds and warned that if arrested again, he could face a prison sentence. The court proceedings and sentence appears in the local South African Newspapers and on SABC TV. Jimmy and Chubby find the whole thing very amusing; Doctor Gus in jail!

Sept 24, 1976
In a twenty-minute radio and television broadcast, Ian Smith stuns his white supporters by announcing Rhodesia will be a multi-racial state.

After much speculation and rumours, it is officially announced that Southland Cables have been bought by Unitech Cables from Port Elizabeth. The effect on Jimmy's position at Southland isn't clear, as Unitech have their own data processing department with their own management structure. The Head Offices of Southland and Unitech Cables are relocated to Edenvale, just outside of Johannesburg.

87

Rumours abound that the data processing departments will be consolidated and moved to Edenvale.

Oct 3, 1976
Rhodesian black leader, Bishop Abel Muzorewa, returns to a tumultuous welcome after fifteen months in exile.

Chubby is made a partner at Miller, Keane and Bedford, which is rebranded as Miller, Keane, Bedford and Murphy.

Oct 25, 1976
The Transkei becomes the first black "homeland" or "Bantustan" to be given independence. No foreign governments recognise the move.

For the first time since opening the business, Williams Electrical Services becomes more profitable than Williams Motors. With this in mind, Ian looks to expand. He takes a course covering the programming and installation of Programmable Logic Controllers (PLC). PLCs are often used in factories and industrial plants to control motors, pumps, lights, fans, circuit breakers and other machinery. Ian sees this as the next step in providing a total electronic service to large corporations and factories. He opens up another company and names it Williams Electronics.

Oct 31, 1976
Rhodesian commandos launch a retaliatory raid across the border into Mozambique.

Dec 2, 1976
Jimmy Carter, a Democrat, is elected as President of the United States of America.

Ian, having completed the training in PLCs, applies for the import of required equipment from Nokia of Finland and inexplicably gets sole agency of their product. He hires Nick Powell, a recent graduate with an Industrial Engineering Diploma, to look after the expected PLC business

Having discussed the possibilities of PLCs with Jimmy, he is introduced to the factory manager at Southland Cables, Brian Coleman. Coleman agrees to a pilot project on one of the small PVC cable lines.

88

With Nick's assistance, Ian puts together a small PLC that will control raw PVC input for the extrusion process and measure the quality of the finished product. Statistics on throughput and machine efficiency will also be recorded. The newly implemented process will save the cost of one employee.

Dec 20, 1976

A guerrilla gang crossing into Rhodesia moved in on a British-owned tea plantation and killed twenty-seven African workers and their families with Russian AK47 automatic rifles.

After a successful two-week trial, Southland sign a contract with Williams Electronics to implement the PLC system on all four extrusion lines for small gauge PVC cables and telephone wire.

Dec 28, 1976

Winnie Mandela is released from prison as the deaths from Christmas rioting rises to twenty six.

CHAPTER 25
1977

Jan 2, 1977
Ian Smith rejects the peace proposal of British envoy, Ivor Richard.

On January 4, 1977, four days after his twenty seventh birthday, Chubby marries Fiona. The wedding, held at the Methodist Church on the Bluff, is attended by a huge crowd of family, friends, sports colleagues and business associates. The reception is held at the Durban Collegians Sports Club on the Bluff (essentially a Grosvenor High School Old Boys Club) where Chubby, as co-founder, is president. Jimmy is best man and Fiona's sister and cousin make up the bridal party.

Jan 31, 1977
Four hundred Mission children in Rhodesia are kidnapped for guerrilla training by black nationalists.

On February 3 Williams Electronics signs a contract with Unitech Cables of Port Elizabeth to supply and install PLCs. Ian hires a second PLC expert and promotes his nephew, Clive, to manage the business. Ian, wanting to get back to his first love, decides to expand the Williams Motors brand.

His first move is to find the company who owns the vacant property of the defunct Bluff Ford dealership. The company, Wakefield's, are only too keen to make a deal as the property has been vacant for more than two years. He next approaches Standard Bank with the idea that he will have a STANNIC clerk on site to arrange financing for vehicle sales through their bank. Putting up 2625 Marine Drive as surety, he arranges a substantial loan against the property.

He arranges an interview with the National Dealership Manager at Ford Motor Company in Pretoria. He proposes a deal to reopen Bluff

Ford with a new brand, Williams Ford. The building will be refurbished and offer on-site financing by STANNIC. He negotiates a deal that stock will be sold on consignment, payable either at time of sale or at ninety days from being taken into stock. Surprisingly, Ford agree and a deal is signed to open Williams Ford by April 1, 1977.

While he was on a roll, he decides to push his luck. He offers to sponsor an up and coming young Durban racing driver, Tim Hunt, if Ford will provide him with one of the new Cortina V6 GTs. Ian promises that once he tunes the vehicle, it will be unbeatable. Ford Racing agree on the condition that it is not called a 'factory racer'. Ian agrees.

Feb 7, 1977
African guerrillas massacre seven white missionaries (three Jesuits and four Dominican nuns) at St. Paul's Roman Catholic Mission at Mrewa, thirty seven miles east of Salisbury.

With Dee heavily pregnant, Ian enlists his sister, Miriam, to take over the office management of the Crossways branches of Williams Motors and Williams Electronics.

On Feb 19, 1977 Dee gives birth to a second child, a daughter named Elizabeth.

Ian signs an agreement with Chubby's firm of Miller, Keane, Bedford and Murphy to handle all his marketing requirements.

Feb 25, 1977
Idi Amin orders all American citizens in Uganda to meet with him and forbids them to leave the country.

Gus is arrested for the third time for protesting the proposed 'World Teams' rugby match against the Springboks in Pretoria. He is arrested with his girlfriend, Stacey. Appearing before the Marylebone Magistrates Court, he is given ninety days to leave the country, otherwise he will be deported back to South Africa.

Mar 18, 1977
Zaire: Troops are flown to Shaba Province in an effort to combat troops invading from Angola.

One week before the opening of Williams Ford, Ian entered his souped-up Williams Ford-prepared Cortina V6 GT in the open 50 lap race at

Roy Hesketh Racetrack in Pietermaritzburg. He would be in direct competition with the factory version of the same vehicle. It was a superb drive by Tim Hunt who finished a respectable third behind a pair of Porsche 911s. The factory Cortina came in eleventh.

The driver and owner were interviewed after the race. The consensus was that this was the best performance ever from a Ford Cortina in the open category; everyone wanted to know how they managed it with a standard non-factory car. Ian, ever ready with a quote, praised Tim and said that the car was prepared by expert mechanics at the soon to open Williams Ford on the Bluff.

On the back of extensive advertising, Williams Ford opened on Friday April 1, (Ian's 27th birthday) April Fool's Day. The advertising promised the best deals in Durban, on-site financing and a free tank of petrol on new car sales from Williams Motors.

The six newly employed salesman could barely keep up with the inquiries. Discounts of up to 10% offered on all vehicles had attracted a large crowd. There were the always present 'just looking' customers but the day ended with eleven sales of on-site stock and orders for six more to be delivered from the factory. This was on a work day; prospects looked excellent for Saturday morning.

The normal hours for a Saturday were from 8-12. At 12 o'clock, the on-site STANNIC clerk still had a waiting queue of six people hoping to finalise their deals. Ian decided to keep the doors open as long as there were customers in the show room; the doors eventually closed at 5pm. The day's activities had resulted in a further nineteen sales. As the banks closed at 11am, nine of the sales would only be able to be confirmed on Monday. In two days, thirty sales were concluded with twenty-one confirmed. Of the thirty sales, twenty-two came with a trade in. Ian now had a Used Car inventory.

The Director of the National Ford Dealerships called Ian on Monday morning to congratulate him on achieving record sales over an opening weekend. His concern was that Ian was selling vehicles at a lower price than Ford's recommended price. Ian's answer was what was the average vehicle sales in the other Durban area Branches over the same two day period? When told it was 3.5, Ian's reply was that he would rather sell 30 vehicles at a R100 profit than 3.5 at R300 profit.

With the spectre of deportation hanging over him, Gus decided to take up Stacey's offer to join her in Perth. Gus presents himself to the Australian Consulate in London seeking to emigrate to that country. With his medical degree and his distaste of the Apartheid system, which the Australian Government is equally disgusted with, Gus is granted temporary immigrant status and is free to settle in Perth.

Jun 8, 1977
**Commonwealth leaders issue a warning to Southern African
whites to change their ways or face more bloodshed.**

Val and Cyril make the trip down to Hillcrest for their granddaughter's first birthday. Cyril takes a picture of Sharon using his Polaroid; while it is developing, he produces two pictures, one each of Val and Lynne at the same age. Placing the three pictures side by side it is impossible to tell them apart, it is only the obvious age of the prints that make it possible to tell who is who.

On July 3 Jimmy and Chubby are called up to what was supposed to be their final 'three week' camp with NMR. With the three-month call-ups still in place, they are fortunate that the military powers that be have decided that the Angolan and Northern South West Africa terrain is unsuited to tank warfare; the camp reverts to De Brug and Bloemfontein. What they failed to see was that winter in the Free State was not ideal conditions for crews to be sleeping with their vehicles. The nightly temperature hovered around -12 to -14C.

Jul 18, 1977
Ian Smith calls for a general election.

Friday July 28, 1977: after ten years' service, Chubby and Jimmy return to Durban where their commitment to the South African Defence Force officially ends. A copious amount of alcohol was consumed on that train home from Bloemfontein.

Aug 6, 1977
**Twelve Rhodesians die as a bomb rips through a crowded
Woolworth's store.**

Aug 21, 1977
Sixteen people are massacred by guerrillas in Umtali, Rhodesia.

August 26: Gus marries Stacey, who is three months pregnant, in a civil service in Perth. With the marriage, he immediately qualifies for Australian citizenship, which he takes up but retains his South African nationality.

93

Aug 31, 1977
**Ian Smith wins the general election with eighty percent of the
overwhelmingly white electorate vote.**

With the burgeoning reputation of Williams Electrical, Ian is asked by
ESCOM to tender to install PLCs at one of their substations as a pilot
project. The potential is enormous if the pilot is a success. Realising that
a successful tender and pilot will stretch his resources beyond his current
capacity, he institutes a recruitment drive. He employed his other two
sisters, Angela and Celia, to help Miriam with the offices at the Garage
and Electrical Offices.

Sep 12, 1977
**South African black civil rights leader, Steve Biko, dies while in
police custody.**

Sep 15, 1977
**One thousand two hundred students are arrested in Johannesburg
when they gather to mourn the death of Steve Biko.**

Sep 25, 1977
Over fifteen thousand mourners attend the funeral of Steve Biko.

Ian's tender with ESCOM is accepted and he is contracted to provide
PLCs to fifteen substations in the greater Durban area. Williams
Electronics starts to garner a lot of interest with a number of the larger
more well-known electronics companies hovering around.

Oct 20, 1977
**South African Government clamps down on the press by arresting
at least sixty people, banning two black newspapers and eighteen
black organisations. Donald Woods, editor of the East London
Daily Dispatch newspaper, is served with a banning order.**

Williams Electronics successfully delivers on all fifteen ESCOM
substations. Durban area ESCOM request approval from their head
office in Pretoria to precede with the remaining one hundred and twelve
substations in the greater Durban area. ESCOM head office refuses
permission. The excuse given is that head office doesn't think Williams

Electronics would be able to support that number of installations due to its size.

Oct 23, 1977
South African Prime Minister, B.J. Vorster, says there will be no move to majority black rule, regardless of international pressure.

ESCOM put the supply, programming and installing of one hundred and twelve PLCs at their Durban substations, out to open tender. Ian tenders and even though less cost, loses the contract to electronics giant, CONTEC. The Johannesburg giant begins the process to source the necessary hardware and software. Ian, in the meantime, employs four more PLC programmers and begins their training on the Nokia hardware.

Nov 14, 1977
Pretoria, South African police officers swear that they did not assault Steve Biko but admit to leaving him naked and shackled.

CONTEC approach Nokia to source the required hardware needed to drive the PLCs. They are directed to Williams Electronics, who are the sole distributors in South Africa of the Nokia hardware. Ian, having anticipated CONTEC's need, had already placed an order with Nokia for one hundred and twenty units.

Nov 24, 1977
One man, one vote principal accepted by Ian Smith. Talks are held with Bishop Abel Muzorewa and Reverend Ndabiningi Sithole but exclude guerrilla leaders, Robert Mugabe and Joshua Nkomo, whose armies have been doing all the killing.

CONTEC place an order for the necessary one hundred and twelve units with Williams Electronics. They are quoted thirty percent more than the estimated price used in their tender with ESCOM. CONTEC attempt to reduce the price by appealing to NOKIA; they are referred to Williams Electronics, where they are given short shrift. CONTEC place the order giving Ian and his company a healthy profit, pretty much what they would have made had they had won the tender.

95

Twelve weeks after the death of Steve Biko in a Port Elizabeth police cell, a Magistrate rules that the police could not be held responsible for Biko's death.

The software needed to run the PLCs is custom written and for the ESCOM contract, it was written by Ian's programmers. For some reason that no one at CONTEC would own up to, it appeared that they were under the impression that the software was preloaded onto the hardware. When they were unable to make the PLCs perform as expected, they approached Ian for assistance.

Although the software was transportable across all the hardware, Ian decided to protect his investment. The source code was modified to check the serial number of the hardware, and only if a match was found on the unit would the software work. CONTEC, in an attempt to recover some of their costs, decided that they would only need Ian's assistance for three of the installations. Ian quoted them the unheard of rate of R100 per hour for software implementation. He quoted ten hours per installation for loading and testing the PLC, which totalled R3,000 for the job. He would use this project to train his new PLC programmers. The contract signed with CONTEC stated that the software would be loaded and tested by Williams Electronics; no mention was made about the ownership of the source code.

CONTEC calculated that the investment was worthwhile, as they would use their own staff for the final one hundred and nine installations. The contract would start on January 3, 1978.

CHAPTER 26
1978

Jan 1, 1978
Donald Woods, banned over his attack on the South African Government over the death of Steve Biko, escapes to Lesotho by hitch-hiking over three hundred miles and swimming across a flooded river.

Two days after starting the contract, Williams Electronic successfully installs the first three ESCOM PLCs on behalf of CONTEC. Bill Varner, chairman of CONTEC, although relieved that three of the hundred and twelve substations have been successfully implemented, wants assurance that the remaining will come in under budget.

Feb 15, 1978
Ian Smith produces a plan for blacks to win power in Rhodesia. all citizens over the age of eighteen will be allowed to vote for the one hundred seat assembly. Twenty eight seats will be reserved for whites. The settlement is immediately rejected by US ambassador, Andrew Young, as neither Joshua Nkomo nor Robert Mugabe have been brought into the deal.

After two weeks of attempting to install the next PLCs at ESCOM, the CONTEC installation team admits defeat. The CONTEC project manager calls Ian to complain that the hardware is defective and demands one of his technical staff reports to the Wentworth substation to sort out the problem. Ian reminds him that there is no support contract in place but in the interest of customer relations, he would send one of his programmers out to investigate.

Knowing exactly what the problem was, Ian accompanied his programmer. The PLC was started up and the program immediately displayed the error message "Software not compatible with processor. Load correct object programs."

Ian explained that this was not a hardware problem but a software incompatibility issue. The problem was easily solved by recompiling the programs on each individual processor. He was told that they did not have the source. Ian, acting dumb, asked how they wrote their programs without source code? He was told that they just copied the programs from one of the other successfully running computers. Ian just shook his head and explained; the processors were sold as a programmable computer; the software specific to the ESCOM requirements was owned by Williams Electronics. The assumption was that they would write and tailor their own software.

Ian directed the project manager to read both the ESCOM tender that CONTEC made the bid on, and their order for the processors that Williams Electronics were asked to supply. Ian bade the project manager 'good day' and left, accompanied by his programmer.

Ian returned to his office to find a message to call Robbie Varner, Bill's son, head of CONTEC. Ian decided to wait and let Varner stew for a while. He didn't have long to wait. Miriam called him to say Varner's assistant was on the line and could he hold for Mr. Varner. Ian told Miriam to tell the assistant to get Varner on the line and then he would take the call.

Thirty seconds later, Miriam put the call through to Ian, 'Williams here, what can I do for you Mr. Varner?'

'You can explain to me why you have supplied us with dumb computers that do not work as we expected them to. As per the contract, you will rectify this immediately,' bellowed an obviously irate Varner.

'First of all, Mr. Varner, I suggest you read the order you gave us. We have fulfilled that requirement as per the order. Secondly, as I don't know if your position in CONTEC is because of some technical qualification or if it is a nepotistic appointment, so I will take the time to explain to you how a dumb computer works. What you bought is a piece of hardware that will respond to a set of instructions and perform those tasks repeatedly and without fail. The instructions that we used on our ESCOM installations were developed by my company and are owned by us. Do you understand this?'

'I do not like you attitude or insinuations. I will have the order reviewed and if you are in any breach of it, you will be hearing from our lawyers. I will inform ESCOM of this conversation and I am sure you will hear from them as well,' barely able to speak, Varner slammed down the phone.

Two days later the phone rang with a call for Ian from the CONTEC project manager, 'Mr. Williams, I have been authorised to purchase the necessary software needed to make the PLCs perform as intended. What I need is the purchase price for the sole rights to the aforementioned software and also the signature on a Restriction of Trade Agreement on you not using that software in the future.'

'Let me make this easy for you and your company to understand. The source code for the software is not for sale to you, at any price. I know your company got this tender from ESCOM using nefarious means; I also know what ESCOM's margins are, so I think you are pretty well screwed. If your boss, Varner Junior, hadn't been such an arsehole, I may have made some concessions but let him explain that to Daddy. We are done here,' said Ian, as he hung up the phone.

March 1, 1978: Stacey gives birth to a son. Gus names him Ross in deference to his Mother's maiden name. Gus is adamant that his son will grow up in a country where the colour of your skin doesn't determine your future. Gus commits his future to Australia, and with two partners opens up a state of the art Medical facility, covering a multitude of services.

Mar 3, 1978
Zambia, thirty eight people die in a cross border raid by Rhodesian troops on a suspected terrorist base.

Despite trying for a second child, Lynne is unable to fall pregnant. She makes an appointment with the same doctor she had seen when having the problem in the past. She is given the disappointing news that she will not be able to have another child.

Mar 21, 1978
Salisbury, absolute white rule in Rhodesia ends as three black government ministers are sworn in.

The March edition of Computing SA led with the story that CONTEC withdraws from the ESCOM substation project, citing sourcing problems with the overseas supplier. They hint that possible sanctions are to blame due to South Africa's Apartheid policies. No mention of the fines incurred on failed deliverables.

ESCOM counter the CONTEC statement by citing their failure to deliver one hundred and nine of the one hundred and twelve systems ordered. ESCOM suggests that the order may be re tendered in the near future.

A powerful force of black guerrillas crosses into Rhodesia from Mozambique in an attempt to wreck the political settlement between Ian Smith and moderate black leaders.

On April 3 a CONTEC truck arrives at the Williams Electronics stores with a consignment of one hundred and nine Nokia computers; the delivery note states 'return of goods for credit'. Ian refuses the consignment and turns the truck away.

Later that same afternoon, the CONTEC purchasing manager calls Williams Electronics and demands to know why they refused to accept the Nokia computers for return for credit. Miriam, expecting the call, is ready with the original contract. She quotes; CONTEC request the purchase of one hundred and twelve Nokia phase twelve processors for delivery to CONTEC technical Office in Durban. She also quotes the signed delivery note from CONTEC Goods Receiving that the purchased goods were received in pristine condition. She confirms that the goods would not be accepted for return credit.

The next mistake that CONTEC make is getting Varner Junior to call and demand to speak to Ian. Ian takes the call.

'Williams, I insist you take back this Nokia equipment and refund us at the purchase price we paid. You have no idea how difficult CONTEC can make your life.'

'Varner, as we are using last names only, I will not cave under pressure to your threats. I was prepared to take back the equipment depending on your attitude but unfortunately you making threats has just pissed me off. If you are trying to save face with your Daddy, maybe if he called me and showed me some respect, I would be amenable to cutting a deal. Good day.'

Two days later, a messenger delivered a letter addressed to Ian from Bill Varner. The letter is in the form of an apology about the way his son had acted when negotiating a request for the return of the Nokia equipment. Varner stressed that the threats made on his behalf were in no way a reflection of the way he intended doing business. He had the greatest respect for small businesses, as that was his path to where he was today. He acknowledged Ian's reaction and apologised unreservedly on behalf of his company. He asked for understanding of his son's behaviour, as he was under immense pressure being the son of an extremely successful father. He hoped they could come to some arrangement on the return of the equipment, more to teach his son a business lesson than a need for recovering money. He signed off the letter with the comment that he was sure he would meet up with Ian in the future.

Ian decided, apart from blowing his own trumpet in highlighting that 'he was an extremely successful father', it was an acknowledgement of wrongdoing. He decided he would frame the letter; not many people in business got an apology letter from Bill Varner.

Later that same afternoon, CONTEC purchasing manager called asking for Ian. Ian listened to the man profusely apologising for his and his bosses' approach to trying to return the Nokia equipment. He had reread the purchase agreement and acknowledged there was no refund agreement but hoped Ian could make some arrangement. Ian agreed to accept the returns at an agreed price that was 10% less than their purchase price plus a restocking fee of R1,000 per unit. Unsurprisingly, this was accepted.

Jun 15, 1978
The South African Government disbands its Information Department amid accusations of the misuse of public funds.

Jun 24, 1978
In the worst massacre in Rhodesia's six-year old war, twelve Britons, including wives and children, one a three week old baby, were bayoneted and bludgeoned to death at a lonely Mission Station near Vumba in the Eastern Highlands.

After a delay of three months, ESCOM released a tender document for their requirement to place one hundred and twelve PLCs to be commissioned for their Durban Area substations. Ian submitted his original tender, but to make ESCOM aware that he knew how the previous tender was awarded, he put a fifteen percent increase on the deliverables. Williams Electronics were the only company to tender and were awarded the contract. For the next eighteen months Ian's PLC programmers would be occupied.

Jul 18, 1978
The South African authorities refuse to give Nelson Mandela the thousands of sixtieth birthday cards he received.

Aug 22, 1978
**Jomo Kenyatta, known as Mzee (the old one), president of Kenya
dies at about age eighty.**

With the success of Williams Ford on the Bluff, Ian decides it is time to
expand. With his track record, Ford immediately agree to his request and
suggest that Amanzimtoti would be a good location. No other major
manufacturer has a presence in the town. Ian scouts the area and puts in
a bid for a property which is accepted.

Aug 31, 1978
**Prince Charles refuses to talk to Idi Amin at Jomo Kenyatta's
funeral.**

Sep 4, 1978
**An Air Rhodesia Viscount with fifty six people on board crashes in
remote bush lands near Lake Kariba after being struck down by a
Russian made SAM-7 missile. Some eighteen survivors stagger out
of the wreckage only to be gunned down by AK47-wielding
guerrillas. Joshua Nkomo's Cuban trained and Russian armed
guerrillas claim responsibility.**

Sep 10, 1978
Ian Smith imposes Martial Law on parts of Rhodesia.

CONTRON, a subsidiary of CONTEC, complete the purchase takeover
of Unitech Cables and Southland Cables. They confirm Robert Varner
as Chief Executive Officer of the new member to the CONTEC group
of Companies.

Internally the decision is to create a Johannesburg head office position
for all departments of the new organisation. The data processing
department is to be one of those positions. Jimmy is unsure of exactly
where he will fit into the new group. All key personnel will in future be
required to give three months' notice in the event they resign. Jimmy
falls into this category.

Sep 20, 1978
**South African Prime Minister, B.J. Vorster, announces his
resignation due to "health reasons."**

Sep 28, 1978
The new South African Prime Minister is sixty-two-year old former Minister of Defence, Pieter Willem Botha, who has a reputation of being a hawk on such issues as South West Africa and separate development.

Sep 30, 1978
Three hundred people have died in the bloodiest month so far in the Rhodesian guerrilla war.

On Friday October 6, 1978, Williams Ford 'Toti' opens with a special launch on new 1978 models at attractive prices. With the Ford launching new 1979 models in just over two months, Ian cuts a deal with them to help reduce their 1978 inventory. Ian appoints his top salesman from the Bluff branch as his sales manager.

Oct 22, 1978
Rhodesian forces strike deep into Mozambique territory and kill more than one thousand five hundred in attacks on two separate guerrilla bases.

Nov 7, 1978
Information Minister, Doctor Connie Mulder, resigns in the wake of the "Infogate" scandal. A thirty-seven million pounds fund had been set up to "outsmart and neutralise" the country's enemies.

Ian Barnes is recruited from Phillips South Africa, who were the original owners of Unitech, to be the new Group Financial Director of CONTRON. He is in effect Jimmy's new boss. Barnes, a man with a Napoleon complex, implements a host of new rules that will govern both the Accounting and Data Processing Departments. He also takes an instant dislike to Jimmy, the feeling is mutual.

Nov 24, 1978
Ian Smith extends Martial Law to three quarters of the country.

CHAPTER 27
1979

January 1, 1979: Ian, Dee and their two children, Jimmy, Lynne and their daughter join Chubby and Fiona at their Durban North mansion for his 29th birthday. With the wives looking after the children, the three friends take some time to talk about the previous year and what the future may hold.

'So, Ian, what's it like to be Natal's answer to Harry Oppenheimer?'

'I tell you what, Chubby, I might not be the next Oppenheimer, but I am having a lot of fun. I never thought when I left school and became an appie that I would one day own my own business. I see your company is doing okay, you don't seem short of a buck or two.'

'Yeah, we are doing okay but I would like to break away and form my own agency. Maybe that's going to be the plan in the year ahead. What about you, Jimbo, other than that gorgeous wife of yours, you don't seem to have much going on?'

'I think the shit is going to hit the fan shortly at Southland. There is this little cunt called Barnes who I don't see eye to eye with. I reckon we are heading for a show down soon.'

'What I don't get is that out of the three of us you are probably the smartest one. You need to get out of this corporate world and break free,' stated Ian.

'I think you are right, Ian. If things go as I see them, I'll be coming around to your place looking for a job.'

'Mate, if I thought you were serious, I would offer you a job right now. I hear Gus is settled well in Australia, still on the anti-Apartheid kick though. I doubt if we will see him here again.'

Back at work the next day, Barnes, visiting from head office, calls Jimmy into his office. He hands Jimmy a document and requests that he signs it. Jimmy, not one who would normally read a company document before signing it, informs Barnes that he needs to read the document to see exactly what he is signing. Barnes informs him that he needs to return the signed document by Friday, three days away.

Jimmy returns to his office to read the document. The gist of the document is that as an employee of the CONTEC group, all key personnel are required to sign a non-disclosure agreement, that among other things prevents them from leaving the company and working for a competitor for period of three years from date of termination. It lists competitors as any company involved in the electronics business, cable and related activities or certain unspecified computer related functions.

Jimmy's first thought is to sign the bloody thing; it would be impossible for CONTEC to enforce it. He decides to discuss it with Lynne. She reads through the document and in principal agrees with her husband but sees possible limitations to his future with CONTEC. He would have to take whatever crap they handed him in future.

Friday morning, with the unsigned document on his desk, he is called down to Barnes' office. Taking his time, he walks down, knocks on the door and enters.

'I take you have signed the document, Wilson?'

'You take it wrong. I am not signing it. It is a restriction of trade that handicaps me if or when I leave this organisation.'

'Maybe you don't understand, it is not an option. It is required if you wish to continue working for the CONTEC group of companies. All senior executives, me included, have signed the same document.'

'That is your choice. You may be petrified of your boss but I am not and will not sign it.'

'I am your boss. Are you saying you are not afraid of me? That would be a big mistake.'

'You are barely five foot six; in what universe would I be afraid of you?'

'That's it, Wilson, either sign this or give me your resignation.'

'Nope, I am not resigning.'

'Well, I will fire you then.'

'Excellent! I will see you in the Labour Court unless I get a letter saying I have been laid off and three month's salary.'

'Get out of my office! I will not tolerate your insubordination. This issue is not over.'

Just before the end of the working day, Lorraine, Barnes' secretary knocked on Jimmy's door, she walked in and handed him a letter to be signed. The letter was to inform him that his job had become redundant and his services were no longer required. He would be paid in full for three months up until the end of March. He would be allowed to retain all his benefits, including the use of his company car, through that period.

Jimmy signed the letter and handed it back to Lorraine. 'Jimmy, we will be sorry to see you leave. I am so glad you stood up to him; he really is a nasty little man. Good luck for the future.'

Jimmy picked up the phone to tell Lynne the news. He then packed up his personal things and left. He had no regrets; it was going to turn out to be a dead-end job. He had, however, broadened his computer experience, especially in the IBM market. Although it didn't seem like it at the time, it was the catalyst that would lead him to the future his talents deserved.

Ian's accountant presents him with the financial statements for Williams Motors, showing a small but profitable growth. Williams Electrical is in a similar situation. As both companies are Bluff standards, Ian ignores the suggestion that compared to his ventures it might be time to sell the businesses. Both Ford dealerships show a healthy profit margin; the Bluff operation had the largest vehicle turnover in the Durban Metropolitan area. Despite this, opposition dealers didn't follow the Williams business model.

The most profitable of all of the ventures was Williams Electronics. The only downside was that his total programming manpower was dedicated to a single client in ESCOM. The upside was, as the sole importer of Nokia equipment, all competitors in the PLC market had to order their equipment from Ian. This gave him the perfect insight into what was happening in the market.

On final reckoning, Ian showed a personal after-tax payment due of R136,000; this after taking only a monthly salary of R750. His take home pay was one of the lowest of the senior employees across all of his companies. Ian, ever looking for new challenges, stated his plan for opening at least one more dealership and looking for other opportunities in power grid management systems and data modulators.

Jan 30, 1979
Eighty percent of the votes cast by the ninety-four thousand white registered voters vote to end the thirteen-year long struggle in Rhodesia and accept black majority rule.

Feb 12, 1979
Nationalist guerrillas use missiles to bring down an Air Rhodesia airline, killing fifty-nine.

The previous ban on Professional companies being prevented from advertising is lifted. Now doctors, dentists, lawyers and accountants are free to advertise their services on the open market. One of the first to make use of the new law were accounting companies. In the past they were only able to advertise for staff recruitment; they now flooded the market with advertising their services.

Chubby, ever ready for an opportunity, signed up one of the largest firms, Erickson and Whitmore (E&W) to do their marketing. Eager to get into the Information Technology (IT) management services, E&W embarked on a recruiting drive. Previously, their recruitment was geared towards B. Com. students and they had little knowledge of what was required to service an IT Management Services function.

Chubby, aware that Jimmy was looking around for a new job, puts him in touch with the managing partner at E&W Durban Office. Jimmy calls the number Chubby had supplied and gets an interview with Philip Tucker. He is painted an amazing picture of a career path that a Principal Consultant with E&W can expect. He offers Jimmy a position at a salary of R1,500 per month, which is slightly more than he was getting at Southland. He agrees to start on April 1.

Mar 29, 1979
Idi Amin flees Uganda as his regime of buffoonery and murder collapses.

Friday 30 March: Jimmy drops his company car off at the Southland Cables plant in Pietermaritzburg; he is officially off the books.

On Monday April 2 he reports for work at the E&W offices in Durban. He is astonished to find that the planned Management Consulting Services Department was unable to recruit any other suitable candidates in the Durban area and as such all services will be run out of the Johannesburg Office until further notice. E&W offer to assist his move to Johannesburg.

That night Jimmy discusses the situation with Lynne, who is initially annoyed. They are not desperate for money and could survive for a few months but based on the lack of success in finding a position in the Durban area, maybe it was time for a change of scenery. They agree Jimmy should take the job in Johannesburg.

The next day Jimmy informs Tucker that he will take the position at the Johannesburg office and will start there Monday the 9th. Lynne tells her boss that her situation has changed; ideally a transfer to their

Johannesburg Office would be ideal, if not she would have to resign. Her boss, knowing her value, promises to arrange a transfer and assist with the moving costs.

With her transfer arranged to start on the May 1, Lynne calls her Mother. 'Hi Mom, I need a favour. Can Jimmy stay with you guys from Sunday for a few weeks?'

'Of course he can, why aren't you coming with him? We would love to see little Sharon.'

'There was a mix up with his new job. Those idiots at E&W were unable to recruit the necessary people in the Durban area and forgot to tell Jimmy in time. So now his job is at their Johannesburg Office.'

'So, is he going to work here, and you stay in Hillcrest? That is a recipe for disaster; you are not having marital troubles are you?'

'No Mom, we are all moving up there. I am transferring to our Johannesburg office. I start there on May 1. I will be up there on about the 24th. We will need to look for a place.'

'No, you won't, you will stay here until you are settled. Wait until I tell your Dad, he will be over the moon; we will have to keep an eye on our husbands though; you know what they are like when they get together. I am so excited.'

Apr 6, 1979
Doctor Connie Mulder is expelled from the Nationalist Party in South Africa in the wake of the "I"nfogate" scandal.

Jimmy arrives at the Zales' residence in Northmead Benoni just before 5pm on the Sunday before he starts work at E&W. He finds Val and Cyril in the back yard with a fire going. Before he can utter a word, Cyril hands him a cold Castle. The agenda for the evening is set; a *braai* and then darts in the garage. Jimmy knows immediately that he will start work tomorrow with a hangover.

Jimmy arrives at the E&W offices at the Bank of Lisbon building in down town Johannesburg. The old audit mentality is obvious with the firm's need, as with the other large accounting firms, to be near the financial area adjacent to the Johannesburg Stock Exchange. Traffic is horrendous and parking impossible.

He is introduced to the Management Consulting Services (MCS) team. The managing partner is a Certified Accountant (CA) named Gerry Robertson; Jimmy's direct boss is another CA, Tony Barton. Neither men have any IT experience, but the message is clear: billable hours is the name of the game; good old Audit mentality. Jimmy is informed that as a Principal Consultant, his charge out rate is R125 per hour.

As he is introduced around, it becomes obvious to him that the computer systems knowledge of the group is virtually non-existent. Ninety percent of the staff are either B Com. or BA graduates. There are two Bachelor of Science graduates, neither of whom has held a job in the computer industry. There are two others with some exposure to computers; Mara, a throwback to the hippy days, and her assistant, who are responsible for the office word processors and printers.

The first week is taken up with the Company Mission Statement. Highest priority is Billable Hours; every photocopy, phone call incoming and outbound must be allocated to a client wherever possible; again, an Auditor mindset. The MCS silver bullet is a project management tool called the System Lifecycle Management Tool (SLMT), which was developed in Houston, Texas, aimed at the American market. The tool consists of eight manuals, each in excess of three hundred pages, that will take a Project from Initiation through Installation.

MCS consultants are expected to become experts in the use of this product and then train selected E&W audit clients in its use. Not only is there a cost for the tool there are a copious amount of billable hours. Built into the process is a presentation that will allow an E&W partner to log up to fifty hours at R250 per hour. The process is destined to fail as only large Audit clients, who in most cases already have experienced project teams in place, could justify the cost of SLMT.

Apr 13, 1979
Rhodesian troops destroy the home of nationalist leader, Joshua Nkomo, during cross border raids into Zambia.

Lynne and Sharon arrived in Benoni. After the initial excitement of Jimmy greeting his wife and daughter, Lynne detects a problem with her husband.

She takes him one side, 'There is something wrong, is it my folks? I know they can be a bit over the top but it's only temporary.'

'No, your folks are great. It's the job. I think I have made a huge mistake; the whole department are a bunch of fucking bean counters. They think opening a department to provide computer solutions is about working each client through an eight volume manual, writing copious

109

reports that offer no actual solutions but a list of options and then billing them ridiculous amounts of money. We haven't covered it yet but I think we are supposed to bill the client for toilet paper when we take a dump.'

'What are we going to do with you? I think you should start looking around; there is a much bigger market up here. Wait until you find something before you resign.'

'I know it's easier to find a job when you have a job. I'll suck it up in the meantime. As I am the only one who even knows what a computer looks like, maybe some client will need actual help.'

Apr 24, 1979
Fifty-four-year-old Bishop Abel Muzorewa is elected as the first black Prime Minister of Rhodesia. Joshua Nkomo and Robert Mugabe denounce the election. Neither Britain nor the United States recognise the new government.

With Lynne starting her new job, Val volunteers to look after Sharon full time. With Jimmy barely able to keep it together, the two of them spend the evenings looking around for a house. Although Lynne appreciates her mother looking after her daughter, she does not want to stay too close when buying a house. She wants to concentrate their search in the Northern Suburbs of Johannesburg.

May 4, 1979
The Tory Party wins the British general election and Margaret Thatcher becomes the first female Prime Minister.

Jimmy is called into a meeting with Robertson, along with Barton and another bean counter looking guy.

'Wilson, this is Will van der Berg, one of the Audit Partners. He has a couple of questions for you.'

'Thanks Gerry. Over the weekend I bumped into an old friend, Rodger Hall, who is financial director at a French-owned company called Teletronics; they are an Andrew Yates Audit client. I was told that Andrew Yates placed one of their MCS staff to assist in an upgrade of their software on what he called an IBM System 36. Apparently, in the three weeks he has been there, no progress has been made. Do you have any exposure to this type of IBM computer?'

'Yes.'

'I mean real knowledge.'

'Yes.'

Van der Berg, out of his depth, does not know what specific questions to ask to confirm Jimmy's knowledge; Jimmy, making him suffer, offers no help.

Robertson, eager to push home a decision, asks, 'Wilson, it would a great coup if we can offer an MCS solution to an Andrew Yates Audit client. Could you confidently meet with Mr. Hall and address his problem?'

'Yes, I am confident, but I would need to see what the problem is first. If you can arrange a meeting with Mr. Hall, I will be able to see what the situation is.'

'Will, can you take care of this. As Mr. Hall is a personal friend of yours, I suggest you accompany Wilson. Wilson, take a set of SLMT manuals with you and see if we can interest them in signing up.'

'Mr. Robertson, with due respect, if we want to solve an apparent current software problem for them, the last thing I need is to try and unload a set of manuals that bear no relevance to their problem,' replied Jimmy.

Robertson, somewhat taken aback, 'Very well, Wilson, just make sure you do a good job and represent E&W in a good light. I would very much like to put one over on Andrew Yates.'

Jimmy and van der Berg made the short journey out to the northern suburbs to the offices of Teletronics. They were escorted into a meeting room and introduced to Rodger Hall and Barbara Webb.

Barbara Webb was an American from Michigan currently working in France as a project manager for Teletronics. She was obviously very irritated, having spent the last three weeks making absolutely no progress in installing a workable set of software. Ms. Webb's skill set was purely as a project manager; she had no technical knowledge of the S36 or the programming language RPG. Andrew Yates had assured her and Rodger Hall that they had the expertise to assist Teletronics.

Jimmy listened while Hall, Webb and van der Berg went back and forth about what was needed and what, if anything, E&W could provide. Jimmy just listened, making no comment or promises. Eventually bored by the chatter, he made a suggestion.

'Ms. Webb, why don't you show me what the problem is and I'll see if I can help?' suggested Jimmy,

Ms. Webb looked at Jimmy with scepticism and said, 'I will do that, but I can tell you that if this is not resolved within the week, I will have to abandon the project and return to France. We will have to source a technical person from our head office and I don't know how long that will take. Rodger, this is the last time I am going to go through another failed attempt. Okay, Mr. Wilson, come with me.'

Jimmy followed Ms. Webb out of the meeting room and down the passage to the computer room. Jimmy hadn't actually worked on a S36, only its earlier brother the S34. He knew the RPG language and given enough time would be okay on the newer model. Ms. Webb pointed Jimmy towards the computer console and selected item #1 on the menu – Daily process. The program started up displayed the heading 'Daily Batch Job' and then immediately displayed an error message and terminated.

'I tell you what Ms. Webb, let me have a look at this. Why don't you go back into that meeting and make sure that colleague of mine doesn't try and sell your company some junky project management tool. I will call you if I find anything.'

'Okay and please call me Barbara. I feel we will be spending a lot of time together.'

'Sure and call me Jimmy.'

Barbara headed back to the meeting and Jimmy got to work. He immediately opened the source code for the Day end job and fixed the one statement that was causing the problem. It was a simple fix that any person with even a basic knowledge of programming would have seen and fixed. Well done, Andrew Yates. He restarted the program and watched for a few minutes to ensure there were no other problems.

Five minutes later Jimmy walked into the boardroom and sat down. The ongoing chatter ceased and the three occupants turned to him. Barbara broke the silence, 'Well, do you think you can solve the mysterious problem that Andrew Yates have struggled with for three weeks? Do you have some idea of the how long it might take?'

'To answer your first question, yes I can, and to the second question it took less than five minutes.'

Barbara shot out of her chair, 'I cannot believe it come and show me.'

The two of them headed for the computer room. The job was still processing, the printer was churning out reports and there was a message on the console requesting that the picking list printer required paper.

Barbara looked at Jimmy open mouthed, 'Oh my God, this is how it is supposed to work. We have been unable to print any picking slip in the factory. I will call them to put paper in the printer and start it up. How the heck did you sort this out so quickly?'

'Lucky, I guess.'

'Lucky, my ass. I don't care how Rodger does it, you are not leaving here until they sign you up. Let's go.'

'Actually, here we call it an arse.'

'I like you already. My fiancé, Sebastian, is the manager in charge of all overseas subsidiaries from an IT perspective and this is my first one and it looked doomed to failure until you arrived. Thank you.'

Barbara reported back that it was all systems go. They would have to verify all the output but at least the process was running and printing picking slips. She insisted Rodger make arrangements for Jimmy to be here for the duration of the three month project.

Van der Berg and Jimmy returned to the E&W offices and went straight into a meeting with Robertson and Barton. Van der Berg relayed the events in Jimmy resolving the problem and also the request of his services for the duration of the project. Jimmy could just see the wheels turning in Robertson's head; 8 hours a day at R125 per hour equates to R5,000 per week.

The first words out of Robertson's mouth made Jimmy cringe, 'Will, as this is a specialised skill, I say we bill them at R150 per hour for Wilson. Also, build into the contract a couple of hours a week for Partner review at R250 per hour. Tony, I think you should do the partner review and produce a weekly status report at normal rates. At the same time you might be able to encourage them to use our SLMT process. Wilson, you are familiar with the process?'

'Yes, I am.'

'Well, do you think you can implement the process there? It would be good to get a site on SLMT that we could use as a reference as we are not making any headway at present,' said Robertson.

'Sir, there is a good reason that you are not making any headway. The process is cumbersome and does not provide a solution. This project is already through installation so SLMT, even if it was of any use, would be of no use here.'

'Well, Wilson, that is a very damning statement. We have invested heavily in SLMT and it is the flagship on which MCS is founded,' stated an annoyed Robertson.

'Sir, if that is the case then we are in trouble. I would rather quit than foist that behemoth on any company. I apologise for the statement but in the nine years I have been working in the computer industry, I have never known anyone to use a tool of that size to manage a project. That may be because I have not worked in a large company with a highly structured IT department. If SLMT is our direction, you should be looking at the huge mainframe companies to implement SLMT.'

'Thank you for your input. I will take it under consideration. Are there any other concerns before we commit you to this project?'

'Yes, I do have some concerns. While I appreciate the need for billable hours, I am not sure it is a good idea to have Mr. Barton doing a weekly review. This is a project run by standards set by their French head office, so I cannot see the need for a review. You have already upped my rate and I think any excessive billing will be very obvious to the client. Based on the discussion I had with Ms. Webb, we could be in for a support function after the initial project. Surely we don't want to bill ourselves out of contention.'

'Reluctantly, I think you might be right. As part of a monthly invoice, we usually supply a detailed report covering what we have accomplished. This task will then fall to you. Agreed?'

'Agreed.' Jimmy would have said anything to get out of the E&W down town offices and actually do some real computer work.

Jun 1, 1979
Rhodesia is renamed Zimbabwe-Rhodesia.

With Jimmy now commuting from Benoni to the Teletronics offices in Woodmead, he avoided the traffic congestion into the city centre of Johannesburg, his demeanour instantly improved. The one bugbear he still had was the E&W dress code, three-piece suit at all times. This was solved on the second day at Teletronics. He was introduced to the Managing Director, Mr. Eugene Wannenburg. Jimmy was wearing the compulsory company tie; dark blue and liberally splattered with the EW logo.

After introductions, Jimmy was given the low-down of the company structure. Normally in the overseas subsidiaries, the Managing Director is a French national. In the over fifty subsidiaries around the world, Wannenburg was the only non-French MD. All other senior positions were held by locals apart from the procurement manager, who was a French National, Silvio Forget. Having to deal with the distribution warehouses in France, it was vital to have a French-speaking procurement manager.

The Teletronics business model was that all components required to run their business were ordered from the head offices in France. The obvious delays in placing an order and having the right product on hand as needed were a key component of Forget's job. It was in this area, working with Forget, that would change Jimmy's life dramatically.

At the end of the meeting, Jimmy stood up and shook Wannenburg's hand. He then took off his tie and handed it to him, 'Sir, I see you admiring my tie and as it is emblazoned with your initials EW I would like you to have it.'

Wannenburg burst into laughter and accepted the tie, 'Thank you. I will wear it with pride. Call me Gene. By the way. our dress code is business casual and while you are here why not join us.'

Jimmy. eager to comply. was thankful that this would be the last day he wore a suit to work at Teletronics.

With Jimmy in a better mood, Lynne pressed him to accompany her in the search of a house. The Teletronics offices were located very close to the area she wanted to move to. Each day after work she would meet him and they would look at properties in the area. Living with Lynne's parents was no hardship, they were very accommodating. Most evenings it was either darts with Cyril or cards with Cyril and Val; Lynne was feeling a bit left out. The close proximity of their bedroom to her parents was also affecting their sex life; Lynne was inhibited and growing frustrated; it was time to move.

Jun 4, 1979
The Muldergate scandal (so named after Doctor Connie Mulder) forces the resignation of B.J. Vorster as the South African President.

After an extensive search of the area, Lynne finally found a property in the suburb of Fourways. A four bedroomed house with a swimming pool; nicely situated to schools, shops and both of their current places of employment. Benoni was a fifteen minute drive away so Val could continue to look after Sharon.

The software that Teletronics was using had been written by a French-Canadian company called SERTI. It was a sales and distribution system (SDS) and offered no other process. Normally, subsidiaries the size of the South African one would find a 'packaged program' for their accounting needs. Currently, all Debtors, Creditors and General Ledger transactions were 'batched' up and sent to a data processing company who provided the required output. It was cumbersome and time consuming.

All the current sales reports out of SDS were in French, which were no help to the Sales Manager. Jimmy decided to write a language conversion module. French text would be sent to the module which would return the English version. He enlisted Barbara's help with translations.

His next task was write interface modules to extract invoice data from SDS and feed it directly into a Debtors system he had developed at Southland and he now implemented at Teletronics. He created a banking module to process payments and credit notes. He used this data to produce Debtors Statements and a detailed age analysis; Rodger Hall was ecstatic. He gave Jimmy permission to write modules for local Purchase orders and a Creditors system. Jimmy also added a module that would extract accounting data from both Debtors and Creditors and feed it into a General Ledger system. This was all done without E&W knowledge, they were under the impression he was just helping out with their legacy system. As long as the billable hours were coming in, they left Jimmy alone.

One of the most onerous but vital tasks at Teletronics was performed by Silvio Forget. His job was to ensure that the correct product was available at the right time. Lead times on orders to France were very strict; prices were in French Francs, so exchange rates had a big effect. There were huge differences in the cost of air and sea deliveries. Prices quoted to local clients could be affected by how and when the product was ordered. Forget spent his entire time manually perusing reports, making decisions and then placing orders on a weekly basis.

Jimmy and Barbara arranged a meeting with Silvio and went through his process in great detail. With all of the inventory data available on the computer plus the sales and purchase orders, most of the data needed for ordering from France was available. By adding reorder levels and lead times for both air and sea and adding a currency conversion, Jimmy could see a way to alleviate a lot of the manual effort Silvio was going through.

With all the information needed, Jimmy wrote the one module that would end up changing his life forever. Three weeks later he delivered a reordering process that allowed Silvio to simulate orders and tailor them to the most effective method of processing and delivery. The final step Silvio would make when the order was ready to expedite, was to create a telex to be sent to the central warehouse in Grenoble.

The telex was in a ridged fixed format and had to be exact or it would be rejected. Watching Silvio type in the telex, it was clear to Jimmy that it was in a record format that would be fed manually into a computer system somewhere and processed. Jimmy asked Barbara to ask her husband if there was a central processor in France that could take a file in this format directly, without having to be entered from a telex copy.

As her part on the project was concluding, she would be returning to France soon. She told Jimmy that her fiancé, Sebastian Barthez, would be arriving on the coming Sunday. He had managed to secure a trip to join her on the premise of doing a valuation of the project. As part of his skill set, he was an expert in inventory organisation and analysis; he would spend a couple of days working with Silvio. She also told Jimmy that she was just over three months pregnant, and apart from Sebastian he was now the only other person who knew.

Sebastian arrived at work on Monday and Barbara introduced him to Jimmy. Sebastian thanked him for the great job he was doing and was also very grateful for helping Barbara in rescuing the project.

'Sebastian, I have been doing some work with Silvio and we have made progress but the one thing I don't get is that fax he has to send. It looks to me like it is in a format that could be loaded directly into a computer. Do you know how they do it in Europe?'

'I do. Teletronics use an IBM provided facility whereby a text file is transmitted to a mainframe computer in Brussels. We have a series of drop boxes there and the order data is automatically retrieved and transmitted to our warehouse system where it is fulfilled. What do you have in mind?'

'We have all the data for me to automatically create the file and transmit it to the IBM mainframe. Maybe we can try a test?'

'If you can do that, it will save Silvio a good amount of time, eliminate any human errors and expedite the order quicker. I will get you the drop box details.'

In anticipation of getting the drop box details, Jimmy manually mocked up an exact copy of Silvio's latest telex file. Sebastian provided the address details for the test drop box. Jimmy transmitted the text file. Fifteen minutes later he received the return message that the test file was processed correctly. Silvio was sceptical but agreed to try the process out to create the text file but not send it. He would compare the file to his manual extract until he was happy with the results. Sebastian gave Jimmy the go ahead to program the process.

Sebastian's other task was to work with Silvio and look at optimising the stores and look at redundant stock. To do this, he needed some reports that would help them plan this correctly. Sebastian approached Jimmy and asked if he could provide some report that showed the value of stock by part number and category.

Jimmy said he could and just over three hours later, using the query language of the S36, he provided Sebastian with the report he needed.

The following morning Sebastian asked for another report that would show the sales history over the last three months by part number and category. Again, Jimmy produced the report in a couple of hours.

Just after lunch Sebastian approached Jimmy with another request, 'Sorry to keep bothering you Jimmy but I need one last report. I need to see all the stock by part and category but aged into date between date last ordered and date sold.'

Jimmy leaned over and passed Sebastian a printout, 'Here you go.'

Sebastian opened the report and looked at Jimmy in amazement, 'How did you know I would ask for this report?'

'Well, based on the first two, I figured this would be the next logical request.'

'Barbara is right you are unbelievable. If you ever decide to leave E&W, give me first option.'

Aug 26, 1979
Bishop Abel Muzorewa announces that his country will now be known as Zimbabwe.

Barbara and Sebastian returned to France. Sebastian reiterated to Jimmy that if he ever wanted to leave E&W, to let him know as he would offer him a position with Teletronics. He also imparted some information that with IBM announcing the launch of their new System 38, that the Teletronics group had made the strategic decision to use that computer as a replacement for the current S36.

Shortly after submitting his August time sheet, he received a call from Barton, 'Wilson, I have just received your time sheet and Teletronics bill for the month. I notice you have only billed for 8 hours per day, totalling 184 hours for the month; yet I notice on 5 separate days you worked additional hours totalling 16. By my reckoning, that is a total of 200 hours for the month. Please adjust the invoice accordingly.'

'The contract we have with them is for 8 hours a day and that is what I billed them.'

'You will bill the client for every hour you work. Is that clear?'

'Can I assume that I will be paid overtime for those hours then?'

'No, you are salaried, not hourly paid,' replied Barton and hung up the phone.

Fuck it, thought Jimmy, it's an eight-hour day from now on. He walked over to Rodger Hall's office and relayed Barton's message. He apologised and said from now on he would be working an eight hour day. If he needed to work later, he would let Rodger know and maybe just take the hours off on another day. Rodger was okay with the suggestion.

Two hours later, Rodger walked into the computer room with a faxed copy of the E&W August invoice. 'What's with this new thing, where your company is now faxing me an invoice instead of posting it? Are they desperate for money?'

'I tell you what. Make out the cheque and fax them a copy.'

Rodger complied. Almost immediately, Jimmy's phone rang; it was Barton, 'What are Teletronics thinking? What use is a faxed copy of the cheque? We can't bank that.'

'I think he is sending you a message. Most companies they deal with send them an invoice through the mail which they then process through their Creditors system and make a payment. He actually asked me if E&W were desperate for money. I had no answer to that.'

Barton hung up the phone obviously irritated. Jimmy sat back and calculated the amount of revenue he had generated in the three months he had been at Teletronics; it amounted to just over R70,000 which was nearly four year's salary to him. Something was wrong with this picture.

Sep 7, 1979
Over three hundred are reported killed in Mozambique by cross-border raids by Zimbabwe troops.

Jimmy finalised the automatic ordering process. He ran the first test but only created the file and did not send it. Silvio checked it against his file and found two differences. On further investigations he found that the differences were errors on his side. He fixed his document but still insisted on sending the telex.

Sep 10, 1979
Joshua Nkomo, Robert Mugabe, Abel Muzorewa and Ian Smith travel to talks in London over the future of Zimbabwe.

Week two Silvio checked his document against the one Jimmy created; they matched exactly but he requested one more test for the following week. He sent his telex.

Sep 22, 1979
Zimbabwe troops launch cross-border attacks into Mozambique despite the ongoing London peace talks.

Week three the files again matched exactly, and Silvio finally agreed to let Jimmy send the file automatically. In the space of five minutes the file was transmitted to Brussels, was picked up by Teletronics, loaded to their system and a confirmation returned to Johannesburg. The confirmation of the order was the same one Silvio got back two days after he sent his telex. A further ten minutes later a report was received confirming the shipment dates and expected arrival dates in South Africa.

With a turnaround time of less than twenty minutes it completed what took Silvio over an hour to type into a telex machine and then had to wait up to three days for shipping details. He still insisted on reviewing the file before he sent it but was very excited with the new process. He rushed off to tell Eugene Wannenburg.

Wannenburg, with Silvio in tow, came striding into the computer room. 'Jimmy, Silvio has just told me about what you have done with our order requisition to France. I have done a quick calculation and conservatively estimate with this turnaround you have saved us around R50,000 per month. I really like the currency exchange function. Well done! I think I should let your boss know all about this.'

'Gene, I wouldn't do that as he is likely to double my charge out rate. It's just part of the service, let's leave it at that. But thanks for the vote of confidence.'

Jimmy submitted his September time sheet and sat back and waited for the inevitable phone call. The phone rang a few minutes later; it was Barton, 'Wilson, I notice that you only billed 160 hours this month. Is there some reason for that?'

'I don't know, Mr. Barton. 20 days at 8 hours per day is 160 hours by my calculations.'

'Don't get smug with me, Wilson. You know I instructed you to bill all overtime hours as well.'

'Mr. Barton, as you so clearly told me, I am a salaried employee and I don't qualify for overtime pay. As I am not part of any incentive bonus scheme, there is no incentive for me to work extensive extra hours for no remuneration.'

'Well, depending on your performance I will consider bonus payments in future.'

'While I have you on the phone, I need to give you some information that will affect us in the near future. I don't know if you are aware that IBM have announced the launch of their new System 38. Teletronics' IT manager in France has informed me that this is the direction they will be taking. If we want to continue supporting them, we need to be conversant with this new technology. IBM are running a three-week course out of their Rosebank office. I suggest you register me for that course unless you have someone else in mind.'

'We have no one else. Can you ask Mr. Hall if they are prepared to pay for your time while on the course? After all, it is to their benefit.'

'Mr. Barton, I am not a contract negotiator. I suggest you contact him; this is not part of my job description.' Jimmy put down the phone and walked directly into Rodger's office.

'Rodger, if Barton calls you and suggests that you pay my hours while I am on an IBM S38 course, please tell him where to stick it.'

Roger laughed and agreed. Shortly thereafter when Barton called, Rodger gave him short shrift. He also explained that without S38 knowledge at E&W he would have to look elsewhere for support. Barton, seeing R25,000 a month disappearing out of the door, phoned IBM and booked Jimmy on the next course.

Oct 3, 1979
The South African Barbarian rugby team begins a tour of Britain amid widespread protests.

Jimmy started his S38 course at IBM. The system was a new concept taking advantage of a relational database inherent to the system. It led to far more possibilities than the previous generations S34 and S36.

Oct 18, 1979
Guerrilla leaders accept Britain's Rhodesia Charter in London.

Jimmy completed the IBM course and returned to Teletronics confident that he knew a way to convert their current SDS system into a relational database RPG3 system.

On the November 11, Stacey gave birth to a daughter named Margaret. Stacey informed her husband that she was done having babies and would not be taking birth control pills. If he wanted sex he would need to take care of contraception requirements; she suggested he gets a vasectomy.

December 3 Lynne celebrated her thirty second birthday; she still looked like she was in her early twenties.

After fourteen years and one month of illegal independence, Rhodesia, now Zimbabwe, will again become a British Colony. At Lancaster House, Joshua Nkomo, Robert Mugabe, and Abel Muzorewa signed an agreement for a cease-fire and a new election. The United Nation lifts the thirteen-year-old sanctions.

Jimmy was called into the E&W office for his annual review. Barton addressed his performance for the current year.

'Your performance this year has been good. You have the highest number of billable hours amongst the Principal Consultants. I am disappointed that you only work an eight hour day, there are employees that put in ten and twelve hour days. You might want to consider your decision in that regard. I have considered a bonus system for you but after giving it much thought, I have decided to shelve the idea as I don't want to set any precedents. As far as a salary increase, you haven't completed a full year yet so I will review it again in June.' Standing up Barton extended his hand, 'Thank you for your service.'

Jimmy shook his hand and left without comment.

So ended the seventies. Much had happened;

Gus had immigrated to Australia, started a family and was the owner of a successful and highly profitable Medical practice.

Ian had two very profitable Ford dealerships, his original Electrical and Motor service companies plus the lucrative ESCOM contract serviced by his electronics company. He was now well on his way to becoming a rand millionaire. A complete family with a son and daughter,

Chubby was now the major shareholder in his advertising and marketing company Miller, Keane, Bedford and Murphy. All that was missing was the child so that Fiona desperately wanted.

Jimmy, less financially secure than the other three, had finally found his niche in life and was happy with his lot. A beautiful wife, an equally beautiful daughter and enjoying his job.

CHAPTER 28
The Eighties

1980

1980 would be a year of turmoil in South Africa. Black unrest leads to riots and bombing. On the international stage pressure is exerted with threats of boycotts and sanctions in an effort to effect change in the country. The Nationalist Party refuses to budge. On the sporting scene, South African sports teams are banned from virtually every International competition.

Banned by the International Cricket Council, South Africa relies on so called Rebel Tours which have no first class standing.

The French Rugby team agrees to play one test match against the Springboks in Pretoria. New Zealand invites the Springboks to tour their country. The tour is marred by violent anti-Apartheid demonstrations. Bizarrely, one of the matches is disrupted by a small plane dive-bombing the field with bags of flour. The tour manages to be completed but will be the last for many years.

January 1, 1980: Chubby's thirtieth birthday and keeping up the tradition of getting together at the start of each decade Jimmy and Ian arrive at the Murphy home in Durban North with their wives. Gus' absence is relieved slightly as he calls from Perth to wish Chubby.

Lynne and Dee helped a heavily pregnant Fiona with the food. She was already a week overdue and in Durban's heat looked very uncomfortable. The general feeling was hopefully that she didn't start labour today.

The three friends discussed their plans and hopes for the next decade.

Ian planned to expand the number of Ford Dealerships he owned. He also hoped to secure the PLC contract with ESCOM for all their major metropolitan substations. He reckoned that would set him up for life. All this before he turned thirty. Who would have thought ten years ago this appie would be so successful?

Chubby planned to buy out his three partners and take total control of his business.

Jimmy, the least successful of the three, was quietly confident that he had found his niche and thought the 1980's was his time.

January 5, 1980: Fiona gave birth to a daughter named Valerie, after Chubby's mother. After a difficult birth she was told she would not be able to have another child.

On January 7 Jimmy received a call from Sebastian. Teletronics in Australia had acquired a new IBM S38 and the plan was to install the SDS software and run it in a S36 mode. The US subsidiary in Baltimore had a version running covering multiple depots and would possibly be a good fit for Australia. What he wanted to know was would Jimmy be available to do the installation; it would be approximately three months in duration.

'I would need to know the dates, but I am sure E&W would be amenable to me doing the contract. You know how they love billable hours. Should I get Barton to contact you?'

'No. I have no desire to deal with that man. Because we are an Andrew Yates Audit client it would be virtually impossible for us to employ E&W in Australia on this contract. The only way to do this is to contract you as an individual and for you to bill us directly. We will pay all travel, accommodation and out of pocket costs plus your normal hourly rate. Your invoice for the hourly rate will be submitted to me at the end of the project and we will pay you direct, your out of pocket costs will be paid by the Australians. Let me know if you can work something out. I would really like to use your skills on this one.'

Jimmy called up Barton, 'Mr. Barton, I have had a proposal from Teletronics in France. They have asked my availability to do a project in Australia for approximately three months. They will pay all travel costs directly and our hourly rate on production of an invoice.'

'Excellent news! Have their man contact me and we will draw up a contract for their signature. Do this project right and we could add "International Consulting" experience to our portfolio.'

'There is one slight problem with the contract. As Teletronics are an Andrew Yates client worldwide, he will not be able to sign a contract with us unless he gets permission from Andrew Yates in Australia and that is unlikely to happen.'

'No contract? That is not how we do business. I assume you wouldn't be calling me on this unless there was some proposal on the table.'

'What they would prefer to do is as follows; all travel and accommodation costs they will pay direct, the hours I work I will send to Sebastian Barthez on a monthly basis. He will accumulate and arrange payment directly to me at our hourly rate. When I receive payment, I will pay that amount to E&W. This seems the only way he can get this through without involving Andrew Yates.'

'I don't like this one bit; it's not how we do business.'

'Okay, I'll tell him we are not interested.'

'No, don't do that. It is too good a deal to turn down. What guarantee do we have that they will not renege on the deal?'

'Why would you even think that? There is one other option; I can resign and do it for my own account. They can't do this project timeously without me, so they don't really need E&W. What do you want me to tell them?'

'Are you threatening to resign over this?'

'No, but it is an option that may come up if E&W turn down the deal.'

'I will check with Gerry and get back to you shortly.'

Jimmy could just see the discussion; scared they won't get paid against turning down a lucrative fee. Rumours circulating were that the E&W partners used to Audit practices, where every thought was billable, were getting frustrated with MCS.

Barton called back, 'I have discussed the issue with Gerry, and we have concluded that to safeguard our position we will need a guarantee from you. By our calculations a three-month project would be a minimum of fourteen weeks and at your billable rate would be a minimum of seventy thousand rand. For us to approve the project we require you to sign a promise to pay for that amount. Failure to pay the amount by a specified date will result in us collecting the money from you via legal means. Is this acceptable to you?'

'Nothing quite like covering all your bases. I accept. I will get the project timeline details to be accurate on the duration, I would hate us to underestimate the number of billable hours.'

Jimmy hung up the phone and called Sebastian to agree to the project and request a timeline.

Sebastian faxed Jimmy the proposed timeline -

March 1 - fly from Johannesburg to New York via Paris; Fly New York to Baltimore

March 3 to 7 – at Teletronics Baltimore office. Take over multi warehouse version of SDS.

March 7 – fly to Sydney via Los Angeles.

March 9 – land in Sydney.

March 10 to May 30 - at Teletronics Frenches Forest; install and tailor S36 version of SDS

May 31 - fly to Hong Kong
June 2 - fly from Hong Kong to Johannesburg
Total hours 13 weeks at 8 hours per day 520 hours.
All flights are business class. Out of pocket expenses of 30 dollars Australian per day will be reimbursed by the local subsidiary. You can send me your invoice monthly or one at the end of the project. Based on the issue with Andrew Yates, I will only remit all the funds to you when I receive your final invoice.

'As a side note Teletronics' normal rate for this is $150 per hour, I know you normally charge us R125 but it is up to you how you deal with E&W. I suggest you bill us at $150 and keep the difference. Glad to have you aboard. I will accompany you on the trip up until March 14 when I will return to France; Barbara and baby Luc send their best wishes.'

Jimmy photocopied the fax eliminating the side note and called Barton for a meeting and arranged it for the following morning. He arrived dressed in a suit for the occasion. He was summoned to Robertson's office where he found Barton and some other man who was introduced as E&W legal counsel. Jimmy handed out two copies of the fax and after a short pause Robertson got the meeting underway.

'Wilson, as Tony mentioned to you, we are concerned about doing business under these conditions but are fully aware of the Andrew Yates concern. It is with these concerns that I have asked Phil Jones here to prepare a document that you need to sign. The gist of it is to protect our interests in the event of non-payment by Teletronics. You will be liable for fourteen weeks consulting services mounting to R70,000.'

'Sorry to interrupt you, Mr. Robertson but if you refer to the fax you will see the project is in fact thirteen weeks consulting services mounting to R65,000. That is the amount I should be liable for.'

'Semantics; I will get the document changed. The further point is that legal feel that as you are employed by E&W, that any software you develop should become the property of E&W. Do you have any objections to that?'

'Yes, I do. Teletronics have been paying us to install their legacy software on their computer and at their design. I won't sign any document with that clause, and I doubt very much whether Teletronics would accept any claim by E&W. I am not sure what you are trying to achieve here. There is absolutely no downside on behalf of E&W; if the client doesn't pay, you claim what amounts to 100% billable hours for three months from me and if you doubt I can pay that, I have an unencumbered property in Hillcrest worth more than that. If the project goes as planned, E&W

will be paid a minimum of R65,000 at no risk and be able to add your "International Consultants' to your achievements". If this is an issue for you, I am more than happy to let Mr. Barthez know we will not be able to do the project. Our refusal in this may also lead to the local subsidiary cancelling our arrangement with them.'

'No, don't let's be too hasty, all I am trying to do is look after E&W's best interests. Can you enquire if the payments can be made on a monthly basis?'

Jimmy, now totally irritated, stood up, 'You saw the fax about billing, I am not going to ask them so if this is a show-stopper, I am done' and he turned to leave.

'Wilson, you need to sit down. We are not used to doing business this way; billable hours need to be invoiced on a monthly basis, it affects our cash flow projections.'

'If one single consultant, that would be me, is having that significant an effect on MCS's cash flow, then we have bigger issues. I will not go back to Barthez with this request so if you have nothing else for me, I will go back to my client as I am not billing hours sitting here having this discussion. If you make up your minds either way, let me know so I can inform Barthez.' Jimmy got up and left.

By the time Jimmy got back to Teletronics he had a message waiting for him to call Barton. He waited twenty minutes and sure enough, Barton called him again. Jimmy, anticipating who it was, answered breathing heavily, 'Hello, this is Wilson, I have just got back to the office, what can I help you with?'

'Barton here. I have discussed the project with Gerry, and we agree on one condition and that is you submit a detailed time sheet to us at each month end, that way we can keep on top of the billable hours. I will fax you the amended legal agreement for your signature. One last thing, as Teletronics will be paying you a daily stipend, the E&W policy of R20 per day allowance for out of town travel will not be paid.'

Jesus, he thought talk about penny pinching, but just to irritate Barton a little more, 'As I need visas for the USA and Australia, I assume E&W will pay for those?'

'No, we won't; that is for your account. Sign the legal agreement and fax it back to me.'

Jimmy, finally satisfied, signed the document and faxed it back to Barton; he then went in to see Rodger Hall.

'Hey Rodger, you got a minute?' getting a positive answer he continued. 'I have had a request from the French to help with a project in Australia. It is a three-month job from March through May. I am confident that things here are under control. If there are any issues, I am a phone call away. Worst case scenario I can probably dial in to the system here. Are you okay with this?'

'Actually, Sebastian called me this morning to discuss the project. He assured me that any problems here will be your prime concern. So yes, I am okay. While I have you here, I need to ask you for a favour.'

'Sure, if I can no problem.'

'We have a visitor from our Holland branch coming out here on the 28th. He is their Silvio equivalent and he will spend time with Silvio looking at our process and specifically your reorder module. I hope you can spend some time with him.'

'That's no favour., it's part of the job, it will be a pleasure.'

'Oh sorry the favour. I forgot. He should be done by February 1 and only flies out on the 4th so I was wondering if you and your wife would like a long weekend at Lion Sands lodge in the Kruger Park, but there is a catch.'

'I'll bite, what's the catch?'

'Can you accompany our Dutch visitor?'

'Sure, no problem.'

'You can bill us for the hours.'

'Don't be crazy, it will be a pleasure. It will help me with Lynne; I'll tell her about the Kruger Park and then sneak in the three months away in Australia. Thanks for the offer.'

That night he got home and told Lynne that he had good news and bad news.

'Give me the good news first.'

'Teletronics have offered us a free long weekend at the 5-star Lion Sands Lodge in the Kruger Park, all expenses paid.'

'Wow, that isn't good news it's great news! What's the bad news?'

'We have to entertain an overseas guest from Holland, he is here for the week.'

'That's not bad news, it'll be fun, my folks can look after Sharon.'

'Actually, that is not the real bad news. The bad news is that I have been asked to do a three months project in Australia. There is some good news in there. Sebastian will pay me $150 per hour and I will bill E&W R125 per hour so in 13 weeks I could make around 30K, tax free.'

'I think it will be good experience for you and of course 30K would be good. Sharon and I will move in with my folks. '

Jan 13, 1980
Joshua Nkomo returns to Zimbabwe for the first time in three years.

Jan 27, 1980
ZANU leader Robert Mugabe returns to Zimbabwe after five years in exile.

Wim Wiesel arrived and was introduced to Jimmy and Silvio. Fortunately, Wiesel was fluent in English and an extremely likeable good looking man; Jimmy put his age at somewhere in his mid-thirties. The week went well with Wiesel impressed by the reorder process. The Amsterdam office was currently using an NCR system but hoped to move onto the IBM S38 in the future.

The weekend in the Kruger Park was a great success. The 5-star Lion Sands Lodge was amazing; on the game drive around the park all of the Big 5 were spotted. Wim was good company and Lynne was at her charming best. A good time was had by all.

February 9 Jimmy celebrated his 30th birthday with his wife, daughter and his in-laws, Val and Cyril. Even at the age of three and a half Sharon has exactly the same looks and mannerisms as her mother and grandmother.

March 1 Jimmy flew from Jan Smuts International airport to New York via Paris; arriving in New York the following day, he caught a connecting flight to Baltimore. Following Sebastian's instructions, he took a taxi to the Baltimore Holiday Inn. Monday morning, he met up with Sebastian for breakfast and the two of them headed into the Baltimore Office.

Mar 4, 1980
Robert Gabriel Mugabe, aged fifty-two, is elected Prime Minister of the new state of Zimbabwe. Joshua Nkomo is elected Minister of Home Affairs in Mugabe's first cabinet which includes two whites.

By the end of the week Jimmy understood the S36 SDS multi warehouse concept. The software, both source and object programs, were copied to a set of magnetic tapes that will be used for loading in Australia.

March 7 the two of them caught a first-class flight to Los Angeles LAX airport. After a short stop in the first-class lounge, they boarded a Qantas flight for the seventeen-hour flight to Sydney, Australia. They

129

landed in Sydney on Sunday morning where they were met by Matt Pecar, the Australian Data Processing Manager.

Matt, of Croatian background, had organised them accommodation at a five-star hotel in Manley Beach right on the ocean. The hotel was owned and managed by one of Matt's Croatian connections who gave them a special deal. A rental car was waiting for them at the hotel. Jet-lagged, they agreed to meet Matt at the Frenches Forrest Offices on Monday morning.

Sebastian and Jimmy were introduced to the Australian management team. The project affected mostly logistics and sales; the financial interfaces were not part of the deal. Jimmy sensed coolness towards him from the financial accountant, Bob Whyte. Maybe he was annoyed that finance was not part of the project.

The logistics manager, Guy Picard, the French speaker, and the national sales manager, 'Wally' Walters, were far more welcoming. The week together with Sebastian was spent going through the SDS system functions with a view to establish what if anything needed to change. By the end of the week all changes were documented and agreed upon; Sebastian, Guy and Wally signed off and Sebastian made ready to return to France.

His parting statement to Jimmy was significant. 'I know the project is for eight hours a day, but this is a very tight schedule and unlikely to be completed by the agreed date. I think we have two options here. With an eight-hour day you could ask E&W to extend your stay, but the Johannesburg office may have a problem with that. Secondly, if you are okay with working longer hours or over a weekend I am happy to pay you the extra; just keep me informed of your progress and hours worked. I must thank you for doing this project and am happy in the knowledge that it will be a success. Good luck, my friend.'

Based on the project plan Jimmy calculated he would need to work 10-hour days whenever possible. At the end of each week he would evaluate what stage of the project had been reached before working weekends.

At the end of March, he faxed his time sheet to Barton for 21 days at 8 hours per day = R21,000. He sent a copy of his invoice, signed by Matt Pecar, by fax to Sebastian for 21 days at 10 hours per day = $31,500 and received an acceptance acknowledgement by return fax.

Apr 11, 1980
Doctor Canaan Banana is chosen as the first President of Zimbabwe.

Jimmy was unable to find a home phone number for Gus in Perth. It turned out it was unlisted but he managed to get his office number which he called.

The phone was answered, 'Stewart Medical Center, how may I help you?'

'I would like to speak to Doctor Stewart please.'

'He is unavailable at the moment; can I take a message?'

'Yes, tell him to call this number and tell him it's urgent as I know all about him and a Mrs. Cathy Bright. Thank you.'

Less than five minutes later Jimmy's phone rang. He answered, 'I am busy, what do you want?'

'I don't believe you left that message, you bastard, I had some explaining to do. What the hell are you doing in Sydney?'

Jimmy went on to explain the situation. They ended up with Gus saying he would book a flight from Perth on Friday the 18th and would fly back home early on Monday morning.

Apr 18, 1980

The Union Jack is lowered on Britain's last African colony for the final time. Robert Mugabe spoke of the white-black reconciliation saying, *'If yesterday you hated me, today you cannot avoid the love that binds you to me and me to you.'*

Gus arrived at Sydney Airport on Friday night just after 8pm, Jimmy spotted him immediately, 'Man, it's good to see you again! I am so glad you could make it.'

'James, me boy, you need to tell me just what the hell you are doing here; it's obviously not with the Bank so that's a good thing.'

On the drive, Jimmy brought Gus up to date on his, Ian and Chubby's situations. Gus told him about his Medical practice, his two children but strangely didn't mention his wife, Stacey. Not wanting to pry, he made no comment.

'Gus, I have to ask you this. I understood you going to London and Guy's Hospital but what's the deal with the protests? You made the local news, by the way.'

'You know I've always been against the Dutchman and their Apartheid policies. I came to realise that I didn't want to bring up my children in that world so when the Brits were going to deport me. Stacey offered me a way out by coming here. The country has been good to me; I have a good medical practice and my kids don't see colour in a person.'

'So that's it, you'll never come home?'

'If South Africa ever gets rid of Apartheid and implements one man one vote, I would like to return. I don't know if I could convince Stacey; she hates anything South African, sometimes I think that includes me.'

'Do I detect a problem there?'

'I don't know. I am happy enough, but I will never get Cathy totally out of my head. I know we are both married, and she seems happy, so I think that ship has sailed.'

The two of them got back to the hotel, dumped Gus' bag and headed for the bar. Thinking they were still eighteen they tied on a legendary drinking session.

The following morning after a hearty breakfast, complete with hangovers, they headed for Manley beach. They rented two surfboards and paddled out to a crowded break line. Looking around they realised that they were surrounded by fifteen to twenty-year olds and they hadn't been on a board for over ten years. Without making complete fools of themselves they managed to have good day's surfing.

The following day they repeated the performance at Australia's world-famous Bondi Beach. Sunday night was a repeat performance of Friday and on Monday morning, both worse for wear, Jimmy drove Gus to the airport for an emotional farewell. Maybe one day Gus would be back home; neither knew it would be twelve years before they would see each other again.

At the end of April, Jimmy faxed his time-sheet to Barton for 22 days at 8 hours per day = R22,000. He sent a copy of his invoice signed by Matt Pecar by fax to Sebastian for 20 days at 10 hours; 2 days at 8 hours; 2 weekend days at 8 hours = $34,800 and received an acceptance acknowledgement by return fax.

On Friday May 2, Ian opened his third Ford dealership, Williams Ford Pietermaritzburg. Chubby handled the pre-opening marketing and advertising which ensured a huge turnout. The close proximity to the racetrack at Roy Hesketh drew several local racing personalities. Using his past experience with opening, Ian ran several specials. He ensured that STANNIC had two clerks on-site for instant financing.

May 23, 1980

Five white South African soldiers and eighty-one Black Nationalist guerrillas are killed in some of the fiercest clashes yet seen along the South West Africa/Angola border.

To celebrate the successful opening of Williams Ford Pietermaritzburg, Ian gave away free tickets to the May 24 production car races at the Roy Hesketh track and included a spin around the circuit with Tim Hunt in Williams' sponsored Cortina V6 GT. Another bit of clever marketing by Chubby.

May 26, 1980
The South African Police arrest fifty-two demonstrating churchmen.

At the end of May Jimmy faxed his final time sheet to Barton for 22 days at 8 hours per day = R22,000. He sent a copy of his invoice signed by Matt Pecar by fax to Sebastian for 22 days at 10 hours; 5 weekend days at 8 hours = $39,000 and receives an acceptance acknowledgement from Sebastian that Teletronics will process a remittance of $105,300. The payment could take up to three weeks. The fax also contained the message thanking him for a successful implementation of the project and the comment 'Any time you change your mind, let me know. Regards, Sebastian.'

Jimmy did the calculation based on the current exchange rate and ironically the dollar amount less the rand amount due to E&W was exactly the same: R65,000; roughly three and a half times his current annual salary before tax.

With the project successfully implemented and handed over to Matt Pecar, celebratory drinks were held in the office boardroom. With the tension over and the project now a thing of the past, a few of the Australians let their hair down. Conversation eventually got around to sport.

Wally, as a cricket fan, bemoaned the fact that the Aussies' last test matches against South Africa ten years ago resulted in a 4-0 hammering. With the ban in place, when would they get a chance of revenge? The banter went backwards and forwards with Jimmy not getting too involved because of the politics. Bob Whyte, who had spent much of the last three months nitpicking on Jimmy's progress at every project review meeting, seemed to have an unnatural dislike of everything South African.

Eventually, he decided to make his feelings known and directed his comment directly to Jimmy, 'My son plays state level under twenty rugby for South Australia; I would never allow him to play sport against South Africa.'

133

'Yes, Bob, we've all heard about your son's rugby prowess,' chided Wally, 'Jimmy, is our guest here, just chill out.'

'No, I won't. It's their fucking Apartheid system and he is just as much to blame.'

'For fuck's sake, Bob, get a grip.'

Jimmy chipped in. 'No, Wally, he is right. I totally agree that we should be banned from international sport where our team is selected based on colour.'

'You do?' said Whyte, with an incredulous look on his face.

'Yes, but I really did object when we were banned from the International Sky Diving World Championships.'

'Why is that, was your team selected based on colour?'

'Well yes, but it was for their own safety.'

'How do you justify that?'

'Well everybody knows that black people's lips burst at thirty thousand feet.'

There was a moment's silence then everybody, bar Whyte, burst into laughter. Whyte, not realising Jimmy was just taking the piss, got up and left without comment.

'Don't worry mate, we all think Bob is a bit of a cunt. We enjoyed having you here, thanks for the job you did, and you'd be welcome back any time. Cheers' Wally raised his beer glass as did the rest of the Aussies.

The next day Jimmy left Sydney and flew to Hong Kong. He spent Saturday and Sunday seeing the sights and sounds of Hong Kong. He bought six sets of the new Sony Walkman as gifts for himself, Lynne, Ian, Dee, Chubby and Fiona. He bought perfume for Lynne and Val and a bottle of scotch for Cyril. For Sharon he bought several battery-operated dolls and fluffy animals.

Sunday night he caught his Cathay Pacific business class flight back to Johannesburg; with the time change the expected arrival time was 7.30 am Monday morning.

After a well-rested night Jimmy's flight landed on time and with his business class ticket and priority luggage he was one of the first through customs. He immediately spotted Lynne; she was dressed in an ankle-length skirt, a blue blazer-like jacket and a scarf around her neck. Three months is a long time to be away, he virtually ran over and kissed her. Gathering his luggage, they headed for the underground parking.

With the luggage stowed, Jimmy climbed into the driver's side and turned to face his wife, 'God, I have missed you. Where is Sharon? I thought you might have brought her along.'

'I dropped her off with my Mom on the way here, we have some business to take care of and won't want to be disturbed. Come here.'

Lynne pulled him towards her and kissed him with a ferocity of three months of desire. Jimmy reached down and unbuttoned her jacket only to find out that the scarf was hiding the fact she had no blouse or bra underneath. She just laughed at his surprise; sat up and lifted her skirt to reveal she was not wearing any underwear either. She reached over and squeezed the bulge in his pants and said, 'You better get us home sharpish otherwise we might get arrested.'

Tuesday morning, he reported back to Rodger Hall at Teletronics; after being welcomed back he was handed a message, 'Your boss started calling here yesterday looking for you, the receptionist put him through to me. I explained your flight was only arriving Monday at 7.30 pm. I am not sure if he believed me. He really is a strange man. How did it go in Australia?'

Jimmy spent the next hour updating Rodger on the benefits of SDS on a S38; he hoped Sebastian would schedule Johannesburg sometime in the near future.

The minute he got back to his office the phone rang; it was Barton. No 'welcome back'; 'how did it go'; just 'when can we expect payment?' Jimmy explained the invoice for R65,000 had been sent to Teletronics, where he was told it had been approved and submitted for payment, which could take up to three weeks.

Jun 16, 1980
Police and blacks clash in Soweto on the anniversary of the 1979 riots.

The first thing Monday morning, June 16, Barton called asking if Jimmy had received the payment yet. Jimmy explained that it was only ten business days since he submitted the invoice, and as France was one hour behind South Africa, their office wasn't open yet. He assured Barton he would be first to know.

Jun 18, 1980
Forty-two are shot dead and over two hundred are injured when residents of the Coloured township of Cape Flats take the law into their own hands and attack gangs of thugs who were roaming the streets looting and burning buildings.

On June 20 Jimmy received payment from Teletronics. He put on his suit and headed for the E&W offices where he presented Barton with a cheque for R65,000. He mentioned that the payment was just over three and a half times his annual salary, so maybe a bonus is in order. Barton reluctantly agreed; he will let him know. Jimmy returned to the client.

Later that day, Barton called Jimmy to tell him Robertson was very pleased with the result of the Australian project and the fact that MCS now has international experience; he would get a bonus of R125 (one hour's consulting billing) which will be in his July pay.

Jimmy thanked him profusely, hung up the phone and contacted Sebastian about his offer. Sebastian offered him an initial deal for 1,200 hours at $150 per hour. He would have to take it on Sebastian's word as he needed him in Singapore as soon as possible and getting an official employment contract would take months. Jimmy accepted the deal but would have to check with his wife. He was required to give one calendar months' notice so he could only start by on August 1.

Doing the math of 1,200 hours at $150 per hour was $180,000 and at the current exchange rate was almost R250,000 for about 8 months' work; at his current rate of pay it would take him more than ten years to make that kind of money. The best part was it would be tax-free if he could get Teletronics to pay the money into an offshore bank.

He called Lynne, 'Hello, light of my life.'

'Okay, what do you want?'

'Because of my stellar performance in Australia, I managed to extract a bonus from Barton.'

'Blood from a stone. How much? Can we pay off our mortgage on the house?'

'Not quite, unless we only owe R125 before tax.'

'Are you kidding me? The miserable bastard. I hope you told him to shove it.'

'No, even though it is only R125, it pains him so much it is worth it, So I will keep it, but that's not why I called. I phoned Sebastian and I took him up on his offer of a job.'

'Fantastic, when do you start?'

'I have to give a calendar months' notice so August 1. The job is initially for 1,200 hours but he said he can keep me occupied for as long as we are both delivering and are happy with the arrangement.'

'Brilliant. We can put us both on my Medical Aid. What's the pay like?'

'Speaking of pay; I haven't told you I received the funds from Teletronics. $105,300 so I paid E&W their R65,000.'

'That doesn't sound right, there is some mistake.'

'No, the $105,300 is what I billed the French, it works out to R130,000. The funny part is that it is exactly the same amount as E&W got. That arsehole Barton would shit himself if he knew.'

'So, you cleared R65,000 tax free? I knew there was a reason I love you.'

'There is even better news. The 1,200 hours is at $150 per hour, which works out to about R250,000 which is about 10 years pay at my current rate.'

With the impending French rugby tour of South Africa, Chubby signed a lucrative contract with the South African Rugby Board for the advertising and marketing the tour.

July 1, Jimmy, dressed in his three-piece suit, drove directly into the E&W office and handed in his one months' notice to Barton's secretary, Rose. He then walked over to the office he shared with two other consultants. Before he reached the office, he was stopped by Rose, 'Tony wants to see you right away. He seems to be agitated.'

Jimmy knocked on Barton's door and without waiting for an answer, walked straight in. 'You wanted to see me.'

'What is the meaning of this?' said Barton, waving Jimmy's resignation letter.

'It's my one month's notice which I am obliged to give.'

'I know what it is. What I want to know is why? You state "to pursue other opportunities."'

'That is correct. I have been offered an opportunity to do an installation for Teletronics in Singapore.'

'Ha! I think not. When you joined E&W, you signed a contract that stated that you would not be allowed to take up a position with one of our clients doing the same function as you were with that client for a period of one year. So, I will tear up this letter. I will allow you to go to Singapore, just let me have the details.' Barton tore up the letter and with a self-satisfied flourish, tossed into his waste-paper bin.

'Mr. Barton, you may want to retrieve the letter and paste it together. I will acquiesce to the "no client rule", just let me have a copy of the contract with Teletronics and I will withdraw my resignation.'

'We don't have a written contract as such, but you have been doing work for them on our behalf.'

'I agree on the work aspect and you have been well paid for that, with no effort on your part, I might add. I believe Teletronics are an Andrew Yates client; I don't recall a clause in my contract forbidding me to join the opposition.'

'Wilson, what's this all about. I let you go to Australia; that was a big risk for us.'

'I don't know what sort of a risk. You had me sign a document saying I would owe E&W R65,000 if Teletronics didn't pay, so you were not at any risk. What really clinched me resigning was your constant hassling me for payment when the process had been explained to you a number of times; added to that, the insulting R125 bonus for three months' work.'

'We can revisit the bonus and discuss an ongoing bonus plan.'

'Too little, too late; I need to get back to our client. There is much to do before I leave for Singapore.'

'What about our client? Who will support them if you are in Singapore? Can we place someone there in your absence?'

'Sure, just let me have that person for a month. Assuming he or she has S36 and RPG2 experience I could probably hand over to them.'

'We don't have anyone else with those skills. Can you train somebody in a month?'

'Lack of forward planning, Tony; you have put all your eggs in the SLMT basket and how is that going for you?'

'I don't like your attitude, Wilson. I accept your resignation. You better make sure that you continue to support Teletronics to the fullest in this last month. I am going to call Mr. Hall and offer our continued support after you leave.'

Jimmy turned and left Barton's office, 'Goodbye Rose, this is probably my last visit to the office. It's been nice knowing you.'

Jimmy got back to Teletronics and found Rodger Hall waiting for him, 'I have just had a very interesting call from your boss. He is very concerned about you resigning and would like to place one of your colleagues here when you head for Singapore. He wants to arrange a meeting with me. What is he smoking?'

'He sees a steady revenue stream disappearing over the horizon. If you have some spare time you should arrange a meeting, it might be fun. He will try and sign you up for the System Lifecycle Management Tool (SLMT). It is of no use to you but that is all they know. I will give you a list of questions to ask him, so come on and have a meeting, just for me. I want to see him sweat.'

Rodger agreed and called Barton, who arranged to come out the following day. As suspected, Barton arrived for the meeting armed with a set of SLMT manuals and accompanied by one of the Principal Consultants, who was an expert on SLMT. Barton launched into his

SLMT spiel. Jimmy, having heard the spiel a number of times, had supplied Rodger with a list of questions to ask at key points in the presentation. Each question received a negative answer which slowly but surely made the use of SLMT at Teletronics redundant.

Barton, exasperated, decided on a different point of attack, 'Rodger, as you are probably aware, Wilson has resigned and is due to leave for Singapore at the end of the month. As you are an important client of ours, we are concerned that a lack of support would expose your organisation to serious consequences. We would like to offer our ongoing support to you.'

'Thank you for your offer, Tony, but I think we are covered. We have head office's guarantee of support; Jimmy will have a copy of our system with him in Singapore and we are only a phone call or fax away. As an Auditor, I know this will probably hurt but Jimmy will make any production fixes we need at no charge. That's what you call client service. You have lost a superstar there. Tony, thank you for the presentation but at the end of this month we will no longer need E&W support. Good luck with SLMT. I am sure it will work in some organisations but unfortunately, not in ours.' Rodger stood up and shook the hands of the two E&W employees and ushered them out.

'Thanks Rodger, I enjoyed that. He will probably send you an invoice. Please don't pay it.'

'I had fun as well. That Barton really is an annoying man. I won't be paying any invoice from him.'

July 31 Jimmy sent his last time sheet through to Barton and officially left E&W. On Sunday August 3 he boarded a South African Airlines flight for Singapore. He was booked into a furnished apartment, which he would vacate when Barbara arrived in two weeks' time. Barbara was bringing her young son, Luc, with her. The Singapore Office sourced a Philippine maid to look after Luc and clean the apartment.

On Sebastian's instruction, Jimmy was paid out of pocket expenses of 60 Singapore dollars a day. This was to cover meals and transport. Jimmy decided to take the Mass Rapid Transport (MRT) to and from work and eat local food. Total expenditure most days: under 15 Sing dollars a day.

Jimmy opened a bank account in the Cayman Islands and instructed Teletronics to deposit his consulting fees in that account.

By the time Barbara arrived, Jimmy had loaded SDS and started converting it to Native S38. He would take the opportunity while in Singapore to rewrite the programs using the new S38 features. With the new design, he would own the source. Future installations would be much quicker and Teletronics would benefit so Sebastian had no issues with the arrangement.

Singapore was an eye-opener. Temperature all year around was between 31C and 33C; hot and humid. With nothing much to do, Jimmy searched the island for electronic bargains and gifts for family and friends back home.

Aug 6, 1980
Cabinet Minister, Edgar Tekere, is charged with murdering a
white farmer in Zimbabwe.

On October 29, the French rugby tour to South Africa began. They played four matches, three against select sides which they won and the fourth against the Springboks which they lost. Chubby garnered a six-figure fee for advertising and marketing. He also made an even larger fee by selling space on advertising boards that surrounded the pitch for the test match. It was a unique idea and would be the standard at future matches.

Due to the success and revenue stream, it was an easy sell to the provisional Rugby teams as well.

Nov 4, 1980
Ronald Reagan defeats Jimmy Carter in the United States Presidential
elections.

Dec 8, 1980
Cabinet Minister, Edgar Tekere, is cleared of murdering a white
farmer.

John Lennon, aged forty, is shot dead outside his Dakota Building
apartment by Mark David Chapman, aged twenty-five, to whom
Lennon had given his autograph earlier in the day.

After being away for just over four and a half months, Jimmy changed his ticket and headed home for Christmas. He told Barbara he'd be back on January 5. Loaded up with gifts, he flew back to Johannesburg on SAA arriving home at 8.30 am on Sunday 21st. He spotted Lynne and Sharon and rushed over only to be stopped by his daughter jumping into his arms. Disappointingly, Lynne was fully clothed but looked stunning anyway, no makeup and well-tanned.

140

With Lynne on vacation they picked up Val and Cyril and headed for Hillcrest for Christmas. With the three girls in the back of the car, you couldn't help noticing just how alike they looked. Three versions of the same woman.

With just over $120,000 in his Cayman bank account and over R50,000 in his local account, things were looking good. He also had nearly 6,000 Sing dollars left over from what he referred to as his 'lunch money'. He would have to buy Lynne an air ticket to come and visit him in Singapore.

CHAPTER 29
1981

1981 would see big changes in neighbouring Rhodesia soon to be renamed Zimbabwe. Black rule was on South Africa's doorstep. Racial tension caused riots in London. Huge demonstrations against South Africa's Apartheid policies on three different continents. The Springboks made one of their last rugby tours as worldwide sanctions were brought to bear on the country. Despite the pressures, the Nationalist Party refused to budge.

Jimmy, Ian and their families made their way to Chubby's Durban North mansion for his 31st birthday. With the women sitting around the pool with the kids, the three men headed for the bar in Chubby's den.

With Jimmy being away most of the year, the conversation centred on what he had been up to. He told them of his time in Singapore and Australia.

'I know Sydney is on the opposite side of Australia to Perth but it's a pity you couldn't get together with Gus.'

'You are right, Ian, but I met this really cool cat, here are a couple of photos I took.' Jimmy handed him three photos.

'Jesus, you arsehole! Why didn't you tell us you got together? Two middle aged surfers – where were these taken? Here, Chubbs, have a butchers at these idiots.'

'That one at Manley Beach and the other two at Bondi Beach. Check the topless chick in the background, nice pair of tits.'

'So, how was Doctor Gus, our favourite anti-Apartheid demonstrator?' inquired Ian.

'He was hard to read. He is making good money there, has two kids who he insists will be brought up in a society where the colour of your skin has no consequence. His wife hates everything South African; he did seem a bit negative when talking about her.'

'So, we won't be seeing him anytime soon. The Dutchman won't end Apartheid and let the Kaffirs vote, thank God.'

January 3 Jimmy flew back to Singapore but not before giving Lynne a return ticket leaving on February 6 and returning home on the 14th. He told her that she would be his birthday present.

Jan 15, 1981
Over three hundred people have died in clashes between the two black ZANLA and ZIPRA guerrilla organisations in Zimbabwe.

With Sharon safely under Val's care, Lynne caught an afternoon flight to Singapore where she was met by her husband at 8 am on Sunday morning. They took a taxi directly to the Ana Hotel where Jimmy was staying. A quick shower later, they headed for the bed. After a frenetic session, Lynne rolled over and was immediately asleep. *Maybe I should have bought her a business class ticket,* thought Jimmy.

Lynne spent her days working her way through her husband's lunch money. A shopper's paradise, she stocked up on silk clothing, perfume, a designer watch, Ray Ban sunglasses and a camera. She bought gifts for their daughter and her parents. Jimmy had to warn her about her luggage allowance. He suggested that she wear a low-cut top and short skirt when she travels home. That would distract the check-in clerk at Changi Airport when leaving and the customs guy when she got to Jan Smuts.

After a week of indulging themselves, Jimmy accompanied his wife to the airport. Dressed in a short skirt and a plunging neckline, she did distract the young Chinese guy at check-in who let her overweight suitcase through at no extra cost. Back at Jan Smuts the ploy worked again as she strolled through customs without her luggage being searched.

Feb 15, 1981
Ten months after white Rhodesia became black Zimbabwe; Prime Minister Robert Mugabe uses a white-led air raid to crush a rebellion by guerrilla supporters of Joshua Nkomo.

Mar 30, 1981
Ronald Reagan, the President of the United States, is wounded in an assassination attempt by John Hinckley III, a twenty-five-year old disk jockey.

At the end of March, after eight months in Singapore, Jimmy flew home. He took the month of April off to spend some time with his wife and daughter. Sharon, nearly five years old, had started pre-school and was growing up quickly. With the success of the Singapore project, Sebastian decided to upgrade the South African office to Jimmy's modified S38 version of SDS. This way, having Jimmy at home, he could optimise the new version and be with his family at the same time.

As part of his upgrade, he would also develop a manufacturing and job-costing module which would also be used in Singapore.

Apr 4, 1981

London, rioting between black and white youths turns Brixton ablaze. Two hundred and thirteen people arrested, and two hundred and one policemen injured.

On July 22 the Springboks embarked on their rugby tour to New Zealand amid doubts that it might be terminated before the scheduled end of September 12. Prior to their arrival in Auckland, the 'Stop the Tour' organisers promised to disrupt the games at every opportunity.

The second tour match on July 25 at Waikato was cancelled due to violent protests. The protestors broke down the fences around the ground and stormed the field. Running battles between the police and protestors turned violent. The police admitted they underestimated the number of protestors.

The following five matches leading up to the first test match all went ahead under huge police presence. The first test match on August 15 went ahead with the police searching spectators entering the ground. Continual surveillance of the perimeter of the ground was done for the duration of the game.

The very next match on August 19 was cancelled when violent protestors broke into the ground before the game and dug holes on the playing surface and burned down one of the stands. The South Canterbury Police called for the cancellation of the match as they could not guarantee the safety of the players or the spectators. Left wing agitators demanded the tour be abandoned.

The next six matches went ahead and were met with continual protest. The New Zealand population was divided over the tour; non-rugby supporters wanted the Springboks to leave immediately. As the tour was seen as a clash between the two best Rugby Teams in the world, fans insisted it must go on.

144

The final match of the tour was the third test to be played in Auckland. The series was tied at one test apiece. This would be the decider. The match was played with huge security around the ground keeping protestors out of the stadium.

In one of the most bizarre things ever seen at a sporting event, a small aircraft started buzzing the field. After a number of dangerous passes, one of the plane's occupants started dropping five-pound bags of white flour on the playing field. A number of these landed very close to players and if they had made contact, a serious injury would have been the result.

The game managed to be completed without any players being injured. The All Blacks won the game with a dubiously awarded penalty in the last minute; final score 25-22. The match was refereed by a New Zealand referee.

The Springboks left New Zealand happy to be away from violent demonstrations and headed for the USA for a three-match tour. After the trauma of New Zealand, most of the players would have preferred to return home rather than partake in what was a meaningless tour to the USA. They were consoled by management that as rugby was a non-event in the States, at least there would be no demonstrations.

Were they in for a shock; the first match against the Midwest All Stars, scheduled to be played in Chicago, was secretly rescheduled for mid-morning on Saturday 19th at Roosevelt Park in Racine, Wisconsin, due to anti-Apartheid demonstrations. The strategy worked as only 500 spectators attended. Two demonstrators were arrested.

The New York City match on September 22 against the Eastern All Stars was moved up-state to Albany. The long serving Mayor of Albany, Erastus Corning, maintained that there was a right of peaceful assembly to 'publicly espouse an unpopular cause,' despite his own stated view that 'I abhor everything about apartheid.'

Governor Hugh Carey argued that the event should be barred as the anti-apartheid demonstrators presented an 'imminent danger of riot,' but a Federal court ruling allowing the game to be played was upheld in the United States Court of Appeals. A further appeal to Supreme Court Justice Thurgood Marshall was also overruled on the grounds of free speech.

The match went ahead with around a thousand demonstrators corralled 100 yards away from the field of play, which was surrounded by the police. No violence occurred at the game, but a pipe bomb was set off in the early morning outside the headquarters of the Eastern

Rugby Union resulting in damage to the building estimated at $50,000. No one was injured.

The final match of the tour, on September 25 against the US National team, took place in secret at Glenville in up-state New York. The thirty spectators recorded at the match was the lowest ever attendance for an international rugby match.

The next day the Springbok rugby team flew home; most wondered what the point of the USA leg of the tour was all about. This would be the last rugby tour for many years. Despite the obvious hatred of the South African Apartheid policies, the Nationalist Government refused to budge.

On November 23 Jimmy flew to Hong Kong to do an implementation of SDS. The Office on Hong Kong Island was only manned by a small admin staff. The plan was to install only the Sales and Distribution modules, no interfaces to any financial systems. The whole implementation was planned to be completed by December 11.

Dec 2, 1981

Forty-four mercenaries, disguised as tourists and under the leadership of Colonel "Mad Mike" Hoare, hijack an Air India flight to South Africa. The attempted coup to overthrow the Seychelles Government of left wing leader, Albert Rene, is thwarted.

After the success of her trip to Singapore, Jimmy bought Lynne a ticket so she could spend her 34th birthday in Hong Kong. As with Singapore, Lynne spent her time sightseeing and shopping. They flew home together on Saturday, December 12. As he had a business class ticket, he upgraded Lynne's ticket.

With the Johannesburg S38 in place, Jimmy asked Rodger Hall what he intended to do with the old IBM 36. Rodger told him it had been written off the books and had no value. Jimmy offered to take it off his hands. He upgraded the Fourways outside granny flat into an office and installed the S36. He could use the system to write code in S38 format but would still need to compile and test it on an actual S38.

CHAPTER 30
1982

1982 would be the year that South Africa attempted to circumvent the International Cricket Councils (ICC) worldwide ban on the Springboks. By offering huge amounts of cash to current and recently retired Test players, they would be enticed to tour South Africa and play Test matches. These tours would be called 'Rebel Tours' or the 'Kruger Rands Tours' and would not receive ICC recognition nor would they carry the 'first class' tag.

On the home front, the Nationalist Party continued with their Apartheid policies. So called terrorist groups like the ANC and SWAPO ramped up their activities against white rule. The war along the Angola border intensified and resulted in casualties for the SADF, SWAPO and the Angolan MPLA. News coverage of SADF casualties was heavily censored in the South African news outlets. The average South African, not in the SADF, had no clue of what the situation was along their borders.

Jimmy's first scheduled installation of the year was in Taipei, Taiwan. It had become an increasing problem booking his flights and accommodation through the travel office in France. At Sebastian's request, Jimmy was asked to book his own flights which would be refunded by Teletronics. They would pay for a business class round trip; the local subsidiary would book and pay for accommodation and also pay the daily allowance in local currency cash.

Jimmy decided that it was probably a good idea to book his flights through the same travel agency that he had booked Lynne's trips to Singapore and Hong Kong. He called Mayfair Travel and was put through to Gillian Barker, who remembered doing Lynne's trips. He explained he needed to fly from Johannesburg to Taipei in Taiwan round trip. He wanted the most direct flights possible, leaving Saturday February 13 and returning March 6. He wanted two totally separate quotes, one in business class and one in economy.

Gillian called him the next day telling him that he could collect the quotes, or she could have them delivered. He chose to pick them up himself.

The flight to Taiwan would leaving Johannesburg 08.00 on Saturday, and with a connection in Singapore, would arrive in Taipei on Sunday at 19.30 local time. The return flight would leave Taipei on March 6 at 09.00, and with a stopover in Singapore, arrive back in Johannesburg 17.30 on Sunday afternoon. All flights were on Singapore Airlines; Business class: R11,290; economy class: R3,660. Jimmy instructed her to book the economy flights, a handy profit of R7,630.

The plan to fly economy would be a big winner going forward. The plan for the local subsidiary booking and paying for the accommodation would not always be a win; Taipei would be one of those.

Jimmy flew to Taipei and with not getting much sleep in his economy seat he landed not well rested. Giving the taxi driver his hotel's address, they headed into the city. One thing he would learn about the Chinese is that 'workers' have a distinct class they fit into. Jimmy was not seen to be at an executive level, very few in the Taipei office were, and as such he was given accommodation befitting of his position. The hotel was an absolute dive, his room was directly under the Jacuzzi on the 2nd floor and it seemed to run twenty-four seven. When he complained, all of a sudden nobody understood English.

Of all of the countries Jimmy worked in, Taiwan was by far the most unpleasant. Fortunately, it was only a three-week assignment and with the profit on the air ticket and his fee it netted him around R30K.

Feb 17, 1982
Robert Mugabe dismisses Joshua Nkomo and two other black ministers as the twenty-two-month-old Zimbabwe coalition government is brought to an abrupt end.

Feb 28, 1982
Geoff Boycott and eleven other English cricketers arrive in Johannesburg despite a ban on playing cricket in South Africa.

In an effort to keep Springbok cricket relevant, the South African Cricket Board welcomed Geoff Boycott and his 'England' cricket team. They would play against select and full Springbok teams but the ICC would not recognise their validity. Although most of the team were in the twilight of their careers, there were a few who were not. The 'rebels' were more than adequately compensated but the ban loomed over all of the team.

Mar 19, 1982
**The rebel English cricketers touring South Africa are given a
three-year ban by the Test and County Cricket Board.**

With the Test and County Board imposing a three-year ban on the rebels, Chubby approached Cricket South Africa (CSA) with a proposal to further compensate the rebels by signing them up for personal appearances, speaking engagements and selective advertising.

Mar 20, 1982
**Doctor Andries Treurnicht launches the ultra-right-wing
Conservative Party in South Africa.**

April 3 Jimmy flew to Düsseldorf via Stuttgart to join Barbara for an initial four months on what would be the first major European subsidiary to use SDS on S38. It was a very high-profile project especially with it being in such close proximity to the home office in Paris.

He was booked into the Holiday Inn in Ratingen just a short walk away from the Teletronics offices. After a long flight he decided he would take advantage of the hotel sauna. Not knowing the etiquette, he played it safe and kept his shorts on under the towel. He found the sauna unoccupied and settled in for a good cleansing sweat.

He hadn't been there ten minutes when the door opened and a forty-something female walked in with a towel wrapped around her. Jimmy mumbled a greeting which she acknowledged; divesting herself from the towel, she sat on it completely naked. Jimmy tried not to stare and that went well until she spread her towel out on the upper bench and laid down on her back. With her knees pulled up and her unshaven legs spread, there was a very hairy vagina at eye level. Welcome to Germany.

Monday morning, he took a taxi into the Teletronics Offices in Ratingen where he met up with Barbara. This was only her second project since Singapore; she had been assigned to the project for at least one year. She had her son, Luc, with her and had managed to arrange for her Philippine maid from Singapore to accompany her. Jimmy's main task was to Germanize SDS and train their local IT staff to make use of the inherent data for additional reporting.

Because the daily rate at the Holiday Inn was expensive, the Germans arranged a furnished one bedroom flat for Jimmy within walking distance to the office.

Both Jimmy and Barbara found the Germans way too serious and as this was the third project they had worked on together, they were very

149

relaxed with each other. Jimmy, often not too good at remembering names, had trouble with the IT manager's name. When referring to him while speaking to Barbara he called him Herman.

'His name isn't Herman, it's Klaus.'

'Well, I can't seem to remember his name so to me he is Herman as in Herman the German.'

'What about the computer operator?'

'Have you seen the size of that lunch box he brings to work? Well, he is Herman Lunch Box.'

'What about the programmer?'

'You've heard how he keeps snorting; Herman Horse.'

With Barbara almost wetting herself, 'Great idea, that's how we will refer to them.'

The project went very well and with all of his initial tasks completed, Jimmy headed back to Johannesburg at the end of July. Although the money was great, Lynne found it frustrating that her husband was away for long periods of time. Six-year old Sharon cried for days each time he left.

With his next assignment in Amsterdam in September, Jimmy took a three week break to recharge his batteries and spend some time with his family. He took on the role of stay at home Dad, which Sharon loved.

Aug 10, 1982

Two hundred South African and SWAPO (South West Africa People's Organisation) guerrillas are reported killed in clashes along the Angolan border.

In September, Jimmy headed to Amsterdam for the Holland installation. The Dutch were a friendly liberal nation; this installation was a pleasure to do, by far the most enjoyable to date.

After two weeks at home, Jimmy traded exciting Amsterdam for boring, expensive Brussels in November; SDS for Belgium

CHAPTER 31
1983

1983 saw the first government-sanctioned sporting event where a black team openly played against one of white South Africans. A team made up of mostly current West Indian Test players undertook a 'Rebel' tour to the country. As with the English, they were well compensated. They all received a lifetime ban by the West Indies Cricket Board, but as they are being paid more than they would earn at home over their entire career, the feeling among the team was 'so what.'

Chubby signed them up on the same deal he had with the English. One additional request from the players was for a steady supply of *dagga,* the South African equivalent of ganja.

Jimmy spent most of the year in South East Asia. A return to Singapore to add the manufacturing module in February, March and April was followed by a short visit home. Then it was off to Kuala Lumpur in Malaysia in June and July. The next stop was directly to Bangkok in Thailand. On completion, Lynne joined him for a one-week trip to Phuket.

May 20, 1983
At least sixteen people are killed and one hundred and ninety are injured when a car bomb exploded outside the South African Air Force Headquarters building in Pretoria. The Minister for Law and Order, Louis Le Grange, blames the bomb on the banned African National Congress.

Jimmy convinced Rodger Hall to employ a computer supervisor. The person would need basic skills in operations and job control. He would be trained in how to troubleshoot and provide Jimmy with any computer error messages. He would be taught how to make program corrections on Jimmy's instructions. He would be shown how to write simple queries for ad-hoc reports. With him being away so much, it gave Rodger on-site backup. Rodger agreed and with the French Head

Office's push to hire people of colour, a job advert was placed in *Computing SA*. They narrowed down the choice to a black man, an Indian and a coloured. Jimmy interviewed the applicants and with Rodgers agreement, the job was offered to Ryan Herman, who was coloured.

Jun 29, 1983
The South African Government extends the banning order on
Winnie Mandela.

On July 1 Lynne was promoted to Marketing Director at her Pharmaceutical Company, as she no longer called directly on customers, she handed in her Volkswagen Passat and got a Mercedes Benz; the vehicle given to all of the Company's Directors.

Nov 3, 1983
A national referendum in South Africa by whites only comes out in favour. of power sharing with Coloureds and Asians but excludes blacks.

CHAPTER 32
1984

After the success of the previous year's cricket tour a second West Indies tour took place. Chubby again took care of the marketing, advertising and public appearances.

Continued terrorist activities were seen throughout the year, becoming even more brazen. Intimidation by black terror groups on the local black communities became a common occurrence. A vile new method of punishment was let loose by blacks on other blacks whom they deemed to have not obeyed the boycott of white businesses; it was called 'Necklacing'.

Necklacing took the form of placing a car tire over the head of the victim; it was filled with petrol and pulled down over the person's chest and arms and then lit. Not only did the person die a painfully horrible death but it sent a message; disobey us and this is what will happen to you.

One of the most horrendous examples of this occurred in Port Elizabeth, where an eleven-year old black boy, having begged some money, went into the closest shop to buy bread as he was starving. He was spotted entering the white-owned shop and reported to the 'comrades'. He was abducted and given the 'necklace'. He died a horrible death surrounded by a cheering, dancing mob. The message was clear: break the boycott and you will die.

The most ridiculous part of the whole incident was that having begged for the 10 cents, he was supposed to catch a bus to the township which would have cost him 15 cents, and then buy the loaf of bread from a black-owned shop for 25 cents. Not only were they killing their own but ripping them off as well.

In January, Jimmy flew to Jakarta for the Indonesian installation of SDS. It was a small subsidiary only took four days to complete. Lynne flew into Singapore where Jimmy, using his 'lunch money', had bought tickets to Bali for a week's holiday. They then flew back to Singapore; Lynne flew home and Jimmy continued his upgrades

On March 1 Ian opened his fourth dealership in Port Shepstone. Using the same tried and proven method, the launch again proved a roaring success. With all of his business enterprises pulling him in every direction, he appointed a Dealership Manager in each of his four Ford Dealers. He got a daily sales report to keep on top of the situation.

His deal with ESCOM was progressing and on budget; it was due for completion by year end. To fill that void he looked at Ford Motor Company to propose adding PLC's to their production line.

Chubby, ever looking to expand his business, came up with one of the best advertising campaigns of the year; destined to win multiple awards. It would put his advertising company at the forefront of innovative ads.

With Jimmy away in Norway, Chubby approached Lynne with a project. He had been given a tender to create an ad campaign for an anti-ageing skin product for a leading cosmetic company. What he wanted to do was use Lynne, Val and Sharon in the adverts.

The shot started with a close up of Val's face, still a very attractive 55-year old. The camera pulled back as she rubbed the anti-ageing cream on her face. The camera then moved back in and slowly focused on Lynne, dressed in identical clothes to Val, giving the impression that the cream had transformed her to look 20 years younger. It showed a close up of Lynne rubbing cream on her face. The transformation is seamless. The camera then retreated and returned to show Sharon, also dressed identically. This gave the impression that all three were the same person; the ad ended with the message 'You only need a dab to get that youthful look back.'

The ad was an instant hit and ran daily on SABC TV. It stopped after one week and with a gap of two days, a new one ran. The new ad was the exact opposite of the first one, starting with Sharon morphing into Lynne and then Lynne into Val. Seven-year old Sharon spoke the words 'I hope I can be as pretty as my Mom when I grow up'. Thirty-six-year old Lynne uttered the same words. Fifty-five-year old Val ended by saying, 'It's not only in the genes. Ponds beauty cream helps me look young again.'

With the huge success of the two ads, there was a clamour by the media to find out more about the three Pond's girls. Chubby, anticipating the reaction, signed them up to his agency and handled the requests for interviews. The three of them appeared on the morning breakfast show on SABC. Seated next to each other the resemblance was uncanny.

The magazine program, Carte Blanche, did a fifteen-minute segment on them. Photos were shown side by side of them at a year old and five years old; absolutely identical. A photo of Val at thirty-six was superimposed on Lynne's face; it fitted seamlessly into a single entity. While Val was a little nervous, young Sharon handled it like a veteran.

When Jimmy returned from Norway, he was met at the airport by his wife and daughter. He spotted the two of them surrounded by a crowd of people and it looked to him like they were being asked to pose for photos. As he got nearer, he noticed that some of the crowd were handing Lynne and Sharon magazines and the two of them were signing the front cover.

Sharon, spotting her Father, broke away from the crowd and ran at him jumping into his arms. Lynne, seeing the two of them, apologised to the crowd and joined them. They headed for the underground parking.

'What the heck was all that about? Who were those people?'

'Daddy, they are just our fans. They wanted photos with us and our autographs. We are famous.'

Lynne handed Jimmy a copy of the *Fair Lady* magazine and on the cover was a huge photograph of Val, Lynne and Sharon with the caption 'Is it really just all in the genes?'

On the way home Lynne explained the 'Ponds' ad and Chubby's part in it. Yes, they were celebrities and couldn't go anywhere together without being mobbed. It started out as a bit of fun but was now becoming a problem. Their fifteen minutes of fame.

Jun 2, 1984
President P.W. Botha arrives in London amid mass protests, for the first visit by a South African leader for twenty-three years.

Jimmy's final international assignment of the year was to Denmark. The Danish were really a good-looking nation. He had never seen so many beautiful women in one place. He had a room at a small hotel in Copenhagen, just a short bus ride away from the offices in Ballarup.

The IT manager had a drinking problem and was also pretty useless from a technical point of view. All of the SDS training was geared towards the computer operator, a typical statuesque blond Scandinavian beauty. After the first couple of hectic days, it was time to relax on Friday after work. It was here that Jimmy was introduced to the sauna culture of the Danes.

There were three very distinct groups of employees: the factory workers, office staff and executives. Each of these groups of employees had their own sauna. On Friday, after work, Jimmy was invited for drinks with his office staff colleagues. They congregated in the office staff canteen for drinks and snacks. After about twenty minutes, everyone got up, gathered their drinks and headed to the sauna area. Then to a person, they began disrobing and everybody – male and female – totally naked, headed into the sauna. It was the least sexual thing Jimmy had ever seen; naked people of both sexes sitting around like it was the most natural thing in the world.

As people became too hot, they got up, jumped in the cold plunge pool, got out and had a seat and a drink and repeated the process. Quite an experience.

Sep 4, 1984
In Sharpeville, deputy mayor Sam Dlamini was hacked to death by mobs of black students then doused in petrol and set alight. This, the day after South Africa's new constitution came into effect giving Asians and Coloureds limited political power.

Dec 10, 1984
The Nobel Prize for Peace is awarded to Bishop Desmond Tutu for his non-violent struggle against apartheid.

CHAPTER 33
1985

1985 saw a dramatic increase in terrorist activity on the South African borders and also in the black townships. Bombing attacks on soft targets showed a marked increase. The government placed restrictions on press reporting. More police and military call ups were made to combat rioting in black townships. The Nationalist Government remained steadfast that it would not cave in to foreign interference in the domestic policies of the country.

Quote of the year by P.W. Botha, *"I am not prepared to lead white South Africans on a road to abdication and suicide."*

On the first of January, Teletronics announced the buyout of Merlin Gerin and Square D; they rebranded the business as Groupe Schreiber. Jimmy spent the first four months of the year changing the brand name on SDS. Working from the South Africa office, he completed the task and released the new version of the software.

Feb 18, 1985
At least eight killed and several hundred injured when South African Police clash with back squatters at the Cape Flats district of Cape Town.

With the money she had made from the Pond's ad campaign, Lynne treated herself to a fire engine red Porsche 911 convertible. Jimmy, much to his dismay, was not allowed to drive it.

Mar 21, 1985
South African riot police shoot seventeen blacks dead at Langa Township on the twenty-fifth anniversary of Sharpeville.

Apr 16, 1985
The South African Government says it will end the ban on mixed race marriages.

In May, Jimmy left for Milton Keynes in England to install SDS at their new warehouse. Having got the process down to a fine art, it was starting to become a bit boring. He did have a good laugh when the Managing Director's secretary sent out a letter to all Schreiber customers informing them of the relocation of their new warehouse. She typed the letter misspelling 'wherehouse' and the auto correct changed it to 'whorehouse'. She did not notice the mistake and sent out over one thousand letters explaining the whereabouts of Groupe Schreiber's new whorehouse.

Jun 15, 1985
South Africa celebrates its first mixed race marriage.

On July 1 Ian won the ESCOM contract to install PLCs in all major metropolitan substations. He opened additional support offices in Johannesburg, Cape Town, Bloemfontein, Pretoria and Port Elizabeth. He now had over fifty staff working full-time on the ESCOM project.

Jul 21, 1985
South African President P.W. Botha announces that a state of emergency will be imposed on thirty magisterial districts after a year of unrest that has left over five hundred people dead. The South African Council of Churches condemns the move "as a desperate act aimed at stemming the tide of liberation."

Jul 23, 1985
The South African Police detain four hundred and forty-one people under the emergency laws.

In August, Jimmy travelled to Dublin to install SDS in Ireland. As installations went, this was one of the easiest so far. He absolutely loved Ireland. The people at Schreiber were great, so relaxed and easy going. The Irish people in general were among the friendliest in the world, always ready for a night on the town. He developed a taste for Guinness. He was booked into a hotel that used to be a castle; four poster bed and a fireplace in the room, just beautiful.

Aug 10, 1985
Leading anti-apartheid campaigner, Reverend Alan Boesak, is arrested as forty die in racial riots.

Aug 15, 1985
President P.W. Botha told a Nationalist Party meeting in
Durban that he refused to consider immediate changes to the
country's apartheid policies and *"would not give in to hostile
pressure and agitation from abroad."*

Aug 16, 1985
Bishop Desmond Tutu says the chances of peaceful change in
South Africa are "virtually nil."

Aug 23, 1985
Six blacks are killed in clashes with Security Police and over five
hundred black school children are arrested for boycotting classes.

Sep 6, 1985
President P.W. Botha closes all the Coloured schools in the
Western Cape where thirty have died in a week of clashes with the
Police.

Sept 11, 1985
The South African Government says it will restore citizenship to
fifteen million blacks living in the "homelands."

In October, Jimmy returned to Milton Keynes in England to add the
manufacturing modules for SDS. The Union representing the factory
workers threatened to go on strike as they saw that the SDS manufacturing
module would result in a reduction of three jobs. The strike was averted
when the company signed a document stating that no lay-offs would
occur. God bless the British Unions.

Oct 7, 1985
Several hundred blacks riot in North London after the death of a
black woman during a police search of her flat. A white forty-year-old
Police Constable, Keith Blakelock, was hacked to death by the mob.

Oct 21, 1985
British Prime Minister Margaret Thatcher boycotts apartheid
sanctions against South Africa during a Commonwealth Prime
Ministers' meeting in Nassau, saying sanctions will only hurt the
blacks.

Nov 2, 1985
The South African Government implements severe restrictions on
press reporting.

Nov 21, 1985
Thirteen blacks are killed in clashes with Police at the black
township of Mamelodi.

Dec 23, 1985
Six whites die when a bomb is exploded at a shopping centre in
Durban during the Christmas shopping rush.

CHAPTER 34
1986

On the home front 1986 was similar to the previous year. Intense pressure on South Africa from the International Community, the National Party refused to budge, violence, murder, mayhem and rioting. Black labour presented a new force in an attempt to force change in the country. Strikes in key areas of the economy brought gold mines to a standstill. Police brutality in quelling disturbances resulted in many deaths.

1986 was also a year where many large international companies began to disinvest in South Africa by pulling their operations out of the country. While these announcements were hailed in the international communities, they had very little effect on the economy.

Cricket South Africa announced that an Australian cricket team would tour South Africa. Cricket Australia immediately placed a lifetime ban on those players who took part in the tour.

Demonstrations against the tour were seen in all major Australian cities. Gus and his wife, Stacey, took part in the Perth demonstrations where Stacey was arrested. Gus made the news on SABC TV where he was interviewed.

Chubby again handled the advertising and marketing on behalf of CSA and the rebel tourists.

Jan 2, 1986
England cancels its cricket tour to Bangladesh at the last minute due to row over continued ties with South Africa.

Feb 18, 1986
South African authorities ban Television men from filming riot-torn Alexandra Township outside Johannesburg where eighty are dead and over three hundred injured.

On March 6 Ian opened his fifth dealership on the Natal North Coast in Stanger and named it Williams Ford North Coast. Using his tried and trusted methods, number five would service a large area of Northern Natal.

Apr 2, 1986
Bishop Desmond Tutu calls for international sanctions against South Africa in an attempt to end apartheid.

May 1, 1986
One and half million black mine workers go on strike in Johannesburg.

May 19, 1986
South African forces carry out raids on Zambia, Zimbabwe and Botswana terrorist bases.

May 22, 1986
Right-wing extremists wearing swastika style armbands and brown military-style uniforms break up a meeting being held by Foreign Minister Pik Botha. Twelve people injured.

May 25, 1986
Thirty thousand blacks are forcibly expelled from their homes at Crossroads squatter camp near Cape Town.

On June 1 Jimmy headed for Vienna in Austria for a one-month project to implement SDS. With Lynne's promotion and salary increase, the Wilson family could live comfortably without his Groupe Schreiber payments. He arranged that all future payments, including airfare refunds, be paid directly into his offshore account as a safeguard against future unrest in South Africa. He again missed his daughter's birthday.

Jun 12, 1986
In a nationwide sweep hundreds of black activists, church workers and trade union leaders are arrested under the continued state of emergency laws.

Jun 13, 1986
Bishop Desmond Tutu meets P.W. Botha for the first time in six years to protest at the ongoing state of emergency.

Jun 16, 1986
**Millions of blacks stay away from work on the tenth anniversary
of the Soweto uprising.**

Aug 18, 1986
**According to the South African Government eight thousand five
hundred and one people have been detained under the state of
emergency regulations.**

Aug 27, 1986
**Police shoot twelve dead and wound seventy after a night of rioting
in Soweto. The homes of black councillors are set alight and burnt.**

September 7 Jimmy headed for Madrid to implement SDS version in
Spain.

Sep 7, 1986
**Desmond Tutu is enthroned as Archbishop of Cape Town
becoming the first black head of the Southern African Anglicans.**

Sep 25, 1986
The South African Government tightens press restrictions.

Oct 2, 1986
**The United States Senate overrides President Ronald Reagan's
veto on sanctions against South Africa.**

Oct 22, 1986
**General Motors, IBM, Honeywell and Warner's, the four largest
American companies, abandon their operations in South Africa as
part of the United States sanctions against South Africa.**

Bowing to pressure from the US government, several large companies
disinvested in South Africa. General Motors sold their Port Elizabeth
plant to a local conglomeration and it was renamed Delta Motors who
continued to manufacture GM vehicles.

IBM, who didn't actually manufacture or assemble their product in
South Africa, went through the motions of disinvesting. The company

was 'sold off' to IBM staff in South Africa and they continued to sell and support IBM products.

The new company made the announcement that it would not sell IBM products to the police, military or agencies enforcing apartheid. The company was formed to protect IBM staff in South Africa.

Both the GM and IBM disinvestments were seen for what they were, window dressing to appease the United States Congress. Neither corporation saw any effect on their bottom line.

Nov 24, 1986
London, Barclays Bank announces it is disinvesting in South Africa, where it is the largest commercial bank.

Dec 30, 1986
Oil giant ESSO pulls out of South Africa.

Year-end sales figures for the Williams Ford group showed Ian to be the biggest mover of Ford motor vehicles in Southern Africa. Ian's accountants informed him that he now had a net worth of just fewer than one million rand.

CHAPTER 35
1987 - 1989

A second Australian Rebel Cricket tour took place. Public interest in these tours was on the wane. With SA Breweries as the main sponsor and TV advertising, the tour broke even financially. That would be the last of the Rebel tours.

On the political front nothing changed. Violence continued to rise and was dealt with by brute force from the police and army troops. South African troops were still stationed on the northern borders of South West Africa to combat SWAPO insurgents. The borders with Zimbabwe and Mozambique also became a favoured route for ANC terrorists.

Jimmy had only two SDS installations to do in 1987, Turin in Italy during March and April. Lisbon in Portugal during May.

With twenty Schreiber subsidiaries installed around the world, Sebastian made the decision that 1987 and part of 1988 would be used to consolidate. Jimmy would be based in Johannesburg with Ryan Herman as his assistant. All new requests would be validated by Sebastian's team in France before being forwarded to Jimmy for programming.

Jimmy would consolidate all base SDS programs, those that were the same in all subsidiaries. Programs specific to each subsidiary would be held in libraries unique to that subsidiary. Ryan would take ownership of cataloguing each unique library. New or changed programs specific to a subsidiary would be bundled and shipped to the country they referred to. No change would be allowed to any base program.

Jan 2,1987
All future editions of Enid Blyton's Noddy will be shorn of the traditional black gollywog in an attempt to excise any taint of racism.

Jan 3, 1987
South African envoy to London, Dennis Worrall, quits to stand against the Government in a whites-only general election.

Apr 12, 1987
**Archbishop Desmond Tutu says he will breach the emergency laws
by praying for the release of all detainees.**

May 6, 1987
**South Africa's ruling Nationalist Party begins its fortieth year in
power by gaining one hundred and twenty-three of the one
hundred and sixty-six seats in the House of Assembly. The hard
line "no-concessions-to-blacks" Conservative party wins twenty-
two seats to become the official opposition.**

Nov 25, 1987
**Sixteen missionaries are massacred by black guerrillas near
Bulawayo in Zimbabwe.**

On June 21 1988 IBM announced the launch of the latest addition to its catalogue of computers; the next in the S34, S36 and S38 range. In a break from tradition they named it the AS400 as in Application System 400. With the S38's running out of steam, it was a welcome announcement.

Groupe Schreiber made the strategic decision to replace the S38 with the more powerful AS400. Schreiber were assured that the S38 programs will run successfully on the new AS400 but performance would be greatly enhanced if the programs were converted to native AS400.

Sebastian tasked Jimmy to convert the S38 programs into native AS400. He outlined the plan. Schreiber would begin ordering AS400 for those larger subsidiaries who were experiencing processing bottle necks, for example, Germany, Singapore and England. The first AS400 would be assigned to Johannesburg where the programs would be converted or rewritten to fully utilise the AS400 functions.

The converted programs would run in parallel with those running on the S38 version. The plan was go-live in South Africa by the end of the first quarter of 1989.

At Schreiber's expense, Jimmy took a three-week course on the AS400 at IBM offices in Rochester, Minnesota. On his return to Johannesburg, he found that their AS400 had been delivered. He spent the next few weeks writing and testing a program that would read the S38 source code and convert it into AS400 code. After two and a half weeks he had the program ready and working.

He set up a process where Ryan could load the S38 program, run it against the conversion code and compile it into an AS400 version. Jimmy would check the output and run a test, compare results and either catalogue as correct or trace the difference and manually correct it. It was a bit of a mind-numbing process but it did ensure that the new version worked correctly and was also infinitely quicker than rewriting the program.

March 31, 1989 Jimmy ran the parallel March month end on the AS400 while Ryan did the same on the S38. The AS400 version completed the month-end task in twenty-three minutes and sixteen seconds. The S38 version took its normal two and a quarter hours. They spent the whole weekend checking both sets of results which they found matched exactly.

Sunday April 2 Jimmy called Sebastian with the news. They decided to use the AS400 for business for the month of April, after which, if it was successful, they would package the new version and send it to Singapore. The package would contain detailed instructions on how to load the system. With the conversion program a success, Jimmy instructed Ryan to start converting the South African and Singapore specific programs.

Sebastian supplied Jimmy with a plan of the sequence of launches for all current S38 subsidiaries. The schedule extended well into the 1990's.

In September 1989, Erickson and Whitmore announced that they have merged with Andrew Yates to become Erickson and Yates (E&Y). E&Y now became Groupe Schreiber's Auditors. Jimmy didn't have long to wait before he got an unexpected phone call from Barton.

Jimmy picked up the phone and answered, 'Wilson here, what can I do for you?'

'Barton here, I presume you are aware of the E&Y merger. I am calling on behalf of our Groupe Schreiber Audit Partner, who has suggested that MCS do an evaluation of your computer systems. When would that be convenient for you?'

'I wondered how long it would take for you to call. As far as I am concerned, no time is convenient for me, but as I am not a Schreiber employee, I suggest you call Rodger Hall. Cheers.'

Shortly thereafter, Rodger walked into the office, 'I have just had your buddy Barton on the phone wanting to do an evaluation of our computer system. What are your thoughts now that they are our Auditors?'

'I am sure they will be part of any annual audit but in the meantime, we could have some fun with them. I doubt that they have anyone who has even seen an AS400, let alone knows what to do with one, but it's your call.'

'I'll set something up for tomorrow. I will find out what he needs and let you know.'

On the dot 8am, Barton, accompanied by a consultant, Bodo Andersen, arrived at the Schreiber office. Both dressed in their dark blue three-piece suits and Andersen carrying the eight volume SLMT manuals. They were led up to Rodger's office where Barton outlined the evaluation process. A report would be produced detailing the system security rating and how the whole process measured up to the industry standard of SLMT.

Rodger called Jimmy and invited him into his office. Jimmy, knowing E&Y were coming in, dressed for the occasion, he was wearing a short sleeve red and blue checked shirt and a pair of khaki trousers and *takkies*.

'Jimmy, you know Tony Barton, this is the consultant who is going to do our evaluation. Bodo Andersen, this is Jimmy Wilson, our computer consultant, he is assigned to us from our head office in France.'

'How are you doing, Tony, nice to meet you Bodo. What say we get the show on the road? If you will follow me.'

Jimmy led the two of them down the passage and into his office next to the computer room.

'Have a seat gents and tell me just what it is you are going to evaluate.'

'Well, Wilson, as you know we are now the Schreiber Auditors and as such.'

'Let me stop you there, Mr. Barton, here we address people either by their first name or prefix their surname with a Mr. or Mrs. It's just a matter of respect. I am your client, not your employee.' He could see Barton seething.

'I apologise, what I was saying is as your Auditors, it would be remiss of us if we did not report on the status of your systems, which if at risk, could have grave consequences. Andersen here will do the evaluation and based on his findings, we will produce a report highlighting any deficiencies and what controls could be put in place. So, can we get started?'

'Sure, where would you like to start?'

'Security is a good starting point. I can see the computer from here. Who has access?

Waving his access card, 'You need one of these, there are only three in the company, Rodger has one, Ryan Herman, the computer supervisor has another and then this one of mine.' He watches Bodo making notes.

'Who has access to these terminals scattered around the building?'

'Anyone who has a user id and password. ID's are issued by the security officer, Ryan Herman, I am his backup. ID's allow the particular user access only to the area that their job needs.'

'Can we get a printout of the users and their passwords?'

'No, those details are kept on the computer and can only be viewed by me or Ryan. As an AS400 expert, you will be able to see them if you wish.'

Ignoring the comment, Andersen ploughed on, 'What I would like to do next is look at your system documentation and map it to the SLMT standards and highlight any gaps found.'

'Our systems documentation is kept on the computer in libraries. I assume you can navigate around AS400 libraries. I must point out though, it is not our objective to fit our processes into your SLMT ones. You may not be aware, but I have had exposure to SLMT when I worked at E&W where I found them to be of no use at all.'

Barton couldn't contain himself, 'Mr. Wilson, may I suggest that you open yourself up to the possibility that SLMT may be of help to Schreiber?'

'You know as well as I do that SLMT is of no use at all to a fully completed project. If used at all, it should be at project initiation time. I have printed out a lot of relevant documentation that I am sure Bodo can evaluate and report on. If that is acceptable to you, maybe you can start there.'

Barton nodded. Jimmy led the two of them to an empty office where he had left a box of computer printouts. If there was one thing any IBM computer did very well was produce copious reports that told you very little and referred to any number of IBM manuals. The box contained detailed program flowcharts that meant nothing if you didn't know the programming language. He also printed out a whole bunch of memory dumps which had no bearing on system documentation. Added to the pile were reports on system performance showing memory and processor usage by minute.

He left the two of them with the comment, 'I am right next door if you have any questions. If I am not around, Ryan Herman can help you. Have fun.'

Jimmy kept an eye on Barton and Andersen; he could see they had no clue. Andersen kept referring to the SLMT manuals looking for help. He knew Rodger was a stickler for time and would always leave by 5pm. He had arranged a lift into the office that day with Lynne in her 911. She said she would come up to his office at 4.30 and wait with him until Barton was ready to leave.

Lynne was well known at Schreiber and had visited the office several times; she was waved in and she made her way to her husband's office but not before greeting Rodger. As she entered his office, he looked next door and nearly burst out laughing. Andersen's eyes nearly fell out of his head and lip-reading, Jimmy made out the words 'he's married to the Pond's girl?'

Jimmy and Lynne walked out through reception just ahead of Barton and Andersen. Lynne had got the pole visitors parking spot, right in front of the main door and by arrangement she hopped into the passenger side and passed the keys to her husband. Jimmy cranked up the engine and with the top down, headed for the exit. Looking in the rear-view window he could see the astonished look on Barton's face. Making a right hand turn out of the gate, Jimmy headed in the opposite direction to where Barton would be going. Two hundred meters up the road Lynne made him pull over and exchange seats; he had his one and only drive of her 911.

With the future development of SDS on the AS400, Jimmy decided to purchase his own AS400 which he installed in his 'office' at the Wilson home in Fourways. He loaded up a series of Computer Learning Modules on the old S36 and donated it to Alexandra Township High School.

The eighties ended with Ian, Jimmy and Chubby all relatively wealthy and healthy. Gus was still stranded in Perth but remained adamant that he would not return to South Africa while Apartheid was in place.

On the morning of December 31 Lynne drove Jimmy and Sharon to her parent's home in Benoni. There they handed Sharon over to Val and Cyril, who would follow them down to Hillcrest for the New Year. Lynne drove her 911 and Jimmy had to just suck it up.

CHAPTER 36
The 90's – A Decade of Change and Turmoil

The enormous international pressure on South Africa and its Apartheid Policy was finally beginning to take its toll on the Afrikaner led National Party. The first step towards 'One man one vote' took place in 1990 on February 11 with Nelson Mandela's release from prison. The release of the African National Congress leader garnered worldwide coverage. A new beginning for South Africa.

January 1 Chubby's fortieth birthday was celebrated at his and Fiona's Durban North home. Those in attendance were Ian and Dee, Jimmy and Lynne, Gus still living in Perth Australia sent his best wishes but was unable to attend. Conversation turned to the events of the last couple of years.

'So, Mr. Murphy, what's it like to hit the good old four oh? It's all downhill for you from now on.'

'Don't you believe it, Wilson, you're next so keep the wise cracks to yourself. I got a telegram from Gus that was a bit cryptic. Apart from the birthday wishes he also stated, "See you guys soon". I'm not sure what that means, as he hasn't been back here since 1970-something.'

'I got a letter from him a couple of weeks back. I'm not sure this is for general consumption but he indicated his marriage was on the rocks. He reckons there will be big change in South Africa in the coming months and years and he wants to be part of it, but his wife hates anything to do with this country and won't move. So maybe we will see him sooner rather than later. I sure hope so, I miss the bugger.'

'Hey, Williams, you are quiet over there. What are you doing? Mentally counting all your money? So, how is business?' asked Chubby.

'Pretty good, I must say. Electronics business is flourishing, I picked up an excellent contract with Telkom. I love dealing with this government, you know exactly where you stand. Find the right contact and they tell you what they want when tendering, you pay up and get the business. I hope a black government, when it happens, plays the same way. I am thinking of selling off two of my garages, it's tough to find good managers, we'll see what happens.'

'What the fuck are you going to do with all your money?'

'Jimmy, my china, you can never have too much money. I don't see you or Chubby scratching for a few bucks. I reckon we see what happens with this ANC deal before we make any plans for the future. If they are anything like the normal Kaffirs in Africa, they will probably fuck this country up beyond belief.'

'Well, I know I'm getting tired of the constant overseas travel and Lynne is giving me beans about the amount of time I am away. I miss the two of them greatly and don't want to lose out on seeing Sharon growing up.'

'Jesus, mate, I don't know how she does it, but your missus looks better every time I see her, and your daughter is the spitting image of her mother. You are going to need a gun to ward off the boys when she starts dating. I think my Fiona still bears her a grudge for looking so good.'

'If you had seen Lynne's mother, Val, you would have seen where the looks came from. All three of them together are scary, it's uncanny. The times away are hard but the home comings are out of this world.'

'So, Chubby, what are your plans for the future now you've reached middle age? Jimmy is still squirrelling away his tax-free dollars offshore saving up for something, who knows?' asked Ian,

'I reckon with this whole "release Mandela" and the ANC, the next step is allowing us to play international sports again. There is going to be huge exposure of our sportsman to the rest of the world. I am glad you asked because I am busy setting up an agency to represent sports stars and maybe you guys would like to join me?'

'Sounds interesting, what do you think, Ian?' said Jimmy.

'Give us some details, Chubbs.'

'The basic plan is to sign up top sports stars to the Agency. We will represent them in a number of areas; contract negotiation, endorsements. image rights and personal appearances; in fact anything that will generate a fee for them and us. My lawyer is busy drawing up a business and legal plan, so let me know if you want to invest. No pressure entirely up to you, but I can tell you the possibilities are endless. The first big test is whether they will let us play in the next cricket world cup,' explained Chubby.

'I'm in, what about you, Ian?' said Jimmy.

'In, just have your lawyers send mine a copy of any agreements. What are you going to call the agency?' replied Ian.

'I am glad you guys like the idea. I would love to make the same offer to Gus. It would be great if the four of us could be in business together.'

'I have his address; send him the details as well, it might hasten his return. I reckon Murphy and Associates is a good name, after all everyone knows who you are,' said Jimmy.

The party adjourned and the guests headed home. Chubby contacted Gus and he agreed to invest. Ian sold off two of his five service stations, banking just over two million rand in the process. Ironically, it was the lowest academic achiever of the four who was the most successful businessman in the group.

It took just over six months to get Murphy and Associates up and running. A huge media event was planned for the launch, nearly all of the 'stars' signed up were present. Due to his connections, Chubby had secured the signatures of eleven of the current Natal rugby team, three ex-Natal and Springbok cricketers and two from Western Province.

Television presenters for Carte Blanche were signed up plus the 'White Zulu' Johnny Clegg. The media attention was huge, barely had the event finished screening than the calls started coming in. A team of 'sports agents' hungrily signed up clients left and right. The catch phrase for 'celebrities' and sports stars would become – 'let me give you my agent's number, we can set something up'. Unfortunately, like any good thing, competitors started to open up, but Murphy and Associates were the first and remained the gold standard.

On September 25 Jimmy received a call from his brother, David, informing him that his father had died of a heart attack. Jimmy hadn't seen much of his family over the years and not seen his father for the last six years. It saddened him that his parents had never returned to South Africa. His sister Maureen was married and lived in Rhode Island in the USA. Brother David settled in Milton Keynes in the UK, married with twin daughters. Jimmy booked tickets for himself, Lynne and Sharon and flew to England for the funeral.

The funeral took place in Millom, Iris' home town. Every aunt, uncle and cousin turned out, Maureen and her husband, Peter, flew in and David and family drove up from Milton Keynes. It was the first meeting between Lynne and any member of the Wilson's extended family. As an only child, she always longed to be a part of a large family, and even in a sad time she managed to integrate herself and her daughter into the hearts of her husband's family.

By midyear 1991, with the production of the first year's figures, it became obvious that Murphy and Associates was a huge success. Profits were enormous, to avoid as much income tax as possible it was decided to plough most of the money back into the company and open two more branches, one in Johannesburg and one in Cape Town. A strategic decision was made that each office should be fronted up by one or two well-known sports stars; image was everything.

Jimmy, still working with Groupe Schreiber, took on his latest assignment – Greece, based in Athens – the contract was for three weeks ending on July 19, he had a four-week break before going to Denmark. Usually he would return to Hillcrest before heading for Copenhagen, this time he decided to fly his wife and daughter to Greece for a two week holiday. He called Lynne and made the offer, 'Yes absolutely, but I'm not sure about Sharon. Your sister has invited her to Rhode Island for the rest of the summer, I don't want to disappoint Maureen and Sharon is so keen to go.'

'Ok with me. I'll have you all to myself. I will book you a flight to Mykonos and I'll meet you there.'

'Mykonos, hmm, that's the island with the topless beaches, right? I'm too old for that, maybe somewhere else?'

'It's only topless if you want to, you can wear a full cozzie and still look great.'

'Okay, send me the details, you are the best. I love you.'

Saturday 20 Jimmy took the short flight from Athens to Mykonos; Lynne would be arriving on a flight landing just two hours after his. Her flight landed on time, an anomaly for Greece; she alighted dressed in a bright red mini dress, bare-legged wearing a large white hat, she always knew how to make an entrance.

'God, are you a sight for sore eyes. Anyone chat you up on the flight?'

'Don't be silly. I am all aloof above the mere peasants you find on these flights, only one man for me. Kiss me and let's find our accommodation.'

'You'll love the place I booked, great location, fabulous view and I got them to paint the ceiling your favourite colour. You will be seeing a lot of it so I figured get it painted.'

'Who says you are going to be on top? I'm going to throw you down and have my way.'

The taxi drive into the town was about fifteen minutes, although the taxi driver tried his best to prolong the trip. By the time they reached the hotel, both were champing at the bit. They barely put down their bags before they were both naked, Jimmy never tired of looking at his naked wife. She was nearly forty four, looked twenty years younger and had the energy and vitality to go with it. By the time they were sated it was dark, neither had the energy or desire to leave the bed in search of food, so they immediately fell asleep.

Jimmy was woken by a slap on his bare bum, 'Come on, old man, the sun is well up in the sky and room service is on the way. Get yourself showered and ready for a day in the sun.'

'Go away. I think you killed me last night, I need more sleep.'

'If you don't get up, I will kill you. We are going to eat and then head for a beach called Paradise. We can take a taxi, bus or walk; I suggest the taxi, at least for the first day, until we get our bearings.'

Jimmy showered and pulled on a T-shirt and his swimming shorts. He returned to the sitting room to find Lynne dressed in a sarong, split to the waist showing off her legs, a sheer white peasant blouse showing her red bikini top underneath all topped off with her big white hat. Breakfast arrived, Greek yogurt, orange juice, croissants, jam and strong coffee and was hungrily consumed.

The taxi ride to Paradise Beach was short. It wasn't quite 10 am when they alighted; already hot, it was a beautiful clear sunny day. Beautiful clear blue sea and with almost white grainy beach sand. Paradise consisted of a building with five bedrooms for rent, a camp site for tents at a dollar a day and what looked for the entire world like large packing cases with two single beds for ten dollars a week. There was a shop selling beach stuff, soft drinks and light snacks. The outside restaurant served typical Greek meals and served wine, beer and ouzo.

The two them settled onto their newly acquired bamboo beach mats, rubbed each other up with sun tan cream, lay back and soaked up the sun. Not half an hour later Lynne asked Jimmy to get her a bottle of cold water from the shop. He joined the slow moving queue, purchased two bottles of water and made his way back to Lynne.

He got back to where he thought they were sitting, to find three completely naked 'Mediterranean' looking young men seated around a naked lady, who bore a striking resemblance to his wife, lying on her stomach. Doing a double-take he said, 'Lynnette, what's going on here, who are these yahoos?'

Without raising her head. 'The one on my right is Giuseppe, an Italian; he thinks he is in with me, the other two who understand English are local Greeks, all old enough to be my kids. Tell them to go away.'

'Okay boys, hit the road, this lady is my wife, bad luck.'

The three hopefuls got up and left. Lynne rolled over onto her back and sat up, Jimmy nearly had a heart attack. 'Oh my God, Lynne, you are bald, when did you shave your pubes? I would have noticed it last night.'

'I did it this morning while you were sleeping; I heard it is the new way to go. It feels fucking amazing; I have been as horny as hell since I did it. I think it's going to be unreal for oral sex, I can't wait! Do you like it?'

'I don't know, it looks strange at first and what's with all the clothes off? I thought you said you wouldn't even take your top off. I turn my back and you are *kaalgat* with half the male population surrounding you.'

'Well, I was quite happy to stay fully clothed until I looked around and saw so many naked people no better looking than me, so I went for it. The only problem is that I am so turned on I am soaking wet; I don't know if I will be able to keep my hands off you. Your turn, get that cozzie off and join me.'

Jimmy sat down on the mat and slipped off his cozzie, 'I think I'm going to have to spend a lot of time on my stomach. I get a boner looking at you fully dressed, naked on the beach I'm fucked.'

'James, my boy suck it up. You better rub some of that suntan stuff on your willie, I don't want it getting sunburnt as it will be no good to either of us like that.'

About fifty feet from the edge of the water, there was a reef which extended about twenty-five more feet out to sea. You could walk across the reef which was submerged one foot below the water. The other side of the reef the water was ten feet deep.

Eventually the heat got to both of them; it was time for a cooling off swim. Jimmy debated on whether to put his cozzie back on; Lynne made up his mind for him. She grabbed him by the hand and pulled him to his feet and the two of them walked hand in hand into the water. Jimmy immediately ducked under, keeping the water line above his waist, his semi-erect penis now submerged.

Lynne, knowing his discomfort, swam over to him flung her arms around his neck and kissed him passionately on the lips. She circled her legs around his waist pushing his penis downwards with her bum.

'Hey, this is not fair. It's easy to see when a bloke is excited but you women have no telltale sign. I am going to have to stay in the water until everyone goes home.'

'No, you won't, follow me,' said Lynne as she released Jimmy and headed for the reef. She swam onto the reef and stood up. The water came to just below her knees; she walked across and dove into the water on the other side. 'Come on, Jimmy boy, let me sort out your problem for you.'

Jimmy swam over to the reef pulled himself on to it but didn't stand. Instead he doggy paddled across to the other side and join his wife.

'I know I can be a bit of a slut at times but I always wanted to fuck in public with a chance of being watched. Bring that cock of yours over here and put it in me.'

To anybody paying attention to them for the next ten minutes, it was very obvious what it was that they were doing. With Lynne doing most of the sexual work and Jimmy trying to keep them afloat, there was quite a lot of movement. Jimmy had an orgasm, Lynne did not but the purpose of the exercise was successful. 'Maybe now you will be able to lie on your back safely. Let's go back and get some rays, I want to go home with an all over tan.'

For the next twelve days they spent days on the beach, nights eating, drinking and making love; not a care in the world, totally into each other. They rented scooters and explored the island. They stopped off at 'Super Paradise', the fully naked gay beach just over hill from Paradise Beach. As a beautiful couple they were eyed out by both men and women of the same sex. Eventually it was time to go home. They flew to Athens and caught an SAA flight to Durban via Johannesburg.

Sharon had arranged to spend the rest of the year in the USA with Maureen. She would complete her school year at Providence High School. Needless to say, she was a popular attraction; beautiful with an exotic accent.

Two weeks later Jimmy flew to Denmark, accompanied by Lynne. As Sharon was still in the USA, Lynne felt she could join her husband and when he was working, she could explore on her own. A busy three weeks work-wise and Jimmy was next scheduled to travel to Hong Kong after a one week break back in Durban.

As a gesture of goodwill towards South Africa, the Indian Cricket Council invited the team to India for a three series of One Day Internationals (ODI). The matches would be a fifty over contest. South Africa's first cricket tour since the ban over Apartheid. It would also be the first time an official South African team of any sort would tour India.

The tour was an amazing success. India won the series 2-1 which was watched live by tens of thousands of spectators and a television audience of millions. The tour generated millions of dollars, of which very little were passed on to the South African players. This was highlighted by Kepler Wessels, who had recently returned from Australia where he had played international cricket for that country. The South African cricketers were paid a small match fee, a bonus fee for a win and a daily stipend, typical of the good old 'amateur days'. This did not sit well with Wessels and the press got wind of the discord and it was widely reported.

Chubby, never one to miss an opportunity, approached the SA captain, Clive Rice, and his deputy Wessels, and after much negotiation signed both up to his agency. The plan was to have Rice and Wessels pass the deal onto the rest of the team that toured. All players except 32 year old Tim Shaw signed up. The Cricket South Africa (CSA) was approached and a proposal was presented to the effect that in future, players should be 'contracted' to CSA on a year to year basis. The players would then be paid a fixed salary based on their perceived value to the team.

Three categories would be set up at international level. Category A would be for established players or those deemed vital to the success of CSA. Category B would be for players who were likely to be part of current team setup. Category C would be for up and coming players. The purpose of the contracts was to ensure the availability of those players whenever needed by CSA. It also meant that any off season activity had to be met with the approval of CSA. The amount paid in each category would need to be sufficient to negate the need of players to find additional sources of cricket playing income.

By brokering the deal, Murphy and Associates garnered the market on cricket representation. It proved so successful that the same process was presented to the provincial cricket unions.

With the loosening of sporting sanctions, South Africa in general now had a universe of international sport to follow live or on TV. Chubby's next strategic move was to sign up as many black soccer players as he could lay his hands on. His first signing was Jomo Maponyane, a legendary soccer player in his day and now owner of the popular Jomo Cosmos.

Within weeks, everywhere you looked there was Jomo's face advertising something or the other. This was the catalyst for an endless stream of black athletes signing up with the Agency. It was a license to print money.

The 1992 Cricket World Cup was held in Australia and New Zealand with South Africa attending for the first time. Former captain, Clive Rice, was controversially left out of the squad; there was some suggestion it was because of his affiliation with Murphy and Associates, strongly denied by CSA. Chubby, with so many clients playing in the tournament, decided to attend the entire month long tournament. He secured tickets for all South Africa's pool games and the options for further rounds if they progressed. He offered these to various company staff, potential clients and his three co-owners.

Jimmy, as an ardent cricket fan, took up the offer for him and Lynne to attend four pool matches and the semi-final and final if South Africa made it through. The first match against Pakistan on March 8 and final due on March 25. Lynne was not a big fan but loved travelling, so she accompanied him. Ian, not a great fan either, decided he would watch the last pool match against India and any subsequent matches if the team qualified. Gus planned to see the first game against Australia in Sydney and then join up with Jimmy and Lynne.

February 26 South Africa versus the hosts, Australia, played to a full house at the Sydney Cricket Ground. Chubby met up with Gus for the first time in over fifteen years in the VIP section. Chubby, up to his neck in wheeler dealing, could only stop for a short chat, with a promise to hook up later. South Africa stunned Australia thrashing them by nine wickets. Gus failed to connect with Chubby and flew back to Perth more than a little pissed off.

March 7 Jimmy and Lynne checked into their hotel in Brisbane to find a note from Gus leaving his room number. Immediately on reaching their room, Jimmy called Gus, 'Gus, my old mate! I am so glad you made it. We have just arrived but I'm ready for a drink, your place or mine?'

'Hey man, great to hear from you, I heard you were bringing the lovely Lynne with you. Why don't the two of you come up to my room and let's spend some of that money Chubbs has been making for us?'

Jimmy and Lynne caught the lift up the three floors to Gus' room and knocked on the door. Lynne elbowed her way past her husband and threw her arms around Gus, 'Doctor Angus, I am so pleased to see you again, you look a bit run down. We will fix that, James, let's sort out his minibar.'

Jimmy and Gus shook hands then hugged each other. Their joy at seeing each other was interrupted by Lynne shrieking, 'Cathy, what the hell are you doing here? I haven't seen or heard from you in years!'

'Gus invited me over for the cricket, we've kept in touch all these years. I am so excited to see you two. God, you make a great couple.'

'Cathy, you look amazing, hardly changed since we last saw you.'

'You are very kind, Lynne. I am now fifty years old and feeling it. Gus tells me that for the next couple of weeks we are going to live like kings and forget the troubles of the world. He really is a good man.'

With everyone supplied with drinks, Gus and Cathy brought Jimmy and Lynne up to date. Cathy's second husband, Richard, had died two years ago, a victim of an armed robbery while drawing cash at an ATM in Johannesburg. Jimmy recalled the incident but at the time had not associated it with Cathy. They had been married nearly eighteen years but had no children.

Gus told them his marriage was all but over, he and his wife Stacey had been living apart since the middle of last year. Before marrying, Gus had signed an ante nuptial agreement which protected his medical practice. Divorce proceedings had started but the sticking point has been child custody. His two children, Ross and Margaret, were still at school and Stacey wanted sole custody. Gus was trying to gain reasonable access and the possibility of them, when ready, going to a university of his choice. Stacey was fighting the request but might relent if sufficient financial compensation was made available to her. He was also currently going through the process of selling his practice with a view to returning to South Africa and being part of the new generation.

Jimmy pulled Gus to one side, 'Sorry to hear of your marriage problems but just a word of caution, if you do come back to SA, leave as much money as is legal in Oz. The ANC will win the election and we have no idea how they will approach governing the country. They are making promises of housing and jobs for everyone and anyone with a grain of intelligence knows that is not possible. Also, hang on to your Aussie citizenship.'

'Jimmy, you are overreacting on the ANC plans. Mandela will be president and he advocates one nation for all its people. I think eventually SA will become a normal country and race no longer the defining criteria. Be positive, man I am.'

While this chat was going on, Lynne and Cathy were also in deep conversation, 'You and Jimmy seem right for each other, how do you do it?'

'It's easy. I love him unconditionally and he does exactly what I tell him. Any problems, I just take off all my clothes, end of argument. Just joking; we are perfect for each other. What is going on with you, if I may ask?'

'Gus and I have kept in touch over the years. He was happy for me when I married Richard as was I when he married Stacey. When Richard died, Gus wanted to attend the funeral, Stacey threw a fit, so he didn't make it. I think that was the start of it for him. He contacted me two weeks go with the offer of a trip to watch the cricket. He told me you were all coming so how could I refuse? So here I am, just so happy to see you all.'

'Please tell me you are sleeping with him. You two were so good together and I know he never stopped loving you.' With Cathy blushing, no answer was needed.

For the next week the foursome buzzed around Australia taking in four matches in places as far afield as Brisbane, Canberra, Melbourne and Adelaide. In that time, there were only fleeting sightings of Chubby, he was like a man possessed, looking after the interests of his clients, making contacts, signing up cricketers, going international. Ian joined the group in Adelaide where SA managed to qualify for the semi-final to be played in Sydney against England.

The semi-final was a travesty. South Africa held England to 236 for 4 in their fifty overs. South Africa were well on their way at 226 for 7 with nearly 10 overs left when the rain came down. With the rain delay and the inefficient way that the game was eventually resumed, the ridiculous target of 26 runs required with one ball to go was set. Brian McMillan blocked the ball and walked off, England advancing to the final. This ridiculous ruling would eventually lead to a change of the rules when a match was delayed by rain. Too late for the South African team who had to head on home.

Ian flew directly back to SA with a refuelling stop in Mauritius. Jimmy offered for Cathy to accompany him and Lynne back to SA with a two-day stopover in Hong Kong, she agreed and the three of them flew first class on Cathay Pacific. They spent two days in the five-star Hong Kong Sheraton. The girls went shopping while Jimmy contacted Groupe Schreiber to discuss his next assignment.

He was informed that his presence was needed in Dublin, Ireland for four weeks, starting April 13. From there he was needed in Amsterdam, Holland for two weeks starting immediately after Dublin. After Amsterdam it was four weeks in Bangkok, Thailand. That would mean three countries in ten weeks away from home without a break. He said he needed to confirm with his wife and would get back to them when he arrived back in SA.

When the girls returned that evening, Jimmy told Lynne about his next proposed assignments.

'Oh man, ten weeks. I don't like that at all. Do we still need to do this? We have plenty of money coming in.'

'I can't just drop them; they have been very good to me and paid me a lot of money over the years. I tell you what, why don't you quit your job and come with me? We can have a ball and be paid to do it. If you won't quit your job, then take two or three months off. When this one is done, I will speak to Sebastian and let him know.'

'Okay, I will take leave and come with you. Then you can make up your mind on your future.'

Jimmy and Lynne arrived in Dublin the Sunday before he was due to start work. They hired a car on company expense and checked into their hotel. The hotel – once a country estate – was now converted into a ten-room hotel. The rooms were exquisite with four-poster bed and a fireplace in each room. While Jimmy worked, Lynne explored Dublin and the surrounding areas. Both fell in love with the country and its friendly citizens. They vowed to return one day for a vacation.

Amsterdam was an eye-opener for Lynne. Jimmy had made a few trips previously and was used to the sights and sounds. On the second night he took her on tour of the red light district where the ladies in the windows plied their trade. Lynne was fascinated, especially when one very attractive lady attempted to entice Jimmy into her room.

The lady, seeing Jimmy holding on to his wife's hand, opened her door and looking at both of them said, 'Come on in, I'll do both of you.' Jimmy nearly crapped himself, Lynne on the other hand looked across at Jimmy and said, 'What about it? It might be a bit of fun.'

'No chance, are you crazy?'

'Just testing you but if you said yes I would have gone for it,' laughed Lynne.

They arrived in Thailand for the final leg. Again Lynne spent the days sightseeing and shopping. The second weekend they flew down to Phuket and spent the weekend at the beach. Finally, it was home to Hillcrest. A few days later he called Sebastian.

'Jimmy, good to hear from you. Thanks again, all three subsidiaries are pleased with your software implementation, great job. How did your wife enjoy the trip?'

'She loved it. Why I'm calling is that I want to cut back on the travel; it is affecting my family to some extent. Maybe we can come to some arrangement where I do very few installations and only short time ones.'

'As you know, Hong Kong is reverting back to China in 1997 and this will open up Mainland China to us. This is an enormous market, very strategic and I was hoping to rely on you to help us there. It's an eighteen-month project starting early next year, and we would plan to relocate you, and your family if you so wish, to Beijing for the duration. We will pay top dollar for your software and services. Can I rely on you?'

'I will have to discuss this with my wife. Can I get back to you in a couple of days?'

'Sure, you can. We really need you on this assignment so let me know as soon as possible.'

Lynne was adamant that she wanted no part of eighteen months in Beijing, and there was no way she could live for that length of time without her husband.

'Jimmy, we have enough money. I am done with all of the travelling, please tell Sebastian no.'

'Okay, I will tell him that I have an alternate proposal that if he accepts, we all win. I can't just dump them.'

Jimmy called Sebastian the next day, 'Sebastian, I cannot commit to eighteen months in Beijing, but I would like to propose two options that may suit both of us. As you know, I have my own IBM AS400 and I own the source code for the subsidiary applications. I believe I can tailor the programs from here given the subsidiary's detailed specifications. I can test the new programs and package them for installation with detailed operating instructions. For existing subsidiaries that require changes, I can support them from SA. With the new high-speed data lines, I can log directly onto their computers and do trouble shooting. With email I can keep in contact with all of the installations. With video conferencing the same applies, it will be like I am on-site. I will consider on-site meetings and training but only for periods of no longer than ten days. A lot of this is at Lynne's request and I agree with her. Any comments?'

'I think this would work in many cases but I am not sure it will for Beijing. What is option two?'

'Option two is that I sell Schreiber the source code and you take care of all new and existing installations. I will go through a detailed handover, as well as providing copious documentation. Any programmer training will also be provided. Obviously, any source code change would negate me being able to support it. Based on the China project, this may be your best solution. What do you think?'

'I believe option one will work for us in all situations bar China. I will speak with my bosses and propose that we setup our own team for Beijing and purchase and take control of the source code and isolate it just for China. That will allow your existing code to continue under your control until such time as you no longer can or want to continue. At that time, that source code will be signed over to us at no further cost outlay. If okay with you, I will get this approved and have a new contract sent to you for signature. Do you have a figure in mind for source code?'

'Sebastian, you know the value, we have it running in thirty-two subsidiaries, make me an offer.'

'Okay, I will get back to you. Thanks Jimmy, I want to keep this relationship intact. Say hello to that lovely wife of yours.'

'I will and my regards to Barbara.'

Three days later Jimmy received an email from Sebastian with a detailed contract attached and the instruction 'please sign and return at your earliest convenience.' To summarise and ignore the legalese, the main details were as follows: A $6,000 per month retainer for forty hours miscellaneous support would be paid, any hours over forty would be compensated at $150 per hour when documentation was provided. Any new subsidiary would be a fixed payment based on the size and effort; historic data would be used to calculate the effort and subsequent fee. A one-time payment of US$ 2,000,000 for the sole ownership of all source code would be paid once a restraint of trade agreement was signed. The agreement could be terminated by either party with a one months' notice period.

Jimmy responded that the terms were acceptable, he would have his lawyer examine the contract wording and, on his approval, Jimmy would sign the necessary documents. The following week Jimmy forwarded the signed documents to Sebastian with an attached payment plan. The monthly retainer would be paid into his Standard Bank account, the one-time payment and any fixed fee payments would be paid directly into his Cayman Island bank account.

Everything signed, sealed and payments made, Jimmy approached Lynne, 'I have heard back from Sebastian and I have some good news and some bad news.'

'Let's have the good news first.'

'We will not be going to Beijing.'

'Great but what's the bad news?'

'I will still continue working for Schreiber.'

'Oh no. You couldn't get out of it?'

'I could but they made me a good offer.'

Jimmy explained the details of the offer for support and ongoing projects.

'Great, that means you can still make money but work from home. My husband, you are a genius.'

'Oh sorry, I forgot to mention they bought all my software, I no longer own it.'

'They paid you for it? How much?'

'Two million.'

'Two million Rand, fantastic! Maybe you can buy me a new car now.'

'No, two million dollars US and yes you can have a new car, the new VW Beetle is quite nice.'

'The Beetle is just fine, but I suppose that means you never want sex with me again?'

The early evening of December 1, 1993, the telephone rang at the Wilson home in Hillcrest.

'Get that Jimmy, it may be Sharon. I am expecting her to call, I will be there in a minute.'

'Hey there, Sharon, how are you doing?'

'Sharon?'

'Gus, you old bastard! How the hell are you? It must be the middle of the night in Perth, what's going on?'

'I'm calling from the Edward Hotel. I arrived earlier this morning a bit jet-lagged so I booked in for a kip. I'm feeling a whole lot stronger now.'

'How long are you here for? Check out of there and come and stay with us. Give me the word and we will come and pick you up.'

'I thought you might say that. I have a rental car so I will see you in a couple of hours.' Gus put down the phone, picked up his already packed suitcases and headed for the car.

'Who was that?'

'Gus, he is on his way. I told him to come and stay here rather than in a hotel.'

Just over an hour later, Gus pulled into the drive. Lynne, pushing her husband aside, made a beeline for him, virtually jumping into his arms, 'Gus, my darling, it is so good to see you again. You look a whole lot better than the last time I saw you. Does Cathy know you are here?'

'Good to see you too Lynne, gorgeous as ever. No, Cathy doesn't know I am here yet, she thinks I am arriving on Saturday. I just wanted to get my head sorted out before I see her.'

'Come in. Jimmy dear, get his other bags, I'll get the drinks in. I cannot wait to hear what has been happening in your life, Gus.'

Bags delivered to the guest room, Jimmy headed off to the patio where Gus and Lynne were waiting. 'I see we all have drinks so Gus, tell us what is happening and why are you here?' said Jimmy

'Well, it's a long story. As you both know I have alluded to having some marital problems, well they finally reached a breaking point just after I got back from the Cricket World Cup. We had been at loggerheads for many months before that, but when I returned, she accused me of having an affair. If she meant Cathy, she was right, and I admitted to it. She went nuts and for whatever reason, told me she had been seeing someone on the side for the last couple of years. I had suspected as much but didn't really care as our sex life had been virtually over since Margaret was born.'

'Can I get everyone a refill?' asked Lynne. Getting a positive response, she headed for the kitchen. 'Don't continue until I get back.' She returned minutes later and passed out the drinks.

'Cheers Lynne. I told her I thought we should split up and get a divorce. Her first reaction was; 'I hope you don't think this will come cheap'. She has always been very materialistic so I was expecting it. I told her that we had an ante nuptial contract but I was prepared to compromise, especially in regard to her agreeing to reasonable child custody and visitation rights. Based on previous arguments, she wanted full custody giving me very limited visitation rights. What she came up with next stunned me. She would give me full custody of both children if I agreed to her financial demands. She wanted a tax-free cash settlement of five hundred thousand Australian Dollars, the transfer of the house into her name, mortgage-free, a new BMW X5 and fifteen thousand dollars a month for two years to allow her to get back on her feet. Added to this, if I sold my medical practice within the next five years, she would receive twenty five percent of the sale value.'

'Fuck me, she really wants to take you to the cleaners. I hope you told her to take a hike,' said Jimmy.

'No mate, I agreed to everything and the divorce went through two weeks ago. I am returning to SA to be part of this whole new beginning, I reckon there's now real hope for this country.'

'Well, we need to see about the new hope. The ANC will win by sheer volume or intimidation. But what about your Medical Practice?'

'Oh, that's taken care of. I reached an agreement with the Western Australia Government. I transferred ownership to them in exchange for a grant that will pay for me opening clinics in this country in underprivileged areas. They will pay all the costs for building, materials and training. So Stacey gets twenty five percent of bugger all, at least the last time I fucked her it felt good for a change.'

'You sneaky bastard, good for you! If Jimmy messes me around, your settlement will look like chump change. I can't wait until Saturday, please call Cathy now and tell her to come over. Jimmy, call Chubby and Ian and give them the good news. We need to throw the biggest party Hillcrest has ever seen,' said Lynne.

'I called Cathy she is on her way over; she sounded a little annoyed that I didn't call her before coming over to you.'

'Ian, Chubby and wives are on for Saturday. Double celebration. Gus coming home and your 46th birthday. Time for a real skop.'

Durban North to Hillcrest was under most situations a forty-five-minute drive, Cathy made it in just over half an hour. On hearing her car turn into the drive, Lynne and Jimmy left the porch and headed inside to give them a bit of initial privacy. Five minutes later, a beaming Gus and tearful Cathy came into the lounge holding hands like a couple of teenagers.

'Cathy, so glad to see you. Looks like Gus is back for good so stop bawling and come and have a drink. Jimmy, get Cathy a G&T, she could do with one.'

'Thanks Lynne, I didn't know whether to kiss him or kill him, but I am so glad he is here. Ross and Margaret will be arriving as soon as the school year is over, I am looking forward to meeting them. I hope they will like me.'

'How can they not like you? You will be fine. So, what are your immediate plans, Gus?'

'Cathy is quitting her job at the bank, she is going to help me setting up the clinics. Our first stop is Ixopo. I hope to see my mother for the first time in over twenty years. I would like to open a clinic there in memory of my Father. I am still a bit out of sorts due to the travel so I'd like to hit the sack.'

'Okay, I understand,' said Lynne, 'We'll entertain Cathy for a while. I'm sure it's too early for her.'

'Oh no, I am also a bit tired.'

'Just joking my friend; be gentle with him. See you in the morning.'

Early the next morning after a hearty breakfast, and much teasing, Gus and Cathy headed for Ixopo. The drive was through rural Natal, much of it in a poor state of repairs. Gus reckoned the ANC, based on their election campaign promises, were going to have a big job on their hands in restoring this area of Natal. Arriving in Ixopo, they drove directly to the hospital and walked up to reception.

'How may I help you?' inquired the nurse on duty.

'I would like to see my mother, Matron Stewart, if possible.'

'Matron Stewart is your mother? She has never mentioned any family except her husband who died many years ago. Hold on a minute, I will speak with my supervisor.'

The nurse waddled away down the corridor and turned into an office marked 'Matron'. A few moments later another rather large lady came out of the office and walked over to them.

'I am sorry, who are you? I am the Matron here.'

'I am Angus Stewart, Doctor Stewart that is. I am Edith Stewart's son and if she is around, I would like to see her please.'

'I am very sorry, please come with me. Edith has a room at the back of the hospital. She is suffering from Alzheimer's and has good days and bad days. She may or may not recognise you. We have looked after her for the last few years in recognition of her wonderful service to this hospital. Here is her room; please go in.'

Gus and Cathy opened the door and entered the small room. Sitting in a chair in the corner was an old woman who Gus did not recognise. On hearing the noise, the old woman looked up and her face broke into a huge smile.

'Hamish, is that you? Where have you been? I knew you would come back. Come over here and sit next to me my darling husband and tell me about your day.'

'Mom, it's me, Angus, your son.'

'Oh Hamish, don't make silly jokes, Angus is still at school, he won't be back for hours, come and sit down. Who is that strange woman with you?'

'Mom, it's Cathy, my wife. I am a doctor now, just like Father was.'

Edith started screaming hysterically, 'No Hamish, I am your wife! Send that whore away. I will not have her near us.'

Edith's screams alerted the hospital staff and Matron appeared and tried unsuccessfully to calm Edith. 'Please go and wait in my office. I will give her something to calm her down.'

Gus and Cathy left the room and headed for the Matron's office. The screaming abated and Matron reappeared.

'I am sorry. she has mainly bad days but other than the Alzheimer's she's as healthy as a horse. I am Matron Burns. by the way,' she said, extending her hand. Gus introduced Cathy and himself.

'It's funny she has never mentioned you, but I can see why she reacted the way she did. You are the spitting image of your father and a Doctor to boot.'

Gus asked if he could see the hospital administrator and maybe arrange a meeting with him and some of the senior medical staff as he had a proposal to present. Matron Burns picked up her phone and called the hospital director and relayed Gus' request. On ending the call, she said, 'The Director, Mr. Allan Thompson, will see you immediately. I will escort you to his office.'

Gus and Cathy followed her down the corridor, she knocked on a door marked 'Director' and entered. The man sitting behind the desk was maybe a few years older than Gus and so could not possibly the Mr. Allan Thompson who had looked after his well-being as a child.

'Doctor Stewart, pleased to meet you. My father has spoken of you in the past, he was the previous Hospital Administrator; unfortunately, he passed away several years back. I am very sorry about your Mother's condition, there is not much we can do other than make her comfortable. What can I do for you?'

After introducing Cathy, Gus sat down and laid out his plan to Thompson. He wanted to open a clinic that would predominately treat those unfortunates unable to afford normal medical expenses. The clinic would be a non-profit organisation and be funded by an organisation who wished to remain anonymous. The clinic would be manned by experienced nursing staff and have a doctor available. It was envisioned that any serious medical need would still be serviced by the existing hospital. With the likelihood of an ANC victory in the election, there would be a greater say in the treatment of blacks and many hospitals would not be able to cope so the clinics would help. The first clinic of this type would be here in Ixopo and be the model for all future clinics which would be mainly in rural areas. Strict business auditing would be done by the sponsor's auditors. As he completed his presentation, he asked if Thompson had any questions.

'I have many but I am sure you have a detailed plan and timeline for my perusal. Any involvement in my part should be well documented. What will the clinic be called?'

'I haven't really given it a thought. Any suggestions?'

'What about the "Hamish and Edith Stewart Clinic"? Both of your parents made significant contributions to medicine in this area.'

'Sounds like a good name. Thank you for your time. I will be in touch soon.'

Gus' two children arrived in Durban on Saturday 18. They were met by Gus with Cathy staying at home in Durban North. On the trip from the airport, Gus brought his children up to date on his situation. They did the same telling Gus that their mother had shown no emotion when dropping them off at Perth Airport; if anything, she seemed glad to be rid of them. He told them that he had registered both of them at Northlands High School which was coed. He told them all about Cathy whom he intended to marry.

Arriving at the house in Durban North they were met by a nervous Cathy. She needn't have worried, both kids took to her immediately. They were shown to their rooms and had the chance to clean up before a light lunch. A quick swim after the meal and they both hit the wall totally jet-lagged. With the two kids taking a nap, Gus and Cathy decided to do the same.

Gus, with his mind firmly set on the clinic project, threw himself into it, ably assisted by Cathy. With the land approved by local town council,

Gus planned to have the clinic up and running before the April elections. Unfortunately, the local ANC member who would be running for election in the area got word of the project. He approached Gus for details and the offer to help expedite. Gus naively agreed and provided the details.

Less than a week later, billboards started appearing in most of the Natal province. Pictures of the proposed Ixopo clinic with smiling black faces of doctors, nurses and patients were everywhere. The slogan 'See, we deliver what we promise, free medical for all. Vote ANC and secure your future.'

Gus, initially pissed off by the blatant lies, realised that any publicity that would help establish more clinics was okay with him.

April 26 to 29, 1994 the first fully democratic elections were held in South Africa. As expected, the African National Congress (ANC) won the majority vote. Nearly twenty-two million votes were counted with the ANC accumulating sixty-two percent of the vote. An historic time in the history of South Africa. The result was hailed around the world, the demise of Apartheid had finally been accomplished through the ballot box. With Nelson Mandela elected as President, the 'Rainbow Nation', led by its first ever black President, was born. Peace and prosperity for all was forecast by the ANC.

Gus voted for the ANC, Ian for the Nationalist Party while Jimmy and Chubby did not bother to vote.

1994 was to be a year of political adjustment in South Africa. The ANC's election promise was affordable housing and jobs for all. A small government subsidised stand-alone two bedroomed unit with living room, bathroom and kitchen. Solar and electrical power provided to a manufactured home. The first units were badly constructed and in many cases simply fell apart. The availability of the new units was being allocated by a council motivated by bribery. Unrest was gathering.

Many rural blacks, anticipating the other ANC promise of jobs for all, had moved into the cities where accommodation was impossible to find. Squatter camps began to spring up near the major towns and cities. New jobs were not being created as many companies were waiting to see what the political situation would be like in the new South Africa.

Unable to find work to feed their families, many blacks took to crime. Robberies, home invasions – and the new national sport of car hijackings – escalated. ANC members, especially the 'comrades' who took part in the struggle against Apartheid, were given highly-paid government jobs, for which they were sorely unqualified. Infrastructures like mail, garbage collections, electricity supply and general road works began to fall apart.

Gus still believed that having an ANC government elected by free and fair elections would prevail. These were teething problems and would soon be solved for the general good of all of South Africa's people. Positive signs from the International Community were evident with the 1995 Rugby World Cup Competition being awarded to the country; a predominately white sport was adopted by President Mandala as a unifying event for black and white.

By the end of 1994 Gus had three rural clinics up and running. All were operating within the parameters set up under the anonymous auspices of the Western Australian Government.

1995 began with the announcement that a 'Truth and Reconciliation Commission' was to be setup to address the ANC's call for 'truth' about the apartheid years. This – combined with the ruling National Party's demand for amnesty for many of the perpetrators of apartheid – would create the hybrid "truth and reconciliation" commission led by Arch Bishop Desmond Tutu. The Commission hoped it would heal the wounds of the past, give dignity to victims, and permit the emergence of a post-apartheid "rainbow nation" led by Nelson Mandala. To further heal the wounds, the commission recommended that there be a "wealth tax," which would punish those who gained from Apartheid.

Ian. sensing that a number of business may come under threat. decided to cash in on his various enterprises. The CEO of Africa's largest electronics company, CONTEC, Dr. Bill Varner. had made numerous offers to buy out Ian's electronics company and thus corner the market in Programmable Logic Controller (PLC), power grid management systems and data modulators. Ian had rejected all offers in the past. Through a third party, Varner was given an indication that Ian may be willing to negotiate a sale.

Varner had his lawyers contact Ian with a one-time non-negotiable offer. Ian, having heard of Varner's aggressive negotiating skills, was expecting something along those lines. The cash offer was to purchase the company lock, stock and barrel for five-hundred million rand and a ten-year restriction of trade.

Ian's book valuation was for six hundred and fifty million rand but realised in an uncertain market this was not likely to be achieved. He decided to counter anyway; he accepted the cash offer but as there would be a restriction of trade, he wanted one hundred thousand shares in CONTEC, with a share option of a further four hundred thousand shares at the ruling selling price on the day that the contracts were signed. He would also agree to a time limit of two years to sell or purchase the share options.

Surprisingly, Varner agreed, and the sale was concluded; it would come into effect on January 1, 1995.

The final step was to divest himself of his three remaining garages. His son Douglas was due to finish his B Com degree in the next couple of weeks. As an early twenty first birthday present, Ian decided to sign over the three remaining garages to his son. Now unencumbered by any business issues and a bucket load of money, Ian and Dee could take some time to enjoy the fruits of his labours.

January 1, 1995 Chubby celebrated his 45th birthday with the news that his agency had won the local marketing rights for the Rugby World Cup. Now a very wealthy man, he continued to make money for himself and his three silent partners. With offices in all major centres of South Africa and London, New York and Sydney, he was attracting the unwanted attention of the ANC.

With the ANC making a lot of noises about 'affirmative action positions', pressure was being put on high profile companies to employ blacks in senior management positions. Murphy and Associates was on the ANC list of targets. Chubby called a meeting of his partners. Gus, unable to attend, said he would go with the majority decision.

Consensus was that they would have to appoint at least one, maybe two, blacks to the board of directors. One active voting member and a non-executive member with no voting rights would be appointed. He or she would have to be well connected politically; they would be given an impressive title, a big salary and a large company car. Their names would be added to the letter heads and any company literature. Provided the rest of the board voted as a group, the new director would have no effect on major decisions.

Ian and Chubby took on the task of identifying and employing the new directors. It was also decided to offer Jomo Maponyane a ten percent stake in the South African section of the business. Each of the current four partners would give up two and a half percent of their shares. Another high-profile black as a partner could only help, even if he was not an ANC member.

With the majority of the profitable business in the three international branches and a weak Rand, the financial effect on Jimmy, Gus, Ian and Chubby would be minimal. The directorship was offered to and accepted by a nephew of Nelson Mandela. The non-executive director was offered to one of Jacob Zuma's wives, killing two birds with one stone, a female and a high profile member of the ANC's wife.

By the middle of 1995 Jimmy decided it was time to call it quits on the Schreiber deal, he confirmed it with Sebastian, and they agreed to amicably end the contract. To celebrate, he took Lynne on a month-long Mediterranean cruise, ensuring that one of the stops was Mykonos. Lynne refused to rule out the possibility of repeating her all over tan.

With Douglas running his three garages and Margaret in college, Ian found himself at a bit of a loose end. Having worked his whole life since the age of fifteen, he needed a new project. With more money than he would ever need, it would have to be something fun and enjoyable.

Chubby, having spent most of his working life in the marketing and sports agency business, decided to join his three other partners and take a less hands-on approach to the business. He wanted to spend some time with his family and spend some of the vast amount of money he had accumulated.

With three of the four taking time to relax and cut back any working hours, it was only Gus who was still committed to any project. Having had over a year of ANC rule, he was beginning to doubt his commitment to the vision of the Rainbow Nation. Even with the strict controls imposed by the sponsors, it was becoming difficult to stop corruption and blatant thievery from occurring at the various clinics. It was almost seen as their right to take what wasn't theirs. Much of the time it was to the detriment of the very people they were supposed to be looking after.

The hours he was putting in and the amount of travel was wearing him down. He spent more time away from his family than with them. Cathy never complained; she was happy when he was at home with her and the children. Gus decided it was time they got married.

On Saturday August 12, 1995 Gus and Cathy tied the knot in a short ceremony at Saint Mark's Catholic Church in Durban North. With Jimmy as best man and Lynne as bridesmaid, a union that had taken decades finally happened. With Gus' extended family – his two children, Chubby, Fiona, Valerie, Ian, Dee, Douglas and Elizabeth – in attendance it was an emotional gathering, only Sharon was missing unable to make it due to university in Boston and the short notice.

The party made their way to the Durban Country Club where all those of legal drinking age proceeded to run up a huge bar bill. A lavish meal was laid on with no expense spared. The tab was picked up by Murphy and Associates.

In a quiet moment the four friends got together to drink a toast to friendship. Gus, very emotional and close to tears, thanked them for being there when he was in need. He was very happy that they had all made their fortune and could now enjoy themselves.

'What about you, Gus? Surely it's time to cut back and enjoy Cathy and the kids?' asked Ian.

'Ian, you may be right, but I still believe in what I am doing. For years under Apartheid we were taking advantage of the black population. The ANC will right this wrong given the time.'

'Gus, I think you are in dream land. The NATS were corrupt in many ways but this ANC lot is going to make them look like amateurs. They reckon it's payback time, they will loot this country and fuck the economy up, mark my words,' stated Ian.

'Well, let's agree to disagree. So, what are you lazy bastards going to do now that you are all unemployed?'

'Funny you should ask. I think we should open up a pub/restaurant and locate it on the Bluff. We don't need to make any money on it, but it could become a place where good friends meet.'

'Good idea, Ian. Just think all those years ago when we used to sneak into the old Harcourt Hotel for a round of Lion Ales. We four scruffs from the Bluff have come a long way since then.'

'Jimmy, you hit the nail on the head, we'll call it Scruffs. I have done some research and have a plan laid out. Let's get together soon and get started.'

Two weeks later the three of them met up (Gus was unavailable due to his clinic commitments), and Ian presented his concept with architectural plans, interior design for pub and restaurant, potential sites, parking lot sizes and external signage. The business plan – with cost and sales estimates and timeline to opening – showed a plan for the pub to be up and running in time for the Christmas Season.

'So, here is the general idea. The interior will have a sports bar concept, flat screen TV's all around the pub and maybe a couple in the restaurant. We decorate the pub with sporting memorabilia, concentrating on local Bluff and Durban personalities, Rugby, cricket, football and surfing. We find photos of personalities and Bluff characters blow them up into larger than life size and have them cover the wall in the pub. I would like some high-tech system for ordering of food and drinks and tied to it, a process keeping a check of payments, sales and stocks. Jimmy, I reckon you could come up with a system to do this, give you something to exercise that brain of yours. I want us to be able to provide the best food and drink at prices no one else can beat. We will make a profit but nothing major. The idea is to have some fun while giving the

Bluff somewhere to spend their money and get bloody good value for it. What do you think?'

'Just how long have you been mulling this over? So much detail already.'

'Just since Gus' wedding, Chubbs. I reckon with your connections the sporting memorabilia will be a piece of cake. I have a site in mind, just opposite the Old Bluff Drive-in, easy access and plenty of parking spaces. So, what do you guys say?'

'I'm in. Jimmy, what about you?' said Chubs.

'Damn sure, I'll check with Gus but I am positive he will join us. I reckon the ANC are wearing him down. I have some ideas on a system and as money is no object, it will blow you all away.'

'Okay, it's set then, I will get my lawyer to draw up a legal contract to cover us. I will see someone on the town council to secure the piece of land and have it correctly zoned for our business and at the same time apply for our liquor license, I will probably have to grease a few palms. I am used to this; it will be black ones instead of white this time, but the same old rules apply,' declared Ian.

In a surprisingly short space of time, the land was purchased and rezoned the same day, the liquor license was approved and plans for the building signed off. Chubby began sourcing the necessary memorabilia and met with the local S.A. Breweries rep, Cliffy Barnard. Barnard knew of Chubby from his rugby playing days but was sceptical of opening a pub on the Bluff. All of the bars were attached to hotels and the volume of trade was very low. Anyone on the Bluff wanting a night out always headed into Durban.

Barnard reluctantly agreed to open an account for the new, yet unnamed, pub. The breweries required a deposit of R6,000 to be held in case of non-payment of delivery. Beer would be ordered by telephone and delivery was to be paid in full on each delivery; cash or cheque. Any default would cause the suspension of their account with the breweries and all deliveries would cease until resolved. Barnard warned that historically new pubs/restaurants failed in the first three to six months. Breweries would not contribute to any advertising and no special deals for the opening. Chubby just smiled, signed the contract and handed over a cheque for R6,000.

Dealing with SA Breweries would prove difficult and at times unpleasant, but that's what you put up with when they had an over 90% market share. Based on the fact that their market leader, Castle Lager, was the beer of choice by most South Africans, it was a take it or leave it situation.

With all the necessary contracts signed, it was time to source all the other suppliers that were non-SA Breweries. Food menus for the pub and restaurant needed to be drawn up and approved. Tables, chairs, knives, forks, etcetera, were ordered. With pressure from the wives, these tasks were given over to the ladies. Led by Lynne, Dee, Fiona and Cathy got to work, with the caveat that they remember the place was called Scruffs and not the Regent.

Jimmy got to work on the ordering system. He virtually locked himself in his Hillcrest office, coming out only to eat and sleep. The continual arrival of high-tech computer equipment seemed like a never-ending stream. When asked what it was, he would only reply, 'I need it. Go away.'

With three weeks to opening, everything was ready and in place except the cash registers and the front signage. The name of the pub was still a closely guarded secret and all advertising just said, 'a new and exciting venue was opening soon.' Jimmy gave Ian and Chubby a call and told them to meet him at the pub by ten o'clock that morning; he was ready with the 'tills'. Before leaving Hillcrest, Jimmy asked Lynne to contact all the wives and if possible, come to the pub and bring as many of their kids as were available.

Just after ten, with the crowd assembled, Jimmy started his spiel, 'Okay folks, I know there is a lot of equipment around, but I am going to give a limited demo of what this thing does. I have spent a ton of money on this stuff, way over budget, but I had so much fun doing it that I am prepared to pay for it out of my own pocket. Okay, follow me and try and keep up.'

Taking them into the back office, he switched on the large computer screen and logged in with a user ID and password. 'This is the main controller. I have loaded in all the items we will be selling, made up some quantities and prices for the purpose of this exercise.'

Pushing a function key, a list of staff members appeared, 'Each staff member has a unique ID and a card like this to identify them. If anyone leaves, the card is reusable. I have also loaded all our tables and numbered them; by using this function you can assign waiting staff to tables as you can see. Using this function key, you will see a real time stock situation plus sales of each item. I have set reorder levels for everything and a purchase order will generate when those levels are reached. Any questions before we get to the good stuff?'

'Wow, there is more? How the hell did you come up with this?' asked Ian.

'Just slapped it together in my spare time. We'll do the pub first. Ross, you will be a waiter, here is your card. I have already programmed you in. Lynne, you are a customer and wish to run a tab. I have swiped your credit card and I give you this card for ordering. Your orders will accumulate on your credit card but will not be processed until you check out. Okay, you and Dee are going to order food and booze. Tap your card on the screen at your table.'

Lynne tapped her card on the screen; immediately it displayed a photo of Ross and showed the message; 'Hi, I am Ross. I will be your waiter.' Below that was a choice of food or drinks. Touching the drinks tab displayed a further choice of beer, wine and cocktails. Lynne selected wine and was presented with further choices, she chose a bottle of red. The screen went back to display food or drinks. She selected food and was presented with the bar menu. She selected ribs, fries and a salad, Dee selected bar snacks.

'Okay, follow me. Ian, I have you in as a barman. Look at your screen and you will see the drinks order. Pretend you have the drinks ready and tap the done tab. Ross, check the waiter station screen. You will see your name highlighted, tap next to that.'
Ross tapped the screen and the drinks ordered for table 7 were ready for pickup was displayed.

'Okay, Ross, pick up the drinks and deliver to table 7; smile, your tip may depend on it. Okay folks, follow me to the kitchen,' ordered Jimmy.

At the centre point in the kitchen was another screen; this one displaying the food order for table 7 – waiter Ross. Jimmy tapped the screen next the order, the display changed to show 'food being prepared', a further tap changed it to 'food ready'.

'Pretty straight forward, right? Ross, check the waiter station, see the food is ready, collect and deliver. Lynne, go ahead and indulge, more booze, maybe a desert, coffee. Fiona, you go and handle the kitchen, Ian, stay at the bar and Ross, do the deliveries. Lynne, assume you are done, tap the screen for checking out,' instructed Jimmy.

Lynne obliged and was presented with a confirmation screen listing all their purchases and a total rand amount. There was an option for a tip; money or a percentage, Lynne chose a generous 25% and hit accept. Ross got a signal that a bill was printing for his customer. He picked up the bill and presented it to Lynne for signing. Grateful for the size of the tip, he leaned in and kissed Lynne on the cheek and then did the same to Dee.

'So, folks, that's how the food and drink will be handled. What do you think?'

'You may have gone over budget but it's bloody amazing. What do you think, Ian?' asked Chubby.

'Gob-smacked, you are amazing. Great ideas and it will be fun to watch people using it. It is so simple, it's unreal. Great job! What about those who have no credit or debit cards and want to pay cash?' said Ian.

'I am glad you asked. I pre-empted that by setting Lynne up on that first screen. Cash customers can still order on the screen in the same way but when checking out, the waiter will collect cash. Now, onto the boring management stuff, follow me.'

Jimmy led the group back into the office. He logged on to the screen and pressed the 'Live' tab; the screen displayed the live situation. It showed all the sales as of that moment split into categories of food, wine, cocktails and beer. Options of 'sales by waiter' with accumulated tips. Options for showing 'Opening stock by item,' 'Quantity sold,' 'Stock on hand,' 'reorder levels.' There were options to generate a purchase order for restocking. Options to change prices globally by product, to change prices for a select time period that could be used for a Happy Hour concept.

'I know that it is a whole lot to absorb but we will have wealth of data available and it will make stock taking easy and any 'leakages' easy to see. I have had some fun doing it,' said Jimmy.

'I have no words for this. It will revolutionise the way we do things. I reckon the customers will love it. Fantastic job.'

'Thanks, Ian, I concentrated on making the customer happy with quick and correct service. I did indulge a bit and if you have time, I can show that as well.'

'There's more? Right, let's see what you have,' said Ian.

'I am still fine-tuning this and have loaded some dummy data. When I press the F10 function key you will see a schematic of all of our tables and bar area. By paging up and down you will notice a time clock in the top left corner. You will see a heat map by area which changes by the time of day. What this shows is sales volume by quantity in red and sales value in Rands in green. Just an idea that may be useful in tracking where our business is being generated, which may help with staffing. There is one other thing I need to show you, so it is back to one of the pub screens, follow me.'

Taking Lynne's ordering card, Jimmy tapped the screen twice. Immediately an image of an old jukebox appeared. He scrolled through a list of songs and tapped one by Tina Turner, '*Simply the Best*'; seconds later the song started with Tina coming through the multi-speaker surround system.

'So, anyone can start up the jukebox and select the music; they will be queued up in sequence. The volume can only be controlled by one of our management cards,' said Jimmy.

There was a stunned silence from the onlooking group. 'Okay, one last thing I added is from an idea I saw in many pubs in the UK. They have regular "trivia nights" so I added a module for us to offer it to our patrons. We can load it to start at any time, on any day. People can play simply by tapping their card and selecting the Games tab. The questions are displayed and answers chosen from a list. I reckon we offer drinks and or meal vouchers to the winners. Now I am done.'

'Jesus, Jimmy, it is incredible what you have done, this is going to be so much fun! I can't wait for opening day.'

On Friday December 8 Scruffs on the Bluff opened to an enormous crowd. Invited guests included a number of those whose large images adorned the walls in the pub. All four partners, their wives and children were in attendance, the only absentee was Sharon, still at university in the USA. The only Breweries representative, Cliffy Barnard, was suitably impressed by the turnout and the atmosphere. He approached Chubby, 'Hey Chubby, great turn out, it is a good idea to sell low price on an opening. The word will get around quickly seems like you may be onto a winner.'

'Thanks, Cliff, but I am disappointed in the lack of effort on the Breweries part to get the word out. But hey, we will have to work together.'

Opening night was a roaring success. At the push of a button just how successful it had been was obvious. Virtually everything needed reordering and apart from SA Breweries, that was done by generating purchase orders. Breweries, unfortunately, would have to be phoned.

The price of booze and food was set low for opening night and the thought was to restore them to what was normal in the bars and hotels in the Durban area. Ian went over the numbers and made the discovery that although they had sold low, they had still made a reasonable profit. He contacted his partners and suggested they keep the prices the same as for opening night. All agreed.

The first hint of an issue came from the marketing department at SAB. Cliffy requested a meeting, Ian agreed to see him.

'Ian, thanks for seeing me at such short notice. I just wanted to say that your first three weeks have been unbelievable; the amount of our product you have moved has exceeded all of our expectations, congratulations. We are wondering just when you will adjust your prices upward from your opening day.'

'Cliff, we are very happy with our prices and intend to keep them at this level for the foreseeable future. What seems to be your problem?'

'Well, based on our experience, we expect a Castle pint in the bottle to sell for between R3 and R3.50, you are selling for R1.10. As you no doubt know, the cost of beer less the return on empties is 98 cents giving you a markup of 12 cents? A Castle draft normally sells between R4.00 upwards to R5.00; you are selling at R2.00. Again, making around 12% markup. Based on our recommended selling prices, you should be looking at a 300 to 400% markup on beer. We are very concerned with your current practice. Our recommendation is for you to fall in line with other establishments selling our product.'

'I fail to see why SAB should be concerned about our pricing. According to my sources, we are moving more of your product after only three weeks of operation than any other bar or restaurant in the whole of Natal. You should be here thanking us instead of what seems to me like hassling us.'

'We have had endless calls from our other customers complaining that you are affecting their businesses with your pricing. Many have insinuated that we are giving you special deals that allow you to sell at your current prices. Many have threatened to boycott us and go elsewhere.'

'I say bullshit to that threat. You are a monopoly, where exactly will they get product from?'

'Ian, I would hate for us to suspend your deliveries over a small issue like this. Please, think it over.'

'I have and we will stay at status quo. If this is a threat on your part, it won't work on me. If you intend to stop deliveries, please put it in writing, close our account and have our R6,000 deposit returned immediately.'

'I am disappointed. I am sure you will hear from our management if any action is taken,' said Cliffy over his shoulder as he departed.

The next morning Fiona called SAB to place the beer order only to be told that deliveries had been suspended until further notice. She called Ian with the news. Half expecting the news, Ian told Fiona to contact the other partners and inform them of the situation. Also, to call the SABC, *The Mercury* and *Times* newspapers to inform them there would be a news conference at 5 pm at the pub.

Ian called his partners, explained the situation and told them of his plan. They divided up the tasks and got to work. Ian called all the local distributors of non-SAB breweries and explained to each of them SAB's stand and his plan to only sell non-SAB product. By the end of the morning, he had secured deliveries of Windhoek, Hansa, Heineken,

Amstel, Becks, Sam Adams and half a dozen lesser known imports. All suppliers were invited to the news conference as guests. Almost all of the suppliers agreed to sell to Scruffs at cost plus 5%, very happy to put one over on the behemoth that was SAB.

Chubby contacted the chairmen of all the bigger sports clubs on the Bluff and outlined his plan. All agreed to participate. He also called a business connection of his to order a large banner but only if it could be ready today. He secured the promise it would be delivered by 3 pm that day.

Jimmy's task was to preload all the new product on the system with selling price exactly one cent lower than the SAB equivalent prices. Assuming all went to plan, the loss would be minimised but a loss nevertheless.

At exactly 4.30, Scruffs stopped selling. Invited guests started arriving, the TV and newspapers, eager for a story, setup outside the building. Regular customers stood around looking confused as the crowd grew in size.

At exactly 5 pm Ian, Jimmy, Gus and Chubby emerged from inside the building. they, in turn, were followed by a representative from each of the new beer suppliers.

Ian took the microphone and addressed the crowd.

'Thank you all for coming. My partners and I have an announcement to make.' Ian raised his hand, and on that signal, the banner across the front of the building unfurled.

'As you can see, we have announced our pub as an "SAB-free Zone". You are probably wondering what that is all about, let me explain. When we started this venture, we agreed to offer food and drink at affordable prices. In this economic climate we wanted people of the Bluff to be able to enjoy a night out without bankrupting them. Our feedback has been that we are delivering exactly what they need. Unfortunately, we have encountered a problem. SAB have stated that they will no longer deliver their product to us and closed our account with them. By the way, Mr. Erasmus, we are still waiting for the return of our deposit. So, why would they stop deliveries? The excuse we have been given is that we are selling their product at a lower price than they approve of.'

Ian paused, leaving the crowd muttering and shaking their heads, the TV cameras recording every nuance. Ian continued.

'Despite us being happy to sell at our prices, we were strong-armed by SAB that if we didn't sell at their recommended prices, they would stop delivery. Hence, the SAB-free zone. We will not sell their product from this day on. Let me introduce these gentlemen standing behind me.'

One by one, Ian introduced the suppliers by name and extolled their products. The crowd, now hyped up, cheered loudly at each introduction. Once all had been introduced, Ian continued.

'So, it raises the question, will the beer be as good and cheap as the Castle? The answers are yes to both, except we will be selling the complete range of beers mentioned just slightly cheaper than Castle.'

The crowd went nuts.

'So, finally to keep this a SAB-free zone, what could we do with our remaining stock? SAB might take it back and refund us, but I really don't want to deal with them any more. So, we have decided to donate our remaining stock to our local sports clubs. Mike, come on over.'

Mike Smothers, chairman of Fynnlands Sports Club, stepped forward.

'Mike, it is my pleasure to donate twenty cases of Castle to your club.'

Mike, previous primed, shook his head, 'No thanks. I will vote for us to stop selling SAB after their treatment of your pub.'

Each of the five sports club chairmen gave the same reaction; it had helped that each club was given a R10,000 anonymous donation prior to the meeting.

Ian, holding an open Castle Lager bottle, turned it upside down and poured the contents on the ground, 'Looks like no one wants it. We are making a statement; we will not be bullied and told how to run our business by SAB. Until such time as they stop interfering in our business, we will not sell their product. That's all I have to say folks, thank you for coming. The first round is on the house.'

The 7 pm news on SABC opened with the story, giving it extensive coverage with some cutting sound bites. They ended saying that SAB were approached for a comment but none was forthcoming.

The late evening edition of the *Times* carried a shortened story with the headline 'SAB's Castle knocked over by little David.' The morning edition of the *Mercury,* given more time to get to press, covered the story on its front page. The headline read, 'Big Bully SAB put in its place by a bunch of Scruffs.' SAB were still unavailable for comment.

When the final costs were tallied, Scruffs were down just over R125,000. They saw it as value for money. Ian got Fiona to call SAB and ask when they could expect the refund of their deposit. More to annoy them than needing the money.

Reaction countrywide was instantaneous. TV coverage continued, with various bar and club owners interviewed for their reactions. In every instance, they agreed with Ian about SAB's bullying tactics and their utter disdain in dealing with the smaller bars and clubs. SAB, sensing they were losing the PR battle, decided to go on record with a comment.

CEO Erasmus read what looked like a prepared statement, 'I would just like to go on record and apologise to the owners of Scruffs for what has been a great misunderstanding. Our employee, Mr. Clifford Barnard, who has since been terminated, took it upon himself, with no authorisation from any senior member of SAB, to suspend deliveries. We have never and will never dictate to any business on their practices. I am very sorry this has happened and would welcome meeting with the owners of Scruffs to come a solution where we can resume business with them.'

Ian, watching the broadcast, just smiled and waited for the phone call. He didn't have to wait long.

'Is that Mr. Williams? This is Mr. Erasmus' personal assistant.' On receiving a positive response, he continued, 'Will you hold for him, please?'

'Hold on, when you have him on the phone, you can call me back,' said Ian, hanging up the phone.

Seconds later the phone rang again, 'Mr. Williams, this is Erasmus. I think we need to discuss this embarrassing misunderstanding and come to a solution that suits us both.'

'I agree. I will set up a meeting for Sunday morning 9 am at our pub, I suggest you bring one of your legal guys and we will have our lawyer present. Try to be on time. as we open at 11 am on Sundays.'

'You want me to come there? Why not do a teleconference?'

'On big deals like this. we do face to face, see you on Sunday. Goodbye.'

Ian called Barnard and told him to be at the pub on Sunday morning.

Sunday morning. on the dot of 9 am. Erasmus and two other gentlemen arrived, all dressed in suits and carrying briefcases. They were greeted by the four owners, who just happened to be dressed in shorts and golf shirts, bearing the Scruffs logo.

'Welcome gentlemen, take a seat, sorry it's in the pub but we don't have an office big enough for all of us today.' Ian introduced his partners and carried on with, 'Let's get down to business.'

'First off, I would like to apologise for the misunderstanding that took place. I feel we can get your business back online immediately. What other concerns do you have?' said Erasmus.

'I am glad you asked,' said Ian. 'I have prepared a list of things that need to happen for us to resume business. You two,' he indicated to the two lawyers, 'you will need to take notes, as I only have this copy with me today. I will get our lawyer to send you an official copy, if everyone agrees. Firstly, we want an official apology in the way you dealt with us announced in the press. We will lodge a deposit of R100,000 with you, from which you will draw down our orders, we will replenish the deposit weekly with a bank transfer. We do not want the ridiculous process of paying for each delivery, when you have a large amount of our money on deposit. For new orders we will no longer phone them in, we will fax you our order, which will be in the exact format of your current order form. Maybe if your systems can handle it, we can send the order in a PDF format, or maybe even better, a text file that can be loaded directly into your system. We have somebody on board who could help your IT department make this happen, no charge. Lastly, we need SAB to take the responsibility for ordering the deliveries to be stopped. We know Barnard was acting on orders from above and has been made the scapegoat. We want him reinstated as our rep and won't do business until he is. Hey Cliffy, come on out here.'

'That is a lot of demands. We need to discuss them,' said Erasmus.

'You are the CEO; you have until 10.59 this morning to give us an answer. You can inform Cliff now about his reinstatement. We will leave you alone to make up your mind. Come guys, let's have a *dop*.'

Unsurprisingly, Erasmus agreed to all the demands. Ian offered them lunch, which was gratefully accepted, a round of Windhoek lager was placed on the table and unbeknownst to Erasmus, a wide-angle photo was taken. The photo would take pride of place in the pub with the caption, 'Don't mess with a Bluff Scruff'. Barnard was happily reinstated and all was well. Erasmus was genuinely impressed with the computer system and wondered if they would be prepared to sell it to other pubs. Jimmy just laughed and shook his head.

The whole SAB saga generated huge media attention for Scruffs. TV, magazine and newspapers queued up for interviews. All recorded and photographed interviews were held in the pub or with the pub in the background. The team took a strategic decision that the ladies would front the interviews, much better to use four good-looking women than four old farts. The prevailing question was, 'What's next for Scruffs, will you open more of the same?'

This led to Ian declaring to his three partners, 'Guys, this has been a lot of fun but I don't know about doing more. We did this for the people of the Bluff, our people; I don't think we should do more of the same elsewhere. What do you guys reckon?'

'I can't speak for all of you, but I've had a ball. Putting together this pub and its systems was more fun than I ever had working a real job. The question is, if we do more, where and why? Gus, what about you?'

'Well, Jimmy, the original plan was to provide something like this for our community, give something back. If we do go on, I would suggest building them near a University. Varsity students are always pushed for funds but still need to unwind. That would be my suggestion.'

'Gus, I reckon you are onto something, what do you say, Chubbs?'

'Good idea, I say we build three more. I went to Natal University, so one there. Gus, one near UCT, your old stomping ground, so that would cover Cape Town and Durban city. We should also look at Johannesburg, maybe near WITS.'

'Hey fellows, how's this for a plan? Ian, it was your idea so we assign Scruffs on the Bluff to you. Chubbs, you take on Natal U, Gus, obviously UCT is yours and I, for no other reason than it is the only area left, will do WITS. Once up and running we compete with each other. The annual loser has to suffer a yet to be decided forfeit. Are we on?' asked Jimmy.

Always up for a challenge, the partners shook hands on the deal. Matches were drawn to see who would start first with the result that Gus would start followed by Chubby with Jimmy in last position. Each Pub would be of exactly the same configuration and theme. The only difference would be the large poster photographs would be of locals based on the location. The only consistent photo display would be of Erasmus and the Windhoek Lagers.

Gus having been busy with what was going to be his last clinic, had relocated to Cape Town and rented a house in Constantia. The clinic situated in Mitchell's Plain, just outside of Cape Town, was proving to be the most difficult of them all. There was a lot of mistrust in the area and a lot of gang activity. Intimidation was rife and less community participation had led to Gus calling time on his arrangement with the Australians. A replacement – a politically well-connected black doctor – had been identified and recruited for future clinics.

With 18-year old Ross doing a science degree at UCT, Gus made the decision to put an offer in on the house he was currently renting, it was accepted. Gus held a family meeting to decide if they should relocate to Cape Town. Cathy and Margaret agreed immediately and so the Stewart family moved to Constantia; they rented out Cathy's Durban North home as she was reluctant to sell.

Ironically, work on the Cape Town Scruffs began on April 16, the same day as the start of formal hearings of the Truth and Reconciliation Commission. With Dee looking after the Bluff pub, it was left that Cathy, Lynne and Fiona would handle the ordering and supervision of the pub and restaurant. Jimmy took care of the 'tills' and hooked them all up to his central computer in Hillcrest.

The pub was officially opened on Friday July 5 1996. All four partners, along with their wives and family attended. Just as before, the opening of the second Scruffs was a huge success. Gus, now totally removed from his association with the clinics, appeared more relaxed and content than he had been since his return to South Africa some two and a half years ago.

Almost immediately work began on the Durban version of Scruffs. Now a pretty well-oiled machine, the implementation took a little over six weeks from start to finish. With Chubby fronting the Durban pub, the opening became a media headline. The turnover instantly exceeded the original Bluff pub. Ian, a little miffed, promised that his pub would get back first place status.

As a group, it was decided to delay the Johannesburg pub. Work would only start on November 1 with a view to opening on Friday December 13. The Friday the 13th target date proved to be a bad omen. Labour strikes in the building industry delayed the opening day to January 3, 1997.

The delay meant the expected Christmas holiday trade was missed. The late opening also meant the initial student trade from WITS didn't happen as the University was closed for the summer holidays. Despite these setbacks, the pub and restaurant turned a profit from day one. Jimmy and Lynne, who had moved into their Fourways house for the duration, decided they would look for a management team to run the WITS branch; both of them missed Hillcrest and would prefer to live there.

Jimmy had installed a network in his Hillcrest home, with all four pubs hooked into a central monitoring system. From a screen in his office, he had access to real-time data of the entire operation. One of the first things he did was install a real-time bar chart showing sales volumes and cash receipts of all four pubs side by side. Giving Ian, Chubby and Gus the same access. it became a daily competition of who was 'winning'.

On May 10, Lynne and Jimmy flew to Logan Airport in Boston, where they were met by Sharon, Jimmy's sister, Maureen and her husband

Peter. The purpose of the visit was to attend Sharon's graduation from Brown University in Providence, Rhode Island, Maureen and Peter's home town.

Jimmy hadn't seen his sister since his mother's death and hadn't seen his daughter for over a year. It was an emotional reunion. The first thing he noticed was Sharon's slight American twang and the unbelievable likeness to Lynne. When Lynne and daughter stopped weeping, Peter loaded everyone into his Caddy for the drive to Providence.

The gowning ceremony was scheduled for Friday May 23 giving them almost two weeks to see the sights and sounds. Sharon had graduated *cum laude* with Bachelor of Science degree. Maureen had hoped she would continue on and do her Masters, but Sharon made it clear she wanted to go home to Hillcrest.

The gowning ceremony was an eye-opener for Jimmy. Over one thousand students were being awarded their degrees, each applauded by the audience as they received their diplomas. When Sharon was called, to Jimmy's surprise she seemed to get the loudest applause and biggest cheer. Looking at his sister, he shrugged his shoulders. 'You ain't seen nothing yet *boetie*, just wait till the mob get hold of her. We will be here for hours. To say she is popular is an understatement. She has half the male population wrapped around her little finger,' laughed Maureen.

When Sharon finally emerged, Jimmy noticed a young man trailing just behind her like a puppy dog. Sharon, after accepting congratulations from her family, turned to the puppy dog, 'Mom, Dad, this is Jake Higgins III, a friend of mine. Jake, this is my mom, Lynne and my dad, James.'

Jimmy extended his hand to Jake, who looked a little confused. He had the 'Oh my God, there are two of them.' Look, thought Jimmy. 'Nice to meet you Jake. Yes, I know, they look identical, I sure am one lucky bastard.'

Lynne leant forward, shook Jake's hand and kissed him on the cheek, 'Don't take any notice of him.'

Jake, still with the goldfish look, seemed unable to talk. 'Jake, unfortunately we are going for a family meal so I will have to see you maybe tomorrow before we leave for home on Sunday. Give me a call and we will fix a time. Congratulations on your degree. I think you will do great at law school. Come on folks, time to celebrate,' urged Sharon.

Peter had booked them into the exclusive Newport Yacht Club for cocktails and a meal. Sharon, still legally too young to drink, had to doctor her champagne with orange juice. She proposed a toast, 'To my folks. I love you so much, thank you for allowing me to attend Brown.

To my Aunty Maureen and Uncle Peter, I cannot thank you enough for suggesting Brown and the three years you have been my surrogate parents, I love you both.'

'Right, my girl, what are your plans and where does Jake III fit in?' asked Jimmy.

'Dad, Jake says he's in love with me and wants to get married. I am twenty, for God's sake! Anyway, he's not my type, he just follows me around. As for my plans, with your permission of course, I would like to take off the rest of the year and do some travelling. Next year I would like to enrol at Natal U and do my Masters, then the year after do an MBA at UCT, maybe stay with Gus and Cathy.'

'So, where would you like to travel?' asked Jimmy.

'I believe Mykonos is great in summer, maybe a week or so there to start,' replied Sharon, with a cheeky look at her father, 'Don't worry, Dad, I've seen the photos; just kidding.'

A soulful Jake Higgins III pitched up unannounced the next morning. Lynne watched her daughter gently explain that she was going home and would miss him dearly but she needed to spend time at home with her parents. She bade him farewell with a hug and a kiss on the cheek. She looks just like my mom, if only my dad was still alive to see her now.

A first-class flight on Virgin Atlantic, with a short stopover in London, got the Wilson family home to Durban early Monday morning. Collecting Sharon's copious amount of luggage, they retrieved their car from the long-term parking lot and headed home to Hillcrest. After spending the bulk of the flight asleep in their First-Class beds, they were well rested.

'Dad, I'm going to have a swim then can I borrow the car? I want to go to the Bluff and see what Scruffs is like. I've only seen photos. I have to see the real thing.'

'You can borrow the car but remember we drive on the left here. Why don't we all go? I'll call Ian and Chubby. I am sure they are dying to see you.'

Lynne called Ian and Jimmy got hold of Chubby. By the time they reached Scruffs, it was just after lunch and the place was about half full, not bad for a Monday. Sharon parked the car and the three of them got out. They were met at the door by a waitress who instructed them to follow her; a table on the patio had been setup.

They walked through the pub and out onto the patio where they were greeted by the whole Durban clan, bar Chubby's daughter, Valerie, who was at school.

Sharon did the rounds, hugging and kissing first Dee then Ian and Elizabeth. She followed up with Fiona and Chubby. She sensed someone was missing, "You are wondering where Dougie is, aren't you?' Dee said. 'He was called away with some issue going on at one of his dealerships. He is worse than his Father, he promised to be back shortly.'

'Thank you all so much, I have missed you terribly. Thank goodness, I can legally have a drink here, not like in the States. Cheers everyone!' Valerie sat down between Lynne and Elizabeth.

'Hey girl, do I detect a bit of a Yankee twang there? That will have to go if you want to be a Bluff Scruff. It's great to have you back,' said Ian, raising his glass.

The next minutes were taken up with Sharon answering questions about her time in the USA and about her plans for the future. There was a sudden lull in the conversation and Sharon looked up to see a very tall dark-haired man coming across the pub floor. She turned to Margaret and whispered, 'Oh my God, do you see that gorgeous hunk coming this way, isn't he fabulous?'

'No, he's not, that's my dumb brother.'

'That's Dougie?' exclaimed Sharon.

'Yes, Dougie, the same one who is an absolute workaholic, hasn't got time for fun,' said Margaret.

Dougie strode up to the table with a big smile, 'Hello folks, sorry I'm late, business called.' His eyes roamed around the table and came to a dead stop, his mouth dropped open. Struggling for words, he spluttered, 'Aunty Lynne, there are two of you.'

'Don't be daft, Dougie, this is Sharon, surely you remember her. You spent a lot of time teasing her when you were all much younger.'

'I haven't seen her since she was about five. Sharon, welcome home, you look great. Margaret, move up and let me sit down.'

What happened next surprised everyone. Sharon and Dougie, sitting side by side, locked eyes and just stared at each other grinning slightly. Jimmy looked across at Lynne and silently mouthed, 'He's got the thousand-yard stare, can you believe it?' Lynne smiled back and whispered, 'So has she.'

With lunch finished, the conversation centred around the current political situation in the country, particularly around the big increase in crime. Taking the opportunity, Sharon asked Ian, 'Uncle Ian, I haven't actually seen all the workings of Scruffs. I wonder if someone can give the tour?'

Before anyone could answer, Dougie chipped in, 'Good idea, Sharon, let me show you what our parents have put together, and it is quite impressive.' He stood up and helped Sharon to her feet.

'What do you know about the systems at Scruffs? Dad should do it,' complained Margaret.

Before anyone could make a move, Dougie and Sharon disappeared heading for the back office.

Ian turned to Jimmy and said, 'Well, that was unexpected. I have never seen Douglas lose his composure like that. Maybe your daughter will lighten him up a bit.'

'Hey, man, I have never seen her react like that to any male, you could see the electricity. If that catches fire, we'll be in-laws; what a thought,' said Jimmy.

'Hey, while we're all here, Fiona has come up with what I think is a great idea and I'd like her to bounce it off you. Ok Fee, tell them all about your idea,' said Ian.

Fiona, not used to being the centre of attention any more, blushed and cleared her throat.

'It's just an idea at this point. We all know how much money is spent by advertisers to attract new business, but I don't think most do enough to keep their current customers as well. After working with Jimmy's system, I think there is a possibility we can offer something unique. I know we keep our suppliers and staff records on file. What if we add our regular customers on the system? What I have in mind is to offer a loyalty bonus to regulars. They can open an "account record" with us. We collect name, address, phone, sex, date of birth, email address and some other data like payment method. We issue them with their personal card with a password. Every time they order we award points or something. They can accumulate points and "cash" them in for free meals etcetera. We can email special deals/ events/ happenings to them. When it's their birthday, maybe offer a free meal. I have also heard a lot of talk on our Scruffs attire; I think we could sell T-shirts, caps, golf shirts, sweat shirts and maybe wind breakers all with logo and the location name underneath. So just some ideas, what do you all think?'

'Fee, you are a bloody genius. We could pay for this by saving on our advertising budget. James, me boy, what do you reckon, is it doable?'

'Ian, I love the idea. Fee, let's get together as soon as possible, come out to Hillcrest and you can help me map this whole thing out. You have just jolted a few additional ideas out of me with this suggestion. If, sorry, I mean when it works, we pilot it at the Durban pub. Keep this top-secret folks, we don't want to give our opposition any clues. Until in place, we will refer to this as the "Fee Module".'

Ian stood up and much to Fiona's embarrassment proposed a toast, 'To Fiona, not just a pretty face but a marketing genius as well. Cheers Fee, well done.' For the first time in her life Fiona felt she was truly accepted as an equal partner.

Dougie and Sharon eventually returned from their tour of the facilities. Sharon approached her father. 'Dad, is it okay if Douglas gives me a ride home? He wants to take me on a trip around the Bluff as so much has changed.'

As this was happening, Ian tapped the screen twice and the jukebox appeared, with no one taking any notice he selected a song by *The Doors*.

'Sure baby, have fun, we will leave a light on for you.'

As they turned to leave, Ian hit the button and turned up the volume. They had barely taken a step when *The Doors'* song 'Light my Fire' blared out. Embarrassed, Dougie turned to his father just in time for the chorus to start with the lyrics, 'Come on baby, light my fire.' Blushing, the two of them left in a hurry to a raucous round of applause.

Lynne, sleeping with one ear tuned in, noticed Sharon arriving home just after one o'clock. She smiled and rolled over back into a deep sleep. The following morning, just after ten, Sharon emerged, all showered and dressed up.

'How was your evening?' asked Lynne.

'Mom, it was great. Douglas is such a nice man and so interesting. He has invited me to meet him for lunch. Can I borrow a car? I have to meet him at his Pinetown Dealership; he said he has promised his staff a special treat and wants me to be there for it. A bit weird, right?'

Jimmy, overhearing the conversation, thought, 'I know what their treat will be.' 'Take your mom's old Beetle. You were a bit ropey yesterday driving on the left. I'll get you a set of wheels once you get a South African license and get used to driving on the wrong side of the road. Have fun.'

Lynne watched her daughter leave, 'She has grown up so much in the last few years, so confident. I have never seen her looking this radiant; I think young Douglas has an eye on her.'

'He had better behave, otherwise I'll cut his nuts off, she is still a baby.'

'She is twenty and it makes me feel so old.'

'Oh please, you are more gorgeous now than when I met you, still the sexiest woman I have ever laid eyes on.'

Grabbing Jimmy by the hand, she pulled him towards the bedroom, 'Come on Buster, show me what you've got, make me feel twenty again.'

'Fee is coming over shortly, we don't have the time.'

'You'd better be quick then, old man.'

By the time Fiona arrived, Lynne and Jimmy were showered and dressed drinking coffee on the porch. Lynne noticed that Fiona looked different somehow; less nervous, with a bit of a spring in her step and smiling for a change. 'Hey Fee, you look fabulous, I love that dress. James, I will leave the two of you alone to do your thing, just holler if you need anything.'

Fiona and Jimmy retreated to the computer room. 'I love your ideas and I know we can make them work. I agree with adding our customers to our existing database. I think, added to your suggestions, we collect the person's nickname to make it real personal and friendly. The point's idea is genius and I like the Scruffs merchandise but maybe we don't sell it. What if they can only "purchase" stuff with their points? Make it a bit more exclusive.'

'Yes, damn good idea, only the real regulars get to wear our stuff. Replied Fiona.

'I like the idea of the personal ordering card and I have an idea on that. It is really easy and quick to personalise the card. What if we add a photograph to it as well? I don't know if you are aware of it, but all of the screens have a built-in camera. What I envisage is we take a picture when we enrol them, add it to the card and file it on the system. When the customer taps the screen with their card, we snap another picture and compare it to the one on file. Using some face recognition software that I have found, we compare pictures, if a match no password is needed. It will also help with lost or stolen cards.'

'Jimmy, you are unreal, what a great idea. I have a question then. If we know who it is and have their ordering records on file, can you prompt them with a message like "Howzit 'nickname' your usual?" and then show their "usual" and a "Yes" tab? That's real personal.'

'A bloody fantastic idea, Fee, you are in the wrong business. What are your ideas about the merchandise?'

'Well, I thought that when they reach the points level needed, we guide them to a list of gear. We let them place an order for a specific item. They enter size and colour. On the front of all items is our logo and location, on the back we print their name or nickname. We order the item from our suppliers so each is absolutely unique.'

'Brilliant idea. I tell you what, let's keep this all to ourselves, play down what we are doing. When tested and ready we pilot it at the Durban Pub. We will blow them away. I have work to do on this. I think if you can identify say, ten regulars, we can set them up and maybe back calculate some points. We will only contact those you identify when we ready to go and only if they agree. I will start on this immediately, I reckon we have update meeting once a week and as soon as I have any part ready I want you to give it a workover. Fun times ahead, thank you, Fiona, you beauty!'

For the next three weeks, Fiona and Jimmy worked feverishly. By June 21, Sharon's twenty first birthday, they were almost ready. Still going strong, Sharon and Douglas were obviously the centre of attraction, but Fiona and Jimmy were grilled on the 'Fee Module.' Jimmy using Sharon's birthday party as an excuse not to steal the thunder, managed to put off all questions.

Sunday morning July 6 interested parties were invited to be at the Durban pub at 8 am. Gus, Cathy, Ross and Margaret flew in from Cape Town. They were joined by Ian, Dee and Elizabeth, Sharon and Dougie, Chubby and his daughter, Valerie, plus the ten customers. Jimmy and Fiona took centre stage and introduced the ten customers by name.

'Folks, we are here today to demonstrate the "Fee Module", which will be demonstrated by its instigator, Fiona Murphy. Fee, it's all yours,' said Jimmy.

'Thanks, Jimmy. We have set up a big screen for the demo as it will make it easier for all to see. To save time I have added nine of our guests to the system already and they have their customer cards. Matt here volunteered to be a "new customer". Matt, if you will join Jimmy in the office we will get started.'

Matt left to join Jimmy and a few seconds later the overhead screen came alive. 'As you can see, Jimmy is registering Matt on the system, it is very quick and very simple. Jimmy has tapped the save button, they should be out here any second now,' explained Fiona.

Jimmy and Matt reappeared with a grinning Matt flashing his new customer card. 'As you can see, Matt has his card with photograph. Matt, if you could go over to the screen on table 3 and tap your card,' ordered Jimmy.

Matt obliged and the screen activated and seconds later a message appeared, 'Welcome back, Matt, can I order your regular drink?' An image of a Windhoek draft appeared, flanked by 'Yes' and 'No' tabs. Matt tapped the 'Yes' tab and the register at the bar pinged, showing the order.

'So, what happened there was the screen took a photo of Matt as soon as he tapped his card, compared it to the one on his card, which we have on file, recognised him, checked what his normal drink is and offered it to him. He chose to order it but could have said, "No" and the normal process would have clocked in. Gillian, if you could clock in on table 4 but select "No" for favourite drink,' said Fiona.

Gillian obliged and after selecting 'No' was presented with the daily specials menu. She chose a mixed grill and a glass of Merlot.

'Notice the top right of the screen and you will see "Points; 300". These have accumulated; we added them for effect, Gillian tap the points and let's see what happens,' said Fiona.

She followed orders and was presented with a screen offering 'Food' and 'Merchandise'; as instructed she chose 'Merchandise'. A list of all Scruffs merchandise, with their point value, was displayed. She chose a T-shirt for 55 points. Prompted, she selected pink, size 34 and the name Gilly. The screen confirmed her choice and the message, 'Item will be delivered on Tuesday July 8.'

'Gary, pick a table and log on. We have set Gary up with today as his birthday. He has been sent an email telling him he is eligible for a free birthday meal,' said Jimmy.

Gary tapped in and the screen broke into the tune of 'Happy Birthday, Gazza (his on-file nickname). At the end of the tune, he was presented with a food menu, he selected his meal and then the system showed him the drinks menu where he selected his one free drink.

'There are a number of other features, like being able to easily change the greeting messages, very simple to do. What I'd like you to do is pair up with our guests and have some fun. Jimmy will answer any questions,' said Fiona.

The next half an hour was punctuated by the jukebox blaring and the sounds of amazement from all corners. The fun and games were interrupted by a flashing screen at table 11. Everyone stopped to see what was happening. Sharon and her partner Basil were looking at their screen that was displaying a message 'Bas, this doesn't look at all like you, Mate. Your waiter will be with you shortly.'

Jimmy burst out laughing, 'My own daughter trying to defraud the system. Lynne, what did we do wrong bringing her up?'

'Sorry Dad, I just wanted to see what would happen if I logged on with Basil's card, sorry.'

'It is okay, I knew someone would try but not my own daughter. It's a safety guard to deal with stolen, lost cards or lending your card to someone else.' Jimmy tapped his card on the screen and the flashing stopped.

'Can I have your attention, please? Jimmy needs to reset the system for opening time so if there are any questions, let's have them now.'

'Great presentation, Fee. Only one question from me. When can I have this for the Bluff pub?' asked Ian.

'Me too,' said Gus.

'I can install immediately but I think let it run for a week here in case of teething problems. After that I suggest Fee spends a week at each site as there is some training needed. Draw straws folks,' said Jimmy.

The straws were drawn Ian, Jimmy and then Gus.

'One last thing before we end. I would like to thank my ten volunteers for their effort and keeping the secret. We did cheat a bit as they had some training and for that we gave them a choice of merchandise. Guys, come on and pick up your stuff. Oh, and Chubby, food and drink for the whole group of us is on the house and on your budget,' said Fiona, bowing to the applause.

By the end of August, the new systems were in place in all of the four pubs. As for the initial launch, there was huge media coverage. As designer and programmer, Fiona and Jimmy were in great demand for interviews. The prevailing questions were always 'whose idea was it?' and 'would Scruffs consider selling the application?' The answers were always the same, Fiona and no.

Fiona was unanimously elected as CEO of Scruffs based in Durban. Jimmy found a manager for the Johannesburg operation and handed over day to day control to him. Ian offered management of the Bluff operation to Cliffy Barnard; it was only Gus who retained full management of the Cape Town branch. He was happy with the relaxed, unpressured day to day that the pub offered with his family close at hand.

Sharon embarked on her overseas trip after a tearful farewell to Douglas. Douglas lasted exactly two weeks before he approached his father to please look after his garages and dealerships, as was heading off to Spain to meet Sharon. He said he would be back in two weeks but it took closer to four before the two of them returned.

Lynne, with Jimmy and Sharon, celebrated her 50th birthday quietly. Lynne, distraught at the thought of turning 50, was inconsolable. Being the middle of summer the two girls were dressed in matching red bikinis. Jimmy spotted the two of them standing side by side at the pool, he dashed into the house and came out with his digital camera and snapped off a couple of shots.

'Hey girls, come here, I want to show you something.' Displaying the first photo of the two girls from the back on the camera screen, he covered the heads with his finger. 'Guess who is who on this one.'

It was impossible to tell. He scrolled to the next photo a frontal view and did the same, with the same result. He removed his finger and said, 'To someone who didn't know you, they would not be able to tell you apart. So now stop your sniffles, you look 35 and from now on you are 35.'

The end of 1997 saw Elizabeth complete her teacher's diploma, Ross finished the third year of his law degree at UCT. His sister Margaret, following in her father's footsteps, passed her second year towards her medical degree.

As a celebration of his 48th birthday, Chubby invited his three friends and their extended families to his Plettenburg Bay mansion. Everyone attended, including Ian's 81-year old mother, Betty, and Lynn's mother, 69-year old Val. It was the first time that most of them had seen Val, Lynne and Sharon together at the same time. Their resemblance was uncanny, three versions of the same person but at different ages. Dougie just smiled as he knew exactly what his future wife would look like right through until she was 70, all he had to do now was marry her.

With everyone seated in close proximity, Chubby stood up and announced, 'Can I have your attention for just a moment? I would like to thank you all for coming today, please make yourselves at home and enjoy the food and drink. I want to thank my three mates for being part of my life. It's been a fun ride for four scruffs from the Bluff. I need to take the three of you aside for a few minutes, but for the rest of you enjoy; cheers!'

The four friends retired to Chubby's office in the basement of the house. Once all were seated, he said, 'Boys, I have had an offer for the international arm of Murphy and Associates. Some American billionaire wants to buy the company lock, stock and barrel with the exception of our local operation. They want to keep the brand name initially but will probably change it down the line. There will be a restriction of trade agreement. What are your thoughts?'

'Well, I don't know about you guys but I am more than happy to opt out. What about you, Gus, and you, Jimmy?'

'I am with you, Ian, take the money and run. Gus?'

'Me too, I am happy with things in Cape Town, more money than I could conceivably spend, and I see my family every day. Sell.'

'What about the local operation?' asked Jimmy.

'Well, James me old cobber, I reckon we get rid of that as well. Let's get hold of Jomo and see if he can get some of his buddies together and buy us out. With all of the shit we take operating under the fucking ANC, I reckon best we let it go black. Let them deal with this government. It might also look good on our part selling to a black group. Offer Jomo a nominal price and let's get out of it,' said Chubby.

'Do we all agree with Ian?' Getting a positive response, Chubby continued, 'Okay, I'll get the ball in motion. Don't you want to know what the offer is?'

To a chorus of 'yes', 'A one-time cash payment of five hundred million US paid into any bank of our choosing.'

To a chorus of 'fuck me' with one voice, 'Where do we sign?'

'Before we adjourn, what about Scruffs? None of us need the money, what do we do with the pubs?' asked Chubby.

'Well, Chubby, I say we keep them, they identify us, and they are still pissing off SAB, which is a good thing. I, for one, will never sell mine because it is the original. We need to make a pact on this,' declared Ian.

'I agree with Ian. Other pubs will open using our concept, I'm sure someone will clone our software, technology is always moving. I won't sell mine; I would rather close it than sell it,' said Chubby.

'I reckon we should never sell; if we close one, we close them all. No one else is going to provide food and drink at the margins we do. They are all in to make bigger profits and get into line with SAB,' said Ian.

Chubby arranged a meeting with Jomo to inform him of their plans and offer him the chance to buy them out. Jomo – a very wealthy man in his own right – decided if they were selling out, he would look for investors to buy their share. He wasn't interested in total ownership but the revenue stream was useful.

With the announcement of the sale of Murphy and Associates International, inquiries began on the availability of the South African enterprise. The possible availability of a 90% stake in the business was leaked to the press. Interest from investors was immediate; the chance of a large profit was obvious to the four partners.

An approach was made to Chubby by a prominent black businessman to purchase the entire 90%. The man – known to have strong ties to the ANC – was offering an amount of twenty-four million rand in cash. Chubby put the proposal to the others.

'Sounds like tax payer money to me. I personally don't need the money but it seems a fair price,' said Ian.

'Me neither, what about you, Jimmy?'

'We have flown under the radar with our SA earnings from a tax point of view; I would rather not draw any more attention to ourselves with a large – obviously public – cash payment. I want to settle the deal. What about if we donate the funds from the sale to selected sports foundations with a stipulation that it be used to further opportunities in underprivileged areas?' said Jimmy.

'Great idea, a tax deduction and good publicity in the press. I second the idea,' said Ian.

With Jomo holding on to his ten percent stake, the remaining ninety were signed over. The whole process left a bad taste in the mouth.

The ANC government claimed that the previously white-owned business was now a truly African affair. They had managed to secure the business and at the same time were able to funnel twenty-four million rand into deserving sporting foundations. The first thing the new consortium did was rename the business to 'The Comrades Agency.' A not-so-subtle reference to those so-called 'Comrades' who were part of the struggle against Apartheid. The next move was to replace the entire management structure with actual 'Comrades' who were woefully unqualified for the job.

Two months later, Jomo sold his share in the company, and within six months a once thriving business was run into the ground. It was later confirmed that less than ten percent of the sales price ended up with a sporting body. Welcome to the new South Africa.

Ian, growing discontented with the situation in the country, decided it was time to look at a future elsewhere. He bought two properties: one in Aspen, Colorado and another just outside of Toronto in Canada. If – or when – the situation in South Africa became untenable, he would leave. Almost all of his fortune was offshore and really, only Scruffs would be an issue. His son, Dougie, was already a very wealthy young man and he would be going nowhere as long as Sharon remained in South Africa. Elizabeth, now a fully qualified teacher, managed to secure herself a teaching position in Tokyo, Japan, teaching English. She was due to leave just after her twenty-first birthday on February 9.

Jimmy, now shot of all his local business interests with the exception of Scruffs WITS branch, decided to buy a yacht. An extensive search for just the right thing led him to Barcelona. There he purchased a seventy-six-foot Nordhavn Trawler for one point six million dollars, Lynne spent another three hundred thousand refurbishing it to her tastes. After all the necessary courses and instruction, Captain Jimmy Wilson declared the vessel ready. On June 7, 1998 the newly named *Scruff One* was launched on her maiden voyage. The plan was to cruise the Mediterranean, stopping where they felt like it for as long it suited them. An open invite was issued to his three friends to join Lynne and him whenever they wished. The ship slept eight comfortably.

Chubby, having placed Durban Scruffs in Fiona's name, found himself at a loose end. With all of his other business interests liquidated, he decided to run for president of the Natal Rugby Union. The Natal rugby teams of the last many years had failed to achieve anything of note. Chubby, with backing from the majority of the board, promised to bring a more professional and business-savvy approach to the Union. He was unanimously elected and threw himself into the project of restoring Natal rugby to its previous heights.

Out of the four of them it was only Gus who seemed content to carry on with Scruffs UCT being his only area of involvement. He was content to spend his time with Cathy and their two children. Both children, Ross on the way to a Law degree and Margaret with medical studies, were his pride and joy. The twenty-seven clinics that had been setup were drowning in bureaucratic red tape and fraudulent practices. When Gus had removed himself from the process, the Western Australian Government and their sponsorship had been placed under the ANC minister of Home Affairs. As each clinic began failing the audit process, it became obvious that the funds provided were not reaching their correct destination. With a failure to get to consensus on audit investigations between the two governments, the Western Australians decided to pull their funding. The ANC were unable to operate the clinics without the funds and they folded one by one.

To keep up the tradition for Chubby's 49th birthday, Jimmy invited his three friends and their wives to celebrate the occasion on his yacht. They were flown into Mykonos and driven to the harbour where they were ferried out to the yacht. Only Gus and Cathy hadn't had the experience of *Scruffs One*.

Friday January 1, 1999, the first day of the last year of the millennium, was a gorgeous sunny day. First item on the menu was breakfast, Greek-style. Chubby was toasted and presented with a collection of birthday gifts, mostly of the fun variety. The one that caused the biggest laugh was Lynne's present of a pink thong swimming cozzie. Not missing a trick, Chubby disappeared only to return, clad in his new cozzie.

Straight after breakfast, Jimmy took the boat on a trip around the Island pointing out all points of interest. The final stop was to anchor the boat a hundred yards off Paradise Beach. Loading up their swimming gear and hopping aboard the dinghy, the party headed for the beach. Chubby, still wearing only his thong, was first off the dingy and grabbing the anchor rope, pulled the little boat up onto the beach.

Although it was January, the temperature was in the mid-eighties and the beach was quite crowded. As usual there was a mixture of fully clothed, partly clothed, topless and completely naked. Having come from a southern hemisphere summer, the visitors were reasonably well tanned, Jimmy and Lynne, having spent much of the previous year in the sun, were extremely well tanned.

The four men headed for the outside bar and ordered a round of ice cold Heineken drafts and settled down to watch the goings on. The four women laid out their beach mats and towels and began divesting themselves of their dresses. For four middle-aged women of affluent lifestyles, they were all in excellent shape. 59 -year old Cathy in her blue one-piece cozzie, 52-year old Lynne in a tiny red bikini, 50-year old Fiona in a white one-piece and 48-year old Dee in a black bikini made up a good-looking foursome.

With the four men watching their wives, they could see some discussion led by Lynne going on. A bit of head shaking and then some nodding, it was Lynne first, she reached behind her back and undid her bikini top and dropped it at her side. She was followed by Dee. Fiona, wearing a one piece, freed her arms and rolled her cozzie down to her waist, an obviously nervous Cathy followed suit.

Still with their backs to their husbands they stood up. As one they turned around and flashed their breasts at the men, then turning back around, linked hands and ran down to the edge of the water and jumped in. With the water up to their necks the four of them divested themselves of what remained of their cozzies. They stood up, waved their cozzies in the air and threw them onto the beach and then swam over to the reef. Hanging onto the side of the reef they motioned to their husbands to join them.

After a brief discussion, Ian stood up and shouted, 'We are just fine here, having a couple of beers, enjoying the sights and sounds. You enjoy your swim.'

'Well, can you please throw our cozzies back into the water?' shouted Dee.

Ian just turned his back and ignored her.

'I can see where this is going,' said Lynne. 'They are not going to comply, we are stuck here. Well screw that, girls, follow me.'

Lynne with her all over tan and shaved pubes led her three girlfriends out of the water and picking up their cozzies, walked casually back to their mats and sat down. Giggling like teenagers, they slipped the cozzie bottoms back on but remained topless. The men in the meantime feigned disinterest. Chubby, unable to contain himself any longer, walked over to the girls.

'Can I bring you ladies something to drink, a cocktail maybe?'

'No thanks, I think we'll come over and join you all,' responded Lynne. 'I just need to make a quick trip to the beach shop and then we will be with you.'

Lynne, still topless, grabbed her purse and headed to the shop. She emerged minutes later with a packet. With Dee helping her, she picked up a towel and held it up shielding Cathy and Fiona. After a bit of wriggling around behind the towel, the two girls emerged wearing only the bottoms of two newly purchased bikinis. Now all similarly attired, they walked over and joined their husbands. With a deadpan face, Lynne asked, 'Okay, about that drink you were bragging about?'

Jimmy signalled to the waiter and ordered a round of drinks. With the women unfazed by sitting topless, it was left to the men to accept it. One couldn't help looking at each of the girls. Jimmy looking across at Cathy, couldn't help thinking, 'I remember seeing her naked the best part of thirty years ago and she looks no different now, she is in great shape. Probably having had no kids helps.'

After the first round of drinks everyone relaxed; sitting around chatting with half naked wives seemed like the most natural thing in the world. A few more drinks and a light lunch later Jimmy called time.

'Okay folks, it is time to head back to the boat, Ladies, best you get dressed and we can be on our way.'

'We are dressed. Ian, if you and Gus can pick up our towels and things, we will see you on the dinghy,' chirped Dee.

The couples spent the next six days cruising around Mykonos and the surrounding islands. Anchoring off deserted beaches, swimming in deep water and generally getting a lot of sun. By the time the trip was ending, all six of the visitors were well tanned. The girls were proud of their tanned boobs and although envious of Lynne and her full body tan, none of them were brave enough to go completely naked. Lynne, not wanting to be seen flaunting herself, kept her bikini bottoms on.

As the trip drew to its conclusion, discussion turned to future plans. Ian and Dee were going to their Aspen home for some skiing, all were invited. Chubby was getting ready for the Super Rugby Season with his Natal Sharks team. Gus and Cathy just looking forward to getting home and seeing their children.

Jimmy and Lynne were heading for Barcelona, where they would berth their yacht and head to Cape Town. He had received a message from Sharon that he needed to be in Cape Town for his birthday, as she was being gowned with her Master's degree and she also had an important announcement to make.

The friends said goodbye and the visitors departed to the airport for the flight home via Athens. They vowed to all meet up soon.

Jimmy and Lynne took a slow cruise to Barcelona where they moored the boat, purchased two first-class tickets to Cape Town and boarded the plane for what would be a fateful trip back to South Africa. They arrived Sunday morning February 7 and were met at Cape Town airport by Gus.

'Welcome, you two. I got a call yesterday from Ian, he and Dee are arriving this afternoon. He didn't say why the sudden visit but who cares why. You are all staying at my place, I have arranged, at the request of your daughter, that we have a "session" at the pub for your birthday and to celebrate her Master's degree. Looks like she may be following in her old man's footsteps.'

After the gowning ceremony Lynne, Jimmy and Sharon headed for Scruffs. With its close proximity to UCT there was a large group of newly-gowned students celebrating like only students can. The general mood was very festive. The trio located their host and headed towards the reserved area. Present were Gus and family, Ian, Dee and to Jimmy and Lynne's surprise, Dougie.

After congratulations all around, everyone took their seats except Dougie who turned and looked directly at Jimmy, 'Sir, I have a request to make. I have asked Sharon to be my wife, she has agreed. I am now asking your permission to allow me to marry your beautiful daughter. I love her dearly and promise to honour and take care of her to the best of my ability.'

Jimmy, close to tears, could barely speak he nodded and then composing himself, 'Dougie, I have known you since birth, your family are our family, absolutely you have my blessing. Lynne, might be a tougher sell.'

Lynne, bawling her eyes out, stood up and rushed over to Dougie and hugged him, 'I want lots of grandchildren. When is the wedding?'

'We haven't set a date yet but we both want it to be soon.'

Sharon, who had remained silent, walked slowly over to her Father, put her arms around his neck and whispered in his ear, 'I love him, Dad, almost as much as I love you. Thank you, we'll make you and Mom proud.'

Sharon spent the next few minutes showing off her huge engagement ring. Dougie accepted congratulations from his emotional Father and crying Mother.

'Jimmy, who would have thought thirty-six years ago that we would reach this point, soon to be part of the same family. I love you, man,' said Ian.

'It's going to continue to get raucous here with all these students. I have booked a table at the Mount Nelson for the two families. Yes, I knew about it but Sharon asked me to keep it secret. So, I have a limo waiting, enjoy the evening. We will close up and see you back at our place, probably very late, enjoy yourselves. Congratulations, it couldn't happen to nicer people.'

Normal closing time on a Tuesday was 11 pm. Bit by bit the crowd started thinning out. By ten to eleven there was only one table left occupied. Four young twenty-something black men had been drinking steadily most of the evening. Gus noticed their waiter carrying a tray of twelve beers over to the table. With ten minutes to go until closing, Gus was concerned, he walked over to his terminal in the office and looked up who they were and what they had consumed.

The credit card on hold was for one Thomas Sithole, not a regular but running up quite an extensive bill. The name somehow looked familiar but Gus couldn't place it. Deciding to pre-empt any issues, he walked over to the table.

'Hi fellers, I see you are enjoying yourselves, everything to your satisfaction?'

'Fuck off, whitey, we don't need your condescending attitude. We'll call you when we want another round so leave us alone,' said the one who seemed the main man.

Must be Thomas Sithole thought Gus,' No need to be rude, Mr. Sithole. I am the owner and we are closing in five minutes so unless you want to waste all these beers, better drink up quick or lose them.'

'Oh, so you know who I am. We will drink the beers in our own time, so I say again, fuck off.'

'Okay sonny, that's it. Time for you and your buddies to leave. You have thirty seconds to vacate the premises or I call my security company; they just love cleaning out troublemakers. Go and don't come back. I don't need your business, and no. I don't know who you are.'

Sithole stood up and glared at Gus, 'You are making a bad decision and will regret it. I will tell my Uncle about your racist attitude. Come on guys. let's fuck off from this shit hole.'

Gus followed them to the door and closed it behind them. He turned to go back into the pub and finish off the closing process. Unfortunately, he failed to ensure that the front door was securely locked. With Cathy and Margaret closing down the kitchen and Ross doing the same to the bar area, Gus was left in the office finalising tomorrows orders.

All of a sudden, he sensed someone behind him; as he turned to look, he took a heavy blow to the head and semi-conscious, he fell to the floor. By the time he cleared his head, he found himself securely tied to his office chair which had been wheeled into the pub.

Looking around he saw Cathy, Margaret and Ross being held by Sithole's three grinning accomplices.

'See what happens when you fuck with Thomas Sithole, whitey. We own the country now and we do what we want,' spat Sithole, smashing Gus across the face with one of the still full beer bottles.

Gus could feel his nose break. 'Leave the others alone, your issue is with me.'

'Oh no,' looking across to the person who was restraining Ross, 'Moses, show this white pig what we mean.'

Moses, with a maniacal grin, smashed the beer bottle he was holding and jammed it into Ross' neck opening a huge gash. Ross dropped to the floor bleeding profusely. Gus, realising Ross would bleed out in seconds, screamed at the top of his voice, 'Cut me loose, he will bleed to death, I am a doctor, let me attend to him.' Helpless, Gus watched his son die.

Sithole just laughed and nodded to the two men restraining Cathy and Margaret. Both girls were punched in the face dropping them to the floor. Gus, fearing the worst, struggled against his bonds only to receive another blow to his face. Margaret's clothes were ripped off and with Sithole and Moses holding her down, she was brutally raped. With Cathy screaming and Gus begging, Sithole just laughed.

When the first one, later identified as Nelson Moyana, was finished with Margaret, Moses Maseka took his place and he was followed by Sithole. When Sithole was done, he climbed off Margaret and kicked he viciously on the side of the head rendering her unconscious. The fourth thug, Dumisani Sonke, turned the unconscious girl over onto her stomach and raped her anally. When Sonke was finished, the four of them took turns to kick her in ribs, Gus could hear them breaking.

Tired of their sport with the unconscious Margaret, they turned their attentions to Cathy who screamed hysterically throughout the ordeal. Gus, unable to help, begged Sithole to stop; all he got for his trouble was a further blow to his face. For the next hour, Cathy was subjected to repeated rapes both vaginally and anally. Between rapes she was severely beaten to the head and ribs, Gus was powerless to help.

After what seemed like a lifetime, Shithole turned to Gus and said, 'See, white man, you cannot even protect your women; we will kill all the whites, your time will come. Now you can sit here and suffer your loss, just like we have suffered.' With that, he struck Gus across the head which left him sprawled on the floor still tied to his chair.

Back at the Stewart home Ian and Jimmy were getting concerned that Gus and his family had not returned. By two o'clock, after repeated calls to the pub, they decided to check up. Arriving at the pub they found the front door closed but not locked. Suspecting a problem, they ran into the pub and the carnage that awaited them.

They found Ross in a pool of blood, obviously dead; Cathy and Margaret both naked and severely beaten but thankfully still breathing; Gus was unconscious and strapped into his office chair. Ian, with Jimmy's help, picked up the chair and freed Gus who immediately regained consciousness. He opened his eyes to see his two friends and let out a cry that was almost inhuman; his family had been decimated.

As a trained professional, he pulled himself together and barked out instructions to his friends. 'Ian, phone for an ambulance, tell them there is a doctor on-site and to bring rape kits. Jimmy, call the cops but wait a few minutes, I want the ambulance to arrive first. I don't trust the police and I want to take DNA swabs for evidence. After you've called the cops, backup the CCTV disks. Everything will have been recorded, I want an extra copy, just in case. I am going check on the girls.'

Jimmy and Ian left Gus alone to tend to Cathy and Margaret. Cathy was awake but unresponsive to any questions from Gus, she appeared to be in shock. Margaret was unconscious, possibly in a coma. Both had severe head and face trauma and both were bleeding from the anus and vagina.

Ian and Jimmy, tasks completed, returned, 'Jesus, Gus, what the fuck happened here?' asked a still stunned Ian.

Gus went through the sequence of events; at the end he said, 'The cunt that started it said his name was Thomas Sithole and hinted his uncle was someone of importance. Any ideas?'

'There is a Mopani Sithole who is Minister of Police – an ANC bigwig. We better hope that it is not him. These Kaffirs are totally corrupt, good idea to get evidence before the cops arrive.'

'Ian, I have been an advocate of the new South Africa but tonight has brought it home to me how wrong I have been. They've raped and murdered my family and they are doing the same to the country. Hopefully justice will prevail and these bastards will be locked up and the keys thrown away. It's a pity we no longer have the death penalty.'

The conversation was interrupted by the arrival of the ambulance. Gus supervised the taking of vaginal and anal swabs for DNA purposes. He helped load his wife and daughter into the ambulance. He told the attending medics that he would wait for the police before following them to the hospital. Ross' body would have to remain until the police finished their investigation.

As an afterthought, Gus collected the beer bottle that was used to slash Ross' throat and the one that he had been repeatedly smashed with against his head.

The police arrived exactly forty-three minutes after the call had been placed. A seriously overweight black sergeant appeared to be in charge, he was accompanied by two black constables. He introduced himself and his two associates. His first question was that this being a restaurant, could Gus possibly provide him and two colleagues with some coffee and something to eat.

Ian completely lost it, 'There has been a murder and two rapes, and you want something to fucking eat? Jesus Christ, what the fuck do you think this is? Do your fucking job if you are capable; it's taken you almost an hour to get here.'

'Sir, don't you shout at me. I am a police officer and it has been a busy day. Where are the other two bodies?'

'There is only one body, my son Ross, over there under the tablecloth. The other two are not dead, just raped and beaten and on the way to the hospital.'

'You should not have moved them until we the police got here.'

'I am a doctor. I moved them because they needed medical help and they may well have been bodies by the time you took to get here. This is your crime scene; I suggest you investigate.'

The three policemen mulled around aimlessly talking in Xhosa, no one taking any notes. The sergeant lifted the cloth off Ross and dumbly asked Gus, 'How did this one die?'

'Jesus, he was stabbed to death with this broken bottle! I have it in a bag for fingerprints. Can I release my son's body for the medical examiner now? By the way, where is he or she, surely you called them out?'

'No, I will do that later. It is very late now; you must come to the station and make a statement. We are finished here.'

'Gus, go, Jimmy and I will photograph everything here. Make sure these idiots take those rape kits and beer bottles into evidence. Take the CCTV disks. I will make another copy, just in case. Call one of your doctor connections and get a medical examiner out here now, we will wait. Don't take any shit from these fools. Call us if you need anything.'

Gus and the cops left. 'Jesus, what a mess. How the hell does this happen to the one guy who had the most belief in the New South Africa and has done more for black development than anyone I know? These Kaffirs are going to wreck this country. Jimmy, give Lynne a call and tell her and Dee what has happened. I'm sure they'll head for Groote Schuur to see Cathy and Margaret.'

Gus was taken to Constantia police station where he made a detailed statement, laboriously documented by a black female constable. Gus read it and signed the document. He gave the sergeant the rape kits, the two beer bottles and CCTV disks and insisted they be logged as evidence. This was reluctantly done. Free to leave, he ordered a taxi and headed for the hospital.

He arrived to find Lynne, Dee and Jimmy waiting nervously in the emergency waiting room. Both girls were in surgery. Ian called to say the coroner had been and Ross' body had been removed to the mortuary. Gus checked with the admitting nurse and was glad to find out that a second set of rape swabs had been taken and recorded.

Despite his protestations, Gus was taken into an emergency room where he was attended by a young doctor. It was established that he had a broken nose, fractured cheek bone, two broken ribs and cuts that required stitching. He allowed the cuts to be stitched up and his broken ribs to be strapped. The nose and cheek bone would have to wait until he had news on his wife and daughter.

It was nearly seven in the morning when a weary looking doctor emerged from surgery. Seeing Gus' beat up face, he knew immediately who the husband was. He walked up to Gus and shook his hand, 'Doctor, your daughter is out of surgery, she had a ruptured spleen which I had to remove, extensive damage to the genital regions from the rape and severe head trauma. Her left leg was dislocated at the hip, I reset it. I have put her into an induced coma to combat any possible brain swelling. It is too early to tell but the prognosis is not good. She may also have some spinal damage. What kind of savages did this to her? My colleague is still attending to your wife. My sympathies on the loss of your son, I don't know what this country is coming to.'

Gus thanked the doctor and turned to his friends. Lynne and Dee were crying uncontrollably, Ian and Jimmy with faces set in stone. 'I am going in to see Margaret. I am not sure if she will know I am there but I must see her.'

Nearly four hours later the second doctor emerged from surgery and headed over to Gus. The doctor shook his hand and guided him to one side. 'Sir, your wife is out of surgery and been moved to the ICU. I have given her something to make her sleep. I have never seen anything like this before. She has a broken jaw, both arms broken, her left leg fractured above and below the knee, several broken ribs, severe damage to her vagina and anus, a punctured lung and some internal bleeding. Hopefully no permanent damage to her liver, we will keep an eye on that. We have repaired everything physically that we can. With the beating she has had, I would be worried about her mental state. You can go in and see her, she will be out for the next five or six hours. I recommend you go home and we will call if any change or either one regains consciousness.'

Gus thanked the doctor and followed the waiting nurse to the ICU. There he found Cathy, hardly able to recognise her amongst the bandages and plaster. Her face swollen and badly bruised. He vowed that he would see justice done over this senseless crime. He kissed her on the cheek and told her he loved her. He returned to the waiting room, gave his friends an update and said they should all go back to the house and get some sleep. He on the other hand, would get his broken nose set and then go down to the morgue and see his son.

While Dee and Lynne headed back to Gus' house, Ian and Jimmy drove over to the pub. The doors were still locked as Ian had left them; there were no other signs of life. Ian unlocked the doors and they entered the premises locking the door behind them. All that remained as a reminder of the carnage of the previous night were the broken beer bottles and the dried pool of Ross' blood.

Their shocked silence was disturbed by a loud banging on the front doors. Both men walked over to the door to find a large white man and a black man carrying a camera. Not sure if it was the press or the police, Ian opened the door and inquired, 'What do you want? We are closed.'

The white guy flashed his badge and said, 'I am Detective Badenhorst. I am here to survey the crime scene and ask questions. Who are you?'

'Ian Williams and my business partner, James Wilson. We are friends and partners of the owner, Angus Stewart who is currently at the morgue with his dead son. We can help you with answers.'

'Thank you. I am sorry for your loss. I have read the statement where your partner had accused four black males of beating him, killing his son and raping his wife and daughter. These are very serious accusations and in these new times we must be careful before accusing anyone.'

'Come with me. Detective. I would like to show you something so we can stop beating about the bush,' said Jimmy, indicating Badenhorst should follow him to the office.

Jimmy switched on the office screen and pulled up the credit card of Thomas Sithole showing a photo and address details, 'Detective, make a note of the name and address please. Now as for evidence, watch the footage from the CCTV.'

Jimmy fast forwarded to the point where Gus was struck on the head and then onto the scene in the pub. Ian, who hadn't seen the footage, gasped when it started. Badenhorst sat stony faced. Jimmy stopped the video at the point where Ross was killed and that was where Cathy and Margaret had their clothes torn off and were beaten to the floor.

'As you can see, there is the evidence and it only gets worse. We have given a copy of the disks to your Constantia police station, plus vaginal and anal swabs along with the beer bottle that was used to kill my friend's son and the beer bottle he was beaten with. I trust there is enough evidence to arrest these animals, particularly Sithole.'

'Thank you, sir. I will need to take the CCV TV recorder with me into evidence,' said Badenhorst.

'Why, you have a copy of the disks?' said Jimmy.

'Police protocol. Please do not speak to the press until we have made an official statement. It is a very sensitive issue.'

'Why is it a sensitive issue? The evidence is as clear as day,' said Jimmy.

'Thomas Sithole is the nephew of the Minister of Police, Mopani Sithole. I am just following orders, I cannot say I agree with them but under today's affirmative action, it is what it is. So again, no press,' stated Badenhorst.

Badenhorst and the camera man left taking the CCTV recorder with them 'Don't worry Ian, we have copies here and I copy the stuff automatically to my central server. Badenhorst looked a bit nervous; we are going to have to be careful that the cops don't fuck up this case,' remarked Jimmy.

Jimmy called a cleaning company to come and remove Ross' blood stains and those where Cathy and Margaret were raped. Ian went into the kitchen to rustle up some food and coffee. Jimmy printed a sign 'Closed until further notice' and stuck it on the front door.

Just after 2 pm the telephone in the office rang. Ian got up and answered it, 'Can I speak with Doctor Angus Stewart please? I am Jake Alberts from the *Cape Argus*.'

'Mr. Alberts. Angus is not available. The police have told us not to talk to the press until they have made a statement. so thanks for the call but "No Comment".'

'Hold up, the police have made a statement, obviously you haven't seen it. I can read it to you and maybe you can comment on it.'

'Typical; okay, I will put you on speaker phone so my partner can also hear you. Go ahead,' said Ian.

'Okay, the gist of it is, "Four black youths have been accused of attacking a prominent white Cape Town doctor in one of his many business operations. Late last night at the popular bar, Scruffs, a bar near UCT, a scuffle broke out when the owner evicted the four youths, reasons unknown at this time. Some damage was done to property and minor injuries occurred. It appears there were racial undertones which caused the confrontations. There is no evidence at this time to corroborate the doctor's accusations. The investigation is following up on some leads." I am not sure why they would make a statement on a minor happening like this, in my opinion it sounds like a cover up. Any comments?'

'*Cape Argus* you say. Get yourself up here and we will give you the real story, just make sure your paper is brave enough to print it,' demanded Ian.

With Alberts agreeing, Jimmy switched on the TV to SABC TV1. Scrolling down the bottom of the screen was breaking news; 'Rich white Cape Town doctor racially abuses four black students and evicts them from his bar. More to follow.'

'Christ, the bullshit has already started. How the hell are they going to cover this up? We need to get the truth out there real quick. I don't think we can actually show Alberts the tape, but we can tell him the story and he can "follow the bodies" as they say. I don't know how Gus is going to get over this. Shit, that was quick, Ian, see who is knocking on the door.'

To Ian and Jimmy's surprise it was Gus. Ian let him in and the two of them went over what had happened since they last saw him. Gus in turn brought his two friends up to date. The coroner confirmed that Ross had died virtually instantly. Margaret was in an induced coma and Cathy conscious but was not able to recognise anyone or communicate. The doctors say it could just be shock added to the amount of pain killers she is on.

A further knocking on the front door alerted them to the arrival of Jake Alberts. He had arrived with copies of the all early evening newspapers.

The Sowetan, a black ANC-supporting paper, carried the headline; 'Prominent white Cape Town doctors attacks four black students after racial outburst'. The story line went on to describe multi-millionaire white doctor engaging the students in a racial outburst and then physically attacking them. The students defended themselves and some people were hurt. The piece ended with the note that this was the same doctor involved in setting up the non-profit clinics. Without actually blaming him, they noted that he removed himself from the project once the ANC-led investigation showed financial irregularities.

The white-owned papers all carried a small front-page story describing the incident. All mentioned the millionaire white doctor and four young black students. All suggested it was a racial attack and self-defence on the part of the students. Other than Gus' name, no others were referenced. Only the *Bloemfontein Chronicle* hinted that the police were holding back key information.

'I have seen the various TV news casts and all have a similar theme. You, Doctor, instigated the situation and any damage that was done was in self-defence. Do you care to comment?'

'No comment, just follow me,' said Gus.

Gus led them into the pub, 'That is the blood of my son, Ross, 20. He is in the morgue at Groote Schuur, you can see him there. I am going to show you some CCTV footage and I will print some hard copy images from there. Follow me.'

Gus led Alberts into the office. He pulled up the credit card record for Sithole, together with his picture. He pressed a button and a hard copy printed of the photo which he handed to the reporter.

'Name Thomas Sithole, 24. First year student at UCT currently doing a "Fine Arts Degree." He has attended the university for five years, still doing a first-year course. Notice his orders from last night. They ordered – among other things – twelve beers five minutes before closing time. Now turn your attention to the screen.'

Gus played the video showing the start of the confrontation and up to them leaving, 'Are you clear what happened? Good, here is a copy of the four of them at the table.'

The next scene Gus showed was him bound to his chair with Sithole smashing him across the face with a beer bottle, he printed a copy. He moved the video on a few frames until he stopped it showing Cathy, Margaret and Ross being held by the other three blacks; he printed a copy and handed it to Alberts.

'That is all I am going to show you. The police have a copy and so do we. They have the DNA and fingerprint evidence. I suggest you visit the hospital and morgue and check the condition of my family. I will give you a document allowing you access. Any questions?'

'Just one. Do you have any idea why the police have played down this incident?'

'Follow the perpetrators, especially the leader, and you will see why. Justice needs to be done here. Thank you, just print the truth.'

Alberts thanked Gus for his time, shook hands with all of them and left clutching his printed copies.

The late edition *Cape Argus* ran with the lead story. 'Evidence suggests a cover up by the Police.' The story went on to say that new evidence shows that the four black students were the real perpetrators of the incident at Scruffs. The writer claimed that he had incontestable evidence that the doctor had been beaten, his wife and daughter were in hospital with severe injuries and his son was in the morgue. No names were mentioned but it was claimed that the architect of the whole affair was the nephew of a prominent ANC cabinet minister.

The editor of the *Argus* was summoned to the Constantia Police station to be interviewed about his newspapers slanderous allegations. The meeting lasted all of five minutes; the editor produced three photographs of the key incidents and the Police Commander backed down.

Now that the name of the leader of the group was out in the open, the police were compelled to follow up on the allegations. Although the police were under the impression that they had the video evidence under control and could keep the incident out of the public eye, it was obvious the whole thing would escalate.

The telephones at the Stewart home and at Scruffs rang incessantly. The news media were hungry for the story. Gus vowed to speak to no outlet other than the *Argus* and the *Bloemfontein Chronicle.*

The police, now under pressure to make arrests, brought in Thomas Sithole. Under pressure, he named his three accomplices. The police announced the arrest of Thomas Sithole, 24, student at UCT; Dumisani Sonke, 25, unemployed; Moses Maseka, 24, unemployed; and Nelson Moyana, 24, unemployed. No mention was made of any connection to an ANC Member of Parliament.

It didn't take long for the media and public to make the connection between Thomas Sithole and his uncle, Mopani Sithole.

Just two days after the attacks, the four blacks appeared in the Cape Town Magistrates court before the black Judge, the Honourable Sikele Machopene. The charges were read out accusing all four of the same crimes; affray with cause to bodily harm. The defendants were not asked to plead, and the Judge asked if the defendants' lawyer had anything to add. The lawyer made a statement, 'Your Honour, the accused vehemently deny the accusations and I request the charges be dropped. It is obviously a plot to discredit my clients and cover up what was a racial incident.'

'Counsellor, you do not demand in my court. The trial date is set for February 25.'

'Your Honour, my clients are all upstanding members of the community and no flight risk, I appeal that they be allowed out on bail.'

'Granted. R500 per person, payable to the clerk of the court. Dismissed.'

The packed courthouse were stunned. R500 bail for what could be a rape and murder case. Gus, Ian and Jimmy were flabbergasted, this was complete bullshit.

As the accused were leaving the courtroom, they passed close by Gus; Sithole leaned across and said, 'See Doctor, you can't touch us. Be very careful because you are next.'

Ian had to restrain Gus who was ready to climb over the railing and attack Sithole. 'Leave it, Gus, the courts will take care of him. There is enough evidence to bury the bastards.'

For the next two weeks leading up to the trial, the media was full of speculation. Was the 'White Doctor' the perpetrator, was he a throwback to the old Apartheid days? Were the Police covering up due to one of the accused being the nephew of the Minister of Police? All would be revealed on February 25, 1999.

The trial opened to a packed house. Gus, Ian, Jimmy and Chubby were seated in the second row directly behind the prosecutor's table. Lynne, Dee and Fiona chose not to attend. Cathy and Margaret were still in hospital. It was obvious who the 'White Doctor' was as Gus was still showing all the effects of his beating. One half of the court was made up of blacks, many dressed in the traditional ANC colours of green, yellow and black. The other half were the press and those who managed to get a seat.

The prosecutor was black and the defendants' lawyer white. All four accused chose to be tried at the same time.

Calling the court to order, the white judge, the Honourable Justice Ralph Martindale, read out the charges. The charges were listed as breaking and entering, assaulting the four members of the Stewart family and a manslaughter charge for causing the accidental death of Ross Stewart. No mention of rape.

Gus stood up and shouted out, 'What about the rape of my wife and daughter? What nonsense is this?'

'Sit down, Doctor. Any more outbursts and I will remove you from my courtroom.' Gus, still fuming, sat down. Nodding towards the prosecutor, the Judge said, 'Counsellor, go ahead with your opening comments.'

Dingaan Mopanyane stood up bowed to the judge and turned to address the court. 'We will show the evidence before this court that the accused are guilty of the charges laid upon them. We will prosecute to the fullest letter of the law. Thank you.' And sat down.

Shit, thought Gus, this guy is useless, what a pathetic opening statement. Well, at least the evidence will show truly what happened and they will get done for murder.

The lawyer for the defence, Counsellor Philip Watson, stood and began, 'Your Honour and Members of the Court, we refute the charges that the prosecution has brought as nothing more than mischief-making. There are no eye-witnesses, only the word of an Apartheid idealist, elitist, privileged white doctor. We challenge the prosecution to prove any of these charges. Thank you.' He sat down.

'Mr. Mopanyane, call your first witness.'

'I call Sergeant Alfred Nduna.' The fat sergeant from the initial investigation waddled in and sat down. 'Sergeant, in your own words, can you tell this court what you observed?'

'The call came into the Constantia Police Station about a disturbance at the place called Scruffs. I, with my two constables, arrived on the scene. It was very early in the morning. I requested some food and coffee for me and my men as we were hungry. That man,' he said pointing at Ian, 'told me to fuck off and do my job. It was very upsetting.'

Laughter broke out all around the courtroom. 'Just tell us what you saw. Continue.'

'I observed a body that was covered by a tablecloth. I could see it was dead. I asked where the two other bodies were and the man told me they had gone to the hospital. I told him he should have waited for the police to arrive and he said if he waited that long, they would both be dead.' Again, laughter echoed around the room.

'What happened next?'

'We were finished our examination and I instructed the Doctor that he come with me to the Police station to make a statement.'

'Did the doctor offer you any evidence?'

'Yes, he gave me the beer bottles used to beat him with and plastic bags with DNA swabs that he said were from his wife and daughter. He also gave us what he said were video disks containing evidence. We then left and he came to the police station and made a statement.'

'Thank you, Sergeant, no more questions.'

Watson stood up. "Sergeant, you say the two alleged bodies were not in the building when you arrived.' Getting a positive answer he continued. 'So it was not possible for you to have taken the swabs or even observed them being taken?' Again a positive answer. 'So, it is my belief that the swabs or the DNA found on them cannot be admitted in evidence. A person who may have actually perpetrated the crime could not prove the swabs were from his wife or daughter. Is that correct?'

'Yes.'

'So, you saw no bodies of two supposedly raped females and were given DNA swabs from some unknown source?'

'Yes.'

'What about the beer bottles? Did you find any fingerprints?'

'No.'

'So, no evidence that my clients were even there, other than the say so of Doctor Stewart,' said Watson.

'Yes Sir.'

'Thank you. Your Honour, I move to request that both the DNA and beer bottles be removed from the evidence as they were not collected under police supervision. Moving the so called bodies without police permission is tantamount to destroying evidence. Any further reference to either item should be excluded from this trial.'

'I agree,' replied the Judge. 'Councillor, call your next witness.'

'I call Detective Badenhorst.'

Badenhorst took his seat in the witness box. 'Detective, tell us in your own words what you observed.'

'I arrived later in the morning and found Messrs. Ian Williams and James Wilson, who informed me that they were business partners of Doctor Stewart. They related what they understood had occurred the previous night.'

'Did they offer any evidence?'

'Yes. They showed me a screen display with a picture and details of a Mr. Thomas Sithole and what food and beverages he had purchased.'

'Is Mr. Sithole in the courtroom today? If so, can you point him out please and continue?'

Badenhorst pointed to Sithole and continued. 'Mr. Wilson printed a copy of the photograph for me. I warned him not to make false accusations as the photograph might have no significance as to what had happened. He told me that the whole incident had been recorded on CCTV. I told Wilson that I would have to take the recorder in as evidence, which I did. I then left and went back to the station where I entered the recorder into evidence.'

'No further questions.'

'Detective, what do you think the reason was that you were shown a picture of Mr. Sithole?'

'I believe it was to guide me towards seeing Mr. Sithole as one of the so-called perpetrators.'

'Did you believe that this was crucial evidence and could somehow prove Mr. Sithole guilty?'

'No.'

'What did you find on the CCTV recorder?'

'We played through the recordings and found nothing of consequence until at exactly 10.52 pm. At that time Doctor Stewart approached Mr. Sithole's group and told them to drink up as it was closing time. Mr. Sithole, who had just received a new round of beers, replied that they would leave when they had finished drinking. Doctor Stewart objected and told them to leave immediately. At this point Mr. Sithole told the Doctor to fuck off. It then deteriorated into a slinging match with the Doctor threatening to call his security team and have them taken care of.'

'What happened next?'

'Mr. Sithole and his group left and the doors were locked behind them. They left their unfinished drinks behind.'

'What time was this?'

'They left the building at 10.59pm.'

'Was there any physical confrontation?'

'No.'

'What else was seen on the video recorder?'

'Nothing, it ended at midnight.'

'No further questions, Your Honour.'

'Thank you, Counsellor. At this point I suggest we break for lunch. Court will convene in one hour.'

During the break Gus sought out Dingaan Mopanyane. 'Mr. Mopanyane, the police are obviously lying about the video evidence. I have in my possession copies of the entire incident. Can you ask the judge to enter them into evidence? Also, where are the swabs that were taken at the hospital? I also want to know why you do not allow me to be seated at the prosecution table as I am the victim here?'

'Doctor, let me make one thing clear, I am the prosecutor here, not you, so let me do my job. As for you not being at the prosecutors table, it is the state bringing the charges, not you. Now go away and let me gather my thoughts.'

'I will tell you this, Mr. Dingaan Mopanyane, if your ineptitude allows these killers to walk free, I will personally send copies of the CCTV disks to all the media outlets I can find.'

When the trial resumed, Mopanyane asked the Judge if he could approach the bench. The Judge agreed and Mopanyane was joined by Watson.

'Your Honour, during the recess I was approached by Doctor Stewart who indicated that he had copies of the CCTV disks that will prove that the so-called altercation extended past 10.59 pm. I request that they be entered into evidence.'

Martindale looked over to Watson, 'Any objections, Counsellor?'

'I strenuously object. It is over two weeks since these charges were brought against my clients, in that time anything could have been done to those disks to add compromising data to the detriment of those accused. It is well known that Mr. Wilson is some kind of computer genius and I am sure that he would do anything to assist his partner. They should not be allowed into evidence.'

'I agree, permission denied. Please continue with your next witness.'

'I call nursing sister Julienne Peters.'

'Miss Peters, were you in attendance in the emergency room at Groote Schuur on the night of February 9 of this year?'

'Yes, I was.'

'Did you attend to two white females who were brought in as alleged rape victims?'

'Yes I did. Because of the allegations of rape, I followed protocol and took vaginal and anal swabs as evidence.'

'What were the conditions of the two victims?'

Objection, Your Honour, what is the relevance of this line of questioning? There are no charges of rape in these proceedings.'

Turning to Mopanyane the Judge asked, 'Where are you going with this line of questioning?'

'The DNA on the swabs will link the accused to the scene of the crime beyond 10.59 pm and also prove this was more than just affray.'

'Were these swabs entered into evidence and if so can they be produced?'

'The swabs were handed over to the Constantia Police Station and it appears that they have been misplaced.'

'Counsellor, you should know better than to waste this court's time with unsubstantiated testimony. Your witness may be excused as there is no relevance in her testimony. Please call your next witness.'

'I call the ambulance driver, Juan Fernandez.'

'Before you proceed, Counsellor, what is the purpose of this witness?'

'Your Honour, I will show that the two females were collected from Scruffs and delivered to Groote Schuur.'

'As there is no relevance in that testimony, do not waste any more of our time. Call your next witness.'

'I have no further witnesses Your Honour.'

'Mr. Watson, you may call your first witness.'

'Your Honour, I call Doctor Eugene Smithers.'

'Doctor, state your name and profession for the court.'

'I am Doctor Eugene Smithers, a Medical Examiner for the Cape Town region.'

'Doctor, were you called out to the establishment called Scruffs in the early hours of February 10 of this year?'

'Yes I was. I received the call at 7.45 am and arrived on the scene at 8.05 am.'

'What did you observe?'

'I was met by Mr. Ian Williams who directed me to the dead body which he identified as one Mr. Ross Stewart.'

'Was there anyone else present?'

'No.'

'Were you able to establish cause and time of death?'

'Yes. The cause of death was that the carotid artery in the neck had been severed by a sharp object; he would have died almost immediately. I established the time of death to be between the hours of 1.30 am to 2.30 am. Definitely no later than 2.30 am.'

'Was any reason for the delay in calling for your services given?'

'I was told the delay was due to the ineptitude of the police department. Mr. Williams said that Sergeant Alfred Nduna of the Police Department forgot to call for an ME, and a call had to be made to one of Doctor Stewart's medical friends to ask for our services.'

'Did you find this a little strange?'

'Yes, I did.'

'Thank you, Doctor, no further questions.'

'Mr. Mopanyane, your witness.'

'No questions, Your Honour.'

'Mr. Watson, call your next witness.'

'I call Mr. Thomas Sithole. Mr. Sithole, please state your name and profession for the record.'

'I am Thomas Sithole. I am a student at University of Cape Town.'

'Sir, do you frequent the establishment called Scruffs on a regular basis?'

'No, this was my first visit. We were celebrating the gowning of some of our comrades at the university. This place was the closest.'

'Can you tell us in your own words what occurred on the night in question?'

'Me and my three comrades were having a few drinks. We ordered a last round just before closing time. At about five minutes before closing Stewart approached our table. We were unaware of who he was or what position he held. He bluntly told us to drink up as he was closing; he was very aggressive. I told him we would finish our drinks, but he told us to leave immediately. Unfortunately, I told him to fuck off, which was wrong of me. He told us to get out in thirty seconds or he would call his security team who in his words "they just love cleaning out troublemakers". We got up and leaving our drinks behind, we left the building. I heard the doors locking behind us.'

'Did you at any time have any physical contact with Mr. Stewart?'

'No.'

'Did you at any time feel physically threatened by Mr. Stewart?'

'Yes, he threatened to call his security team and we all know just how much enjoyment those thugs get smacking us black boys around the head.'

'No more questions, Your Honour.'

'Mr. Sithole, how long have you attended UCT and what course are you following?'

'I have been a student at UCT since 1995. I am doing a Degree in Fine Arts.'

'What year are you in study-wise?'

'First year.'

'So, going into your fifth year at UCT you are starting as a first year Fine Arts student? Are you not also the chairman of the Black Students Organisation who are radically active in trying to exclude white students from attending UCT?'

'Objection, Your Honour. What is the relevance of these questions?'

'I will show how Mr. Sithole has a history of baiting white people and because of this, he is the instigator and perpetrator of all of the incidents of the night in question.'

'That is all supposition; change your line of questioning.'

'Based on that ruling I have no further questions.'

'Mr. Watson, call your next witness.'

'No further witnesses; the Defence rests.'

'With all witnesses called, this is a good time to break for the day. Counsellors, prepare your closing arguments; we will reconvene at 10 am tomorrow morning.'

As the crowd left the court room, Gus made a beeline for Mopanyane. Before he could get anywhere near him, he was blocked by two very large Bailiffs. 'Mopanyane, I warned you. You are totally inept and losing this trial because of it. I will release the disks to the media if those four animals walk free.'

Ian and Jimmy managed to drag the incandescent Gus away and the three of them, accompanied by Chubby, left the court room. They were accosted by a tidal wave of media all asking for a comment.

'No comment at this time,' said Gus to the waiting media. The four of them headed for the waiting car driven by Fiona.

Once in the car, Gus let loose, 'These bastards are going to ensure that they walk! We have to release the disks before tomorrow's verdict comes in.'

'Gus, we need to think this through. No media is going to release them to the world at this time. I don't think it will change the verdict. The charges are breaking and entering, assault and manslaughter. Nothing on rape and murder; let it play out. Whatever the verdict, we release the disks and once out we can go after rape and murder, that will put them away for life.'

The following morning at 10 am the trial reconvened. Mopanyane, on the Judge's instruction, got up to give his closing arguments.

In a rambling mostly incoherent jumble of unconnected statements, Mopanyane failed to prove any of the prosecutions charges. He ended off with the ridiculous statement 'Members of the court, we the prosecution charge you find the defendants guilty and prosecute them to the fullest letter of the law.'

Watson opened his closing arguments with, 'Thank you, Counsellor Mopanyane. The prosecution has failed to provide any evidence that the accused had remained or returned to Scruffs at any time after 10.59 pm when they were shown to leave the premises. The alleged CCTV evidence proves that my clients left the building at 10.59 pm and did not return. The Medical Examiner estimates the time of death of Ross Stewart to be between 1.30 am and 2.30 am by which time my clients had long since departed. My clients admit to there being a non-physical altercation between them and Stewart that was provoked by racial slurs from the aforementioned Stewart. As there is no physical evidence to connect my clients to any charges, you can only bring in one verdict "Not Guilty to all charges." Thank you for your attendance.'

Justice Ralph Martindale faced the courtroom in one of the most bizarre scenes ever witnessed in a South African court room; he announced he had reached a verdict.

'As to the charge of breaking and entering, I find the defendants not guilty.'

'As to the charge of assault, I find the defendants not guilty.'

'As to the charge of manslaughter, I find the defendants not guilty.'

The court room erupted. The black majority in the room began chanting ANC slogans and anti-white threats. 'Viva ANC!' 'Kill the whites!' 'One bullet, one Boer!' The black Press hurried away to post their headlines celebrating black justice. The white press would hint at the ineptitude of the prosecution and police and compare the trial to the O.J. Simpson trial where justice bowed to black pressure.

Gus, Jimmy, Ian and Chubby left the building and vowed to themselves to continue the fight for justice. Outside the courthouse Gus was confronted by Sithole and his three cronies. Sithole walked over and spat at Gus, 'You see Doctor, I told you we will win. The time for whites in this country is over; we will kill all of you. Be very careful as you will be next. Maybe we will come and visit you and finish the job.'

Over the next couple of days, the media frenzy continued. Gus approached a number of the local white-backed newspapers and offered to provide the full uncensored version of the CCTV disks. Surprisingly, there were no takers. Most of them acknowledged to him that it was obvious that the police – maybe as high up as the Minister of Police – had interfered or suppressed evidence but none were willing to make the accusations.

The British newspaper '*The News of the World*' approached Gus with an offer to purchase the disks. Gus refused a large cash offer, instead he offered them free of charge. A representative of the paper was handed a password-protected copy for delivery to his editor. The password was emailed to the editor. On review the editor contacted Gus and said the disks were even too explosive for *The News of the World* and they would not risk publishing any of the visuals. He said they would, however, publish a story on what took part on the night of February 9, 1999 with the footnote that visual evidence was able to corroborate their story.

On Friday March 5, 1999 *The News of the World* broke the story of the murder of Ross Stewart and the rape of his sister Margaret and his stepmother Cathy. The two females were still in hospital; one in a coma and the other awake but unable to communicate.

The fall out was instantaneous, the South African President, Nelson Mandela, contacted his British counterpart, Tony Blair, and demanded that the fabricated and slanderous story published that morning in *The News of the World* be retracted and the necessary apologies be made.

Initially Blair resisted interfering in a newspaper story until he heard the word 'racist.' It was explained that the accuser, the white doctor Angus Stewart, had a history of racist behaviour and was also implicated in an audit failure of hospital clinics where funds donated by the Australian Government were unaccounted for.

Under pressure from 10 Downing Street, *The News of the World* issued an apology to the South African Government and its Department of Justice.

On March 9, exactly one month since the attack, Gus received more bad news. He was called to the hospital where he was informed that his daughter had been put on life support. She had suffered at least six convulsive attacks. Each one had stopped her heart and each time the attending doctors had managed to restart it. The seventh and last one they had failed so they had put her on life support which kept her heart beating and her body breathing. In deference to a fellow doctor, they had left the decision to continue with life support to Gus.

Gus, seeing his young daughter lying there badly beaten, disfigured and unable to breathe on her own, made the decision to turn off the life support machine. Moments later Margaret expired; a tearful Gus asked that she be moved to the morgue so as he could make funeral arrangements.

With a heavy heart, he walked over to the ward where his wife Cathy lay. She had her eyes open and they appeared to follow him. Still heavily bandaged, she lay on her back not moving. She was in what had been diagnosed as a vegetative state. Patients had been known to come out of this condition but it was unlikely. Gus sat down next to her and gently told her the news of Margaret's passing; there was no reaction.

Gus returned to his empty home in Constantia and called Jimmy.

'Hey Jimmy, I called to let you know that Margaret passed away today. She had a number of convulsions and was put on life support. I made the decision to switch it off. Cathy shows no improvement, I think the brain damage is beyond repair. She may last for a day, weeks or years. My life is fucked and those bastards are walking around free.'

'Gus, I'm so sorry. Is there anything I can do?'

'I cannot go back to Scruffs. I know we said we wouldn't sell so I want to shut the place down and would appreciate your input.'

'I will call Ian and Chubbs and let them know and see what they say. Lynne and I will catch a flight in the morning. Hang in there, Mate, we will see you tomorrow.'

Jimmy set up a conference call with Ian and Chubby to pass on Gus' news.

'Sad to hear about Margaret but I think he made the right decision. I think we should hold off on closing down UCT. I do have a concern though. Here at the Durban pub we have noticed a whole lot more blacks have been coming in. Mostly students, we have had a bit of shit happening, mainly racial stuff. The security guys have been called a couple of times.'

'Funny you should mention that; we have seen it happening at WITS. I wonder if there is a connection. What about you, Ian?'

'Yes, we did have an issue. A group of blacks came in the other night and started with a few of the locals. It didn't last long; the locals cracked a few heads and kicked some black bums. We haven't seen anything since then. The action did seem a bit political, with the *Kaffirs* referring to Scruffs being "their bar".'

'Okay; I am going to Cape Town tomorrow. I will keep you posted. Cheers.'

Gus met Jimmy and Lynne at the airport. Lynne burst into tears and hugged Gus. 'I am so sorry for your loss. It is everyone's loss; she was a precious child. I must go to the hospital to see my friend.'

'Ian is arriving in about an hour so Gus; can you take Lynne to the hospital? I will rent a car and wait for Ian. We will come up to the house when he arrives.'

Gus and Lynne left for the hospital while Jimmy waited for Ian.

By the time Ian and Jimmy got to Gus' house, he had arrived back from the hospital with Lynne. With Gus refusing to go the pub, Ian and Jimmy took it upon themselves to pay it a visit. The plan was to dispose of any perishables and make sure the place was still secure.

When they arrived they found two black youths sitting aimlessly on the front door step. The front door and part of the adjoining wall contained posters and some graffiti. Most all of it had similar theme, 'Reopen our pub', 'We demand our pub be reopened', there were a few 'Viva ANC' posters and one claiming 'Sithole for President'.

Ian unlocked the door and the two of them entered, securely locking it behind them. Jimmy switched on the computer screen and noticed the CCTV recorder was still missing. The two of them checked the inventory looking for any perishable items that needed to be destroyed.

Finishing that task, they entered the pub where the bloodstains had still not been removed. Ian offered to contact the cleaners.

Deciding there was nothing else to be accomplished, they walked to the front door to make their departure. They were met by a mob of about fifty or so blacks. All chanting about the reopening of their pub. Looking out over the crowd, Ian spotted Thomas Sithole who appeared to be the central figure.

Sithole approached them, 'What are you two white pigs doing here? Where is the racist Doctor? We demand he opens our pub, we are thirsty for beer.'

'Fuck off, you murdering bastard. You are lucky the Doctor isn't here; he would rip your stupid head off. This is this not your pub and never will be,' said Ian.

'You are wrong white man; we' he pointed to the mob behind him, 'will kill your men and rape your women. We will take your houses and your cars. We will claim all you have taken from us.'

'If it wasn't for the white man, you people would still be running around the bush in loin clothes. So, like I said, fuck off, you are on private property. We will never open this pub again.'

Ian and Jimmy left to the mindless chants of "Viva ANC" and "kill the Boers."

'This is an orchestrated plan going on here. It's too much of a coincidence that it is happening at all of your pubs, bar my one. We need to find out who is behind it.'

'I think you are right, Ian, let's have a chat to Gus and Chubby I have some ideas.'

Back at Constantia, Jimmy set up a call with Chubby, who was in Perth, Australia with his Natal Sharks team for a Super Rugby match.

'Hey Chubbs, we hope things are going well over there, good luck for the game. I am here with Gus and Ian; we want to have a chat about the situation with Scruffs. There seems to be a concentrated effort by the black youth to destabilise the Varsity branches. We reckon there is some ANC bigwig backing them. It may be an effort on their part to force us out and take over. I think we should find out who and pre-empt them with an offer to sell.'

'What about the Bluff pub? Ian, I thought you would never sell.'

'I am not going to sell. The *Kaffirs* tried their luck stirring shit; the local boys put them in the picture. There have been no more incidents. We can make a decision on that one on its own.'

'I am more than happy to be rid of the WITS pub. What about you, Chubbs?'

'I'm glad you said it first, so am I. It has become a burden for Fiona; we don't need the money. I say sell.'

'Gus, I know you want out so here's the plan. Let's find out who is behind this and then we leak out that we are maybe interested to sell and take it from there.'

'I am a bit loathe to sell a thriving, well-respected business to a bunch of corrupt ANC thugs. We built up a huge following and we are good value for money. They just walk in and start milking the cow. It doesn't seem right.'

'Don't worry, I have a plan. It is twofold. One, we take them for a huge amount of money, and have it sent directly offshore. Two, I have a way to ensure that they totally fuck the place up and it will look like it is totally their ineptitude and greed that does it. Are we on?'

With all four partners in agreement, Chubby took on the responsibility of 'leaking' the information to the right sources. Exactly two days later he was approached by a highly placed ANC member of parliament with the request for a meeting. The meeting would have to be kept private and confidential until a deal was reached.

Chubby, due back in South Africa, agreed to meet in Cape Town; his two partners would also be present. It was decided to keep Gus out of the meeting mainly due to the high profile of his court case. The meeting was arranged for Thursday March 18 at a private home in Sea Point.

Present at the meeting were Ian, Jimmy and Chubby representing Scruffs and representing the proposed buyers were a team from the Ministry of Economic Development. The Minister himself was not present but was represented by the deputy minister who was authorised to speak and negotiate on his behalf.

Ian opened the meeting and informed all present that the sale of Scruffs would include the restaurants at UCT, Natal University and WITS only. They would only be sold as a group and not individually.

He then went on to list all the requirements that needed to be met in order for the sale to proceed.

The name of Scruffs was not part of the deal. All signage and other references were copyrighted and not for sale. All liquor licenses would be cancelled. and the new owners would need to reapply. The sale would be for the premises and fittings only. The sale of the computers and software to run them were not part of the sale but could be purchased as a separate entity. All posters and photographs were not part of the sale and not negotiable. All consumable stock is excluded from the sale. If the agreed selling price was met, it would be paid into a bank of our choosing and in US dollars.

'Speaking on behalf of the Minister, we accept those demands. We would require the purchase of all of the computers and the software to run them. Can you detail your selling price, please?'

'The purchase price of each of the mentioned restaurants is two million dollars, total six million dollars. The computers and software will cost an additional four million dollars, giving a total of ten million. If this is acceptable, I will have our lawyers draw up an agreement for signature. On signature, you will deposit the agreed amount with our lawyer and the authorisation allowing him to redeposit in an offshore bank of our designation. We want no tax liability on this sale. What sort of delay do you see, if any at all?'

'I see no reason for any delay. I can have the documents signed as soon as they are ready from your lawyer.'

'Well, I took the liberty to have them drawn up and ready. If you can have your side done immediately I think we can target April 1, 1999 as the day your clients inherit three very popular and profitable restaurants. Congratulations, we look forward to receiving your remittance.' Ian handed over the documents and shook hands.

On the way back to Gus's house, Ian looked at his two partners, 'Can you believe that? Ten million dollars tax-free without batting an eyelid. Economic Development, my arse, I bet some Comrade scores on this one. I reckon we should have asked for more.'

The next morning bright and early Ian received a call from their lawyers noting that all documents had been signed and the cash transfer made successfully. Hand over of the premises would be 5pm on March 31.

'Right, James me boy, we have the money; now let's hear your plan.'

'Okay, this doesn't affect you and the Bluff Scruffs but for the rest of us my plan is as follows:

'I have done a search of all of our regulars on file. Over all of the pubs there are only two black members and they haven't purchased anything for the last couple of months. What I suggest is we contact all of these regulars and invite them to a closing down party on March 30. We ask them to wear some Scruffs attire and offer drinks and food at a fifty percent discount. This way we get rid of all of our stock and set some benchmark for when the new owners takeover. We can auction off all the posters, photos and memorabilia with the proceeds going to charity or some deserving sports club. Any booze left over we donate to a sports club, any food we can donate to a homeless shelter. On March 31 all of our menus, products, pricing and members will be deleted.'

'Excellent idea, maybe we can get some of the press involved. They are always up for freebies,' suggested Ian,

'Not so sure about the press, Ian, but hey why not? You can deal with them. All parties are to start at each pub at the same time.'

'Anything else in your plan?'

'Oh yes, I am only getting started. We stop all purchases by Friday 26 and we close all our vendor accounts, including SAB, and delete them from the system. The new crowd will have to start from scratch. They have bought the computers and software, but software is only the object version, no source code included. They will be able to use it but not change it. So I will have some fun there.'

'Fun? Come on, what fun?'

'Well, currently I backup everything on my server. When we hand over, I will disconnect the pubs from my server, in essence meaning the pubs should do their own backups. The backup function key at each pub is currently disabled as backup is done centrally. I will enable it but it won't actually do anything, just look like it is doing something. I will add a few time-based things just to annoy and inconvenience them.'

'Tell us.'

'No, wait and see but I guarantee that they will be done and dusted within three months tops and it will be all their fault. Now, let's have a *dop* to celebrate.'

With Ian and Chubby returning to Durban, Jimmy and Lynne decided to stay on a few days with Gus. Jimmy, able to change the Scruffs software remotely, got to work on his plan. Fiona sent out the emails to the UCT, NU and WITS regulars inviting them to a 'Closing Down Party'. Only regular members with a Scruffs photo ID card would be allowed entry.

On March 22 it was announced that the popular chain of Scruffs Pubs and Restaurants had been purchase by a consortium of black businessmen; the purchase price was not disclosed. The name Scruffs would be replaced by Amandla (Freedom) but the great value and service would be maintained and even increased. A small footnote indicated the original Scruffs located on the Bluff was not part of the agreement.

Over the next week Jimmy put the finishing touches to his software updates and loaded them to the three Varsity computers. A clean-up program was added that would remove all Scruffs data as of March 31 at 5 pm.

Under the presence of heavy security, the UCT pub was reopened on the morning of March 30. Heavy security was also deployed at the other two venues. Membership only was strictly enforced. There were minor incidents but the whole process took place in a good atmosphere. Many were sad to see the end of Scruffs as a venue but hoped that Amandla would keep up the same traditions.

Surprisingly, the new owners had kept themselves at arm's length. They had been provided with a detailed operating manual for all the computer and kitchen processes. No effort had been made or they had not asked for assistance in staff training.

The morning of March 31 was spent in disposing of the remaining consumables and cleaning up the premises and the removal of the Scruffs signage. Handover was completed at 5 pm with the Scruffs lawyers handing over the keys. The press was on-site to record the passing of the white owners to the new black ones. The new Amandla signage was uncovered to a cheering totally black crowd. The new business would be open to the public on April 1 at 10 am.

The opening of the Amandla Pubs was overshadowed by the news that parliament had passed a resolution that the moratorium on the death penalty would be revoked immediately. At first, most people thought it to be an April Fool's joke, but it soon dawned on everyone that it was in fact true. All capital crimes, specifically murder and rape, would now carry a mandatory death sentence.

A little later the same day, Gus got a call from the hospital. Cathy had suffered a massive heart attack and died. Gus, accompanied by Lynne and Jimmy, made the sad journey to Groote Schuur. Cathy, barely recognisable, lay peacefully at last. Gus requested some time alone with her. Crying softly, he said his farewell, he told her she was the love of his life and he would miss her forever. He also whispered that he would make those who did this to her pay, he would see justice done.

At the same time this was happening, the Amandla pubs opened for business. Having taken over the systems at 5.01 pm the previous evening, the staff had made very little progress. Their new website was not completely configured yet and they were unable to download their menus. Not a single waiter from the old Scruffs pub was re-employed, all were recruited new and were black.

All food and drink orders had been made by telephone with the result that none of the deliveries had been entered automatically into the system. The linking of the products and their purchase and selling prices were not online when the doors opened. Waiter and table data was not in the system. Nobody had ordered the blank cards needed for ordering from the computer screens; because of this all orders were to be taken manually by the waiters.

Confusion and chaos reigned from the opening minutes; patrons, unable to order from the screen, had to wait for a server. The waiter in turn could log on but not place a computer order as the products were not on the system which resulted in the bar screen not being able to alert the barman. So, the order was handwritten, called out to the barman and delivered to the table.

Food orders were the same; with no copies of the menu, waiters had to remember the options and the prices and relate these each time to the customer which was time consuming and often done wrong. The order was handwritten and delivered to the kitchen; when complete, there was no way to automatically tell the waiter the food was ready.

As the chaos ensued, the irritation levels grew. Food was delivered to the wrong tables or it was cold. Service levels dropped steadily. When it was time to settle their bills, customers were presented with a handwritten piece of paper, which was most of the time incorrect. In many cases – especially regarding drinks – there were omissions; waiters were overworked and forgot to enter items. Bills were added up incorrectly, the VAT was either left off or incorrectly calculated. Many customers, irritated by having to wait a long time for their bills, just got up and left without paying.

At the end of the night when it was time to cash up and check stock, it was obvious that it was going to be an impossible task. There was no way to check the cash against what was sold. Manual bills had been misplaced, lost or just thrown away. The same situation was prevalent at all three locations. An executive decision was taken to temporally suspend trading until Monday April 4. They reasoned that having seen the task at hand it would take three days to get all the data on the system and order the blank computer ID cards. Someone suggested they request some assistance or guidance from the previous owners.

Friday morning Jimmy received a call from Scruffs lawyers relaying the request from Amandla for assistance. 'Tell them that I am in Barcelona, Chubby is with Natal Sharks in Argentina, Ian has no interest in helping the opposition and Gus said tell them to get fucked. My suggestion is they make it a priority to follow the operations manual and spend less time decorating the place with ANC placards and posters of 'Comrades of the Struggle'.'

Jimmy relayed the messages and his response to his partners. The consensus was one for 'let them stew'.

'It's good to see them struggle but they will get some semblance of order by Monday. Was this your plan or is there something else you have in mind?'

'No, Gus, this is of their own doing. I knew they wouldn't get sorted in time and hadn't bothered to ask for some training. The fun hasn't even started, watch this space. Friday should be fun.'

Friday evening at exactly 8 pm, with all three bars packed and the music blasting, things started to go wrong. At the end of the song playing there was a distinct pause, this was followed by a well-known Afrikaans song playing, 'We are marching to Pretoria'. The volume started to get louder until it was at maximum. The patrons looked stunned and with an expression of 'which idiot would play that tune?' the song ended, and the juke box went silent.

An enterprising young man tapped his card on the screen and selected a more appropriate number. The song he chose was replaced by 'Suikerbossie' (sugar bush) which started up softly and grew to a crescendo. The crowd turned on the poor unfortunate, shouting abuse. Someone tried to turn down the volume, without any luck. Management was called and had the same result. At the end of that song, the same thing happened again; someone selected a number and to everyone's surprise another Afrikaans number started up.

This continued through the next five numbers before the whole jukebox system went offline. There were a lot of angry murmurings directed towards the owners. All the while, this was being recorded on the CCTV.

At exactly 10.55 pm, the sound system activated and a voice came over the speakers, 'We will now play the national anthem, Nkosi Sikelel' iAfrika, please stand. The well-known anthem started; two notes into the anthem the words were drowned out by static. The static eventually cleared just in time for the second verse, the Afrikaans verse known as 'Die Stem'. This verse and the third verse the English version completed with no problems.

Angry patrons threw bottles and glasses at the speakers as though it was their fault. Scuffles broke out and some furniture was damaged. A number of people left in disgust, vowing never to return. What had started out as a relatively calm evening ended in chaos. Management solved the juke box issue by disconnecting all the speakers.

The following Wednesday, at all pubs simultaneously, the ID card system began to malfunction. New cards started printing all the text in mirror image, the photograph was somehow printing what looked like the back of the head instead of the front. This rendered the new cards useless. The facial recognition system on the screens displayed the faces inverted, thus failing to match the photo on file. Some bright sparks tried turning the screens upside down to no avail. The 'Non Regular' cards still allowed computer ordering, but the 'Regulars' cards were now useless.

On Friday at 4.55 pm a message was broadcast to all computer screens that 'Happy Hour' would start at 5 pm and last until 7 pm. All drinks and food were half price. At exactly 5 pm all prices on the system were automatically halved. Surprised staff were inundated with orders. Managers rushed to try and change prices back to their original value, only to be met with the message 'Prices set by "executive manager's name" cannot be over-ridden.' At 7.01 pm the prices all changed back to their original value plus 15%.

For the next two weeks the systems ran smoothly as designed.

On Friday April 30 at exactly 5.35 pm, what seemed like a power surge occurred at all three venues, for around two seconds the system appeared to go offline and then restart. It seemed there was no damage done and business continued. Shortly thereafter, behind the scenes, a one was added to each table number. This resulted in an order placed by table number six to be charged to and delivered to table seven and so forth. Panic ensued, customers were screaming at servers; servers were shouting at the kitchen and bar staff. All new orders were stopped while staff attempted to deliver the correct order to the correct table.

The issue seemed to sort itself out, no more wrong orders and wrong deliveries. All was fine until it was time for customers to check out. The physical orders had been corrected but the charges were still the one table out. Customers who had ordered and consumed items that should have cost more were presented with a bill for less; they promptly signed their credit card and left post-haste. Those customers that had the reverse situation refused to sign the inflated bill and demanded to see the manager. In most cases the only way to placate the customer was write off the amount and return their credit card with no charge.

At the end of the first month all three venues were unable to produce accurate sales and revenue figures that matched with the stock figures. The owners refused to believe the managers that these were the result of systems problems; accusations of theft and fraud were levelled. With owners not trusting management and management not trusting that the systems were being properly run, it was decided to no longer use the computer system. Amandla reverted to a manual system until further notice.

With a manual ordering system in place, service levels dropped to those of any normal pub. The attraction of cheap food and drink with great service – which was the key to attracting students – no longer applied at Amandla. Prices had never been as low as Scruffs but the black community still gave Amandla their patronage as they saw it as 'Their Pub'. With the service levels dropping and the prices rising, customers started drifting away. By the time the July University holidays came around, the pubs were virtually deserted.

In the meantime, Jimmy and Lynne had returned to their yacht in Barcelona and planned to cruise the Mediterranean for the duration of the northern hemisphere spring and summer. Ian and Dee had invested in a huge fifth wheel camper and decided to go off 'the grid' and tour the USA and Canada. Chubby, still heavily involved with Natal Sharks rugby and the Super 14 tournament, took Fiona with him on his trips. It was only Gus who remained full time in South Africa. Despite numerous offers from his friends to accompany them, he refused. His stated plan was to divest all his South African assets and return to Australia and resume practising medicine.

Gus had no intention of quietly selling up and slinking off back to Australia, he fully intended to keep his promise to Cathy. He purchased a white Nissan panel van and kitted out the rear interior with a mattress and straps to secure both hands and feet. He had the ground floor garage at his Constantia home modified to allow direct access to the basement. As a registered medical doctor, he secured enough ketamine and propofol to render a small army unconscious.

Ready to make good his promise to Cathy, he set out to track down the four thugs who destroyed his family. If the Justice System of South Africa couldn't or wouldn't punish the guilty, he would do it for them. Working on his own, Gus realised that he would have to pick them off one at a time. He did want all four of them present when justice would be served.

He began cruising the known black student hangouts and the known addresses of the four men. It became obvious that it was going to be near impossible to find a time when anyone was totally alone; they appeared to always hang out as a group. Finally, after three days, Gus caught a break. Moses Maseka had a girlfriend that he visited every Tuesday afternoon on his own.

Gus followed him to an apartment block in Sea Point and watched as he ascended to the sixth floor where he was let into the flat by an older white or coloured woman; obviously married and having a bit on the side. Gus parked right near the entrance to the building, got out of the vehicle, opened the back doors and removed a car jack. He placed the jack under the rear left wheel and proceeded to jack up the van to 'change a wheel'. He also raised the bonnet to give the impression that he was having some mechanical problem. All the while he kept an eye on the sixth floor.

Just over an hour later, Moses reappeared walking with a swagger and huge grin on his face. Gus, hunched over the rear wheel, waited until Moses passed by; jumping up, Gus, armed with a syringe loaded with ketamine, plunged the needle into Moses' neck. Spinning the shocked Moses around, Gus bundled him into the back of the van and slammed the doors closed. The whole incident took less than three seconds. With Moses safely incapacitated, Gus jacked down the car, closed the bonnet, started the van and drove off. No one appeared to notice anything. When he reached the corner he pulled over and scrambled into the rear. Moses was still unconscious so put up no resistance while Gus securely strapped his hands and feet and placed tape over his mouth.

Gus drove home, opened the garage door and parked the van. He closed the garage door, opened the van's rear door and dragged out the still unconscious Moses Maseka. He carried Maseka down into the basement, dumped him on the floor and shackled both his arms into chains that were secured into the wall.

He searched Maseka and removed the cell phone he found. He scrolled through the text messages looking for any that were sent or received by his three cohorts. Strangely enough most of the texts were in English and full of Bros, LOLs, and WTFs. He found various messages to all three, most just chat type.

He did, however, find two to Dumisani Sonke that were very similar and exactly one week apart. The first one was telling Sonke to meet him in the parking lot of Checkers near the Sea Point swimming pool as he had some prime *dagga*. The second one was exactly one week later was to meet at the same place as he had two girls organised, sure fucks. So reasoning that the meeting place was key and it appeared that it was only the two of them involved, he needed to send a message that would entice only Sonke.

Maseka started to come around. Gus watched him as he slowly realised that he was chained to the wall in some unrecognised place. His struggle turned to panic the minute he recognised his captor.

'Hello, Moses Maseka, remember me?'

'You cannot keep me here, what are you doing?'

'Oh yes, I can, but don't worry, your friends will be joining you soon and then we will discuss your new trial for the murder and rape of my family. You do know that the death sentence has now been reinstated. If you had pleaded guilty at the first trial you would only have gone to prison but now if the Judge finds you guilty, it will be the death sentence. Maybe if you plead guilty and show remorse the Judge will commute it to life in prison.'

'I am sorry, Sir. I plead guilty.'

'Sorry, but you are getting ahead of yourself. We will have to wait until your good friends join you. I am going to leave you now and you can watch some television.'

Gus switched on the TV and started up the attached video. The video was of the moments that Maseka killed Ross; it was on a permanent loop and would play over and over. Gus turned and left the basement. He went upstairs and sent a text message Sonke; 'Hey Bro, gotta meet, same place in one hour. I found a white Nissan van, loaded with booze. Was unlocked with keys in. Just us, we make big money.'

Gus got an instant response, 'Shoo Bro, be there.'

Gus got in his van and headed for the Checkers parking lot. He made sure to get there a little before the appointed time and to park away from the crowded areas. He saw Sonke approaching so he flashed the van headlights and popped open the passenger door. Sonke saw the van and with a little jig type dance, headed over. Sliding into the passenger seat, he was met with a needle to his neck and seconds later he slumped forward unconscious. Gus leaned over shut the door and drove off.

Arriving home, he dragged Sonke downstairs and chained him next to his sobbing partner in crime. He removed Sonke's cell phone and turning to Maseka said, 'When he wakes up you can tell him all about your little problem. In the meantime, I will change the TV program for you.'

Hitting a switch on the remote, the video changed; it started with Moses killing Ross and continued with the repeated raping of his daughter and wife. Leaving it on a repetitive loop, Gus turned off the basement lights and left the room to the sounds of Moses crying out that he was sorry.

Back upstairs, Gus began scrolling through Sonke's cell phone hoping to find something similar to Maseka, some kind of one on one meeting. Nothing stood out as obvious as the one he used on Sonke. Rereading Sonke's incoming message he had sent from Maseka, an idea came to him. Using Sonke's phone, he forwarded the message separately to both Sithole and Nelson Moyana.

Within seconds, both Maseka and Sonke's phones came alive.

Maseka from Sithole: 'You have a score. why are you cutting me out? Only Sonke, what is this?'

Maseka from Moyana: 'Hey Bro WTF only Dumi not good Bro.'

Sonke from Sithole, 'You go there alone and don't call me. Bullshit Bro.'

Sonke from Moyana, 'Hey Bro WTF why no call to me?'

Gus decided not to respond, let them stew awhile.

A couple of minutes later.

Maseka from Sithole, 'Where are you?'

Maseka from Moyana, 'Why no reply.'

Sonke from Sithole, 'You ignore me?'

Sonke from Moyana, 'Why no reply?'

Gus continued to ignore them and the messages got more and more irate. In place of the texts, the phones started ringing; Gus ignored them and let them go to voicemail. It was getting a bit late in the day and Gus figured it best to try and take the last two in one trip.

Picking up Maseka's cell, he texted Sithole, 'Sorry Bro I was going to send you a message. I have a van of booze maybe 30K. I have a buyer can you come now?'

'Don't fuck with me Bro. Why only now?'

'Had to duck the cops. Meet Buyer in one hour; be at Checkers parking twenty mins, white van.'

Picking up Sonke's cell he sent Moyana, 'Sorry delay Bro had to get buyer first.'

'Where are you now?'

'Have to get to buyer in two hours for 30K. Are you in?'

'Yes come and get me at my home.'

'No be at Checkers parking maybe in just over one hour look for white van.'

Gus loaded up two syringes, got in the van and headed for the Checkers parking lot. Gus turned into the parking lot and made a wide sweep letting the headlights run across the whole area. He immediately spotted Sithole's white BMW parked well away from the crowd. Driving slowly towards it he flashed the headlights three times, came to a stop head on to the BMW and popped open the passenger door. Sithole swaggered over and got into the passenger seat head first only to receive a needle in his neck. With a surprised look on his face, he slumped over unconscious.

Gus leaned over the inert body and pulled the door closed; turning left he headed for the far end of the lot. He stopped the van and walked around and opened the rear doors. With the left-hand side of the van backed up against the wall it gave Gus cover to remove Sithole unobserved; he placed him in the back of the van, secured him and closed the doors. He sat back and waited for Moyana.

Forty-five minutes later, Gus spotted what looked like Moyana wandering around looking for the van. He started up the engine and drove slowly towards Moyana, when he got about fifty feet away, he flashed the headlights. Moyana reacted immediately and grinning, walked towards the still moving van. Gus popped open the passenger side door but did not stop, he passed Moyana making him turn and trot after the van. Moyana caught up and climbed into the passenger seat. Gus hit the brakes forcing Moyana to fall slightly forward where he was met with a needle to the neck. Without pausing, Gus turned the van and headed home.

Arriving home, he dragged first Moyana and then Sithole down into the basement and shackled them to the wall alongside their two comrades. Gus turned off the TV and video. During the process both Maseka and Sonke had remained silent. Gus busied himself setting up a video camera pointing it directly at the four men chained to the wall. Gus waited patiently until Moyana and Sithole regained consciousness.

The two men woke slowly and confused. First Sithole and then Moyana; both stunned to find themselves chained to a wall facing a video camera. Sithole; recognising Gus; was the first to react, 'What the fuck do you think you are doing? Where is the booze? You cannot steal from us, my uncle will be sure to put you away.'

'Welcome, Mr. Sithole, you sure are one stupid fucker. There is no booze; you and these other three killers have been brought here for another reason.'

'And what is that reason? When my uncle locks you up, you will never see the light of day again. I will have you killed in prison.'

'Your outbursts and threats are not making me at all sympathetic towards you. You have been brought here to answer for your crimes towards me and my family. Tomorrow you will be brought in front of the court and admit to your crimes and will be justly judged and sentenced.'

'You are a fool, Doctor, you will never succeed in making it to the courthouse with us. My uncle and his police force will ensure that. You will be dead before you get halfway.'

'I think you are a bit confused, but then anyone doing first year studies after five years is maybe a little slow and stupid. You are already in the courthouse. I will go now and leave you to watch the reasons that you are here.' Gus flipped on the remote control and the TV burst into life, playing the murder and rape video on continuous loop. 'Good night.'

The next morning Gus got up, showered and ate a hearty breakfast. Taking his time, he went slowly down to the basement. He walked into a torrent of abuse, mostly from Sithole. Ignoring the outbursts, he walked calmly over to the TV and turned off the video. He moved the video camera to face the four accused and turned it on.

'Before we start proceedings there are some rules that need to be observed. Any continual shouting out will not be allowed. I will gag anyone who fails to obey this rule. If you wish to speak, just raise your right arm and I will hear you. Is this understood?'

Receiving no comment, he continued, 'You have been charged with the murder of my son, Ross, and the rape of my wife and daughter, both who have since died. So you will be charged with rape and manslaughter on those counts. You have spent the night reviewing your actions. Do you understand the charges?'

Sithole spoke up, 'You cannot try us on these charges, we have already faced the court and been found not guilty. It is called double jeopardy, in case you don't know.'

'Next time put up your hand, Mr. Sithole; I will allow it this time. You were charged with breaking and entry with affray, this is a trial for murder and rape which is what the first one should have been about.'

'As you are all aware, the South African Justice system has reintroduced the mandatory death penalty for capital crimes. The Judge has the authority to override that to a life sentence in certain special cases. As this is a capital case, the death penalty comes into play. A life sentence would be considered if a full confession, a show of remorse and a guilty plea is entered. The confession will be recorded and sent as evidence to the police department. I will ask you one at a time to enter a plea.'

Thinking that all of them would probably follow Sithole, that is where he started.

'Thomas Sithole, how do you plead?'

'This is not a real court. Not guilty.'

'Dumisani Sonke, how do you plead?'

'Not guilty.'

'Moses Maseko, how do you plead?'

'Guilty, sir, please. Sithole forced me.'

'Nelson Moyana, how do you plead?'

'Not guilty.'

Gus picked up masking tape and walking over to the three who pleaded Not guilty and gagged them.

'I have one guilty and three not guilty so I will deal with the testimony of Moses Maseko first. Mr. Maseko, please tell the court in your own words what occurred on the night of February 9. Please talk directly into the camera.'

Maseko explained in great detail all of his actions of that night. He insisted that Sithole had threatened him if he did not take part. He pleaded with Gus to not sentence him to death, he was extremely sorry for his actions. Gus thanked him for his testimony and informed him that he would be sentenced at the end of the trial. Gus walked over and gagged him, at the same time removing the gags of the other three.

Sithole immediately began cursing Maseko, 'You stupid bastard, you have admitted to everything and then you accuse me. You will be dead, I will kill you, you coward. This white pig has no authority over us.'

'Mr. Sithole, I have warned you about shouting out without raising your hand first. Do it again and I will gag you.'

'Fuck you. We will kill all you whites. We will rape all your woman, just as me and my Comrades have already done. Viva ANC.'

Gus calmly walked over to Sithole and gagged him.

'Mr. Sonke, you have pleaded not guilty yet the video evidence clearly shows you partook in the rape of both females. What do you have to say in your defence?'

'Please, Sir, I want to change to guilty like Moses. Sithole forced me to do it. I am very sorry but I am scared of Sithole.'

'I accept your change of plea, Mr. Sonke. Mr. Moyana, you have pleaded not guilty yet the video evidence clearly shows you partook in the rape of both females. What do you have to say in your defence?'

'Sir, Sithole forced us to go back into the building and threatened to kill us if we didn't rape the women. I am very sorry, and I want to change to be guilty.'

'Mr. Sithole, I am going to remove your gag and allow you to speak. You have pleaded not guilty yet the video evidence clearly shows you partook in the rape of both females. What do you have to say in your defence?'

Sithole, screaming in rage, ignored Gus and turned on his Comrades. 'You are weak! This white man has no rule over us. We are ANC and we will kill all the whites in South Africa. This is our land: it is a war. In a war, people die and women are raped. I am a soldier so cannot be guilty of rape and murder, it is my right to do it.'

'The court has heard from all defendants We have heard how the accused entered the building, how Maseko – on the orders of Sithole – cut the throat of Ross Stewart and allowed him to bleed to death. We have heard how all of the accused took turns in repeatedly raping Margaret Stewart and Catherine Stewart. Both females later died from the injuries caused by the accused.'

Gus turned towards the video camera and addressed it directly, 'I have heard all of the evidence from the four accused. They have had the opportunity to watch the proceedings of the night of February 9 1999. I have the admission that Dumisani Sonke, Moses Maseko and Nelson Moyana have all pleaded guilty. Thomas Sithole has pleaded not guilty, yet when asked to defend himself, he has admitted to raping both females. Under this situation, I have no hesitation in proclaiming him guilty of all charges.'

'I will close with the following comment: As a Christian country I believe in the biblical comment "An Eye for an Eye". Here we have three innocent people killed, it should only be right for three people to pay with their life. I will now adjourn this court for the day while I consider the appropriate sentences.'

Leaving the video camera running, Gus left the basement and returned upstairs. Having set up a microphone connected from the basement to his first-floor study, Gus was able to follow the heated conversation going on downstairs. All four turned against each other, accusing everyone but themselves for the situation they were in. Each one claiming that they should not be one of the three to pay with their life. All the while their conversations were being recorded by the video camera. Gus, tired of listening to their ranting, switched off the speaker, poured himself a stiff drink and headed upstairs to bed.

The following morning Gus made his way down to basement ready to bring the 'trial' to a conclusion. He opened the basement door to be greeted by a foul odour of fear mixed with sweat, urine and excrement. The four accused seemed docile and worn out. Gus walked over to the video camera and DVD recorder and changed the disk.

Gus walked over to each of the accused and taped up their mouths. He addressed the four of them. 'I have given a lot of thought to the procedure of this court and come to the conclusion that I cannot be the Judge and Jury. With that in mind, I have decided that you four will be the jury. Given that all four of you have been found guilty, I will give each of you, in turn, an opportunity to review the facts and decide on an appropriate sentence. Take into account the sentence will be based on "An Eye for an Eye". Three of you will be put to death.'

Maseko, Moyana and Sonke all made the same claim that it was Sithole who forced them to commit the crime. They were all scared of him because of the power of his government connections.

Sithole, on the other hand, made his own claim, 'Doctor, you should come to your senses. If you kill any of us, you will be arrested and hung. Let me go and I will ensure all charges against you are dropped. My uncle is the Minister of Police and he will listen to me. You will walk free.'

'I have heard all of your pleas and I am now ready to pass sentence. I will start with you, Moses Maseko. You killed my son and raped my wife and daughter; I sentence you to die.'

Gus walked over to Maseko and cutting the belt around his waist, reached in and using a scalpel, severed Maseko's penis, 'For the rapes, you lose your penis.' Moses screamed in agony. Gus grabbed him by the hair and pulled back his head, at the same he slashed Moses across the throat.

'And for the murder of my son you die the same way.' He stood back and watched Maseko die.

Next was the turn of Dumisani Sonke who hadn't stopped wailing and pleading since Gus came down the stairs. 'Dumisani Sonke, you raped my wife and daughter and those injuries were the cause of their deaths, I sentence you to die.' As with Maseko, Gus relieved Sonke of his penis. He then stepped back, drew a revolver from behind his back and drilled a single bullet into Sonke's forehead.

He then stepped up to Nelson Moyana and repeated exactly the same sentence on him. He then turned to the grinning Sithole.

'You are a clever man, Doctor, and you have a made the correct choice. I will tell my uncle that you showed compassion. Now untie me so I can leave this disgusting place.'

'Thomas Sithole, you raped my wife and daughter and those injuries were the cause of their deaths, I sentence you to die.'

'Waa, Doctor, you said only three to die for three that died. I am free, you promised.'

'Sithole, you are exactly what is wrong with this country. You kill and rape not only the white people, but your own people as well. You take no responsibility for your actions. Your ANC government is the most corrupt in Africa and that is saying something. You lie and cheat, you piece of shit. I, too, am an African, and I will now be an African and lie just as your Sergeant Alfred Nduna lied on the witness stand.'

Gus walked up to Sithole and gave him the same treatment as the previous two accused. He then turned around and addressed the video camera. 'As a medical doctor it pains me greatly to take another human life, but the four you see behind me gave up their rights as humans when they committed the crimes that they have now confessed to. The South African Justice system failed dismally in the case of the rape and murder of my family. The Police obstructed justice at every turn, destroyed evidence and refused to allow video footage of the incident into evidence. It is under these conditions that I carried out the justice the courts failed to do. I have no regrets or remorse.'

Gus switched off the video recorder. He then made five copies of the original CCTV disks, and the same number of copies of the entire proceedings that had taken place in his basement. By the time he was finished it was past midnight. He unshackled each body and carried them one by one up the stairs and loaded them into his van. He printed the name of four newspapers on individual sheets of paper; he attached a sealed envelope, each containing the entire DVD collection, to each of the bodies. He then pinned the name of the four newspapers to the envelopes. He placed the fifth copy in an envelope and addressed it to his lawyer and close friend, Desmond Rabinowitz.

At 4.00 am Gus got into his van and drove towards Cape Town's central business district. His first stop was at the offices of the *Cape Argus* where he unloaded the body Moses Maseko. He drove on to the offices of the *Cape Times* and deposited Dumisani Sonke. The third stop was at the Cape Town offices of the *Citizen* newspaper there he unloaded Nelson Moyana. Finally, he chose the local office of the *Sowetan* where he dropped off Thomas Sithole shortly before 5.00 am.

With most of the city still asleep, Gus drove back to his Constantia home. There he sent the following text message to his three close friends. 'Guys, sometime today you are likely to read or see news headlines about me. They will all probably be true. My family has been avenged. I love you guys, thank you for being there when I needed you. Take care.'

With the messages sent Gus, smashed his cell phone into pieces, dumped it into his trash and waited for the inevitable arrival of the police. He didn't have long to wait. At exactly 7.13 am he heard the police sirens; he got up and walked to his front door, opened it and stood with his hands in the air. He was thrown to the ground, handcuffed and hurled into the back of a waiting police van. He was driven to Cape Town Central Police station where he was secured into a cell with about a dozen others. He was not charged and was not read any rights. He was refused any phone calls.

Jimmy, cruising just off the island of Crete, was the first to react to Gus' text. He immediately tried to call back, receiving no reply, he called to Lynne, 'Hey, Lynne, come up here! I have just received the strangest message from Gus.'

Lynne rushed up to the bridge where Jimmy showed her the message. 'I fear this is bad news, he has done something really bad, I fear. I tried calling him and his cell seemed dead. I'm going to try Chubby; he is back in Durban so maybe he has some news.'

He dialled Chubby's number. 'Jesus, Wilson, this better be important. It's fucking quarter past eight in the morning, I am still jet lagged. What's up?'

'Did you get a text from Gus this morning?'

'Hold on, I'll check. Shit, yes, what the hell is that all about?'

'I reckon he has taken some sort of revenge on those bastards who killed his family. Check the TV or newspapers, call me back. I'm going to try and get hold of Ian, God knows where he is.'

Jimmy hung up and called Ian, 'Wow, you do know it's the middle of the bloody night here. I am in Yellowstone National Park. What's so important to wake me up at this hour? Dee, its Jimmy, go back to sleep'

'Gus sent me a text. I think he has taken some sort of revenge on those bastards who killed his family. I spoke with Chubby; he is going to find out what happened. I am near Crete so I will head there and try and get a flight to SA. Chubby will call back with any info.'

'I'll wait to hear from Chubby. The nearest airport to me is at West Yellowstone in Montana; from there I think Salt Lake City. I will make a plan to get back to SA. It may take a few days.'

The morning TV newscasts and the early editions of the newspapers all carried the story. The SABC news team led with, 'Racist white doctor murders four black youths,' the *Sowetan* with a similar headline. Both outlets made no mention of any confession DVD's, just that all four bodies were genitally mutilated, one with his throat slashed and the other three shot in the forehead. Both also made mention that the same four had been found innocent of previous claims by the same white doctor.

The other three papers led with headlines along the lines of 'Vigilante killings of four black youths.' All mentioned Gus by name and all referenced the original trial and the not guilty verdicts. All questioned the original verdicts but condemned taking the law into your own hands. The presence of the DVDs was noted and that they appeared to show full confessions of all four men.

The overseas press and news stations were divided. The far right praised the fact that justice had been done. The far left were abhorred and condemned Gus as a racist and suggested the death penalty would be justified. The conservative outlets just reported the news that included the fact that there was apparently video evidence of a full confession by all of the deceased.

Chubby, getting the basics of the story, communicated it to both Jimmy and Ian.

Two hours after he was first locked up; Gus was transferred to a single cell on his own. He was still denied any contact with a lawyer, no rights were read to him and no charges laid. He had barely settled into his new cell when had a visitor, one Mopani Sithole, the ANC Minister of Police.

'You, Doctor, have made a grievous mistake. By murdering my nephew, you will be tried, found guilty and hung by the neck. You knew Thomas was innocent but you humiliated him and scared him into confessing to a crime he did not commit. Your so-called video evidence will never see the light of day.'

Mopani Sithole turned his head and addressed the three large black policeman standing behind him. 'Teach the white pig some manners, but do not kill him as he must answer for his actions before the whole country before we legally kill him.'

Sithole turned and left. The three cops entered the cell and proceeded to beat Gus unconscious. Once he passed out, they continued to kick him in the face and ribs, only stopping when they became afraid that he might die.

It took three full days before Gus was able to stand up unaided. As soon as it was possible for him to stand up on his own, he was brought before the local Magistrate where, in a closed to the public court room, he was charged with the premeditated murder of the four men. He was not asked to plead and was not allowed bail. He was refused the request to have any visitors. Though the ANC wanted a quick trial, it was decided to set the date for three months hence on August 16, a Monday. This would allow Gus to heal and not have the brutal beating marks he now carried showing.

Gus' only communication with the outside world was through his lawyer, Desmond Rabinowitz. Ian, Chubby and Jimmy had all returned to South Africa to lend what support they could. Being denied access to their friend, they could only try and generate support and sympathy for him.

None of the news outlets would publish any of the graphic video but the right leaning papers did write or discuss some of the key instances of the so-called vigilante court case. The public, hungry for details, were left in the dark until the entire DVD collection was uploaded to the internet. A far-right white supremacist group posted them to their website under the title 'Black murderers get their payback.' Within no time at all, the site recorded over three million hits.

Public sentiment was growing. The Western Australian Government published an article on how Doctor Stewart, using a good deal of his own money, had worked with them to open clinics throughout rural South Africa with the express purpose of caring for the poor, who were mainly blacks. They were adamant that he was no racist. They condemned his actions in taking the law into his own hands but at the same time suggested that the South African Justice System had failed him. They said they had decided to pull their investment for the clinics due to the corruption of the local governments involved.

In the ensuing weeks, there was a gathering amount of sympathetic support for Gus. The general feeling among the white and liberated black communities was that Gus had suffered traumatic loss under circumstances most couldn't imagine. The fact the Justice System failed him in such obvious and corrupt manner, was garnering sympathy for his actions. When the law fails you and then the perpetrators taunt and threaten you, it must have weighed heavily on Gus.

Local TV news and the printed press were divided along political and racial lines. The right and conservatives against vigilantly taking the law into your own hands but understanding the reasons behind it. The left and most blacks were clear in that he was guilty of murder and must die.

The Times of London published an interesting take on the 'Stewart Trial'.

'49-year-old white South African, Dr. Angus Stewart is accused of being a racist anti-black; he faces charges of murdering four black youths.

Stewart being accused of having a history of racism couldn't be further from the truth. He left South Africa in March 1976 due to his disgust of the Apartheid system. During his time at Guy's Hospital, he was an avid protestor against Apartheid, being arrested numerous times for protesting outside South Africa House here in London.

He immigrated to Perth in Western Australia where he married local girl, Stacey, whom he had met during one of the London protests. Stewart ran a very successful and lucrative medical practice and became a very wealthy man. He and his wife raised two children (both later to become victims in a brutal rape and murder). Stewart continued to rail and protest against Apartheid, refusing to return to his country of birth until a free and fair Government was in place.

In 1992 with his marriage to Stacey failing and the possibility of free elections in his country of birth, Stewart divorced his wife and decided to return home. Stewart sold off his very profitable practice and donated the proceeds to the Western Australian Government with the caveat that the funds met with an equal amount from them and be used in funding medical clinics in rural South Africa. He wanted no mention that he had any part in the funding of the project.

Stewart returned to Durban, South Africa and voted for the ANC in the elections. Like many, he hoped that his country could rejoin the international community as equal partners. He and his Australian backers went on to open nearly thirty clinics, which catered for those who could not afford normal hospital treatment.

When local ANC officials started interfering in the clinics operation by inserting themselves into the process, Stewart resigned. With fraud and corruption prevalent, the Australians ended their financial involvement. Currently there are now only two clinics in operation.

While this newspaper condemns any vigilante taking the law into their own hands, it does sympathise with Stewart. The trial of those accused of raping and murdering his family was a farce and complete miscarriage of justice. One wonders if this one will be any different.

One thing for sure, Stewart is no racist. The eyes of the world will be on this trial; may justice prevail.'

With Gus making no effort to secure himself a top defence lawyer, Ian took it upon himself to make arrangements. He contacted one of South Africa's best-known defence lawyers, Michael (Mickey) Cohen, senior partner of Cohen, Leibowitz and Adelman. Cohen, aware of the publicity and exposure, agreed to take on the case. One of his first steps was to get visitation access to his client for Ian and Jimmy.

At the first opportunity his two friends paid him a visit. They were led into a secure room where they found Gus handcuffed to a table, which in turn was bolted to the floor. It had been over a month since his arrest and the beating he took was still visible. Unable to stand due to his shackles, he greeted his friends.

'Hey guys, man, it is good to see you. Sorry, I can't shake hands as you can see.'

'Jesus, Gus, what possessed you? You had to know they would catch you. If you had let us know what was going on, we could have got you out of the country and put you where they would never have found you.'

'Ian, I know you mean well, and I have no doubt you would have pulled it off. I am resigned to my fate. Ever since Cathy died, I have been unable to sleep without the nightmare of that night. I will never be able to erase that night from my mind; it will be with me forever. I have no desire to live like that. I am sorry.'

'How will you plead? I have seen the video of the "trial"; there will be no doubt in anyone's mind that you killed those bastards?' asked Jimmy.

'I am going to plead not guilty. I don't deny I killed them but I need to ensure there is a case that needs to be heard. If I plead guilty that would be it, all over and no exposure of the real reasons I did it. Mickey tells me that the full uncensored video has had over three million views on the internet. This trial needs to expose the corruption going on in this country; it has to stop otherwise it will just become another black dictatorship.'

On Monday August 16, the court case of the decade opened in the High Court Cape Town. The three presiding judges were all black; Chief Justice Lumka Manyi, assisted by Steven Zondo and Siku Mopanyane. In an unusual move, the Chief Prosecutor was none other than Dingaan Mopanyane, no relation to Siku of the same name. Gus was defended by Michael Cohen, who was assisted by Desmond Rabinowitz.

The demand of seats far exceeded the court's capacity, so a lottery system had been implemented. The public's applications for seats were accumulated and a random drawing took place. Almost 95% of the public seats had been allocated to black people. The press, both local and overseas, made up the balance. Ian, Jimmy and Chubby had been 'appointed' as assistants to the defence and as such were allocated seats directly behind the defence table.

The court opened with Justice Steven Zondo reading out the charges. 'As the Accused, Angus Stewart, you have been charged with the abduction and premeditated murders of Thomas Sithole, Dumisani Sonke, Moses Maseko and Nelson Moyana. How do you plead?'

'Not guilty, your Honour.' Gus sat down to a loud outcry from the public gallery.

Justice Manyi banged his gravel and said in a loud angry voice, 'I will not tolerate outbursts in my court. Any repeat and I will clear the court room. Councillor Dingaan Mopanyane, please proceed with your opening statements.'

'Thank you, Your Honour. We will show that the accused abducted the four victims, drugged them and shackled them to chains in his basement. He held a kangaroo court wherein he falsely accused each of them of the rape and murder of his wife, son and daughter. Then one by one, he brutally murdered them showing no mercy. This same court had previously found all four of the deceased not guilty of the crimes Stewart accused them of. We will provide video evidence of the crime that will prove Stewart is guilty as charged and deserves to be sentenced to the highest order of this court. That is all, thank you, Your Honour.' With that, Mopanyane returned to his seat.

Could this be the same incompetent Mopanyane that had failed me in the previous trial? thought Gus.

Mickey Cohen stood up, 'The defence welcomes that the Prosecution will provide video evidence in this trial. It will prove beyond doubt that the Justice System failed my client in the trial that the very same prosecutor, Mr. Dingaan Mopanyane, so incompetently tried. It will show how my client was forced to watch his family murdered and then see how those perpetrators were then allowed to walk free. He was taunted by them that he would be the next to die. The previous trial was a miscarriage of justice; do not let this one be the same. Thank you, Your Honour.'

'Before we continue, let me make one thing clear. The trial that the defence continues to refer to has no bearing on this trial. I will not allow any further reference to that trial. This is a trial against Mr. Stewart for the abduction and murder of four young men. Is that clear to both the prosecution and defence? Dingaan Mopanyane, please call your first witness.'

'Thank you, Your Honour. I call Mr. Sipho Dladla. Mr. Dladla. please state your name and occupation for the record.'

'I am Sipho Dladla and I am a reporter for the *Sowetan* newspaper.'

'Mr. Dladla, can you please tell the court of what occurred on the morning of May 7 of this year?'

'Yes, sir. Just after 5.00 am, I heard a noise outside of our Cape Town office's front door. I went to investigate and found the dead body of a man lying in the doorway. I noticed a white Nissan van driving away. I went into the office and called the police. I waited with the body until the police arrived.'

'Did you touch or remove anything from the body?'

'No, Sir.'

'Thank you, no more questions.'

'Mr. Cohen, you may cross examine the witness.'

'No questions, Your Honour.'

'Mr. Mopanyane, call your next witness.'

'I call Sergeant Alfred Nduna.' Much to the disgust of the defence, it was the same sergeant from the original investigation and the previous trial.

'Sergeant Alfred Nduna, can you please tell us what occurred on the morning of May 7?'

'We received a phone call just after 5.00 am to say a body had been found on the doorstep of the *Sowetan* newspaper's office. I was dispatched along with two constables. When we arrived we found Mr. Dladla and a dead body. The body was identified as Mr. Thomas Sithole. He was shot in the forehead and his penis had been cut off.'

'Did you find anything else on the body?'

'Yes, it had an envelope attached to the front of the body. I opened it to find a computer disk.'

'Just a single disk?'

'Yes Sir, just one.'

'Is this the disk you found?' Mopanyane showed the disk to Nduna and the three judges.

'Yes, Sir.'

'I enter this into evidence Your Honour.' Mopanyane handed the disk to the judge. 'No more questions.'

On seeing this, Gus leaned over to Cohen and whispered. 'There were four disks in the envelope, there is something wrong here.'

Cohen walked over to the witness box, 'Sergeant, you stated you found only one disk in the envelope, my client said he put four disks in the envelope. Was the envelope sealed when you opened it?'

'Yes Sir, and there was only one disk inside.'

'No more questions, Your Honour.'

Dingaan Mopanyane approached the bench accompanied by Mickey Cohen, 'Your Honour, due to the graphic nature of the contents of this disk, I recommend you clear the public from the court room.'

Manyi addressed the court room. 'We will take a recess while the television and DVD player are set up. We will reconvene in one hour at which time the general public will not be readmitted. The press only will have access.'

Gus took the opportunity to explain to his lawyers, 'There were four disks. The originals have a kind of watermark on them. Running down the bottom of screen, you will find a sequence number. If the disk was copied or edited that number will not be consecutive. I would say they have doctored the data. Can you add my four copies into evidence?'

'I can only ask but I fear they will reject the request based on that they were not in police custody but in yours.'

'What about the other newspapers where I left the other three bodies?'

'Again, I doubt it for the same reason.'

Gus and his two lawyers returned to the courtroom to find a large TV screen had been set up facing side-on to the Judges and the waiting press. On the orders of Manyi, Mopanyane pressed the play button and the TV screen burst into life.

The video started at the point where Sithole makes the statement, 'Doctor, you should come to your senses; if you kill any of us you will be arrested and hung. Let me go and I will ensure all charges against you are dropped. My uncle is the Minister of Police and he will listen to me. You will walk free.' It then jumps in sequence number to where Gus executes Moses Maseka and then continues without any break in sequence number through where Sonke and Moyana are executed. It then resumes at the point where Sithole is executed and resumes again when Gus makes the statement 'I have no regrets or remorse.' To the defence team, the missing sequences are obvious, as is the actual starting point. To the attending press, there is shock and horror at the brutality of what was shown.

With the video now at an end, Mopanyane turned to the three Judges and said, 'The evidence is damning. Stewart murdered, no, executed four innocent men in cold blood and in his own words states "I have no regrets or remorse". The state rests its case.'

The Judge looked across at Cohen, 'Do you have anything to say before I let the public back into the courtroom?'

'Yes, Your Honour, I will prove that what we have just witnessed is not a copy of the original disk. It has been severely redacted and should be removed from the evidence.'

'What proof do you have that it has been redacted?'

'If I may restart the video, I will show the court that this video has been redacted leaving out vital information.'

'I will allow it but turn down the sound, nobody wishes to hear that again. Proceed.'

Cohen turned on the DVD player and started up the video in slow motion mode. 'If you will pay attention to this number on the bottom left of the screen. This is a frame sequence that my client inserted when recording this disk. As you can see, it does not start at one nor does it increase sequentially but rather jumps ahead. This proves that this is a severely redacted copy that someone has made to suit their agenda. I submit that this disk should be removed from evidence and replaced with the originals that my client retained.'

'We cannot accept your client's copy of disks as they were not entered into police evidence at the time of his arrest. I reject both of your requests. Bailiff, you can readmit the public.' Turning back to Cohen, 'You may call your first witness.'

'I call Doctor Stewart.'

Gus stood up and walked over to the witness box where he stated his name and profession.

'Doctor, you have seen the video evidence. Do you agree that it was an exact copy of what you recorded?'

'No, I do not. You could see by the sequencing numbers that it has been edited.'

'Can you give the court the details of what you believe have been edited out?'

'Objection, he can make up anything he wants and has no way to prove his statements.'

'Sustained.'

'During the course of the recording, did any of the deceased admit their guilt in the murder and rape of your family?'

'Objection, we are not trying the deceased here, only the accused.'

'Sustained.'

'As we are not allowed to use my client's original records as evidence, I have no further questions.'

Mopanyane walked over to the witness box, 'Doctor, did you murder the deceased?'

'No, I only did what this court failed to do when they let four men guilty of rape and murder walk free. If you ask if I rendered justice to them and ended their lives, then the answer is yes, I did.'

'No further questions.'

'Call your next witness.'

'I have no further witnesses.'

'This court is adjourned for the day we will resume at 10 am tomorrow. Please prepare your closing arguments.'

Gus was taken back to the cells and the only access he was allowed was with his lawyers. Ian, Jimmy and Chubby returned to their hotel.

'I don't fancy his chances; he looks resigned to a guilty verdict. It looks like they have conspired to make sure he is convicted. Half the world has seen the full content of the videos. This just confirms how corrupt the justice system is in this country.'

'You are right, Ian. Gus has not been able to get over Cathy and his kids' murder. He knows he will be convicted but it will expose just how corrupt the system is. Even if he gets life, I am sure someone will take him out while in prison. This country is fucked up and is only going to get worse.'

'I find it amazing how that useless incompetent bastard Dingaan Mopanyane has gone from the idiot who fucked up the first trial to all of a sudden a top-class prosecutor. If people can't see that as corruption, then they never will. Guys, I reckon we get *vrot* tonight and have a few for our buddy,' said Ian.

'I'm in, what about you, Chubs?' asked Jimmy.

'All in.'

The following morning at exactly 10 am, the court reconvened. Dingaan Mopanyane stood up and addressed the waiting court. 'Your Honour, my closing words are short and concise. We have seen the video evidence and heard the words of the accused. He admits to the murders and should be punished to the letter of the law.'

Dingaan Mopanyane sat down and Mickey Cohen stepped forward. 'As my esteemed colleague has stated, we have all seen the video evidence but what he failed to mention was that it was not an original copy. It had been edited to suit the prosecution and all the scenes that led up to my client's actions had been redacted. My client was severely beaten and forced to watch while his son was murdered, his wife and daughter repeatedly raped with injuries so severe that they caused the death of both of them. He watched as the court, led by Dingaan Mopanyane, failed to convict the perpetrators, failed to allow the video evidence of the crime and then failed to get a conviction. Those self-same perpetrators then threatened, in full view of the court, to kill him next. The Justice System failed him and his family in that instance; do not fail him again. Thank you.'

Chief Justice Lumka Manyi addressed the court, 'We have heard all of the evidence and the closing arguments in this case. My colleagues and I will now retire and consider our verdict. The court will reconvene in two hours' time.'

Exactly two hours later, the three judges returned to the court room.

'I, with the assistance of Justice Steven Zondo and Justice Siku Mopanyane, have arrived at a verdict. We find the accused, Dr. Angus Stewart, guilty as charged. Doctor, do you have a statement to make before we pass sentence?'

'Yes, I have, Your Honour. I repeat what I stated at the end of the video, "As a Medical Doctor it pains me greatly to take another human life, but the four you see behind me gave up their rights as humans when they committed the crimes that they have now confessed to. The South African Justice system failed dismally in case of the rape and murder of my family. The Police obstructed Justice at every turn, destroyed evidence and refused to allow video footage of the incident into evidence. It is under these conditions I carried out the justice the courts failed to do. I have no regrets or remorse." That is all I have to say.' Gus remained standing.

'As we have found the accused guilty of abduction and premeditated murder, this court has no option but to sentence you to death. You will be taken from this court room to Pollsmoor Prison, where at a date to be determined, you will be hung by the neck until you are dead. May God have mercy on your soul.'

The court room erupted. The black majority started chanting 'Viva ANC', 'kill the whites', 'one bullet one Boer', 'Amandla'. The attending journalists made for the exits, eager to call in the story. The handful of whites just looked on in stunned silence. Ian, Chubby and Jimmy managed to break through to the defence desk and console Gus before he was handcuffed and dragged away.

The local and international press, both newspaper and television, had blanket coverage of the sentence. Most black and liberal-leaning left wing outlets praised the sentence. The right wing condemned the outcome and called for international intervention. Many contested that the withholding of key evidence was a miscarriage of justice and that a new trial with full exposure should be held. The advocators of the death penalty cheered, while those who opposed it demonstrated outside Pollsmoor Prison.

Against Gus' wishes, Mickey Cohen arranged for a petition to appeal to the new South African president, Thabo Mbeki. When this failed, he appealed to former president, Nelson Mandela, an advocate of forgiveness; this was also a failure.

By law, all death sentence trials had a right for an automatic appeal, this was overruled, giving further evidence of the failure of the justice system. Appeals for clemency were received from USA President, Bill Clinton, British Prime Minister, Tony Blair and German Chancellor, Helmut Schmidt. All fell on deaf ears

Gus, locked away in Pollsmoor, had no contact with the outside world. He was only allowed visits from his lawyer, Desmond Rabinowitz. It was through his lawyer that he passed and received messages from Ian, Chubby and Jimmy. He supplied Ian with a power of attorney and instructed him to liquidate all of his assets and if possible, move them offshore. His fear was that the courts would freeze or confiscate his assets. Once the funds were out of reach from the ANC, he was to set up a trust that would allow one student a year to be selected to attend university and study medicine. The university of choice was to be the University of Edinburgh in Scotland. Maybe they would find the next Dr. Hamish Stewart.

On October 4, 1999 Desmond Rabinowitz was informed that his client, Dr. Angus Stewart's, sentence would be carried out two weeks hence at 7 am on October 18. Rabinowitz informed Gus, who accepted his fate, satisfied it would all be over soon. The date was released to the news media, which immediately started up appeals for clemency.

On the morning of October 17 Rabinowitz was informed that the sentence would not be carried out the next day as the gallows were not ready and no hangman had been trained. It was postponed until a later date. Gus was informed, much to his dismay.

On December 16, celebrated as the 'Day of Reconciliation', it was announced that the date of execution would be January 1, 2000 at 7 am. The choice of the date for the announcement was a political statement, as the day had previously been known as 'Dingaan's Day', celebrated by the Afrikaners as the day that 470 Voortrekkers had fought off some 20,000 Zulus, also known as the Battle of Blood River.

On the morning of December 21 Gus was moved to the execution cell. No further contact with his lawyer or anyone other than a priest would be allowed. He would spend the last ten days of his life in total isolation.

Ian, having liquidated all of Gus' assets and created the trust, left South Africa and returned to his camper in Yellowstone Park. He was accompanied by his wife, Dee, and their daughter, Elizabeth. He planned to return to Cape Town on December 31. With properties in both the USA and Canada, Ian and family decided to relocate permanently to Toronto.

Jimmy returned to Barcelona with Lynne. He applied for British citizenship on the strength of his mother and grandparents, it was granted immediately. His daughter, Sharon and her fiancé, Ian's son Douglas, having postponed their wedding date until further notice, joined Lynne and Jimmy in Barcelona. The family would return to South Africa on December 31. Jimmy, having moved all his assets out of the country, left only Lynne's house in Hillcrest. Lynne's mother, Val, having refused to leave the country, remained in Hillcrest.

Chubby, having made a huge success in making the Natal Sharks a winning outfit and the province the most profitable one in South Africa, had numerous offers on the table. Along with his wife, Fiona, and daughter, Valerie, he decided to take a full-time position with Sale Sharks in England, effective on February 1, 2000.

On New Year's Eve, the three families and their children gathered at the Mount Nelson Hotel in Cape Town. Still unable to visit their friend, they spent the time reminiscing about the good times and the memories of their friend, Angus Stewart; one of the brightest and kindest people they knew. The ladies cried throughout and the men, especially Ian, Chubby and Jimmy, expressed their anger, frustration and helplessness.

At 5.00 am Ian, Chubby and Jimmy made their way to Pollsmoor Prison where they had been given permission to claim Gus' body.

At 7.25 am the gates to Pollsmoor opened and the lifeless body of Angus Ross Stewart, covered by a white cloth, was wheeled out on a stretcher. Ian claimed the body and instructed the ambulance crew to deliver the body to the crematorium. Ian collected the urn of Gus' ashes which would, as per his instructions, be thrown into the sea off Anstey's Beach on the Bluff.

Jimmy, suddenly realising the date, turned to Chubby. 'We had always promised to get together at the start of each decade to celebrate your birthday but none of us could imagine it would be like this. What a sad way to turn fifty.'

EPILOGUE

January 1, 2000; the first day of the new millennium saw Chubby Murphy's 50th birthday and the final day in the life of Doctor Angus Ross Stewart.

Ian retrieved the urn holding Gus' ashes and with Jimmy and Chubby joining him, chartered a flight to Durban Airport. They made the short trip to the Bluff and Anstey's Beach. Jimmy borrowed a surfboard from one of the locals and carrying the urn paddled out to the break line. He waited for the right wave; with the urn on the front of the board paddled into the wave. He stood up, took the lid off the urn and spread Gus' ashes as he rode the wave. Once the urn was empty, he tossed it into the sea.

Ian, Jimmy and Chubby left Anstey's for the final time and headed for Durban Airport. There they caught a flight to Johannesburg where they were met by Lynne. The four of them drove to the Wilson home in Fourways where they met up with the rest of their families. Later that evening they left Jan Smuts Airport bound for Heathrow in London.

Later, on January 2, 2000, after landing, the friends and their families split with a vow to celebrate Gus' birthday every June 10 together if at all possible. Ian, Dee and Elizabeth caught a flight back to West Yellowstone with connections in New York and Salt Lake City. Jimmy, Lynne, Sharon and Dougie caught a direct flight to Barcelona. Chubby, Dee and Valerie caught the shuttle to Manchester.

Traditionally the first day of January during the Apartheid days was one of defiance by the oppressed black population of South Africa. Starting in the mid-sixties in Durban, large numbers of blacks would descend on the 'Whites Only' South Beach. They would be bussed in from local townships and arrive in their hundreds thousands to swim in the sea. The sheer volumes made it impossible for the police force to prevent them from breaking the law. This tradition continued through the years into the post-Apartheid era where they were now no longer prevented from using the previous 'Whites Only' facilities.

On New Year's Day 2000 over three hundred thousand black and coloured people descended on South Beach. It was a typical Durban summer's day, hot and humid and not a breath of air. With the human throng of bodies, it was impossible for the facilities to cope with such an influx. In no time at all the ablutions were overflowing and urine and excrement started seeping into the street. With a copious amount of alcohol being consumed, tempers started to rise and initially scuffles broke out.

The police, black and white, were unable to restore any semblance of peace and calm. Lifesavers manning the beach were unable to push through the human masses to do any rescues. Unable to use the overburdened toilet facilities, people did their business where they stood, either in the sea or on the sand. Children, separated from their parents, were lost in the crowds with no way of reconnecting.

The Natal Parks Board attempted to close the children's paddling pool adjacent to South Beach due to a health hazard as the pool had been used as a public toilet. Fights broke out between parents and officials. Beer bottles and rocks were thrown. The fountains in the middle of the pool were torn down and the resulting rubble used as weapons. All the time the Police stood by taking no action.

With fights breaking out all over the place, people were taking cover wherever they could find it. Crowds spilled over onto the Esplanade disrupting beach front. traffic. Cars came to a standstill, unable to move in any direction. Irate motorists clashed with beach goers causing more mayhem. Gunshots were heard within the melee causing people to panic and attempt to rush away from the scene. Fires were started with any combustible material that perpetrators could lay their hands on. This attracted the attention of the fire department.

The fire engines, unable to make their way through the traffic, began pushing vehicles forcefully out of the way. More shots were heard causing additional panic which finally jolted the Police into action. A heavily armed platoon of Police arrived and began the impossible task of moving the surging crowd back towards the beach and away from the beach front road. Using only their riot shields and batons they made no progress until someone gave the order to fire tear gas into the crowd.

Total panic ensued. During the confusion, several small concession shops along the beach walkway were looted and virtually destroyed. The police, overwhelmed by the crowd, broke ranks and the now enraged mob tore through their ranks and headed out into the surrounding streets. Cars had their windows smashed; some were overturned and set alight. Most of the tourist-type stores, which were closed in anticipation of possible trouble, now had their windows and doors smashed open. Looters poured into these shops and took whatever they could carry.

With people pouring off the beaches and into the streets, the mob was forced up both West and Smith Streets towards the City Center. Fearing more carnage if the mob made it to the City Center, the police finally made a stand. A double line of men armed with rifles and rubber bullets were strung across West and Smith Street blocking further progress. As the mob advanced, the order was given to fire; a fusillade of rubber bullets struck the leading group, dropping them to the ground. Those behind just trampled over the fallen and continued to advance. A second fusillade was fired with the same result. It seemed that nothing would stop them.

The front line of the police was given the order to retreat and the second line to take their place. Those in the second line had been given live ammunition; they were given the order to fire. The impact was immediate, it was impossible to know how many died instantly. Those struck by the bullets fell and the surge from behind pushed the crowd forward. A second volley of shots rang out with the same results; only this time those behind turned and attempted to retreat.

With the crowd no longer advancing, the police broke ranks to let fire department vehicles through. Using their water cannons they began driving the crowd back towards the beach. As the crowd retreated, the number of dead bodies were exposed. An eyewitness counted over one hundred dead and many more wounded.

It took until late in the evening to restore order and disperse the crowd. The final death toll would never be released but would likely have been in the thousands. The local hospitals treated thousands for non-life-threatening injuries. Hundreds of children, separated from their parents, would remain unclaimed for weeks. The total cost of lost and destroyed property would run into the hundreds of million rand.

The Minister of Police, when asked for a comment on the police action and why it happened, gave the following statement; 'It is a very unfortunate situation but the violence was triggered by racial hatred which has been festering since the murder of four young black men, my nephew included, and the resulting trial which exposed white man's racist beliefs.'

A journalist from the *Citizen* asked, 'But Minister, the crowd and police involved was made up of 99.9% people of colour.'

'That is all I have to say.' He turned away and left.

Watching a repeat of the newscast at Heathrow Airport, Ian said, 'Welcome to the new Millennium, Rainbow Nation style. This is truly the day the Rainbow Died.'

The End

ABOUT THE AUTHOR

James spent his professional life designing and writing software for business solutions. He retired and relocated to Conway SC where he lives with his wife Pippa with whom he shares 5 children. *The Day the Rainbow Died* is his 5th novel to be published but the first one he wrote. The other books are '*Wildfire*,' '*Wildfire the Revenge*' and '*Be afraid.*'